The Anatomist's Dream

The Anatomist's Dream

CLIO GRAY

MYRMIDON

Myrmidon
Rotterdam House
116 Quayside
Newcastle upon Tyne
NE1 3DY

www.myrmidonbooks.com

Published by Myrmidon 2015

A catalogue record for this book is available from the British Library.

ISBN (Hardback) 978-1-910183-20-5
ISBN (Export Paperback) 978-1-910183-21-2

Set in 11.5/14.5pt Sabon by
Falcon Oast Graphic Art Limited,
East Hoathly, East Sussex

Printed in the UK by CPI Group (UK) Ltd, Croydon, CRO 4YY

1 3 5 7 9 10 8 6 4 2

Contents

1

Debut

'It's a taupe,' announced the doctor, poking at the lump with a scratchy yellow finger, 'a French tumour they call it, though couldn't rightly tell you why. Most unusual – got a bit of hair growing on it too, see here?'

Several thin strands grew, wet-wisped, from a lump the size and shape of a duck's egg at the bottom of the baby's head.

'Might kill him,' the doctor carried on with scientific stoicism. 'But probably not, most likely grow a-pace with the rest of him. My goodness though, he does rather resemble the back end of a baboon, don't you think?'

He winked at Frau Kranz, who had never seen a baboon let alone its back end, but understood well enough what he meant.

'*Schweigen Sie!*' she hissed, 'be quiet, sir,' and nodded her head at Shminiak, who had slumped into a stupor by the empty fire, bowing his head, wondering how much more brandy it would take to make everything go away. He'd already clapped his hands about his ears to shut out the baby's awful squalling, moaning quietly: 'For God's sake, make it stop, make it stop, for God's sake . . .'

Frau Kranz, who was the most patient of women, could put

7

it off no longer and chivvied the child up carefully from the bassinet and carried him over to the bed, clamping him onto his mother's sweaty breast. Nelke, exhausted as she was, woke abruptly at the application and tried to swat the intruder weakly away. She refused to believe this monstrosity was of her flesh, that she had given birth at all, the pain of labour nothing more than a terrible nightmare, a twilight dream. But it was no dream, not for Nelke, Shminiak, nor the child who was oblivious of the outside world – a world that seemed peaceful on the surface, there in Staßburg as elsewhere, but the jigsaw puzzle of Europe was beginning to crack along its edges, breaking up from within, harried from without, each piece tugging itself away from the other, the Holy Roman Empire snuffed out years before by Napoleon, a shaky German Confederation created to fill the void. There was civil war in Iberia, and every Italian state clawed at the throats of its neighbours, and soon the entire continent would be utterly fragmented, Metternich packing the prison fortress at Spielburg in Bohemia, its stones reverberating with the cries of the spies and subversives he'd locked inside its walls; but no matter how many he crammed in there seemed an inexhaustible supply, and the secret operatives of princes, kings and Junkers were soon running the country up and down as freely and frequently as the tides run up and down the sands of coastlines the world over. Conspiracy and subterfuge would become bywords for those coming years through which that child of Nelke and Shminiak would grow up, and the slump of 1844 a few years later would scuttle ships and rip the Guilds from nape to knee; potato blight and famine would squeeze the stomachs of labourers and peasants across the land; there would be riots in Aachen and Bavaria, Berlin and Saxony; the Silesian silk workers would break their looms and tools; the Slavs and Poles and Magyars rise up against their masters; the railways would crash and the rivers stutter to a stop with the piling up of the dead.

But all that was yet to come and, as Philbert bullied his way out of Nelke's womb, there was no inkling of the terrible and significant part he would play in these events, no thoughts at all thrumming around inside his monstrous head. Later in his life he would meet people who claimed to understand the language of the wind as it whispered through the trees, who saw omens in the entrails pulled from still-warm lambs, interpreted the future by studying the murfles and mottlements that grew upon men's skin. Perhaps if they'd been there at the very start, attendant at Philbert's birth, they might have foreseen what would happen, maybe had the nous to stop it before it all kicked off. But only Frau Kranz was there with a screaming mother, a drink-sodden father, and the doctor scratching his yellow fingernail on Philbert's taupe.

2

Salting the Meat

Nelke Windberg met Shminiak Bedrobessian in Staßburg, early summer, 1839. It was a holiday, and hot, with boys shinning up greasy poles to get at squawking cocks, couples dancing circles, drunkards bawling, fiddles screeching, men playing ninepins, dogs cleaning up the spillage and puke that fell between the tables set up in the town's square. Nelke was one of those offending bowkers, Shminiak a courteous bystander, slipping an empty piggin bowl beneath her sad debouch. She had obviously drunk more than she was used to, although Shminiak was too polite to point it out; it was easy to drink too much in a place like Staßburg, everyone habitually dehydrated, the soft drift of salt from the mines covering everything, from ground to tables, cups and cutlery, hair and hands and clothes. No one buys salt in Staßburg, went the old saying, you just shake from your shirt. It was in the air you breathed, made worse that celebration day by the dancers kicking up the dust.

Nelke drank as others did, she ate pigs' trotters, jellied tongue, pickled cabbage and cucumber. It was a festival, and she did no more nor less than was expected, except to meet Shminiak Bedrobessian halfway through the day, when he had seen in her what he'd never seen before in any girl, and after he'd cleaned her up he limped her off away from the Wirtshaus, down to the hay meadows by the river, and the next morning they awoke together under the same blanket, deciding there and then that there were worse things they could do than stay together, share shack and rent, with no need to trouble the church with formalities.

He carried on working in the salt mines, hack, hack, hacking away at the salt-bricks with his pickaxe, and she in the flour-mills, churning out bread by the ton.

'Oh my dear Nelke,' Shminiak said, once she agreed to their joining bodies and bed. 'My sweet cherry, the lips of my soul will always kiss your holy name, as will the longing of my breath.'

Shminiak was Armenian and liked to quote his patriarch, Grigor of Nareg, whose *Lamentations Before God* had been such a help to him throughout the shambolic ways of his life. Nelke replied in kind, at least in those early days.

'*Stille, mein Liebchen*,' she so often replied. 'Be still, my love, for we are as one.'

So they were, and the happiness this brought Shminiak caused him to shake off his habitual depression and work all the harder and soon was promoted to *Aufseher*, controlling the town's salt exports to Westphalia and beyond. At home, Nelke was proud and quiet as she grew like an orange, *linea nigra* creeping up from pelvis to bellybutton, stroking the child as it expanded within her skin.

'*Ach, meine kleine kind, meine säugenling, meine apfelkuchen, meine nocke, winzig meine nuß, meine eichel.*' Her words of love and blessing were whispered over and over to her unborn child, her precious apple cake. All her thoughts were of mother-hood and the startling cravings that came with it: she devoured noodles boiled with pickled peppers, apples dipped in fireplace soot, eggs fried and sprinkled over with sugar and salt. She chewed her mouth black with little pieces of coal, peeled sticks

11

right down their cores until she got to their tender centres, her greed growing with her gravidity, the child within her already adored and already named. She listened with joy for the uterine souffles and the double pulse, and laughed when Shminiak tickled her belly with his fingers, both counting down the weeks and months as they came.

And then, almost a month before she was due, all went still, and for three days Nelke held her breath and shook with every moment; couldn't bear the thought that her little apple cake had died within her, her body become a coffin she could not escape. She cried out with relief when the pain began suddenly to rage within her as the child manoeuvred itself for early battle, drumming on her pelvis bones as if trying to snap them through, and then came the sweat and the shouts and the awful swearing as she was racked and attacked by the spasms she could not control. The neighbours all came running then, sending the shiny-eyed, petrified Shminiak down to the ale-house where he rocked back and forth in his chair, the brandy coming across to him at regular intervals as he sang his half remembered hymns of protection from Grigor's *Lamentations Before God*:

'*Cover with Your Hand, O Christ, the roof of my house, mark my door with Your Blood, cover my bed with Your Right Hand. O Jesu protect my couch from ambush and defend my soul's soul in its distress, place Your Arm around my heart and that of my beloved . . .*'

For fourteen hours he sat and rocked and ranted, listening to Nelke's screams ringing down along the cobbled alleyways, the barman keeping the brandy coming, notching up the tally on his slate, wondering if he should really charge such a man at all.

The leather birthing-strap that was placed between Nelke's teeth was worn down to a fragment by the end of it, the bed-posts creaking from grind and press as the child punched its way towards its narrow and bony gate. Right through that leather Nelke finally bit when at last came out her burden, foot-first, still kicking, followed by the rest of it, and then the final travail of the large and cumbersome head that had to be tugged out by force, coming out the colour of red carnations as it bawled as hard as Nelke when it eventually emerged, releasing her from her agony, allowing her to subside into unconscious relief. Frau Kranz from next door had taken early charge and pushed away the world, holding the newborn as if it were her own, cleaning up afterbirth and child, getting him ready for Shminiak come staggering home from the inn, poking gently at the bauble-bump that shone beneath the baby's skin, hard as a plum pip and five times as big.

~

The life that came next for Nelke was not at all as she'd imagined it would be. She could barely look at her torturer, let alone give it a name, and cursed every drop of milk squeezed from her sore and ulcerated breasts and the way her legs had gone all wet and white, shiny like soap, rubbed over by Frau Kranz with fish-oil and glycerine, turning her beauty into the pickings of a fish-monger's stall. She couldn't understand where her little apple cake, already lovingly named Elsa, had gone to, nor the cruel blow she had been dealt inasmuch as a monster had been delivered in her place.

Back to the flourmills went Nelke, soon as she was able, the changeling left with Frau Kranz next door. She went grind, grind, grinding out her anger, knead, knead, kneading out her despair. Her assiduous work did not go unremarked, and a molinet stick was placed into her hands and up the stairs she went, ascending to the high station of the Confectionery Department, her rage and despair put to good use as she whipped and whisked the chocolate into angel folds soft as butter, light as clouds; churning her sweat and tears into the brandy lacing the truffles, the chantilly that filled the tortes, the sugar that was spun around marzipans and chocolates. She saved her best

13

moments for the *nußbeeren*, going at that mocha mousse like a demon, having a special hatred for the hazelnuts she had to hide within, seeing in the whole confection an exact reflection, not of her not-to-be little Elsa, but the horrid taupe of the alien child that had usurped her, duping them both, ripping their promised happiness into ribbons as a conjuror does his flag; a conjurer who has forgotten his trick halfway through and walks off the stage, leaving the broken pieces behind instead of rolling them back together and reproducing the banner again, as whole and beautiful and unscathed as it had been before.

It was left to Shminiak to name his son and to stroke the brown into which his taupe had sulked after its initial shocking debut in purple and red, to twist the little curl of hair around his finger, kiss the beat of blood that ran through it like a second pulse. He sat for many nights in the chair by the fire with the child held close to his heart, while Nelke lay upon the bed, pale and sharp as ghost-thistle, lips opening and closing as she slept her angry sleep.

'My little Philbert,' he whispered at such moments. 'My tiny son. There is love enough in me for both of us, only hush now, and do not wake your mamma,' and then he stroked his small son, his head, his taupe, trying to stroke away the bad times he knew must come.

3

The Leaving Game

When Philbert was two, a man began to visit Nelke and Shminiak. He was dashing and debonair, arriving on a grey-black horse whose pelt shone like molten metal in the sun. He sat and talked quietly with Shminiak of exports, trade-flows, projections and plans. He poured *Kirschwasser* into the gleaming goblets he always brought with him, taking dainty sips, dabbing at his fine moustache with a square of white lace. But when Shminiak was gone abroad to Westphalia and France on his mission to sell Staßburg salt, still that man came and talked quietly with Nelke, still using the language of trade-flows and projections, though of quite a different kind; still sipping softly from his goblet, but dabbing at her lips with his own, brushing his fine moustache across the thin lines of her face, sharing the best of French liqueurs with her, and his wide, green cloak. While all this was going on, Philbert was bundled off next door to good Frau Kranz, drinking buttermilk from her best cracked cup, surviving and thriving despite his mother's parental deprivation of her son.

The world of men is like a vine that throws its tendrils out, binding each one together with talk and tales, and Shminiak, while away, got news of this Frenchman visiting Staßburg in his absence, and of Nelke throwing her doors wide and giving him welcome. Most men would have galloped home in a fury, picking up on the way the stoutest stick he could find, beating his wife to a pulp with it on his return before locking her in the town stocks for a day or two until she understood the meanings of virtue and loyalty. But Shminiak was not most men, and knew about violence and what it begets. He could never forget the bad years he'd spent as a youth, escaping deprivation of one kind only to find worse as he scraped his way from Armenia to the Black Sea shores; the squalid ports, the beatings he had taken, the hard life he'd had before he came to Staßburg where he'd discovered a stability he'd previously only dreamed of. He loved his Nelke and his home, had found a purpose there, was given the great good fortune of a son, no matter that he wasn't perfect.

So, instead of a stick, Shminiak picked up something else on his way home, passing as he did through the market town of Bad Salzyflen and buying what, back home in Armenia, would be a possession worth more than gold. But not in Staßburg, and not to Nelke, who was standing at her table when Shminiak returned with his prize, her tattered apron around her waist, hair dishevelled, hands automatically chopping at the cabbage for that night's soup.

Big 'Halloo!' from her almost-husband, huge smile, little red hairy pig wriggling in his arms.

Nelke stood aghast at the table, knife poised in the thick summer air, unsure into whom she should first heave the blade.

'*Für meine Liebchen,*' Shminiak beamed, plonking the porker down on the table where it proceeded to thrust a snotty snout into the mess of shredded cabbage Nelke had just chopped. Nelke put one hand over her mouth and collapsed weeping into a chair.

'What is to become of me when my husband brings me

16

a pig for a gift?' she wailed, as soon as she was able to draw breath. 'One pig from another, both animals, both filthy. I cannot bear to look at either of you. Get out! Get out! And take that *schweinerei* with you!' she yelled, kicking her young son Philbert out from under the table where he spent so many of his days. The force of her foot bumped him across the floor like a turnip. 'Just leave me alone, all of you! Please, just leave me . . .' Nelke cried out, her misery so evident and present it was shocking in its intensity, her fingers running through her hair, entwining a shred of cabbage there, leaving it hanging, unforgiven, across the sweat of her brow. Shminiak knew all was lost. He turned away, saying nothing. Not even Grigor could help him now. He deposited child and piglet with Frau Kranz before heading his familiar way to the inn.

Good Frau Kranz heard all through the thin, tin walls of their adjoining shacks and asked no questions, taking in the refugees without a murmur, doing her best for both when no one else would. It was a selfless act of kindness that would catapult its way down the years, long after Frau Kranz was gone from life, long after Philbert himself had emerged from the black tunnel of his childhood. An act of kindness Philbert would remember keenly twenty years later when he was passing by a smoking village, another one trampled and stamped out of existence by a filch of foreign renegades who'd deserted whatever army they had once been press-ganged into. In they came and stripped it bare, every ear of barley ripped from every stalk to feed the marauders' horses, every whisker of wheat in the granary bagged and loaded, every animal haltered and taken with them when they went, every man who dared to fight, beaten and shot and kicked into the nearest ditch. And that's where Philbert found a man the following morning, crumpled below a hedge. Almost dead. Not quite. Philbert dribbled water onto his mouth and held his hand, recognising the need people have not to die alone. Philbert, by then, had long left Staßburg and met death face to face in many guises; he'd seen suicide, murder, desertion, and understood the consequences of each. But the care good Frau Kranz gave him in his early years stayed with the man he became and, by the time he sat by the dying man in the ditch, Philbert – who never knew his father's name – had already lived a life most extraordinary, grown like a burr that snags everything it touches, taking away a little fragment from each life, each word, each story, each loss he encountered, of which there had been many.

But the first of these was Nelke, the mother who had never wanted the boy-burr, and who grieved for the non-existent flower of the imagined Elsa who should have been born in his place, and who grieved for this lost child all her life. And it was Nelke who took the decision that one of them had to go and, seeing as Philbert at that time could hardly walk his way past the chicken shed without falling over, she took the burden of leaving upon herself.

～

For Nelke, it went like this: she woke up with a smile for the first time in years, listening to the chickens scratching in the dry mud outside her shack without rancour, knowing it would be the last time she would ever hear them. Shminiak was in Lippstadt doing business, Philbert in his cot underneath the table with his wretched pig, who snottered like an old man, christened with a name that was just as she sounded, which was Kroonk. Nelke didn't know the boy was awake nor that he too was listening and watching, seeing his mother moving quietly about the kitchen, taking a few extra minutes to brush her hair, braid it into a silken snake down her back. She put on her best cotton dress, fingered through the others in the ratty box before closing the lid knowing she would never have to wear another, or sew them when they split, or patch them when they tore. Nelke wanted to sing with the larks she could already hear fluting above the hay meadows and to laugh with the river tugging playfully at its banks beyond. Instead, she crept around her home and picked up a small basket, placing within it the comb and mirror her beau had brought her on his last visit – at last a man who knew the things a woman wanted, as only a fine Frenchman could. She tip-toed past the table and lifted the latch, seeing the sun shine down on her new life and the dusty path that beckoned her on. She sniffed the air, smelt the flour and salt for the very last time, threw her shawl around her shoulders and for a moment, just one moment, she turned to look at the boy beneath the table, wondering if at the very last her heart would waver. But there was nothing but contempt for the shack in which she had been cooped these past few years, and nothing for the child she had never considered her own. Strangely, in that last long look, the only thing she regretted leaving was the one thing never there at all: her little flower bud Elsa who had never bloomed. And it was for Elsa, not Philbert, that Nelke shed a few tears as she took her quick way along the path to the bridge and the man offering escape.

~

Philbert stayed below the table with only little Kroonk for company, hungry and bewildered, waiting for his Mamma to return. Eventually Frau Kranz came in, as she often did, and fetched him up, took him back home with her. But the next day found him back beneath his table, expectant, too young to comprehend that Nelke was never coming back. This went on for several weeks until Frau Kranz began to take the place of Nelke in his head, and he would sit every morning on a chair while she pounded at her dough, rolled out her noodles, trying to explain that sometimes people just disappeared and it wasn't the fault of those they left behind. And eventually four-year-old Philbert forgot his mother's face, her smell, and her anger, the constant dripping of her tears, and for a while there was only Philbert and Kroonk and Frau Kranz, lying beneath their own hedge, in their own ditch, crying out for help, hoping – as people in those places always hope – that help will one day come.

～

The neighbours talked, the neighbours gossiped, the neighbours regarded the disappearance of the Confectioner's girl as something of a scandal, a trope for all the disappointed women, unwilling mothers, flirtatious courtesans they had ever known. And they soon came tap, tap, tapping at Frau Kranz's door wanting more, wanting details, although she never gave them up. Surprisingly they also took much interest in Kroonk, examining her as they examined every newcomer to the town, unanimous in their decision that she was too small, too red and runtish, and absolutely did not like the way she sneezed and snottered. There were murmurings of swine-fever, which Frau Kranz expertly batted aside.

'Stuff and nonsense,' she grumbled, mysterious with her knowledge. 'It's just a cold, little piggy, and don't let nobody tell you different.'

Frau Kranz scratched Kroonk's little red ears, rubbed her down with warm wet towels, fed her, as she had once fed Philbert, with a twist of flannel soaked in milk-bran and mashed-up biscuits, until the sneezing dried out into a purr and the coughing a husk of what it had been, and the neighbours gathered one more time and declared her fit, though fit for what they did not say.

～

They were strange times for Philbert, settling, as mud will do, no matter how fast flows the stream. Nelke left with the summer, and autumn brought Shminiak home, although staying only long enough to bless Frau Kranz and leave her some bolts of cloth from Westphalia, stroking his child's head, chucking Kroonk beneath her chin, admiring what they'd all turned into which seemed, to his eyes at least, a family to which he no longer belonged. He urged Frau Kranz into the bigger shack, removed himself to hers for his increasingly brief and infrequent visits when he drank too much and talked to himself, tried to persuade himself that he was happy too.

And so it went for a few years: boy and pig growing and playing together behind the chicken-shed, paddling in the shallows of the river, snuffling for pignuts in the fields, collecting berries from the woods. Frau Kranz swept and scrubbed out all the years of accumulated muck left behind by Nelke, and made pickles of vegetables and pots of rabbit and pigeon that she sold to neighbours; sewing Shminiak's bolts of cloth into table-cloths, pinafores and curtains, selling the fabulously exotic foreign fabrics to the greyness of the town. They went from cabbage soup to proper wheat-bread and mutton chops; from fried cucumber and potato to salt-fish stew. Kroonk snuffled up the leftovers and rooted the neighbours' middens, though no one seemed to mind, and even began to leave their peels-and-pickings for her in bowls by their back gates.

'How kind,' thought Philbert. 'How generous. How they must love my Kroonk.'

He knew nothing of the tradition his neighbours remembered from better times of Epiphany Pigs, nor heard their whisperings of baked bacon pie, crackling crisping on the spit, fat sputtering into the fire. Nor did he understand the vague memories evoked by the occasional scents of chocolate and cloves as he passed by the mill-house to fetch the bread, nor the even vaguer face conjured up every time he heard the rain drip, drip, dripping from the gutter, Nelke no longer a firm memory; nor did he notice that his father, Shminiak, came home less and less often, nor that his sad brown eyes were now awash with brandy, his beard a tangled mess of sauerkraut and stale crumbs. He didn't comprehend the significance of that last visit when Shminiak hugged Frau Kranz and kissed her hands and cheeks, making her go as red as new-sliced beef, demanding crossly what was what. Shminiak pointed to the pile of cloth he'd left by the door, carefully wrapped in hessian so they would not spoil in the coming winter's winds and rain. He scuffed his boot-heels against the floor and then against each other. He held his son's misshapen head against his waist and went down upon his knees to kiss it fondly, twisting the little curl of hair one more time about his finger, stroking the rounded cheeks that reminded him so much of his beloved Nelke, murmuring sweet nothings to his Little Maus, which was what everyone called him on account of his taupe. Shminiak said his last goodbyes to his boy, handing to him a little wooden donkey with legs jointed at the knees and a silken saddle. He showed Philbert how to work a hand-cranked serinette the ladies in Paris used to teach canaries how to sing, his Little Maus squeaking with delight at the fluting sound of larks when he turned the handle. Shminiak kissed Frau Kranz one last time, kissed his son, and even kissed Kroonk, and then he was gone, just like Nelke before him, neither coming back.

'Your father's taken a very important job in Westphalia,' Frau Kranz told Philbert, dabbing at her eyes with the corner of her dress, fussing about, clattering pans and pots. 'So go outside now, my dear, and play with Kroonk,' and off Philbert went, pleased with his double-jointed donkey and the little serinette.

He was six years old when he stood for a while in the chicken-pecked yard and watched his Papa's horse kicking up dust and salt from the track leading to the bridge. He found some familiar resonance of what had gone before, understanding that something important in his world was changing. He thought he heard a faint, 'Aieee, aieee, Yehovah . . .' drifting down the path towards him.

Last sight for Philbert of his father, and last sound.

Last that anyone in Staßburg ever heard of Shminiak and his Lamentations.

Philbert long remembered the horse and the dust, the track and the bridge, but of those words and of his father, as of his mother, there was soon nothing left.

4

Christmas Present

Winter that year was a cold season when it came, and *Weihnachtsfest* – Christmas time – as drear as it could be. A pall of freezing mist hung low over Staßburg, three men killed by falls of salt-stone cracked from the mine-cliffs by the ice. Worse was to come, hardly a hint of wassailing or carolling that year; very little to celebrate on Christmas Eve, few visitors doing the rounds on *Silvesterabend* to welcome the New Year in. The taverns were quiet because by then over seventy people had died from *Die Grösse Grippe*, an influenza that had stamped over them with the ice, sweeping in from the North like an enemy horde.

Philbert hid from it all beneath his familiar table, Kroonk as always by his side, Frau Kranz making huge pots of gruel to distribute to the sick. Women came in their shawls and their clogs, dipping their tins into her cauldrons before dissipating back into the mud and mist and the evermore demanding and unceasing months of winter. Then Frau Kranz got sick. Not all at once: slower than a cat creeps into a cradle. She hunched a little longer by the fire than was usual, began to sneeze over her sewing, and then to spatter her pretty fabrics by coughing up fine laces of blood. The same neighbour women came in with their shawls and their clogs, clutching their tins, began to stop and rock a little in the chair beside Frau Kranz's bed, cluck-clucking their tongues, trying to feed the same gruel to Frau Kranz that she'd been making for others only weeks before. She lapped at the liquid from their ladles trying to take in all she could, but failed, staining her clothes with the dribbled medallions of the sick. Philbert and Kroonk crawled up beside her on her bed and laid their bodies against her own to keep her warm, wondering what would happen if ever she left, as everyone else had done.

It was a miserable winter for the whole town, a time to be wept over and mourned, and yet somehow endured.

~

When at last March stamped her foot and kicked the cold weather out on its arse, Staßburg was only half the town it had once been. A quarter of its population cut down by the Grippe like thatching reeds and buried; the more well-to-do heading off swiftly into exile, picking up their fine hats and coats as they fled. These last returned with the spring, as the sunshine trickled into the streets and warmed the soil of the fields. The Mine Controllers tied up their 'important business' in Berlin and came back to crank awake the big machines, call those still strong enough back to work at mine and mill. Staßburg survived, and so did Frau Kranz, though she was thin as an egg-shell and had a cough like a rusty chain bending her double with every step. It was cabbage soup and turnip stew all over again for everyone, their deepest pockets scoured clean by winter and sickness. No one complained, just glad to hear once more the shift-bells ringing and the striking of pickaxes from the mines, tasting the tang of salt once more in the air – all signs that Staßburg had arisen.

As if in recognition of this new beginning, the flowers of spring at last began to unfurl within the fields that ran by the river, and the cold, grey skin of the town was browned by the sun. And soon after came something else entirely, further bolstering their optimism as rumours crept into every shack, house and street, starting in some dusty inn on the edge of town where a pedlar had stopped to sharpen the cook's knives. He'd come from Potsdam, he said, and from Potsdam to Magdeburg and from Magdeburg to here, and every step of the way, so the man said, the Fair had been hot on his tail. *They're only a rattle away*, says he, *and sure to be here soon*. The Mine Controllers sent out an emissary as the whispers passed from mouth to mouth and ear to ear, from inn to inn, from tavern to shop until – like a river in spate – it burst through the town, set it abuzz with anticipation. And then, at the very back end of May a cloud of dust was seen on the horizon and they knew at last for sure that pedlar had been right, the rumours true: the Carnival was coming to Staßburg, and not a moment too soon.

~

Staßburg shook itself awake, like a bear after long months of unwanted slumber. The jasmine and late jonquil raised their heads, threading the air with their delicate scent. People stopped worrying about disrespecting the dead and began unfolding their coloured clothes. A yellow neckerchief appeared, a red shawl here, a green shirt there, boasting out beneath dark waist-coats as one blue dress nodded to another on the other side of the street. The Mine Controllers declared a three-day holiday to take effect the moment the promised Carnival appeared. Tidbits began to appear once more outside Frau Kranz's gate; she was uneasy at their implication but unwilling to let go a source of food, picking through them for what she could use, as fed up with the watery soup and dull grey days as everyone else. She tried her best to rally, spent more time up and about, ignoring the blood-spattered blankets and bean-shaped blotches that had appeared on her hands and feet through the thinness of her skin. She'd been ill before, but understood this was not the same; she knew by the slow, erratic beating of her heart that her time might be short and had one last duty to discharge, though not as yet the least idea how to do it.

~

And then in came the Carnival, flying and barking over the bridge into the fields beyond the river, flattening the celandine and corn-grasses, outshining them with its painted carts, colourful stalls and tents, the weird-looking people who peppered and swung here and there amongst its makeshift ginnels. Philbert and Kroonk sat on the opposite riverbank dangling their toes in the cool water, fascinated by the sights, awed by the strange sounds, the smells of donkey dung and people and sawdust drifting through the air, the roars of unknown animals; the people of Staßburg bustling and jostling over the bridge, children laughing and flinging themselves into the river, swimming to the other side, hauling themselves out dripping, ready to go at it once again. The holler and hubbub rose in volume as people thronged the tents and stalls, their voices made louder by wonderment and drink. The smell of frying potatoes and meat blistering on braziers filled the evening air, drawing in every last citizen who had a single coin to spare.

Frau Kranz didn't have even that, so Philbert could only wander outside but never got in to see the shows; he read the signs that shouted with their large lettering of the Extraordinary Feats and Freaks of Nature hidden inside the tents: the Fishman, the Fattest Woman in All the World, the Smallest-Ever Girl. It didn't matter to Philbert; enough just to be a part of something so exotic, threading his way amongst the stalls, seeing all the things the pedlars had brought to sell – all colours of silks and wools and linens, tooled leather boots, gloves and leggings, laces, fancy buttons and buckles, bowls and cups of strange shapes and bright colours, painted clogs, an artisan selling silhouettes of anyone who paid their money over; a man selling potions and phials of strange coloured liquids, jars of leeches which sucked their flat bellies against the glass. There was everything to see, smell and hear, as if every good thing in life had come to Staßburg, shouting out to all who could to come and get it.

Philbert and Kroonk sat and watched from their side of the river, gladdened by the animation across the water, warmed by it, happy to dip their toes and trotters into the water, satisfied to have the privilege to witness something so marvellous.

And then that girl came by, pin thin, legs like a cricket, same height as Philbert but with a face that was pinched and beaked and looked much older than her body, her features bright and without care.

'Do you mind?' said she, setting herself down beside Philbert, her voice sharp as shards of glass. She kicked off her small shoes, once red, now slightly tattered and flaked over with mud, and wriggled her minuscule toes like hatching minnows in the water. Philbert couldn't speak, went red as Kroonk, and apparently had something stuck in his throat, though the girl didn't seem to notice.

'Mmmm!' she breathed and leant back her head, stretched out her arms to the ground behind her. 'This is wonderful!'

Kroonk leant closer, shivering slightly against Philbert's side.

'Lovely pig,' she ventured after a while, and stroked Kroonk behind the ears.

'Kroonk, kroonk,' purred Kroonk as she swapped her allegiance and the girl smiled, Philbert finally opening his mouth and finding words coming out, asking the girl her name.

'Puppelita,' she answered brightly, 'Lita to my friends, and you can call me Lita.'

'I'm Philbert,' Philbert said, emboldened, 'but mostly I'm called Little Maus.'

Lita was amused by the name and giggled, and Philbert correspondingly blushed. And then Lita did what nobody else had ever done, at least not that Philbert ever remembered, and put out her tiny hand and stroked his taupe.

'Little Maus,' she said. 'I like your little maus,' and then she twisted his taupe's soft tuft of hair around her fingers, Philbert so astounded he could only look hard at the water, concentrating on making splashing noises with his feet. Not even Frau Kranz touched his head, and no more did Philbert if he could avoid it. Little Lita was unaware of the boy's ambivalence and sighed again.

'How lovely it must be to dangle your toes in the river all day long,' she said, Philbert once again struck dumb, leaving her to carry on the conversation by herself, which she did. 'Will you be here tomorrow?' she asked. Philbert nodded mutely, trying to smile, Kroonk kroonking so Lita laughed again, picked up her shoes and headed back to the Fair.

That moment was forever fixed in Philbert's memory as if caught in amber, and no matter what else was sent to fill his head, no matter what else would be done to him and his taupe over the years, it remained like an anchor, a starting post, around which the rest of his life would circle forevermore: Lita's fingers against his taupe, Lita's fingers in his hair. He would feel them always, just as then, and later would come to realise this was the single point in time when something inside his head switched itself on and began to blink open its eyes; began to take in all that was going on around him.

Next day found Philbert dangling his feet from dawn through to dusk, toes cold, cramped and crinkled into bladderwrack as he went on waiting right into the night. Only when the moon had risen halfway up the sky did she come, bringing a small bag of violets crushed with almond flakes rolled in sugar, and a bucket of scraps for Kroonk. While they sat there dipping their fingers into the last of the sugar at the very bottom of the bag, Lita asked Philbert about his family and Philbert told her matter-of-factly enough, his tale brief, no more than a sentence, causing the girl to weep inexplicably, putting her arm around his shoulder.

'Poor Little Maus,' she murmured, and then stood up, pulling him after her, taking him off along the bank and over the bridge and into the dust of the Fair, weaving a way through the maze of stalls and show-tents, Philbert's ears buzzing and humming with all the noise. She led him behind a threadbare curtain into a small cubicle, whose canvas walls shook as the crowds outside passed by, making the lamp flicker on its hook, nothing for Philbert feeling quite real.

'This is Tomaso,' Lita introduced a boy whose sad face had two watery eyes in it and another that popped out like a frog from the back of his head. 'His Mama left him too,' she said, automatically picking up a spill of apple-wood, dribbling water into Tomaso's third eye. It blinked slowly, as if in pain, but continued to stare off blindly into the middle distance.

'We're all alone,' Lita said, 'though here at least, we have each other.'

And then she started to sing, and though Philbert didn't understand the words he had a strong feeling he knew what she was saying as she sang, her voice both soft and brittle at the same time, and with a tune so doleful that tears began spilling from Tomaso's eyes, at least the two Philbert could see, for the boy had turned a little away from him, holding his head towards the shadows, Philbert recognising the gesture with shock, because it was something he did himself.

~

Too soon for Philbert it was the last night of the Fair; the neighbours had called in several times to check on Frau Kranz and now stood once more whispering in the doorway waiting for an invitation inside, an invitation that Frau Kranz refused to grant.

'No need for another visit,' she croaked. 'I'm quite well from your last ministrations. Is that you, Philbert?'

And it was, just back from his latest riverbank vigil, though

Lita had not arrived. The neighbours hovered a few moments more, making a fuss of the boy, patting at Kroonk.

'How well she looks,' they said, 'how healthy and plump your little piggy is, Philbert, how smooth her skin.'

'Go away,' Frau Kranz's attempted shout was feeble, 'and get away from the boy and his pet.'

She emphasised the last word as much as she could, for she knew exactly what those neighbours were about and why so all of a sudden solicitous. She'd seen them licking their lips, the awful glint in their eyes, heard the sharpening of knives upon soap-stones, smelled the firing up of a spit at the end of their street and what it meant. Philbert came in, shutting out the neighbours behind the skinny tin door of the shack, as happy as Frau Kranz had ever seen him, Kroonk's little curly tail wriggling excitedly as she trotted in beside him.

'Come here, Little Maus,' she whispered, and the boy and his pig came up to Frau Kranz, who was wrapped in her blood-splattered blankets in her chair by her dying fire.

'There's something I need you to do for me, my Little Maus,' she faltered, laying a dry and wrinkled hand upon his head as he sat obediently on the floor beside her, letting her fingers brush briefly at his taupe.

'You have to go,' she said. 'You have to leave me.'

The boy turned his head towards her, the panic and bewilderment so evident upon his face that her heart took a final dash at life and beat just a little faster.

'They mean to take Kroonk away from you, dear one,' she said, thin tears tracking down her parchment cheeks. 'You must have seen the spit they have set up, down towards the bridge . . .'

The words came from her slowly, keeping her eyes on Philbert's, waiting for the shock of realisation that must come. And so it did, a single gasp escaping the boy as he threw his arms around Kroonk's neck; this small red pig who had been

31

companion, brother and sister to him for as long as he could remember, and silently he wept, and silently he clung to her, Kroonk sitting there on her haunches like an overweight dog, her rounded belly pushing out between her legs.

'I knew this day must come,' Frau Kranz went on, 'I've been racking my brains for a solution, and now I have it. You must go, and you must take this with you.'

She fumbled her shaking fingers beneath her pillow and brought out a small wooden box the colour of newborn chestnuts, with a lustre that hinted of sun-warmed forests far away.

'Look inside,' she said, and Philbert did, lifting out a long, curly tress of hair smelling of chocolate and spices, scents from long ago he half remembered every time he walked past the confectionery shop in town.

'It's your Mamma's,' Frau Kranz wheezed. It had been a day of exertion for her, forcing herself up from bed into chair to endure the overzealous care of overzealous neighbours, trying all the while to come up with a way out of a situation of which she would not, could not, contemplate being even a small part. She had known the moment she woke that a decision had to be made, and now she'd made it, and was about to do the hardest thing she'd ever done in her life, sending away the one person who had ever really mattered to her, the child she'd helped into life and practically brought up those first few years, and done so single-handed in the few years following that. And by sending this child away she knew she was condemning herself to die alone in this little shack, with no one to light up her last few days or hold her hand when she passed into the hereafter. But he was so young, this little boy with his misshapen head, and it was precisely because of that head that she had found an answer at last.

'Hush now, child,' she said, mustering every last inch and ounce of strength she had left in her. 'You must take Kroonk and you must go away, my darling, for I cannot protect you any more.'

The boy was crying freely now, great hiccupping sobs breaking from him as he clutched the box she had given him in one hand and Frau Kranz's skinny fingers in the other.

'You must go, my lamb,' she whispered, snatching breath from the air like scraps of autumn leaves. 'And you must go now. There's a sack beneath the bed. I've packed everything you'll need.'

Philbert unwillingly let go her hand and pulled out the sack as she directed him, small hands trembling as he opened its neck, glancing inside, then placing Nelke's box in with all the rest.

'But where will I go, Mama?' his voice was thin as smoke, hardly audible, but Frau Kranz heard, her heart squeezing almost shut to hear that one word *Mama*, a word she'd hoped to hear all her long life, but never had until now, right at the moment she was having to send this surrogate son away from her, knowing she would never see him again.

'Go to the Fair,' she said. 'Ask them to take you in. Offer to do any jobs for them that you can. Show them your taupe, Little Maus, and maybe that will help.'

She didn't know much about Fairs but she knew they liked unusual, and that was Philbert. She had no more words, so tired it was hard to draw in breath, could only squeeze Philbert's fingers lightly as he lowered his head upon her knees, feeling the warmth of his tears soaking through her skirts, looking down on that taupe of his, at the skin stretched taut over it the colour of spilled tea, that incongruous twist of hair growing slightly off centre; she stroked her Little Maus with all the gentleness her long and childless life had given her, stroked it ever more slowly, slowly, slowly, until she was asleep.

He was too young to understand the full implications of what he was about to do but Frau Kranz's word was good enough for him, so when her hand fell from his head to her lap Philbert moved, stood up, kissed his good Frau Kranz upon her clammy forehead. Then he picked up the sack she had prepared for him but did not go out of the door as might have been expected, for he'd grasped the import of what might happen to Kroonk if he did. Instead he went to the back of the shack and prised up a loose section of the metal-sheeted wall that was thin, corroded by all the salt that pervaded the whole of Staßburg. It gave easily, and soon wide enough for him and Kroonk to wriggle their way through. Straight into the yard then and down past the chicken coop, and from there to the river meadows where Shminiak and Nelke first lay down together, and on into the darkness, bypassing the neighbours' spit that Philbert saw burning merrily away at the tail end of their street, just as Frau Kranz had said it would be. His heart was thudding hard. When he was close by the bridge he picked Kroonk up, pulled her to his chest, dragging his jacket as far as he could across her to keep her hidden, holding the sack up in front of them both for a last protection.

To the Fair, Frau Kranz had directed him, and towards the Fair he went, and over the bridge without any trouble, keeping his head down, moving with the rest of the crowd surging over its back, jostling and laughing as they went to the Last Night of the Fair. He folded himself into the hustle and bustle of folk as they funnelled into the Fair's Ground, slipping a lead around Kroonk's neck as he let her down, wary of anyone who might yet recognise her and try to grab her up, moving immediately away from the crowds and down to the river. He listened to the water moving ever onward to who knew where. He listened to all the people shouting and singing, flinging themselves into this last night of holiday, fully aware that tomorrow it would be back to the mines, back to grudge and drudge, back to normality. He moved away, lay down on the river bank, eyes wide open – Kroonk beside him – wondering what to do, how to find Little Lita, make her understand. He was so tired and troubled that he didn't even realize he'd fallen asleep.

Next thing he knew he was being awoken by a small hand shaking his shoulder. Philbert started, jumped up, his hand gripping tight about the rope that held him fast to Kroonk, his eyes going straightaway towards the bridge, looking for trouble.

'I'll not let Kroonk go!' he shouted, almost before he knew he was speaking. 'I'll not, I will not!'

But the person standing before him was no enemy, no neighbour or townsperson wanting to turn his Kroonk into spit and sausage. Instead it was the one person in the entire world he wanted to see. It was Lita, and she was looking at him so strangely that his throat constricted and would allow out no more words, not even the gasp of surprise he felt but could not express. After his small outburst about the pig she did nothing for a few moments, was merely observing this small boy with his overburdened head and the small pig nuzzling at his knee like a frightened dog. She took a step back from them and glanced across at the river, seeing the lights of the Fair reflecting dimly from the shack she knew to be the boy's home, precisely because it had been from this very spot she'd first spied him – and his odd little pig – dipping their collective feet into the river. She'd seen in him at that moment something she recognised of old, the very reason she'd crossed the bridge that first night of the Fair just to check it out. And she knew why he was here now, though not the particular reason behind it, but she knew, and was kind, and reached out a hand and took Philbert's in her own.

'It's always been like this,' Lita said, in that oddly high voice of hers that had Philbert thinking back to the serinette his father had given him the morning he'd left, hoping it was in the sack he was clutching as if it was a chicken whose neck he'd just wrung. 'And maybe always will be,' she went on. 'Towns we pass through? The people we see? Always someone to gather up with us when we leave. You're not the first, Little Maus, and you won't be the last.'

35

She wrapped her warm-as-tinder fingers around Philbert's lonely own and led him, as she'd done for others before, into a brand new world.

5

Introducing the Carneous Mole

They all left Staßburg along different paths, Nelke with her Frenchman, Shminiak with his sadness and Lamentations, Philbert with his Kroonk and the Fair. Only Frau Kranz stayed, buried in her blankets all the night while her neighbours combed the streets with their newly-sharpened knives. They came back during the night several times, hammering on her doors, shouting out to release the pig, but by then she'd braced a bolt of cloth up against the handle so they couldn't get in and, after performing this last rite of protection for the boy and his pig, she crawled from door to bed. Several days later, one of her neighbours came looking and did what she should have done before and had her man beat down the door with a sledge-hammer. And there was Frau Kranz, curled up like a hedgehog on her bed, surrounded by blood-boltered sheets, her body a sack of rot already leaking out of every orifice.

No mourning for good Frau Kranz, nor the encomium she deserved, only the shack being put to torch and flame – with her inside – once it had been pilfered of anything vaguely useful, the conflagration surrounded by those same women in their clogs to whom Frau Kranz had so assiduously administered during the Great Grippe; paying that kindness no mind at all and spitting into the flames for allowing the boy to escape with the pig they'd been so eager to purloin, assuming it to be communal property having fed it their scraps and chuckings-out, dreaming of all the crackling and moist flesh, soups and pies now beyond their reach. They treated the traitor Frau Kranz no better than they would the coom that gathers at the naves of wheels, or the soot that blackens the oven mouth, pulling down the last of the shack after the burning, and brushing its ashes – and hers – roughly from their hands, as if they'd already forgotten her name.

~

By then, Philbert was many miles distant and so in thrall to his new adventure he immediately forgot everything that had gone before, including Frau Kranz and what might have become of her. He was bemused by everything Lita showed him, by the oddities and eccentricities of the Fair, no one giving his taupe a second glance. That first night, Lita tucked Philbert and his Kroonk away up over the tailgate of her travelling caravan, squashing them into a corner between the drawer she used for a bed and the giant Frau Fettleheim, who claimed to be the fattest woman in all the world, and whose wheezing filled the small space, along with her grunts and grumblings.

'More mouths to feed, Lita,' the huge Frau Fettleheim moaned. 'What were you thinking?'

But Frau Fettleheim was not a cruel person, and she had not refused the extra company of Philbert and his pig despite her apparent objections. She recognised straightaway, just as Lita had done, that both were cast-offs and had nowhere else to go. Everyone in the Fair understood this because, in one way or another, they'd all been there themselves. It wasn't long, therefore, before Frau Fettleheim began to pat Kroonk's head and tickle her ears, especially after Kroonk laid her head on Frau

Fettleheim's knee, at which point she saw in Kroonk rather more of herself than she was comfortable with, this fat little piggling who had been destined, before her escape, to being gutted, sliced, divided and devoured.

'Poor Piggy,' she said then. 'Poor little piggy. And of course you must both stay.'

And so they did, Philbert and Kroonk hugging each other tight that first ever night away from their home, Frau Fettleheim huge and snoring on the one side, Little Lita curled up in her drawer on the other. They both lay awake for a long time, listening to the whelps of dogs, the stamping feet of unknown animals, the gentle plash of the river as it wrestled a tree bough down its length, men and women lurching and leaning against the wood of the small caravan, retching or relieving themselves a few inches away outside, owls later screeching close in the darkness, swooping down on wide black wings, claws skewering the mice and shrews that ran amongst the debris of the carts, and then the final, empty egg-blown silence when only the faintest fibrillation of wind and water were left once human-kind had at last gone away, and all else was left to sleeping.

～

Morning came of a sudden, a huge hullabaloo that grew with every moment like a large bear growling and stretching at the dawn. The Fair people arose in a ripple, one person waking up their neighbours in the adjoining cart or tent, who woke up the next one, who woke up the next. There were general shouts of 'Come on! . . . Halloo! . . . Good morning . . .' and the sounds of animals scratching and yawning, water splashing into kettles, onto faces, onto feet, fires being coaxed back into life, the strong smells of potatoes and cabbage frying together, of acorn coffee and pine-needle tea, pots and harnesses rattling, stalls being broken down, the clacking of wood on metal, great whooshes of canvas being folded and stowed.

Lita woke in a moment, put on her battered red shoes, and

was up. She tidied the last few oddments still lying around, packing Philbert and Kroonk into a corner and telling them to stay quiet and still, folded some of her tiny dresses and put them into her drawer and closed it shut. Other cupboards in the caravan, cunningly concealed in floors and walls, under seating and tables, were revealed and filled. Frau Fettleheim's voluminous garments doubling as tablecloths and covers flicked expertly into the air and caught on the way down, rolled into tubes and pushed between Frau Fettleheim's feet if they could not fit elsewhere. She herself was still asleep, and Lita put her finger to her lips, whispering to the newcomers not to wake her, to stay put, that they would soon be on their way. Outside she went, pushing up the tailgate behind her and closing the wooden hatch of the door. The cart jangled and creaked and jolted as an animal was hitched into its shafts. Frau Fettleheim slept on, her giant, goitre-necked head lolling to and fro, the great bun of her hair gradually sliding to one side, unravelling with the movement, slipping onto her lap like a lazy cat. Then without further warning the cart lurched forward, began trundling over the flattened ground, settling after a few minutes into a gentle rock. Frau Fettleheim awoke briefly, her eyes misty and glazed, grunting something incomprehensible before falling back to sleep.

Cautiously, Philbert crawled upwards and knelt beside the snoring Frau, lifting the corner of the canvas. Up front he could see a man's dark back, hands casually flicking the reins back and forth over the rump of the pony that was pulling the caravan on, and could see maybe twenty, thirty carts in front, doing exactly the same. Little Lita suddenly tumbled into the back end of the cart and he turned towards her, saw she was holding a small basket on her knee. Lita smiled, thrusting towards him the basket filled with warm bread, dark and moist, smelling of pumpernickel and rye. Philbert pinched it off bit by bit, one for him, one for Kroonk, savouring it, glancing out behind Lita, who had turned her attention away. He could see through a chink in the tailgate's canvas the dust bowling up from the wheels of this cart and the one that followed, and the faint glories made by the newly risen sun around the salt crystals that had always made up his world, wondering what would happen now, searching for a last glimpse of the riverbank and the chicken-shed and the shack that lay beyond; but there was nothing but the sunrise and the dust-motes and the flapping of the canvas, until Lita tied it shut.

~

Philbert's new life was unimaginably exciting and exhilarating as he tried to make himself useful in every way he could. He watered Tomaso's third eye relentlessly until Tomaso begged him to stop, take it easy, do it every now and then or not at all. He was sick of having his collar drenched every few minutes, he chided Philbert, pushing him away, telling him to make himself useful elsewhere. Philbert was glad at this rejection, disliking the way that ghastly third eye kept gazing on unperturbed, always ungrateful, and switched his attentions instead to the man known as Herr Fischmann, finding in him a more willing recipient of his care.

Herr Fischmann had skin that flaked and floozied into red-rimmed scales, and he taught Philbert how to rub the tubs of paraffin-wax and jelly into his sores, making his skin shine like the oiled fish-back he was supposed to resemble, discovering that without this constant treatment Herr Fischmann would dry out like desert sand, his outer surface falling in handfuls to the floor, leaving raw red welts behind, scabbed over with dark black blood. He began to understand that Hermann, Herr Fischmann, spent only a tiny proportion of his life as a prize exhibit, the rest remaining hidden, dominated by a never-ending regime of being daubed over with liniments and swabs, or collecting the herbs that went into such treatments, no glamour for *The Half Man, Half Fish* advertised on his

41

hoarding, who was the saddest man Philbert had ever met.

'You cannot imagine what it's like,' Hermann said, as Philbert rubbed Hermann's skin with soothing sage-scented oil, 'to lie in bed and have a million moth-wings flutter at your body, feeling their eggs hatch and writhe beneath your skin, wriggling and squirming, squirming and wriggling. My whole night is like that, Philbert. My whole life. Turn and itch, scratch and turn, itch and scratch. And when I rise in the morning I shake from my sheets the litter of my body, the parts that have escaped me during the night. It's terrible, Little Maus, a terrible curse . . .'

And Philbert supposed that it was. Certainly his own little bodily oddity was nothing in comparison, so unworthy of comment that nobody ever commented on it at all except for the adoption of the name Little Maus following Lita's lead, a pet name he became proud of, relating to his head absolutely and yet absolutely without offence. He'd no third eye, nor was he a giant like Frau Fettleheim, or a dwarf – as he now recognised Lita to be. His taupe, amongst such people, was negligible.

Philbert tended Hermann assiduously, quickly learning how to make his special liniments, soaking gelatine leaves overnight, mixing rose-water with the necessary albumen before adding glycerine of borax, heating and filtering all through a piece of twill. Hermann, in return, was the kindest of men, despite the constant scritch, scritch, scritch of blunt nails against skin and the stink of fish seeping from his pores.

'It's the show,' Hermann sighed, dousing himself in cod-oil, standing in his pail and the green light quivering through his tent. 'They pay and they expect,' he explained, staring at the plate of perch or trout or whatever else had been provided, that stared right back. The crowd came in and clumped about him, holding their noses, touching their fingers momentarily to his scaly skin, grimacing as Hermann forced the flesh of raw fish inside his mouth. They threw pennies into the water surrounding his flaking feet, gagging at the smell of him, the stink of his breath, the stench of his disease, then out they rushed into the fresh air, laughing at the spectacle they'd seen.

One night Philbert brought out his sack, extracting the first of his treasures, holding out to Hermann the long, long, lock of Nelke's hair, hoping it might give him some pleasure. Hermann would not touch it, saying he could not, would not taint it with his fingers. Philbert persisted but Hermann pulled back, reaching instead behind him and slipping a velvet cover from a large glass bottle and placing it on the overturned crate that made his table.

'See?' Hermann pointed. 'This is my treasure, and my mirror.'

Philbert looked, saw a forest of green fronds and a small fish winding between them, a startling thing: blue on yellow with horns like a cow, and almost as square as Nelke's box.

'Beautiful,' Hermann murmured. 'And so happy inside his strange skin . . .'

Philbert loved it, had never seen anything like it, watched it paddle around its bottle, twitching between the weeds. Hermann never did tell Philbert how or where he'd come by this flash of delight, though he did show Philbert later how to chew up bits of meat for it and spit it into the bottle, how to net algae from the ponds and riverbanks they passed, wrapping it around sticks serving as a treat for Butterblume, as Hermann called the fish.

'Every time, before we travel,' Hermann told Philbert, 'we must make sure to cover the bottle with this velvet cloak so that Butterblume can sleep.'

Very important, said Hermann, for when upset the fish released a toxin, and in such a small space all that would achieve was self-destruction.

'Just like a man,' Philbert heard Herr Hermann saying as he gazed sadly into the water where Butterblume was nibbling on

43

the shower of Hermann's skin that had floated down from his dangling fingers. 'Just like a man.'

~

It was morning, it was summer, and three months since Philbert had left Staßburg.

He escaped the gloom of Hermann's tent to attend to his other duties, which by now included waiting on Maulwerf, the Father of the Fair. When first introduced by Lita, Maulwerf studied Philbert top to toe, telling him to turn around slowly, all the while stroking the sharp point of his beard.

'Hmm. The Coconut Boy, possibly. Although who in this country has heard of coconuts? The Boy with An Egg in his Head? That might work.'

'His name is Philbert,' volunteered Lita, 'but we call him Little Maus,' and Maulwerf laughed like a squeaking door, squealing into his beard.

'Very good! Very good!' he gurgled, 'And why are you here, my Little Maus-Junge?'

Philbert mumbled out his brief, all too common, tale, pointing also at Kroonk emerging from Frau Fettleheim's skirts, jumping inexpertly down from the cart, snuffling enquiringly at a curl of discarded carrot peel. Maulwerf became serious.

'I've heard you've been most useful to Herr Hermann,' he said, 'and that is to be admired. But be warned, Little Maus-Junge . . . I am the man who judges who has earned his keep and who has not. And if I find you wanting then you're off. You understand?'

Philbert nodded, his face pale and frightened at this threat of expulsion, then Maulwerf twirled his cane and stabbed it into the ground an inch away from Philbert's foot.

'Good,' he continued. 'That is settled, then. You will see to Hermann, and you will also be my personal valet and sous-chef.'

He lifted his silver-topped, mud-bottomed cane an inch above

Philbert's head, leaning in very close, a faint whiff of garlic escaping him as he gave out his further orders. Every morning Philbert was to brush his velvet jackets, clean his glasses with a special piece of lint, prepare the day's food to his precise specifications, and aid him in his act.

'The Mouse and the Mole,' Maulwerf murmured, chuckling. 'Yes, Little Maus, you will do. And your duties for me will start tonight.'

And so that very evening Philbert helped set up Maulwerf's stall and started to shout out the words he'd been taught:

'Come and see! Come and see! The Man who eats anything! The Carneous Mole! The Man who eats anything so long as it's flesh – foul or fair! Come and see! Come and see!'

Maulwerf sat at his table, bibbed-up and tuckered, white napkin hovering beneath his chin, white teeth flashing at the gathering crowd. The latter did as bid, turning up with off-cuts of maggot-ridden mutton, bowls of slithering worms, raw and festering chicken-combs and mash of beetle, rancid pork, moulded bacon. Maulwerf sat there calmly, smiling at the pile upon his plate, knife and fork poised daintily, and ate what he'd been given, ate every last scrap to the horror of the crowd – although this was what they'd paid to see – swallowing it down in a satisfied gulp. Women's hands stayed motionless on their cheeks, children gagging into their skirts; menfolk laughing half-heartedly before turning away as they went a bilious green. The Carneous Mole ate all before him then dabbed his lips carefully with his spotless bib, bowing to those who'd had the stomach to stay, before turning and walking stately back into his tent. Here Philbert was at the ready holding the bucket and up the whole lot would come, a mangled mess of gristle and skin, maggot and meat, all slimed in the stench of warm vomit.

'How utterly disgusting!' they could hear the excited cries outside the tent. 'How revolting! How does he do it?'

'How easy to make a living,' chuckled Maulwerf, rubbing his hands.

'How do you do it?' Philbert asked, his eyes bright with admiration, his belly churning its way down to his knees.

'No sense of smell, Junge. No trick – can't smell nor taste a thing. Never could. Good plexus control is the key, swallow it down, bring it up. Years of training went into this,' he said, slapping his velvet-bound paunch and letting rip a short ballad of burps. 'Now bring me some proper grub, and a decent decanter of wine.'

So Philbert returned the table to the privacy of the tent, where Maulwerf sat as meticulously well dressed as before, velvet brushed, bib tucked, smile rucked in expectation across his face, Philbert bringing out a plate of boiled and mashed potatoes, some fried leeks (squeaky), an aubergine roasted in its skin (crisp on the outside, creamy within) and, to finish, a bowl of grapes, which sometimes Maulwerf peels and pops into his mouth, spitting the pips out one by one, and sometimes sucks like sweets until they burst and melt in his mouth.

'Better than a mountain of meat,' says Maulwerf, in a well-rehearsed speech, 'better than a bathful of beef . . .' and under the table Kroonk bows her head, polishing his plates one by one.

'Kroonk,' she grunts and falls asleep.

'Quite right,' laughs Maulwerf, delighted to follow suit, his head on the table, his velvet shoulders hunched in the evening light.

Philbert was happy in those times, travelling from town to town, forgetting the last as soon as he arrived at the next. The only person who looked backwards was Tomaso, and only with an eye that didn't see.

'It's bad luck to look back,' announced Maulwerf as Philbert rode at his side, the giant and the dwarf in the cart behind them. 'Look around you, look ahead,' he said, 'but never, ever look back.'

6

Kartoffelkrieg

The Fair circled east with the next spring, going through Paderborn and Holzminder, past Hoxter and over the Hills of Harz. Philbert made Hermann's ointments and liniments, held sick-bowls and chopped vegetables for Maulwerf, brushed his velvet waistcoats until they shone and sang like silk. He washed Frau Fettleheim's stinking feet, learned to roll up the canvas on demand for paying customers, for she was so gigantic she could no longer move from the cart. He patched her ever-expanding clothes and slid open the lid of the water closet over which she sat, gaining the strength and timing needed for such a task. Best of all for Philbert were the moments when he dangled his toes in numerous clear-running streams, Lita at his side, telling him of her life, all fifteen long years of it. She told him of the doctor who'd found her on some sunny Adriatic shore and promised to take her to Rome to see the brilliant doctors there who would make her grow. She wept when she told him how she'd said goodbye to her mother and father, brothers and sister; how she'd packed her small bag and given the doctor all the family's money to pay her way; how she'd left with him and gone to Rome as promised, but not for treatment. Instead he set her up as a side-show, charging the Signores and Signoras umpteen lira to watch her dance, curtsey and prance at their knees, claiming she was the cousin of the famous Sicilian Fairy; carting her on to Florence, Venice, Turin, Milan, Zurich and then Munich. He tied her hair in ribbons, taught her how to whistle like a bird; bought her pretty dresses and slept too close to her at night; tried to make her drink strong liquor, which she refused, and then had shouted and slapped her hard across the face until she finally ran.

'Ran just like my Little Maus,' she whispered, and hung her arm around his neck, for just like her Little Maus Puppelita had run and found the Fair.

～

It was in fact not one Fair but many, all connected, though separate, like a bunch of grapes. In Philbert's part were the Marvellous Marvels: Little Lita, Hermann, Tomaso, Frau Fettleheim and The Carneous Mole. Then there were the food-and-drink men, and the pedlars who came and went as they chose, sometimes with the Fair, sometimes away, always carrying cases bulging with strange tools and inventions: books and beads, knives and ornaments, knick-knacks of diverse descriptions. Also were the dedicated merchants who rolled out great widths of wool and cotton and occasionally, more exotically, embroidered silks; there were the card-men who set up betting games: skittles, reverso, nine men's morris, spot-the-jack. And the artisans who made jewellery, studded belts, embroidered dresses, sharpened knives, sewed gloves, hammered copper, made wheels and mended carts. Lastly were the actors and singers who put on plays and pageants, running dancing troupes throughout the streets, reciting bawdy ballads, disseminating the topical news from one town to the next. All were many and various, attaching themselves to the Fair one day and then gone the next, staying a week or a month before choosing a different path to a different town.

And it was the arrival of one such band one ordinary day,

with such normal quotidian occurrence, that caused that day to end with Philbert's neck in a noose and someone pulling tight upon the rope. They'd no licence, that small group of stragglers joining the Fair somewhere outside Belzig, though every town a person passed through demanded one. Not so onerous in the smaller ones – a few coins to the Mayor or the Bürgermeister or the Schupo, depending on who was the richer, held the most power, or ran the most influential guild. Maulwerf's Fair rarely had problems, for he was well known, had been travelling more or less the same routes regularly for many years and carried a small leather satchel stashed full of introductory letters and high recommendations, one of which would be enough to let him and his Fair pass. But carnivals are loose things, with many threads dangling from their skirts, and people came and went as they pleased. The taxes had been hard those last months in those parts; the winter bad and, as at Staßburg a couple of years before, people had eaten their storehouses inside out with nothing left until the next harvest, only a few sacks of mouldy peas or corn-heads, some spills of flour swept up from the threshing floors mixed with mouse droppings and the tails of dead rats. As the year dragged over from '46 to '47, empty stomachs grumbled and grew bleak with discontent.

Berlin had seen the worst of it, where starving peasants had erected barricades throughout the town, smashing the boots they hadn't boiled for stew through shop windows, storming the storehouses of the rich. The Potato Revolution, as it was known, didn't last long. Men were weak, soldiers stronger. The peasants got the pleasure of breaking down the walls of the crown prince's palace before having their heads stamped into the frosty ground and filthy pavements of Berlin, or got themselves strung up ten at a time on gibbets that scarcely trembled under their combined and paltry weight. The Kartoffelkrieg was over almost before it had begun, but ideas are slippery as eels and move just as quickly and like fire can sneak off into the undergrowth, feeding on subterranean sources, flaring up in unexpected places, and soon all the towns around Berlin had their own little revolutions and their own little parties of rope and wood, and yet still some escaped, and on they went.

The leader of the straggly band Philbert's Fair bumped into was a woman. She'd lost her husband, her father, her brothers and two sons. Several daughters and daughters-in-law had gone missing along the way every time they passed a troop of soldiers, and what happened to them didn't bear thinking about. And so this was a woman with anger sewn right into her bones, and a brace of ugly little grandchildren sucking greedily at her drooping breasts. They melded into the Fair's protection, extras in the semi-permanent acting troupe that had been thinned out, as was normal, by winter, disease and desertion. But they brought a posse of Schupo mercenaries on their heels who swaggered into the camp one evening, blazing pistols and blunderbusses. The Fair was already set up and going well; the village they'd stopped upon still had a few coins to bandy about and a few scrawny goats to roast, so one night out of their lives didn't seem too much to squander for the villagers' entertainment.

'Roll up! Roll up!' Philbert was already shouting at the top of his pipsqueak voice, and Maulwerf already had his table out and laid. Lita was pirouetting on Frau Fettleheim's knees and singing her songs, giant and dwarf complementing each other's size, all of which had drawn the crowds. Across the temporary stage the acting troupe were scraping out their steps, the laughter rising at their farces and antics and the latest popular ballads about princes with necks like chickens and beaks of gold. The night was sparkling with embers blown free from fires by the wind, and the goats had had their throats sliced and haunches skinned and were sizzling on their spits.

The screams, when they started, were only somewhat out of place, and nobody took much notice until that anger-spun woman came yelling through the mud and carts, her children's children hanging like an overweight necklace from her thin shoulders, cursing with all her might the iniquities of the state and the scourge of taxes and the wickedness of the world that had taken so much from her and left her with only poverty and starvation for companions. There was no doubting the woman had gone mad on her trek out from Berlin, drawing that pack of soldiers behind her like hornets after honey. The men on horseback had been sent scouring for the troublemakers and had not far to look. They sent a few shots into the crowd to discourage any upstarts who might complain, killing one man stone dead as he raised his fist to throw nothing more iniquitous than his dice; they sent a lance through one of the dancers because she was wearing an unpatriotic combination of colours, sending the rest of them skittering from the stage, sliding on her blood; they broke up the painted backboards because they depicted a rural idyll with no sign of prince or palace, skewered several of the old woman's followers to its splintered remains because they started flinging handfuls of sugared sweets at the soldiers in feeble protestation.

That woman's voice was hoarse as a boar's by the time she skidded into the mud at Philbert's feet, her throat still wobbling with all the words she could no longer get out, shaking with frustration as she tried to pick herself up, untangle her legs from her skirts and grandchildren as the soldiers came crashing along the cartways, knocking people over, upsetting stalls, sending gaming boards flying, spilling all their tiny counters and carved wooden figures into the ruck of wet grass and mud.

Philbert scooped up one of the woman's dropped grand-children as the hooves hove into view, the sweat and froth of the wild-eyed horses trampling the other child beneath them as they got that woman nicely caught between their flanks, her fists still flailing, her hair all gone wild and getting into her mouth as she found the strength again to scream about injustice and starvation and the families that had been butchered on the streets of Berlin. It didn't last long, those men having done all this before, and they caught her up by her hair and hauled her behind one of the horses with a rope, firing a few more shots at random into the air until her fellow Berliners came forward one by one, eking themselves out from the rest of the Fair, not wanting the people who had taken them in to hang with them.

'My baby,' the woman whispered as she was dragged around the course and came to land back where she'd started, and the soldiers misunderstood and looped their rope around the closest child's neck, ready to throttle her last remaining family before her eyes. Philbert's eyeballs were almost squeezed from his head with the pressure of it, Maulwerf hurrying forward, scrabbling for Philbert's arm as the man on the horse began to haul Philbert up, his feet kicking and struggling, into the air.

'It's the wrong boy!' Maulwerf was shouting, and the baby Philbert had dropped started squalling where it lay and the woman reached out her fingers to touch her.

'The last one,' she managed to whisper, and the soldier laughed as Philbert's feet cleared the ground, coming level with the underbelly of his horse.

'The last one,' she croaked again, and started to crawl away from the horse towards the fallen child, and then at last the man saw the little body towards which the woman was squirming and let go the rope, sending Philbert crashing to the ground between the great iron-shod hooves of his horse.

'I see you, woman,' he said, no colour to his voice, no anger, nor compassion or regret. He merely took his pistol from his belt and shot the child through the belly, the woman he had pursued so far feeling its hot little body's blood running out through her fingers while he slowly reloaded, finally bringing an end to the drama by firing a shot through the back of her neck.

Many years later, Philbert could still recall lying there beside the woman and her child, looking at the dappled, mud-splattered underside of that great horse, the twist at the right side of the girth-strap, the shine of the man's boots and the neat tie of their buckles, the soft leather of his gaiters reaching from heel to knee, the harsh catch of new breath as Maulwerf hauled him by the rope to one side and sliced through the knot with his knife, the enormity of the following barrage of shots and the sudden release of the noose making his ears bleed, so that all that he could hear as the soldiers cleared out was a subdued wave of outrage, men and women weeping as they dragged the Berliners' corpses to one side, the sharp slice and thud of spades going through grass as their collective grave was dug.

~

Such were the times in which they lived, and all this happened again and again before the real revolution began. Philbert couldn't know then that he would play a small but vital part in that revolution, as the trigger is a small but vital part of a gun. And it was such a small thing he would do, such a small mistake, yet it sent other men in other towns upon his heels with their own ropes in their hands and their own pistols at the ready on their belts, pursuing him far harder and more relentlessly than ever they had done this woman from Berlin.

A single flake of snow can start an avalanche, so goes the saying, and for every deluge there must, of necessity, be a first drop of rain to set it off. Snow and rain, so was Philbert. The start of snow and rain.

7

The First Nail

It was under the wheelwright's wagon that Philbert slept with Kroonk for his first couple of years with the Fair. Hermann offered to share his tent but his constant scrattelling and sighing kept anyone within ten yards awake, and sadly Philbert had to go elsewhere. It was also an addendum to the hanging incident, Philbert feeling the need to be outside and free, would wake with his hand at his throat making sure it was still there and not being stretched like a length of washed-out sheep-gut on a rack. He developed a fear of big horses, couldn't bear the touch and scratch of rope upon his skin, had to have a special twine made of leather for Kroonk's lead.

His miraculous escape from a hard death became well known, and he turned into a lucky charm of sorts for people who might not say a word to him, nor speak his name, but would often place their palm briefly upon his head as they passed him by, trying to take a little of the mouse-boy's good fortune for their own.

The one person Philbert felt truly safe with was Otto Stellmacher, the wheelwright, huge and red with work, arms bulging like beer kegs, hard as cooper's bands, and with a massive beard pockmarked with cinder-holes hiding him from cheek to chest. He mended wheels, staves, strouters and strakes; shoed horses and donkeys; cooped barrels and mended ploughs. He tried to teach young Philbert about spoke-dogs and whipper-trees, twisty-bits and clouts, coach-screws and cotter-pins, dowels and gugs; but there was too much to remember, too many names and whats and wheres and which to weld or tap and turn. Philbert nodded as though his neck really had been broken, trying to concentrate before sidling off under pretext of having something else to do, Stellmacher sadly shaking his head behind him, saying that one day he would regret not learning a proper trade when he'd nothing left to sell in this world and nobody left to teach him.

But he was still there the morning Philbert came crawling back, flush-faced beneath the wheelwright's mournful gaze, begging for the lessons he had treated previously with lack of interest, explaining his grand plan as best as he was able, telling Otto about Frau Fettleheim: how she could no longer leave her cart for her size, could hardly move, had begun to smell like a leper-gatherer's cart, worse than the turd-heaps piled high to dry in a dyer's yard; how Lita struggled in her attempts at weekly bed-baths, how the oranges she'd soaked with attar and stuck with cloves to hang as scent-lockets were all too little and too late. Otto listened, thinking mostly of Little Lita, having already noted how pale and pinched she looked, or rather how much paler and more pinched she looked than usual; he knew, as all the fair-men did, that she'd said the night before that she couldn't take it anymore and would have to leave the little caravan that had been her home and the woman who was the closest thing she had to a mother. And besides all that, the Little Maus's idea was rather a good one, having the triple advantage of teaching the boy the rudiments of a trade, airing out the Frau, and letting Lita back into her home. Frau Fettleheim herself was not immune to her own condition and keenly regretted Lita's absence, giving a short, heartrending speech to anyone who would listen as the tears fell down the uncooked pastry layers of her face.

'I cannot bear to be this big, but I don't know how to be any other way. And I cannot bear my own stench, nor that it has finally driven Lita away. Have someone drag my cart down to the river, hack out the boards and throw me in. Walk away and leave me. At least I'll get to be outside again, if only for the few moments before I sink. And I'll get to see something other than the same view of those behind and those ahead, and the roads and the mud and the arse-end of one town followed by the back-end of the next . . .'

Otto was moved by the woman's plight and by Philbert's attempt at a solution, ashamed he'd not come up with the idea himself. He stroked his beard, pulling the gold-and-grey streaks of it into tracks, revealing a small hint of lips moving somewhere beneath the overlying scrub of hair, because it was indeed an elegant solution.

'So once we've built this cart of yours, Philbert, how do you propose to propel it?'

He'd already formed an answer but wanted to push Philbert into thinking of it for himself.

'We could pull it ourselves?' Philbert asked, at which Stellmacher had to laugh, a sound akin to the spilt water he sent over his anvil sometimes to cool it down, then bent down and drew his finger through the sand.

'Like this,' he said, making several lines. 'This is the shaft, and these are called sides; here are the summers, shutlocks and cross keys. We'll build big wheels rimmed round in iron, and place the fore-carriage just above the axle to give it more strength, for my God, the strength they shall need!'

He chuckled, swore Philbert to agreeing he would learn the names of each bit of wood, the square, the aft and fore, the bevel and pin. Philbert hung his head and accepted his fate, understanding that a man should suffer for his friends, unaware how much they would suffer for him in the future.

He took all Otto's instructions and worked harder than he had ever done. Otto's hands were tough and strong as tanner's boards, unlike his which were soft, and wept blisters in their misery. He planed the ash, hewed the oak, lathed the shafts and cornered the keys. They made the cart narrower at the front so that when tipped it would loosen its load the easier.

'Very important,' said Otto, 'particularly considering the load.'

He taught Philbert to rest his wrist on his knee so he didn't chop off his fingers with knife or saw, how to drive in a nail without splitting the board. Philbert watched as Otto fitted the felloes of the rim, shouldered the spokes, swung the hammer to drive them harder into the stock, admiring the way he dished the wheel so it leant in at the top, out at the bottom. And then together they painted the finished product the glorious green that only a mixture of white-lead and arsenic can give, and when dried and all was ready, the cart shining and gleaming, it was late in the evening, but no one wanted to wait and away they went to Frau Fettleheim's, solemnly knocking on the boards, announcing that the carriage awaited its queen.

It was a truly glorious creation, just the right height to shift Frau Fettleheim over from caravan to cart, and the fat lady squawked with delight, kicking up her ankles, sending a ripple through bloomers and chins and her very best dress. Once satisfied everything was in order, Otto took the reins and led the donkey off, slowly at first, Frau Fettleheim sighing with delight just to breathe fresh air, and down the field they went towards the river, people looking up from whatever they were doing as they passed, gasping at the sight, soon starting to laugh, whoop and whistle, flinging caps into the air as they followed the procession, Philbert running alongside the cart making his bows, Kroonk snaffling at the scraps that were flung in celebration, her tail wiggling madly in the excitement, people shouting out:

'The Maus is moving a mountain! Only look! Here comes the Maus and the mountain he has moved!'

Only Hermann stayed behind in the doorway of his tent, waving solemnly as the procession passed him by for the second time, seeing Philbert in the lead with the donkey, grinning like a cockle, and Frau Fettleheim's face wet with tears of joy. He stayed inside because Otto had lit an enormous fire of whin and wood scraps in celebration of Frau Fettleheim's long-awaited release from incarceration, as was only right, and he could not have been happier for her. But he couldn't step any closer to that fire, his skin would not abide it, would start its constant scritch and scratch, knowing there could be no such easy release for him. He watched the celebrations from afar, seeing the leap and crackle of flames reflected in others' faces, the shiver of stars becoming visible in the sudden dark drop of the night.

Only one person thought of him later, when the official wagon-whetting had been done and the gentle celebration descended into general riot, and that was Philbert, who came and stood by the open flap of his tent.

'Everything alright, Little Maus?' Hermann asked from his cot. And the boy came forward, proudly showing him the official wagon-whetting nail Otto had put about his neck on a thong.

'It should be yours,' the boy said. 'For it was you came up with the whole plan.'

Hermann smiled as Philbert took the thong from his over-large head and offered it up. He took it a moment, held the nail in his hand, felt its warmth, and the warmth behind its giving, before giving it back.

'It's yours,' Hermann said. 'It was you and Otto did all the hard work. So tell me, is the Frau pleased with her gift of freedom?'

He saw the boy nod, and saw too that the boy was crying. Hermann said nothing, just placed a single hand upon Philbert's head which seemed enough, the boy subsiding to the floor, curling up, apparently going to sleep. Hermann rolled back onto his cot, trying not to scratch or sigh. He didn't know why Philbert was so upset but understood that sometimes a person doesn't want a crowd but doesn't want to be alone either, just wants to know someone is there, not too far away in the darkness.

He was right about that, but wrong to believe Philbert was sleeping, for he was not. Something about Otto's giving him the nail had brought back a memory: the sudden outline of his Papa shadowed somewhere near the fire, wiping the beer from his beard; made him think of those gifts of the little serinette that sang like a lark, the donkey with its saddle of softest silk, Philbert scanning back through every minute of every day trying to find the memory of where they lay, having the strongest feeling that if he went back slow enough and long enough, he would find them hiding in some crook and cranny of his mind. And he was thinking something else too: that the whole world of his past was deep inside him, and that sure as toad follows tadpole, something good was coming, and then would come the bad.

8

The Arrival of a Stranger

Later that same Autumn, the Fair camped on the banks of a small ox-bow lake some distance from the River Mohne. Frau Fettleheim was happier than ever, Lita had moved back into her beloved drawer. People still touched Philbert's head for luck, for Fair folk were a superstitious bunch, but it was so common-place an occurrence Philbert hardly noticed. He was unaware that his almost-dying with the Berliners outside Belzig had made of him a token, a figure apart from the rest, like a shadow from the one who casts it, someone who has only to reach out his hand in order to touch the other side. The goings on with Frau Fettleheim and her cart only enhanced this image, giving it clarity, making it seem as if this Philbert had brought into existence another facet of the stone into which they had all been cut, able to see things from a different angle. For how else could a child as young as he, and as alien to their way of life, have conjured up a plan the rest of them should have thought of long before? That the root of the solution had come from Hermann and not Philbert, who had only posed the question, was incon-sequential, for the fact remained that had the boy not posed the question the solution would never have been found.

Philbert didn't know of this nebulous something-else the

Fair's folk attributed to him, and they in turn were unaware of the true consequence of Philbert's near-death experience, which was that the lever he'd felt thrown the first time Lita touched his head had taken on a significance he could neither name nor understand. What he did know was that life was short and precious and could be snatched away at any moment and that not a second of it should be lost, nor forgotten. The unsettling thoughts he'd had the night Otto gave him the nail were a small start of his understanding; Philbert became convinced that deep inside his head lay a repository of memories waiting for him to reach them: of serinette, donkey, mother and father. Quite why he found it so imperative to track down those ghosts of ages past he didn't know, only that he sensed them there lurking, tickling like feathers, enough to make him want to bring them back out into the light.

Philbert could not have expressed a whit of all this if asked, and life went on as usual, or as usual as it had become now that Philbert was part and parcel of the Fair. He performed his duties as quietly and solicitously as always, sat often with Hermann after doling out his numerous ministrations, finding a comfort with him not found elsewhere, not even with Lita with whom, young as he was, he was a little in love. Philbert was accustomed to solitude and spent much of his spare time – if not with Hermann – then away from the rest with only Kroonk for company, which was as he liked it.

On one of those Autumn evenings apart, Philbert was sitting on the edge of that ox-bow lake, the banks of the Mohne set ablaze by the low-lying sun, a depth of orange and amber in every reed, on every tree bole, everything exuding a warmth never seen at any other time of year. Philbert was ensconced amongst a heap of fallen leaves, all rustling and rattling by the nudge of the softest breeze, gossiping in small, cracked voices as he watched undiscovered worlds reflected in the smooth water of the lake a few yards below him. It was an evening of content, the Fair's folk camped up a few hundred yards from where he sat, no show to do, no wonders to perform, no villagers or town's people to impress. They sat quiet and comfortable, smoking tobacco, or an approximation of it, around their fires, or mending clothes and bits of canvas, repainting boards, brushing down donkeys, chatting quietly, hanging bowls of hare or pigeon stew over the flames.

Philbert had long since finished his duties, had prepared Maulwerf's macédoine of vegetables, simmered the quince he had picked, peeled and chopped earlier, setting its fragrant flesh into a wine jelly for a late-night treat, wondering if this time Maulwerf would get even a hint of the scents everyone else took for granted. He'd retrieved Kroonk from Tomaso's earlier attempts to have her hunt for truffles, which according to Tomaso were more valuable than gold. It was a task Kroonk had apparently been unable to comprehend, uncovering not a sliver of the fungus, spending her time kicking dead leaves into the air with such abandon and obvious joy that Tomaso despaired of her and had sulked off back to his lace-making, a trade he was learning in order to leave the Fair once and for all. Philbert was glad of it. He'd not liked the bitter twist to Tomaso's mouth when he announced Kroonk's failure, a bitter twist Tomaso tried to turn into a smile without success.

Philbert had relished the feeling of cold water on his feet when he'd paddled in the lake's shallows attempting to perfect the technique Hermann had explained to him of how to stab a fish with a sharpened stick, in the manner of a heron. Things hadn't gone well. Twice he'd stabbed at his prey and hit his foot by mistake, unaware of the illusion of refraction, and twice had mistaken a strip of weed for an eel, at which point he gave up.

He was performing the age old ritual of boy burying himself in fallen leaves, apart from his head, when he heard the noise of a clopping pony and partially exhumed himself, turned his head, seeing a man walking along the track maybe twenty yards distant, lop-eared donkey and small cart in tow. He wasn't much interested at first, for he supposed it was just another traveller, a pedlar most likely, wanting to join up with the Fair, an occurrence not unusual when they were on the outskirts of a busy town; until he recalled they weren't anywhere near a town, busy or otherwise, were deliberately in the middle of nowhere to take their ease before heading into Dortmund. He twisted himself around, observing the newcomer's progress with some suspicion, long enough with the Fair to be wary of strangers popping up from nowhere, never mind that he'd been one himself. The man looked old and stooped, wrapped around with old grey blankets, man and donkey appearing tired and thin, both hobbling slightly, the cart hiccupping slowly over the stones. Philbert followed their progress, wondering which would collapse first – donkey, cart or man – but was interested enough in their passage for him to shuffle himself free of leaves, put on his boots, call Kroonk and slowly meander his way back to camp.

Philbert heard the laughter well before he got there, and was astonished to see the stranger sitting, miraculously revived, amongst a knot of people jostling for his attention, waving their hands above their heads.

'Pick me!' their hands and mouths were saying, 'oh please pick me!'

So another Fair's person after all, and one the rest obviously knew. Philbert was about to head off again, casting one last glance at the stranger, startled to see the man looking right back at him, dark eyes aglint in the failing light. He also noticed that beneath the grey blankets he wore a monk's habit dyed red as a holly berry.

'Ah, at last!' Maulwerf shouted. 'Here he is, Kwert, our Little Maus, a subject I'm sure you'll find most interesting.' Philbert dithered but Maulwerf was not to be put off. 'Here,

Philbert. Now,' he commanded, in his not-to-be-ignored Master-of-the-Fair voice.

Philbert obeyed and came forward, to cries of, 'Oh yes!' and 'Of course, now this will be good,' and 'What do you think he's going to make of that?'

The scarlet man fixed him with his eyes and Philbert had the uncomfortable sensation of being pulled forward like a fish on a line.

'Oh my,' the scarlet man murmured as Philbert came into the fire's light and everyone else fell silent. 'Oh my word, Maulwerf!' said the man, 'but you did not lie. Come on, boy! Come here. That's it. Stand before me so I can see you properly.'

Philbert did as bid, standing like a slave on the block, heart pounding like Otto's hammer on the anvil, the man in front of him looking at him this way and that, his dark eyes probing and alive, flickering and flecked with speckles of gold. His hand came out and pulled Philbert so close he could see the tracery of broken veins lacing the man's long nose, his lips moving and pausing over his yellow teeth, and then very gently, oh so gently, he placed his outspread hand upon Philbert's head, the sleeve of his robe falling back to his elbows, goosepimples rising on hair-less skin, Philbert feeling his fingers, cool and almost weightless, as they probed the line of his taupe, setting off a shower of sparks somewhere deep inside his head. More disturbingly, each spark so engendered revealed a scene or a sound; he saw and heard a man singing and swaying his way down a salt-dusted street, weeping, calling out the name of Jehovah; saw and heard the good Frau Kranz telling him tales of how things used to be; had the scent of vanilla and chocolate right there and so strong, and had the strangest conviction that someone else's tears were running down his cheek and had a glimpse of the tear-giver, long hair pulled back, thin lips that had forgotten how to smile. Then he felt a beard against his skin, damp and unkempt, salt and dust in the air, the awful, all-pervading stench of sickness going through him like the slicing of a knife, sudden and sharp, ceasing just as quickly, leaving him sweating and dizzy, realising the stranger had released him and pulled back, that his eyes no longer glittered, his face unfathomable, the only sounds being the spitting of the fire, the settling of a swan onto the lake, the lifting of the wind from the water as the night came down properly upon them and the stars opened up in a welter in the sky.

'Well now, young man,' the man whose name was Kwert said at last, lifting Philbert's chin with one long, cold finger, looking him bang in the eye, a nail in its hole. 'What have we here? Who are you, boy?'

Philbert would have moved if he could, but felt like a snake caught on a pitchfork.

'Ph . . . Ph . . . Ph . . . Philbert,' he managed to stutter, though no one laughed.

'Philbert.' The man's whisper was long and low, dividing the night in two, him and Philbert on one side, everyone else on the other. He lifted his hand again, holding it a hair's breadth above Philbert's head and closed his eyes, and for that moment there was no one but Philbert and Kwert in the field by the Mohne, silence all around them, and for a split second Philbert saw another few sparks: a woman throwing a small piglet against a wall – Kroonk, he knew it, recognising the pain of her uncomprehending squeal; saw the same woman chop chop chopping cabbage with a knife as if her life depended on it.

'I feel great things for you, Philbert,' Kwert whispered, moving his hand away, taking Philbert's in his own, Kwert's skin cool and smooth as wind-blown apples collected at dawn before the sun filters down into the orchard. He bent his head towards Philbert, touching his forehead with his own.

'There are many things to come, my little Philbert. I see the shadows of yesterday and tomorrow rising up around you, and it will be hard for you to find your way. But if you'll grant it,

I'll guide you through the start of your journey and your achievements will be of great wonder.'

There was movement all around them then as people wrapped themselves close within their cloaks, others turning their heads away, some sniggering with self-imposed bravado at such words, more of them alarmed and worried by them, remembering the time this head-heavy boy was almost hung, remembering the old tale of Death never truly leaving the ones who've already been within his grasp, standing unseen and unbidden at their sides; those survivors more alive than the rest of them precisely because of it.

Philbert was finally loosed as Kwert announced, to no one in particular, that the show was over for tonight, and what he needed now was bread and cheese. There was a slight rustling crescendo as people rose like autumn leaves and the laughter began again, slow and uncertain at first but soon taken over by the general bustle of chatter and talk as everyone melted away from the stranger's fire, some to fetch him the victuals he'd asked for, most to go and take a drink and discuss what they'd heard tonight.

Philbert didn't move. He was as frightened as he was unwilling to leave. He'd no idea what had happened, or if anything had really happened at all, but what he did know was that the path he'd been seeking back into his past had somehow been opened up to him. Lita was the one to lead him away but he heard Maulwerf speaking as they went.

'Well, Kwert,' he said. 'Take some wine. I think you have need of it.'

He glanced back, saw Maulwerf smiling right back at him, and felt Lita's hand wrapped about his own. He didn't understand the shenanigans back by the fire, found them faintly ridiculous now, but was glad to be Philbert, and perhaps even a little proud.

~

Many years later, Philbert would think on that evening, what might or might not have happened if Kwert – with his yellow teeth, thin lips and thinner donkey – had told Philbert he was just a boy with a lump on his head, giving his taupe a quick poke and moving on after giving some vague predictions of long life and children. Maybe then those sudden outbursts of memory triggered by Kwert's touch wouldn't have become the seeds of delusion he would grow up believing: that he had a destiny different from the rest. Maybe the dead would not have been dead. And then again, maybe nothing would have changed at all. Maybe all roads do lead to Rome. Maybe it was only hubris for Philbert the Man to believe otherwise, and that the world would have been different if only he'd stayed by the lake stabbing his foot with his stick, and never allowed Kwert to lay a hand upon his misshapen head.

9

Mr Wharton's Most
Wonderful Jelly

Philbert woke early the next morning, no one else abroad, still obscurely excited by the night before. Kroonk slept on oblivious beneath their cart so he extricated his arm from her shoulder and chose to wander through the quietness of the camp alone. It suited Philbert that morning, liking the thin curls of smoke and smells wisping from abandoned fires, mingling with the snores that crept through the crevasses and cracks of carts and canvas. He poked around several ash piles until he found a warm parsnip, peeling off the blackened skin, popping the melt of pale yellow pulp into his mouth. His stick-stabbed foot had begun to throb a little as he walked, so he went down to the shallows of the ox-bow lake to dip it into the cool water.

He was shocked to find someone there already, and more so that it was Kwert. He was kneeling, head bowed so low he must have been staring almost straight into his stomach if his eyes were open, breathing steadily and loud, mumbling the same refrain over and over, though Philbert could not make out the words. Only later did Philbert learn that Kwert was a Hesychast, and this strange way of kneeling was their way of prayer and meditation. For now, though, the Hesychast Kwert took no ostensible notice of Philbert, nor Philbert of him. Philbert went instead a little way off, sat himself on a promontory, dangling his bruised foot into the water, watching the shards of sunlight shimmering down to the white sand below.

In the quiet, Philbert could hear the man a little better: a strange language, rhythmic, breathing in on one sentence and out with the next, calm and even as the ripples Philbert found himself making with his foot. The whole world seemed to have relaxed with Kwert's chanting, even the ducks and moorhens dabbling gently in the weeds were quiet, and Philbert saw the oiled brown fur of an otter ciphering in and out of the sunlit water, plashing the surface gently with its paws, watching him warily with one eye, contemplating the sky with the other. After a while, Philbert heard the clatter-batter of Kroonk coming down the bank and she came up beside him, laid her head upon his knee. A distinct smudge of charcoal upon the edge of her snout told him she'd been snuffling for scraps, and was still hungry. The interruption roused Kwert and he stretched, hauled himself up and moved towards Philbert. Once alongside, he pushed off his mud-caked boots, Philbert seeing his white feet, the dirt clogged up between his toes, big blisters on his bunion lumps that were burst and raw, as they dipped into the water next to Philbert's own. No wonder then, that the man had been hobbling the night before, making him seem so much older than he actually was. Bad feet will do that to a person, as anyone who has tramped a country up and down for all his years will know.

'Thank you for not disturbing me in my meditations,' Kwert said, his voice gentle and normal, nothing of the frightening intensity his whispers had held the night before.

'That's alright,' Philbert replied. 'It's good to be quiet in the morning.'

He turned his head, found Kwert smiling down at him, saw the stubble was grey on his chin, and was relieved he looked just like anyone else.

'I expect you're wondering who I am,' said Kwert, offering Philbert his hand as if he were a man and an equal and not a boy maybe eight or nine years old, by the best reckonings.

'I am Kwert,' he said by way of introduction. 'Tospirologist and Teller of Signs. I read people's mottlements and murfles, their warts and whitlows, their freckles and their moles. I can read character in their patterns and tell the future from the way they fall. But to tell the truth,' said Kwert, tapping the side of his nose confidentially, 'I make a lot of it up so's to please and amuse the public, as we all must do. A man has to make a living somehow in this world.'

Philbert heard him laugh softly, waiting for what else the man would say, knowing every showman has his spiel, and was not disappointed.

'For instance,' Kwert went on, 'I can tell by the red marks on the back of your pig that she is well loved and loving, has many friends and is not destined for the pudding-prick. And I can tell by the black marks on the end of her nose that she has a fondness for potatoes and roasted swede.'

Philbert smiled, waggling his feet in the water, sending up the silt, clouding the issue, though not for Kwert who added a coda to his previous statement.

'But of course,' he said, 'I was telling the truth about you.'

And before Philbert had time to get startled all over again Kwert stood up, hoisting Philbert with him by the oxters, asking Philbert to help him on with his boots as it was high time they went back to camp and chimed in with the morning's chores.

On their return journey Kwert began to lift up rocks, rootling in the damp earth below them, looking for Philbert knew not what, until finally Kwert called Philbert over and pointed with a long, soil-daubed finger.

'What do you make of that?' he said, prodding the nest of soft-skinned pearls that lay snug in by a tree root. Philbert shrugged his ignorance, and Kwert enlightened him.

'They are the eggs of the earth,' he said, pulling out a large square of linen and scooping the small cluster in, going on to lift more rocks, find more nests and more eggs. He lifted up a couple of snail shells, empty now, quite large, brown on the outer edge, striating into orange and amber, tipping into white at the spiral point.

'Roman snails,' he explained, 'come marching all the way from Italy so we may eat their eggs for breakfast.'

He looked at Philbert in that odd way Philbert would come to know so well.

'It's a sign, Little Maus,' he said, putting his hand gently on the boy's head, and just as before Philbert saw flashes of things he should have been too young to remember, Frau Kranz's talking taking form and substance, a woman hard at work in the chocolate factory of Staßburg, the patterns on the bolts of cloth where they leant against the tin wall of a shack, the taste of salt upon his lips, the grainy feel of it in his hair, the vast, shining amphitheatre of the salt-mines, its surfaces faceted and factored out where the picks had dug and hewn. But these were no jagged fragments, more the rolling in of a smooth, undulating landscape. Last night a key had been turned swiftly in its lock; this morning the door moved slowly open. Kwert himself seemed oblivious of what he had so casually set in motion with so slight a gesture, and went on speaking.

'They are a sign, Little Maus, of all the good things that are yet to come, the bounty of which hides below the surface of life's shell.'

Philbert heard none of this, and only when Kwert removed his hand a moment later did he see the trees and fields again, the river Mohne running quietly by as it had before; for a few moments he had inhabited two worlds, that of the present and the past, each as real as the other. And then his stomach began to rumble, and Kroonk jumbled herself up against his legs, and he came back to this side of life.

~

Back at camp things were awakening, Maulwerf rubbing his hands together before holding them out to a small fire.

'Kwert!' he beamed, as the pair approached. 'Come over and share breakfast,' at which Kwert made some disparaging comment about what Maulwerf could do with his cabbages and carrots and was off for something decent: snails' eggs to flip like oysters on Otto's hot anvil, Philbert to follow on when he had the chance. Kroonk recognised a good thing when she saw it and trotted off at Kwert's heels, Maulwerf laughing heartily as Philbert went to see to Hermann.

While he was rubbing a mint unguent into Hermann's poorly skin, he took the opportunity to ask about Kwert.

'Aaaaghh,' Hermann sighed as the coolness of the ointment eased his itching. 'I can't tell you much. I haven't come across him before, but Maulwerf knows him from way back. He wanders around telling fortunes and selling medicines, as so many do.'

Hermann sighed again as Philbert gently palpated the under-skin of his arms, which were red and rigid as roof-tiles.

'He seems to have taken quite a fancy to you, Philbert, most likely on account of your you know what. He reads them, I gather, freckles and bumps, like others read stars or tea leaves. You should have heard what he said to freckled Hannah last night! Or no, perhaps you shouldn't. I don't know what he'd make of me. I didn't meet him myself, keeping away from the fire as I must do, but I've heard tell that beneath all the gobbledegook he is obliged to spout for the crowds, he is a wise and devout man. A Hesychast, no less. Aaaghh, thank you, Little Maus, that's much better. Much better. Thank you.'

~

Making his way over to Otto's fire Philbert stopped by Kwert's cart, recognising the thin donkey that was busily exploring the oat-bag tied around her neck. One edge of the canvas siding had been hoisted and attached to a spindle on the ridge, exposing about a quarter of the cart's interior to open view. Curious, Philbert poked his head in a little, balancing himself on the cart-edge to get a better look, seeing several shelves with raised edges and rows of bottles secured by a cord across their middles. There were the usual ointments and unguents of varying colours, but one was different: very tall, upwards of twelve inches, yellowish in content and holding something else besides. Within the shadowed transparency of the glass he could see glutinous loops swaying slightly, run through with coloured threads, like toad-spawn on a stick. A hand on his shoulder made Philbert jump, set him rocking idiotically on the wood, knocking all the air from his lungs. Kwert laughed and set the boy gently on his feet, thrusting a poke of something hot into his hands. Philbert looked down into the rough paper cone he'd been given, intrigued by the odd smell, seeing an unappetising bundle of greying blobs, some whole, some burst, some looking like tiny gelatinised snails. It was obviously the cooked repast of earth-eggs Kwert had collected earlier, and made Philbert feel a little queasy.

'Go ahead, Little Maus, eat,' invited Kwert, and so Philbert scooped in a hesitant finger and hoiked a few out, careful not to crush them, popping them quickly into his mouth before he could change his mind. They sprang juice like berries, with a gummy hint of salt and chalk that was not displeasing, indeed was extraordinarily reminiscent of much of the food he'd eaten back in Staßburg, which came as a shock, just that he should remember such a thing.

'So, you were curious were you?' Kwert was saying, pointing at his cart. 'And curiosity is no bad thing, the key to enlighten-ment. So what did you see?'

He lowered himself to the boy's eye-level, and then where he would be if he had, like Philbert, leant in as far as he could go.

'Aah,' he said. 'Of course. My funisi,' and he threw back the rest of the canvas over the top of the cart to reveal the contents in entirety, making the bottles gleam in the morning light. He tapped at the tall jar Philbert had been so intrigued by, setting the blue worm woolding and recoiling at his touch before lifting the jar out, holding it in front of Philbert's face, tracing his finger slowly down the glass.

'This is quite something,' he said. 'A human umbilicus. A trinity of threads: two in, one out. This is what held you to your mother like a boat to the bank, like a leaf to the tree.'

Kwert was off on his spiel again and he unscrewed the jar dramatically, a strong whiff of sour wine and rotten fish puckering Philbert's nose, and then he did more, and took the cord in his finger at one end and pulled it free of the jar, the umbilicus straightened and glistened and aligned in its coils, bouncing gently in front of Philbert's eyes, as if still faintly pulsing with life.

'Like a fish on a line, like a flea on a dog,' Kwert continued, getting into his patter. 'This cord stole life from your mother and gave it to you.'

Philbert dropped his poke of eggs. The feeling of disgust in him was so strong his fingers loosened of their own accord, the funisi twitching and dangling like a hanged man, making him see himself inside his mother's swollen belly, an ugly snail cracking at its shell, sucking at her blood with its hideous straw. It accused him with every slow curling movement as it stared at him with its long and clouded eye. Kwert was still speaking, and chose that moment to lean down and pinch at where Philbert's belly button would be beneath his clothes, his fingers wet and sticky, marking Philbert's shirt with a stinking spot.

'This is where it all began, where you were lowered into the world, a spider on your mother's silk, into this tangled web of life.'

Kwert bounced the horrid noose once more before dropping it back into its jar and screwing on the lid, but by now Philbert was paralysed by nausea at the stink and could not help himself, going down on hands and knees, choking like an old dog in the dirt, nausea riding through him on a tidal bore as he understood the disgust he felt for the funisi was the same disgust his mother had felt for him every day she lived with him, until she could take it no more.

Kwert was mildly surprised at the boy's reaction and squatted down beside him, wiping the dribble from Philbert's mouth with the edge of his robe. But at the sight of that blood-red material Philbert started to heave once more, imagining birth and blood, rip and tear, not an actual memory he was having of Nelke giving birth in such agony and despair, instead a concatenation of later words and comments: that he was a monstrous thing compared to the little Elsa who should have been born in his place, rosy cheeked and perfect in every way.

That Philbert had fainted Kwert was in no doubt: his eyelids flickered faintly as if he was dreaming. He took the boy by the shoulders and shook him gently, bringing him back to field and Fair, glad to see the recognition in the boy's eyes as he began to understand where he was; that there was grass beneath him, and blue sky above, and Kwert beside.

'Are you alright?' Kwert asked, pushing the lad back against the wheel of the cart, disturbed to see the tears running down his cheeks, the awful sadness in his newly opened eyes. He'd had a few reactions to his famous funisi but nothing like this, and it bolstered his belief that he'd been right to come here, because he hadn't come by chance. He'd heard of this Philbert and his head from a few of the folk he'd travelled with up and down the country the year past, and been intrigued. Bumps and the like were his specialty and he wanted to see the boy for himself. He seemed ordinary – everyone said so – but stories of the Kartoffelkrieg hung around him like a premature shroud, and Kwert had wanted to know how that felt. He'd certainly not expected the boy to have some kind of fit right in front of him, but knew what to do, delved a quick hand into the knapsack lying beside him in the grass, bringing out a small pouch of muslin and placing it beneath Philbert's nose. Philbert relaxed as he was overtaken by the scents of flowers: honeysuckle and lemon balm, sweetbrier-leaves and blackberries in the rain. He breathed deep and slow as directed, saw the meadow that stretched out behind his home back in Staßburg sweet and dry in the sun, running down to the river, rolling on and on, and his body stilled. And then Hermann emerged suddenly around the cart-front and was about to pat the donkey when he saw Philbert folded up against one of Kwert's cartwheel's looking pale as a miller's mushroom.

'What's been going on?' Hermann asked, going immediately to Philbert's side, ready to sweep the lad up in his arms if need be and take him away. He could smell vomit, and saw tear tracks on the boy's cheeks, sent a swift angry glance at the red clad Hesychast.

Kwert dipped his head.

'He's had a rather unfortunate reaction to the snail-egg break-fast I just gave him,' Kwert said, and it was no lie, and yet was not the entire truth either. 'And you must be Mr Hermann. I've heard a lot about you.'

Hermann did not respond, busying himself looping his unguent-shiny arms beneath Philbert's own.

'You're a great friend of our Little Maus,' Kwert continued quietly.

'I know that,' Hermann said, bridling at the use of the word 'our' that Kwert had not earned in the slightest. For almost two years this boy Philbert had been solicitous of Hermann's every need, and now was the first time he'd ever been called upon to repay the favour.

'And do you want to be well again?'

Hermann cocked his head, turned and looked at Kwert full on for the first time, taking in his berry-red habit, his head so close-cropped of hair it was almost shaven, the combined effect being to make him a step away from being a monk, though God knew of what order.

'And what, pray,' said Hermann, 'could you possibly do for me?'

'Well I *could* pray,' Kwert said lightly, 'or I could give you what your Little Maus has just pointed out to me, and with it some possible relief.'

~

Several afternoons later, heavy raindrops were making the odd splash and plummet on the canvases of the camp, not yet frequent enough to slow anyone up in their preparations for the move to Dortmund and its environs and certainly not enough to stop the acting troupe at their rehearsals. They'd set up their stage and were going through their motions, many Fair's folk sitting in for the show, Philbert and Lita up front, waiting to be entertained by something they'd not seen before. The acting troupe had a repertoire that varied from town to town, adapting this play or that to each locality, the heft of local politics steering their words one way or another. They acted as surreptitious and uncensored messengers, bringing news from one region to the next, disseminating and depicting events and scandals, or the victories and defeats of ongoing wars and the ever more frequent uprisings afflicting the country up and down; divulging details of the smatter of small revolutions; voicing what the populace could not openly say. And then again sometimes they merely entertained, as they were doing now, employing a handful of popular plots that usually involved two old men – Tingelburg and Tangelrichter in the present case – and the amorous relationships of their respective son and daughter, with much crude and ribald banter about picking cherries and ramming home the horn.

Today it was Hannah playing the beautiful daughter of Tangelrichter, and another actor playing Flavio, Tingelburg's handsome son, both making pretty in a flowery bower, the figure of Harlekin – always Master of Ceremonies – looming behind them like destiny, holding out the dark arms of his cloak, the jostle of red-and-yellow diamonds on his suit the only bright strike in that dull afternoon. Tingelburg and Tangelrichter were about to bawl out their usual bawdy song but they never got the chance, for someone was pushing through the small crowd in front of the stage, shouting and waving his arms, shoving people to the side like puny chessmen. Hermann got to the front and took a long-legged leap onto the stage, and everyone could see there was something different about him, and that he was smiling.

'Only look!' he sang out, arms spinning like waterwheels in a storm spate, an edge of laughter to his voice. 'Just look! Only look!'

And look they did, Philbert and Lita amongst them, watching in amazement as Hermann's face was at once more joyous than they had ever seen it and at the same time funnelled with tears. Then the rain started falling down in earnest like a sign that overtook them all, and everybody began to stand and gape because suddenly they saw what Hermann was on about; that the horrid scales and hardened rims on his body had begun to fall away, leaving pitch-patches of glistening new skin, pink and smooth as baby-butter, tangles of peel and pith washing away as he hung there on his surrogate stage, arms out wide, neck stretched like a swan about to fly up into the sky, tilting his head back as far as it would go, neck craning, mouth opening to catch the raindrops as they cleansed him of pain and itch and disease-ridden skin.

For a few moments everyone was agape, the rain coming down on them unnoticed, trickling down collars, open shirts and sleeves, and then Philbert and Lita were running up the steps to the stage, Lita's long hair stranded wet upon her back, her face a beaming smile, her cries mingling with the sudden shower as she leapt to embrace Hermann, arms around his waist hugging him fiercely, nose to belly. Hermann laughed and laughed and the actors ran around him like flies released from a wheat-barn as he whirled Lita with him in a wild dance, almost toppling them both off the creaking stage, his new skin a-glim in the rain. Hermann took Lita by one hand and Philbert by the other and, after exchanging a brief nod, the three of them leapt from the stage down into the mud, skidding, and laughing before running on, the acting troupe hard on their heels, every one exclaiming and shouting like a pack of town-crying hounds. The Fair's folk they passed stopped at their work, or came out of their tents and caravans to see what all the commotion was about, rubbing their hands on their aprons, holding their hats above their heads, standing, just standing, in the rain as this mad relay of Hermann, Lita, Little Maus and actors ran them by, reaching the river bank and turning a big circle and running them by again, and soon everyone in the Fair was alert to the noise, curious at the cause, intrigued to find Hermann leaping about in the rain like a madman. They stopped outside Maulwerf's tent from where Maulwerf himself, and Kwert with him, emerged, Hermann flinging his arms about Kwert's shoulders, clasping him hard, kissing him on forehead and cheeks, his new body glowing.

'If only the sun could shine like this,' Hermann croaked, his voice giving out on him with all the unaccustomed shouting, 'then the world would never end.'

'Well I never,' murmured Kwert, the moment he was released and got his breath back, and the crowd had swept Hermann off once more, Philbert and Lita trying to keep pace, laughing and slipping in the rain-loosened earth until both looked like toads just nosing out from hibernation from the bottom of a pond.

'Well I never,' Kwert repeated, exchanging a glance with Maulwerf. 'I never expected that. Not at all. Wharton's

Wonderful Jelly or no. The Fabulous Funisi have never done quite this much before now . . .'

And then he pulled his seat outside Maulwerf's tent, never minding the rain, just looking through the failing afternoon at Hermann's progress, seeking out the figure of Philbert amongst the jape and jump of the crowd, until Maulwerf pluffed himself down beside him, sighing.

'My greatest exhibit,' exclaimed Maulwerf, no sadness or rancour to his words. 'Gone,' he said. 'All gone. My Fischmann no more, and I gather from Hermann's effusive greeting it's you I've got to thank for that, Kwert.'

Kwert put his head to one side and wondered about that statement. He'd been in this business a long, long time, as had Maulwerf, and during those many years he'd seen many apparently miraculous happenings and marvels, just like it said on the wooden legend above his cart, but never, never had he seen a marvel, a miracle, such as this; the man Hermann cured of a lifelong affliction. And as much as he wanted to believe in his God and His Saving Powers of Grace, Kwert – of everyone in the Fair – found it difficult to accept.

~

The rain soon went from heavy shower to downright sheet-pour that didn't seem about to stop, and everyone soon retired to their tents to open bottles and gossip and wonder at what had happened, as did Philbert. He and Lita had stood in the rain a while to get rid of the worst of the mud, and then she went to dry herself off and tell Frau Fettleheim the wonderful news of Hermann's healing. Philbert went by habit to Hermann's tent, not thinking that of course Hermann didn't need his usual rubbing-in of liniments and oils now that he was cured. He lifted the flap of Hermann's tent to find that Hermann was not alone, and that Hannah of the freckles had got there before him and was clasped about Hermann's body, Hermann himself resplendent in a fine green shirt. Both disengaged quickly at

Philbert's entrance and Philbert was embarrassed, would have ducked himself away and left them to it, but Hermann spoke up and waved him in.

'Come in, come in, my Little Maus. Come and see this wonderful shirt, given to me by the prettiest actress in all Christendom.'

Hannah giggled and Hermann held out an arm, grasped Philbert by the shoulder and pulled him close. And so there they stood, quite like a cosy little family before a fire, the rain pitter pattering contentedly on the canvas above them.

'How happy I am,' said Hermann, 'just to be wearing such a shirt and not have it catch and claw at my skin, and to be hugging my closest friends without feeling wrapped in thorns.'

Hermann leant down and kissed Philbert lightly on the head, on his taupe, on the little tuft of hair that grew from its centre, and then turned back to Hannah and caught her full on the lips, once, twice and then a third time, his green-clad arms wrapping around her, and her freckled arms about him, and Philbert turned away. He knew he should have felt glad to see them so happy and together, but instead a small and silent dread was gnawing away inside him, burdened by the awful thought that something had been done that should not have been done, and that somebody, sometime soon, would be called to account and have to pay for it.

～

Dawn came bright and fresh, the night washed away by the rain, the air scented with smoke, wet earth and damp leaves and the huge optimism that had come from the news of Hermann's healing, with skin the same as everyone else's and a smile on his face that was as permanent now as it had been lacking before. Otto was up and about, packing away his tools when Philbert rolled out from beneath his cart, feeling more loss than relief that he no longer had Hermann to care for, a vital part of his function at the Fair no longer needed. He went down to the lakeside to have one last paddle before the Fair decamped, Kroonk already there, snortling away at something on the bank, a small heap of scree having slid away during the wet of the night to leave a bare patch of earth glistening in the morning light. He squatted down on his heels, shooing Kroonk away to take a better look. The earth was sandy, already drunk dry of last night's rain, but oddly it seemed a horde of tiny jellyfish had stranded themselves somehow up there on the bank.

'Star-shot,' pronounced a voice, Philbert jumping as the red shadow engulfed him, finding Kwert at his shoulder, startled at how quietly the man could move. 'Some people say it falls from the sky like a comet,' Kwert said, 'the dying remnants of a fallen star. But it's none of that. It's a kind of fungus that springs up overnight in autumn when the weather is damp and the soil is just right. The old folk say it can tell you the future.'

Kwert pushed at the small jellied mounds very gently with his finger, awaiting questions, but Philbert was in no mood for it. He'd had his fill of signs and omens and sudden life changes and could only release a silent sigh. He already knew what the future would bring now Hermann had been restored, given a chance at a new life, and would spend it with freckled Hannah, and no space in it for him. And when Kwert removed his finger and stood up and started heading back to camp, Philbert put his foot hard down on that blasted star-shot and crushed it back into the earth from which it had come.

10

The Monstrous Calf

They arrived early evening in the designated fields on the out-skirts of Dortmund, setting about their stalls, stages and show-tents, getting ready for the crowds who would come flooding in the following morning. The only person who didn't set up shop was Hermann for, as he pointed out, no one was going to pay to see a perfectly ordinary man standing in a bucket of water eating raw fish. That he'd always been a perfectly ordinary man standing in a bucket of water eating raw fish, nobody seemed to consider. Instead, Hermann left his old gold-and-green sign, 'Man Becomes Fish', in his tent and went to help the actors and, more specifically, speckled Hannah, as they went through the paces of their latest plays. Maulwerf grumbled as Philbert brushed his best velvet jacket and polished his shoes and little gold fob watch, saying it was all very well, and he wished Hermann the best and didn't want to deny him his miracle, but it could have waited a few more weeks as the whole thing had left him rather short on shows and not much time to do anything about it.

As it happened, Maulwerf had heard of a two-headed calf being born a month or so before in a hamlet lying to the east of the town, so when Philbert had finished his ministrations he had Philbert whistle up a cart and announced they were off to see if it was worth the purchase. Maulwerf set out sleek and slick, his fob-chain shining like a crescent moon across his tight-buttoned paunch, Philbert beside him in a pair of knee-length trousers Tomaso had grown out of and a new pair of sandals Otto had knocked up out of leftover leather. Their efforts went entirely unremarked by Herr Nicolas Groben, the farmer they had come to see, who was as unkempt as an old straw bale and only spat when Maulwerf offered him his hand. He kept scratching his *Hödensacke* inside his torn and dirty trousers and hoisting his manly bits and pieces first to the left and then the right, to Maulwerf's evident disgust and Philbert's amusement, but as soon as Maulwerf explained his business and the prospect of money changing hands Herr Groben became jovial, although the *Hödensacke*-hoisting continued unabated, giving Maulwerf the unpleasant insight that the man must be carrying more body lice than a hedgehog has fleas. Groben was in good humour, didn't often get such fine gents the likes of Maulwerf calling, so he said, and when he did they were after either his money or his wife, and as far as he was concerned they could take the wife – who was a sour-faced bitch on anyone's account – but as for his cash, that was a much prettier sight, and his to do with as he wished. Times were hard, he told them, and farming a tricky game at best, not that they'd know owt about such things, them being such fine gents. He admired Maulwerf's fob-watch so much that Maulwerf was obliged to take it out, let the man finger it, though kept a tight hold of the chain until he was eventually allowed to put the time-piece back. Groben led them through a yard that was a piss-mire of old turnips and cow-dung, Philbert removing his sandals and going barefoot, but not Maulwerf, who clung to good-breeding and would not consider even rolling up his trousers. Groben led them to the doors of a dirty barn that was collapsed in on one side as if it had been hit by Frau Fettleheim going at some unheard-of speed on her runaway cart. Lying inside was what Maulwerf and Philbert had come to see and, in the residue of some green and stinking straw, there it was: a sack of cow-skin containing a few ramshackle bones, apparently still alive because it stirred vaguely at their approach before sinking back, defeated. Beside this sad excuse for a dam was a calf, suckling lethargically at a withered udder, her hide possibly white, though splattered over with the green of rotting excrement, eyes like saucers, legs like sticks.

Maulwerf was angry, and slapped his cane several times into the slurry.

'This isn't what I came to see, not at all. I was promised a two-headed monster. And this . . . this . . .' he waved his free hand at the pathetic pair before him, 'monstrous it might be, but not worth a bowl of milk.'

Groben gave himself a quick hoist and launched into what passed for a sales pitch.

'I never exactly said as she had two heads. That was more in the way of rumour. Blame it on the wife – I do. Never knows when to shut her gob up, nor nowt else of her come to that. But see this,' he moved forward and roughly turned the calf's neck, her brown eyes terrified and rimmed around with white, her mother rustling where she lay, trying to conjure a protest from brown-frothed lips.

'See here,' he said again, and Philbert and Maulwerf bent down closer, holding their noses against the stench, which was far worse than anything that had come out of Hermann's mouth after he'd been forced to rip raw fish from its bones. What they saw could not in exactitude be called a second head, but coming from the calf's neck there was indeed a sort of rounded stump, as if a leg had begun growing there and then been squashed part-way back again, the size of a small cabbage with a half-formed hoof sticking out at its end.

'I was thinking you might want to take the dam as well, seeing as how they're so attached,' Herr Groben was saying, Maulwerf leaning down, trying not to gag, busy examining the calf, squeezing its neck, palping the whiter bits of its skin, looking at its tongue. Groben went on, undeterred.

'Bit of a bargain, I should say, getting two for one like, two heads was what you came for and, see, I'm offering you them both on a platter, that's what I'm doing.'

Maulwerf said nothing. Groben continued.

'Robbing myself blind is what it is. I'll even throw in a rope so's you can take 'em both now. How's about it, gents? Can't say fairer than that. I'm cutting me own throat as it is, and the missus'll give me a right talking to, and that's like being spat at by a pickle jar, I can tell you . . .'

He didn't rest up, just went on and on, grinding his audience down until half an hour later Groben's fine gents left; Maulwerf checked his fob watch was still in his jacket and that the work-ings hadn't been whipped and then shook the drying mud and crap-cakes from his formerly immaculate trousers and shoes. Taking up the rear, Philbert held the rope that led the monstrous calf, clop-clopping weakly beside him, her lank head hanging, haunch-bones moving up and down like rusty pistons beneath her skin, leaning on Philbert every now and then as she took a wobble over a stone.

The whole episode had been entirely depressing, and neither Philbert nor Maulwerf were inclined to talk. It took them both some time to recover, but Maulwerf eventually began his banter when they were in sight of the Fair.

'You look like a double-act, you two,' he said, having glanced back several times at Philbert leading the emaciated monstrous calf on. 'I could curse that worthless Groben until the world comes to an end, but there you are, trotting along together side by side, and there may be something to it after all.'

Maulwerf had been quiet after that, until they'd got back to camp and he'd taken off his shoes and socks and had his feet soaking in a bowl of warm water to rid them of the dirt, rubbing his hands together as his glasses steamed up.

'Could be something in it yet,' he said to Philbert, as Philbert got the towel ready to take his feet. 'You and your lump, that calf and its neck – if the blessed thing survives the night.'

~

The blessed calf did survive the night, but only because Huffelump, as Philbert had christened her, was taken off his hands the minute they'd got back to the Fair as Lita took charge, dragging the poor thing off for a bath, washing off all the stink and shit, feeding her oats and acorns until she almost burst. The only reason Philbert took no part in this ritual was because almost the moment he landed back he was knocked off his feet by Kroonk, who seemed desperate and distressed, unwilling to leave his side. And she was red – really, really red – far redder than she'd been when Philbert left her.

'What's happened to you?' Philbert crooned as Kroonk nuzzled up beside him, possibly begging for the answer herself. On her heels came Kwert, his hands red as Kroonk.

'What's happened?' Philbert demanded once Kwert had arrived.

'Don't be alarmed,' soothed Kwert, chuckling somewhere at the back of his throat, yellow teeth grinning like a mouthful of pixies. 'It was just an idea, and not a bad one I feel, now that Hermann's left a space, as it were.'

He sat Philbert down and consoled boy and pig alike with a handful of sugared almonds produced rather speedily from his pocket.

'We thought, or rather, Hermann thought,' continued Kwert, 'that a pig wasn't much of a showpiece on her own, handsome though she is.' He scratched Kroonk's ears and Kroonk grunted her agreement through a snoutful of sugarlings. 'So we thought, what if she were redder than she already was? More colourful, so to speak, more of an attraction. What then?'

Kwert caught the look of doubt on Philbert's face and continued hurriedly on.

'Hermann came and asked me how I got my habit so crimson.'

Philbert fixed him with a sullen eye, but remembered how impressive Kwert had looked that first night sitting by the fire, his robe bright and alive as an ember.

'I think he's just being curious,' said Kwert. 'So I tell him how I mix lady's bedstraw with tormentil, a crush of crottle lichen, a dash of limestone, and perhaps a bit of vetch if I can get the right kind. I tell him how I put it all in a pot and boil it layer on layer with the wool, and a handful of sorrel to fasten the dye, and then your Hermann interrupts and says, 'But will it stain a pig?' Naturally, like you, Philbert, I'm aghast, but see at once where the tale is leading, so up I get and go for a pot of dye from my cart where it is maturing into deepest scarlet and says, Right, Hermann, let's give it a try.'

Kwert put his arm around Philbert's shoulder as Philbert's mind began to totter on the brink of appreciating the dastardly plot.

'Normally I'm averse to subterfuge and deception, following as I do the pure ways of life, but to tell the truth it was such an interesting experiment – to paint a pig! What an idea! And of course, it might help my old friend Maulwerf who, through my own intervention, has lost a prize piece. So what harm in that, I thought, and surely my little man Philbert won't see anything wrong with friends helping out friends?'

Philbert's mouth tweaked into a smile as he looked again at Kroonk, her eyes deep black in her poppy-petal skin which shone like sunset, and saw that she really did look quite handsome, and that perhaps Maulwerf himself might appreciate the gesture, and the crowds queue up to throw their coppers into Philbert's tin.

~

Night found Philbert and his newly red Kroonk curled up beneath their cart, warm as fleas in a furball, the camp quiet, everyone resting in the expectation of the morning crush when the Fair opened for business. Huffelump, white and shining after her wash, lay tethered by Kwert's donkey, a bowl of milk and a bag of oats at her still skinny side, happy with her new home, or perhaps too tired to give an opinion. Philbert thought once or twice about that stinking stable she had come from and the mother they'd consigned to oblivion by leaving her there, who would undoubtedly expire quietly now her calf had been removed so abruptly, bones subsiding into the filthy straw while Herr Groben snored solidly in the house beyond, beside his whey-faced wife. Times were coming when Philbert would remember that stinking piss-mired farmyard, and Herr Groben's filthy habits and filthier mouth; times that would slot themselves into their allotted places in his head, his past leading to his future like a banner being unfurled.

11

Sella Turcica

Dortmund, a great hustle-bustle of a city: gangs of musicians sent out into the morning, drumming and piping their way through the streets; others doling out badly printed handbills and ringing tambourines; some of the actors dancing a running pageant to alert everyone to the fact that the Fair had arrived and was not to be missed.

The Red Kroonk Act did not last long on the professional circuit, for not even Maulwerf had been able to come up with a strap line of any great flair. The Boy with a Coconut/Egg/Aubergine/Mole in his Head and his Crimson Pig just wasn't punchy enough, and they ended up bathetically as the Boy With The Monstrous Menagerie, in which Kroonk and Huffelump were the menagerie, whilst Philbert was obviously just The Boy. They even borrowed Hermann's Fish Which Looks Like A Box, but too many people started tapping on its glass and Philbert had to hurriedly cover the poor thing over before it started exuding that poison Hermann had told him about. One man said, a tad unkindly, that a plate of beans and bacon would be more interesting and poked Philbert hard in the head with a dirty finger, but mostly folk just walked away without so much as a backward glance, and the menagerie was swiftly disbanded.

Kroonk's mud-rolling soon hid her artificial redness, and Lita was happy enough to take Huffelump over, feeding her by hand, washing away the near continuous diarrhoea as it dried into dirty crusts about her legs – another little extra that had put the paying public off.

Much to Philbert's admiration, Lita soon had Huffelump trained into a new act about The Life of a Lonely Cowgirl that involved Lita twirling her legs and singing, and Huffelump turning her mournful eyes to the crowd; then up jumped Lita onto the calf's white back and began a pirouette, whisking a whip, crooning of hard times, crueller masters, the wolves of the lonely plains. At the end she would lay down her head on Huffelump's neck and cry with such sincerity the crowd could not help but feel a frisson of pity for the tiny, freakish cow-girl and her misshapen calf, and out came the coins and the hand-clapping.

Philbert still helped out Maulwerf and Otto, so the loss of his short-lived career was not hard to bear. In addition, he some-times went off with Kwert to gather roots and leaves, beechnuts and birch-bark, gleanings of corn, Kwert inspecting his ingredients meticulously before having Philbert grind them up, spitting into the bowl to moisten the mixture then topping it up with water, stoppering it into bottles and leaving the lot to ferment. The result, Kwert announced, went by the name of Quash, a kind of alcoholic tonic that was strong enough to make any man fall over should he imbibe more than his recom-mended daily intake. To Philbert the result looked deeply unpleasant, like rancid milk topped over with grey scum, and was one of the discerning many who would have nothing to do with it. Among the happy few who took to it with appreciation were a couple of newcomers, of whom there were many throughout the Fair's few weeks at Dortmund, these particular two being tradesmen who'd travelled up from Würtemburg during the summer, following the route of the Rhein. Zacharias

Holzhauer touted clocks forged by his family in the Schwarzwald, and Eröglu Erivan Abdal Bey sold saddles and accessories made by his fellow Turkish immigrants scattered up and down the Rhein. The Turk was tall and thin, dark-polished from boots to beard, and apparently knew both Maulwerf and Hermann from years back, as did the Clockmaker who, by contrast to his fellow, was red and stubby, with hair like a blackthorn bush, but they seemed to rub along well and had travelled together for many years.

Philbert was rather taken by Zacharias's clocks, and examined each of them with great interest. His particular favourite was small, six sides of glass set into a cubed wooden frame, its innards exposed to view, small cogs clicking their teeth with precision, banks of wheels whirring first one way and then the other. He had a fancy this was what the inside of his taupe might look like if it was ever revealed to the world, sometimes thinking he could hear a faint tick, tick, ticking somewhere deep inside his skull.

~

'Hello all,' Hermann said as he came into the tent, bending to pat whoever was closest, which happened to be Huffelump, who raised her head sleepily from Lita's shoulder, unfurling a long grey tongue to lick at Hermann's fingers. Hermann carefully removed his fine green shirt and fussily began to place it on a specially constructed hanger that Otto had planed and smoothed out of an ash branch, so as to minimise the wear and tear of his most precious possession. His skin was still pink and smooth as pomegranate juice, though in the dim light from the little brazier it looked as though some of Hannah's freckles had rubbed off on him, small patches of brown appearing around his waist and upper arms.

Once wrapped in a cotton shift, Hermann threw himself down on the cot and asked Philbert what he and Lita had been talking about when he'd come in. He'd not been the slightest surprised or angry to find his tent space taken up by Lita and her monstrous calf, Philbert and his little red pig. He was instead delighted that he could touch people again, stroke animals, take pleasure in wearing his shirt, enjoying being in the company of the people he cared about without annoying them with his itching, or the noxious smell of his ointments.

Philbert told him about the glass clock, and Hermann commented cryptically that time flew by like a hawk outside the open door of a person's life, and that his clog almanac marked it quite quick enough for him. Then he pulled out a rectangular length of dark, polished wood, each edge notched to indicate season, month and week, marked with studs and holes for Quarter Days and Feasts. Hermann took Philbert's hand and traced his fingers along one edge and then another as he turned his almanac around.

'See this little cross?' he said. 'This marks Advent, and this other one is the start of Lent, and these little tacks mark the goose-markets the Fairs follow every year.' Next he pointed out some small scratched letters beside each tack. 'These remind me which town we're going to, so here's DD for Dortmund, and MU for Münster. And, according to this, we should be leaving any day now for GU, OS, and FZ.'

Maulwerf's Fair took a three-year circuit about the lands of Germany, Prussia and the Austro-Hungarian Empire so as not to tire their welcome or clash with other Fairs going the same ways he did. Philbert listened with interest as Hermann laid out the route, finding pleasure in the sounds of towns, the cough of their consonants, the rolling wealds of their vowels, repeating them like an alphabetical mantra, learning their spellings, discovering their rhythms. And it was not just idle interest that made him pay attention. Kwert had been dismayed, though not surprised, to discover that Philbert could hardly read, as neither more could Lita nor Tomaso, and had insisted on demonstrating the glory of words in every way he could, teaching them with tales, telling them stories with words they didn't know, encouraging them to recognise the basic alphabet and their pronunciations by squiggling sticks in sand or drying pools of mud.

Of the three, Philbert was by far the most diligent in his studies, and he repeated these latest names again and again, making up his own mnemonic to remember them, just as Kwert had taught him to do, finding in it an easier knack than he'd expected, a rhyme sequence coming to him almost straightaway from the nowhere-land that was his head: from Dortmund to Gütersloh, from goose fair to stepping stair, from Gütersloh to Osnabrück, from stepping stair to winter lair, and then to Finzeln, and journey's end.

And that was exactly where and when Maulwerf led his Fair as they came up to the cold month of December. Other fairs at this time of year took a southerly trajectory, aiming to spend the winter in more clement climes, which was precisely why Maulwerf took the opposite route, always ready to cash in where others feared to tread. These, he reasoned, were precisely the times when the sudden splash of a fair upon a town's door-steps could urge out its citizens; people who were already beginning to tighten their belts and batten down their doors and quail against whatever hardships the coming winter would bring, folk who would think, *Well why not? Why not one last splurge before we really have to pull in our horns . . .*

It was no surprise then to Philbert when they arrived upon the tattered outskirts of yet another backwater town and Maulwerf called for a quick show-and-stopover before moving on. The place was called Hochwürden, and Philbert would never need a mnemonic to remember that hamlet's name, for it would soon be scratched upon Hermann's almanac by Philbert himself.

12

The Highest of Bridges

'*Die Fastnachtspiel hat begonnen*!'

A roar from the small crowd went up as the blanket was dropped and the stage revealed. The theatre troupe were performing a much-recycled comedy routine that didn't demand too many props or actors. The erstwhile Tingelburg and Tangelrichter were now designated Fraulein Plappermaul and Herr Pluderhosen, who hailed from the Province of Posen. It was the Eve of their Wedding Night, having won each other in the Dance of the Noses competition that had just taken place, with much enforced participation and noisy adjuncts from the happy spectators, Bride and Groom now exhibiting their strap-on papier-mâché hooters with ribald glee.

'I adore your nose, my turtle dove, the way your nostrils flare –'

'I love yours even more, *Liebschön*, and I especially admire the hairs.'

The crowd roared again as Fraulein Plappermaul flicked Pluderhosen's nose with a kerchief while he acted up a sneeze, sending a jet of green ooze – made from Maulwerf's vegetable leftovers – arcing into the front few rows of spectators.

'Your teeth, my peach, they shine like pearls, and fittingly smell of oysters –'

'And yours, my love, are like diamonds, with the gleam of a throwster –'

'They shine like the scales of a newborn fish –'

'And how yours gleam at night from the darkness of their dish!'

And so the play went on, and the crowd roared, and Harlekin rose up at the back like a great black cloud, flinging out small flashes of thunder and lightning from the patterns of his suit, the air heavy with the yellow haze of burning grease from the footlights and tinged with the faint, but unmistakable, background odour of blood, for the Fair had arrived, fortuitously, just after Slaughter Day – a common occurrence in these parts at this time of year – when every animal and fowl that couldn't last the winter through on acorn-must or stored fodder was put to the knife, blood bled into sausages, flesh sliced and diced into huge barrels of brine, or put to hang in the smoke-houses.

Hochwürden, as its name implied, was built high upon the ledge of a sandstone gully, the houses, *Rathaus* and even the church perched along its edge, their dark red stones glowing dimly in the reflections of the many fires that had been lit, seeming to breathe and move with the rising flames, pockets of resin exploding, smoke slinking under handfuls of fresh green wood, off-cuts of beef, mutton and pork dripping into the embers. The narrow streets, scraped back to the bare red rock, heaved slowly in the shifting light, their sporadically chiselled drain-ways threading a backbone down their middles, angled to catch the waste that was now viscous with blood and hair. Slowly, and without hurry, each runnel led to the lip of the chasm by which the town had been built, disgorging its contents into the river churning far below.

On the evening of the Fair's arrival a slight haze hung over the chasm and the bridge that crossed it, the smoke of its charnel fires catching in the myriad droplets that were flung up from the water as it dashed against the rocks beneath, shimmering in the fading light, faint stubs of rainbows appearing every now and then as Philbert walked the bridge's length, turning his head this way and that. Away on the far side stood a forest, dark and hunched and silent, seeming to repel the bridge that had been built to reach it, begrudging the toll the townsfolk took as they pillaged its depths sporadically for the fuel and wood they needed, resenting the intrusion of the pigs and goats who foraged their floors for rotting berries, dropped acorns and mast. It seemed to crouch just beyond reach, looking alien and entirely without welcome, a tangle of low-grown branches hiding the boar that were hunted every autumn just as winter began to drag the sun down from the sky. Hundreds of years before, Philbert knew, men must have seen that bounty just out of reach, and had brought pulleys and ropes, planks and nails, thrown out a crude walkway from one side of the deep-scoured gully to the other, bracing their first bridge against the ancient oaks and beeches that leant away from them, trying to shrug off their nooses and snares. What courage it must have taken for the first man to cross that chasm; Philbert shuddered to think about it.

He'd left the crowds who now were snuggled drunkenly around their fires, the actors having finished their plays and joined them, the few Fair folk who had bothered to set up their booths in a place of such obvious poverty still shouting out their wares to dwindling interest and acclamation. He left the shouting and the swearing and the smoke and stink of blood that had begun to clot within the runnels, making the waste-water hard-running, pooling over the clogs in places, making the streets oily and slippery with grease, and made his way instead to the bridge which, after a few hundred years of architectural acumen, was now buttressed with two arms of stone that rose against the chasm sides, supporting a single, if untidy, sandstone arch. In daylight, people walked across it, ran across it, rode across it, took its width and length with abandon, and even now – though it was late into the night – the light of a couple of braziers crackled where a few old men were huddled upon the nearest of the parapet seats, safe as seagulls on their ledge, drinking acorn coffee splashed with bad brandy, telling stories about fairs long gone by, when that pig had up and run with the blade still halfway across its throat, screaming like a demon, kicking its way down the street and out over the ledge of the gorge into oblivion.

'Still hear him today,' said one. 'Never heard nothing like it, 'cepting the wife, that first time in Finkel's hay barn.'

Sniggers then, as the old men wheezed and cackled into their pipes, remembering their own first times in their own first barns, one of them omitting to say it had been with a pig, though without a knife plunged hard into its throat.

'Mind when young piss-pot Hugo caught himself on fire?' said one, the spittle from his pipe clinging like snot-drops to his beard, making Philbert wary, hanging back in the shadows, yet still oddly fascinated by what might come next.

'Still smell him today,' added another. 'Never smelt nothing like it.'

'Crackled like nuts in a stove, so he did,' commented the first.

'Didn't have no nuts after that, though,' commented another, at which they all coughed again, as they tried to cackle.

'His old wifey never went short, though, I can tell you that.' Another voice, another round of rancid laughter.

'Not so old, neither, I'll have you know. A lot of years in that mare, God bless 'er. Beggin' for it, she was, night an' day.'

'It was charity, is what it was,' came the first voice, and again the pipe smoke rose up in gusts as the old men remembered what another generation would let fade away into the mist that hung about the bridge like thin gauze about a wound. Philbert turned away, obscurely offended, understanding what they were talking about, at least in the abstract, and not wanting to hear more, shivering with the damp, throat itching from the smoke of their pipes. He slid past them through the shadows, made his way right out onto the middle of the bridge, and leant himself against the stone. The thought of the dead drop underneath was frightening, but he liked the cool of the stone against his elbows, beneath his feet, felt a frisson of whispering from the alien forest on the other side.

These old men, he thought, *and those old trees*, both having a malevolence about them he didn't like. He felt bounded by them, trapped in the space between, the stonework of the bridge the only thing keeping him safe, holding him suspended between twin evils, a moment he filed away amongst the myriad other memories he seemed never able to forget; a memory, Kwert had said philosophically, should never be forgotten but rather explored.

One day, one night, one dawn, did the Fair linger in Hochwürden; one day and one night that resulted in drunken men and women lying in disarray about the smouldering carcasses of their fires, lumps of newly slaughtered meat congealing beside tipped-up plates, half-filled mugs of ale still and flat as their owners. A headache settled and brattled upon the entire town, and on Philbert; even Kroonk was slow to stir that final morning. They'd spent the night before, had Philbert, Lita and Tomaso, toting themselves around the various groups of drunkards, giving them close-ups of lumpy heads, third eyes and tiny feet, hoping to scrape up the odd coin from those too far gone to know better. Despite their efforts, the townsfolk were clench-pocketed to a man, and all they'd earned were tooth-torn hunks of half-smoked Wurst so peppery even the smell made them choke, a few swigs of the local ale, brewed to its absolute alcoholic limits, more cloudy and raw than Kwert's Quash, and God knew, that was lethal enough. Tomaso left first thing to seek out the lace-maker, a motherly old woman who was teaching him her trade, the maker of a lace collar Tomaso had once given Philbert, presupposing a friendship that was never furthered, mutually unwanted on both sides. Lita too had absconded, fed up with the crude comments and cruder inspections that had been attempted upon her tiny person, retreating back to the safer environs of Frau Fettleheim, who had not made a single outing for display upon her cart, knowing the moment they landed in this half-arsed town that there was little money to be made, and none worth the turning out of the likes of her.

Philbert, though, had wandered out and about a bit longer, having consigned Kroonk to Lita's safekeeping, sampling some of the town's food and drink, later vomiting it all up again over the side of the bridge before going back to Hermann's tent and curling into uneasy sleep.

He awoke a few hours later, feeling ill, cold and cramped, having an urgent need to breathe air that was fresh and free. He made his way through the debris, human and otherwise, that was littered about the still sleeping and snoring streets, arriving once more at the bridge, immediately enlivened by the fresh breeze that arose from its waters. He felt a slight pang of guilt as he passed the thin threads of spittle he'd left on the stonework the night before, deciding he would go back and clean them off once he felt better, get a bucket of water and un-besmirch the stones he'd sullied, for no matter how debased the inhabitants of the town might be, how desperate for a last hoorah before winter set in, there were certain things Philbert, young as he was, would not tolerate.

The chasm was wreathed in a mist of its own making as Philbert took his way out across the bridge, hearing the water crashing hard against the stones somewhere far below. He could hardly see two yards ahead as he made his way forward, clinging to the bridge's edge with white-knuckled hands, daring himself to go further, gazing every now and then over the side, glimpsing beneath the shifting shadows of mist into the dizzying depths it had failed to hide, peering down onto the cushions of cloud and moss where the chasm narrowed into dripping crevasses of stone folded and worn by millennia of floods, its rocks round as pillows, softened by liverworts and ferns, thin layers of soil anchored to the rocks by the roots of short sturdy trees and shrubs. He was halfway across, thankful to be breathing deeply of the breeze-blown air, the water boiling and laughing in its ginnels, the mist wreathed about him, cold as ghosts, when he heard a voice that near catapulted him out of his skin.

'Hello, Little Maus.'

The voice was low and hollow, as if hewn from the whispering mists and murks that came up from beneath the stonework, Philbert unable to tell at first from where it had come, or from whom. He wasn't afraid, the use of his familiar moniker making it obvious it was someone he knew, and when the clouds spraying up from the river cleared slightly, wafted by the low wind that began to breathe from out the forest, he saw Hermann, perched upon a parapet like a friendly gargoyle, his back to the chasm, elbows resting on his knees, hands held out to the residual warmth coming from the old men's charcoal brazier of the night before, twitching its dying scents of damp ashes and old tobacco into the air.

'Hello, Little Maus,' Hermann said again, and Philbert could see him clearly now, how he was sat all in a droop, as if a key-stone was weighing down upon his shoulders, his neck pushed into the submission of its arch. His fine green shirt was dull and damp, and clung so close to Hermann's skin that Philbert could see the cord of his spine spaced out beneath it. There was no surprise in Hermann's face as he saw Philbert approaching; it held instead an expression of relief, as if he'd been waiting for his Little Maus all along.

Philbert was happy to see him and drew closer, sat himself

down on the parapet seat by Hermann's feet, leaning his back against the brazier, glad of the faint warmth coming from the damp-sunk coals, and more so by the touch of Hermann's leg against his shoulder; comforted by Hermann's presence, feeling protected from the bridge and the muffled tumble of its watery ravine and the empty space beneath its arch, the green-gloved rocks and boulders, the horrid dark of the forest on the other side.

'How fitting you should be here,' Hermann said, nuzzling a toe briefly against Philbert's arm, spreading out his hand above Philbert's taupe like a tent. 'I was just about to leave,' he added almost absently. 'Thought I might slip away with the dawn with no one to see me or say goodbye. But here you are . . .'

'Go away?' cried Philbert, interrupting, jumping up and away from the brazier. 'But you can't leave! Why would you be leaving?' Philbert suddenly realising all at once how much he loved this man, how steady and sure he'd grown within Hermann's orbit, could not bear that Hermann would go, and so suddenly, and for no reason, unable to get out the words he feared he might've blurted out these past few weeks: *Please don't go, Hermann, oh please don't go. I know you love Hannah more than me, but please don't go, or at least take me with you.*

'Oh my little one,' said Hermann, as if he was reading Philbert's thoughts. 'Come sit down again, let me see you.'

And Philbert returned, sat down, Hermann's hand coming to rest upon his uneven crown, the tips of his fingers lightly stroking the soft tuft of his taupe. Hermann sighed deeply and Philbert turned his head towards him, tears already running down his cheeks at what Hermann might say next.

'But it has to go like this, Little Maus,' Hermann said softly. 'I've been speaking to our friend Kwert and he's told me all about you, how he's seen the numinous wrap around you like a cloak. About how you vomited out my evil long before Mr Wharton's Jelly ever touched my skin.'

103

Philbert wiped a hand across his cheek, clutching at Hermann's hand as it cupped his head.

'You're really leaving?' Philbert whispered, grasping at the one straw of meaning he'd taken from Hermann's words.

'I have to,' Hermann's voice was like a husk that has been blown free of its kernel, 'for it's all gone, my dear, all gone, and the game is up. But I do thank you, Little Maus. You must remember I will always thank you, and I don't regret a minute of it, even though it has brought me to my end. You cured me, and now you've killed me. Forgive me.'

And then Hermann extracted his hand from Philbert's and took hold of the wonderful green chemise Hannah had given him on the day of his resurrection, peeled it off of his skin and over his head and placed the wet folds of it gently into Philbert's hands.

'Give this back to Hannah, will you?' Hermann said, his voice calm, falling like petals through the mist and, as Philbert took the gift, he looked up at Hermann, and even through his tears he could see the horrid scales that had returned to Hermann's skin, the ghastly eczematous patches erupting in rocky, untamed islands on Hermann's chest and arms; and the moment he saw them he understood the true import of Hermann's words and tried to free his hands from the green clags of the shirt but he was too late, for Herman had already spread his arms out wide and unbent his knees and was tipping himself backwards in a graceful arc, out and away from the parapet, out and away from Philbert and away from life, giving himself over to the mist, sighing gently as he parted company from everything he had known and loved and was leaving behind, taking his chosen path into the void. Philbert twisted his body out over the abyss hoping to catch at Hermann's legs but was only in time to see Hermann pass through the pillows of rainbow-stained clouds and the mossed-over boulders that seemed to draw back to allow him passage, the water white and eager to take him; saw Hermann's so briefly-beautiful body hit and sink, only to rise up again like a new moon for just one second before being carried away, a soft white bole on the dark waters, Hermann lost forever below the arched arms of the bridge.

Philbert knelt on the seat of the parapet and gazed down and down, his throat dry as skink-skin, his screams thin as reeds, and when Hannah and Maulwerf came shouting and beating their way along the bridge towards him he could only hug his knees and cry, had already closed himself off from the world, a single grain of sand caught in the dark and empty shell of his grief, the green shirt scrunched up tightly against his chest; another lick of time going past him, another clicking of the cogs, another hawk flying past a door that was now closed; Hermann leaving him behind, abandoned once more. Another scratch to put on Hermann's clog almanac, another tack, another cross.

13

The Small Gold Ring

The Fair's folk couldn't leave Hochwürden fast enough. Hermann's death hit them all hard, Hannah and Philbert most of all. They packed up their belongings, put out their fires, rucked up their tents, the town so hung-over it didn't even notice their erstwhile entertainers as they chivvied and clip-clopped their way down the refuse-littered streets, past the blood-clotted runnels, the broken-down houses, the great barrels of brine and newly slaughtered meat.

~

The following days were long and cold and silent, so much so that Maulwerf took the unprecedented decision to skip ahead with his timetable and ignore all further towns they might have stopped at, ordering all instead to head straight for their first winter's resting destination of Finzeln. Anyone who didn't like this decision, he told them, could leave when and where they wanted. Some did. Most didn't, but no one argued, no one having the stomach for it. Hermann had been a staple of the Fair of Wonders for longer than many of them could remember, a man universally well-liked and respected. The hanger-on pedlars were the first to slip away to join the autumnal remnants of other fairs, the Turk and the Clockmaker disappearing a few days later, though in their case they had the grace to speak to Maulwerf personally, having known both he and Hermann well and for many years, offering their condolences and solemn handshakes, apologising that they could not stay but had to make a living, promising to meet up the following year as they usually did. And it was the night following these last two departures when Otto came up to Philbert and proffered a small pouch.

'The Turk left you this, Little Maus,' Otto said, shaking his head sadly, trying to get out the words he'd rigorously prepared but could no longer remember. 'He told me to tell you it was from Hermann,' was all he managed, before nudging one boot into the dirt, and then the other, and then turning swiftly, his eyes glistening as he walked away.

Philbert looked at the pouch, weighing its slight bulk in his hand, trying to push back the tears that had already made his throat and eyes red and raw. He pulled the string from the pouch's neck and looked inside. He could see nothing at all but a small roll of paper that he pulled out with his fingers, finding, to his astonishment that it had been pushed through a small gold ring to keep itself straight. He slid off the ring, holding it loosely in his hand for a moment before he unfurled the paper, seeing there a short sprawl of words he couldn't understand. Philbert had been assiduous at his letters since Kwert began to school him, but he wasn't skilled enough yet to make out anything that wasn't written in bold and delineated letters. Philbert had been avoiding Kwert ever since Hermann's dive off the bridge because although he couldn't, to his chagrin, recall every word Hermann had said to him before he went off the parapet, he remembered the gist:

You cured me. You killed me. Forgive me.

The words hadn't made much sense, but he knew Kwert was somewhere at the root of them, and he blamed Kwert – however unjustly – for what Hermann had chosen to do. So it was a hard thing he did, crawling back to Kwert with that little crease of paper he'd removed from the ring. There were, of course, other people in the Fair Philbert could have gone to for its interpretation but he felt Kwert owed him, and more specifically owed Hermann, and knew too that Kwert would not soften his words but give Philbert a straight answer, whatever the little message said.

Kwert himself was deeply troubled by Hermann's demise and the reasons for it, and sadder still to see Philbert so heart-sore and unwilling to take comfort from anyone, especially him. His pulse quickened, therefore, as he saw the small boy edging towards him through the desultory crowd that evening, though he made no show of noticing, carried on mixing and bottling his medicaments, his Adam's apple as hard and tight in his throat as the stoppers he was jamming into the bottles' necks.

'Philbert,' he said warmly, as the boy came to a halt a yard or so in front of him, Philbert's attention focussed not on Kwert but on his donkey, putting out his small hand to stroke at her lumpy grey fur before wordlessly handing over the piece of paper he'd taken from the pouch. Kwert took it from him and studied it gravely, reading it slowly and with deliberation.

'You want to know what it says?' Kwert asked gently, and the boy nodded. He didn't speak, but followed Kwert's example and sat down next to him on the wet log Kwert was using as a stool. Kwert swallowed, remembering how surprised he'd been at the efficaciousness of the ointment he'd given to Hermann, and how Hermann had approached Kwert a few heady weeks afterwards, just a couple of days before they'd reached Hochwürden, saying that he needed more of the Wonderful Jelly, that his symptoms were returning, that he couldn't go back to the way he had been, not after this brief and euphoric taste of release. Kwert told Hermann then it was not that simple, that the funisi that went into the jelly were hard to come by, especially the most powerful ones – human umbilici – and that anyway timelines and omens needed to align. Kwert was a great believer in the spiritual side of life, convinced that the greater part of Hermann's healing had come not from the jelly at all but from young Philbert, the boy with that special head that seemed to radiate warmth when he touched it, and could not overlook how spectacularly sick Philbert had been only moments before Hermann arrived at Kwert's cart, vomiting up – Kwert believed – the darkness that lay at the heart of Hermann's disease. It was not the answer Hermann wanted but he'd recognised the logic, for he knew – like Kwert, like most of the Fair's folk – that miracles such as had happened to him could not be brought about by medicines alone, but that God must have had a hand in it. Kwert knew that His ways were mysterious and often worked through innocents such as Philbert, whether or not those innocents understood it.

Kwert sat beside Philbert now. He wanted to take away the hurt Hermann's death had so obviously inflicted, acutely aware that Hermann's words on this little piece of paper might do precisely the opposite. But Kwert was a Hesychast, a man of God, and would not hide the truth.

'It says this,' he said, and began to read in a wobbling voice.

'*My dearest Philbert, my Little Maus, the child of my heart if not of my blood, you who have taken more care of me than any man could have hoped for. I want to thank you for all you have done.*'

So far so good, Kwert thought, glancing at Philbert sat beside him on the log, seeing his small form quiver as he drank in the words and the kindness and closeness that were so implicit, fearing to say more, fearing to be the one to strike home the blow that was about to come.

'*Do not forget me,*' Kwert read on quietly, placing his free hand on Philbert's where it lay, cold and clammy on the wood, '*for I will not forget you, no matter where it is I am heading.*

You cured me. You killed me. Forgive me, as I have forgiven you. Yours forever, Hermann.'

Kwert felt the boy flinch and fight against his protective hand, and though no words came out it was as if Philbert's whole body had become a howl, the tears pouring down his cheeks as if they could turn back the world, give him back all he had lost, and it was only then that Kwert truly understood how great had been his misjudgement to assign miracles to random causes, random signs, handing over the responsibility of those miracles to one single event, one act, one person – one boy, who surely didn't deserve to bear such a burden. That Kwert had done exactly that to Philbert, to a child – a child Kwert still firmly believed would go on to do great things – sickened him. He would have cut off his right hand not to have done so, but it was far too late now for platitudes and empty gestures. All Kwert could do from here on in was try to abnegate the consequences of his own rash actions and words, take care of Philbert, steer him along right paths. Damn his visions and predictions. The boy didn't need them, and no more at that moment did he.

Philbert cried that night on the log beside Kwert, cried with such awful abandon that Kwert almost cried too, pulling the boy close to him, drawing his red habit about his shaking shoulders as if it would protect him.

'Hermann has left you, taken the only path he could,' Kwert said, once Philbert finally subsided. 'But be assured, I will never do so. As long as I draw breath I will be here if you need me.'

He hugged the boy close until neither could breathe and had to disengage, Kwert placing his hand against Philbert's head, feeling that strange warmth again.

'You and me, Philbert,' Kwert whispered, rubbing the sleeve of his bright red habit across Philbert's cheeks and chin to mop up the salty residue of tears now stilled and spent. 'You and me, Philbert, and a whole world out there waiting for us, through which we will travel together. Always together. Never alone.'

Words, just words, but words Kwert meant with every beat of his heart as he spoke them, and words Philbert clung to like a drowning man at a raft. He held out the small gold ring to Kwert and Kwert undid the thong around Philbert's neck from which Otto's nail already hung, and on went the small gold ring beside it before it was tied tightly back about his neck, and the piece of paper from Hermann was placed back in its pouch and back into Philbert's jacket where it would remain, Philbert swore, for as long as he lived.

Afterwards, Philbert went to Hermann's tent. It had been commandeered by Tomaso the day after Hermann's death with such casual cruelty that everyone – Maulwerf included – had been too upset to immediately countermand. It was only a few pieces of canvas after all, and someone might as well make use of it. The cart the tent folded down neatly into still guarded Hermann's few effects and possessions. Philbert had previously lacked the courage to go up directly against Tomaso and demand their release, but he did so now. He ignored Tomaso's shouts and threats of what the hell did Philbert think he was doing, for this was his place now. Philbert roughly shoved the older boy aside, going straight to Hermann's small stash of belongings, retrieving the clog almanac, tucking it into his trousers, and then took up the hooded glass housing Hermann's fish.

'Bring that back!' Tomaso shouted. 'That there's a valuable thing . . .'

But Philbert was already marching out of the tent with it and Tomaso, for all his shouting and swearing bravado, made no move to stop him. Philbert held the glass case still as he could between his hands, going straight for the nearby river. Once there, he placed it down onto the scratchy green grass of the bank and knelt beside it, lifting off hood and lid, tipping it gently until its water began to fall in a limpid stream towards the river, the momentum taking the little fish with it. Philbert watched the bright blue and yellow of it wending off a little hesitantly at first, until its short quarrel between captivity and freedom was taken by the current and away it went – just like Hermann – into the unknown.

Philbert knew he was most probably releasing little Butterblume into the wrong kind of water, with the wrong kind of food, that it would most likely last a mere few minutes before being swallowed whole by some winter-hungry pike, but there it was. It had to be done. It could not possibly stay with Tomaso, and it was a whole other miracle it had survived so long in his company. Its release felt like Philbert's own. His way of accepting Hermann's forgiveness, of moving on from Hermann's care and love into Kwert's. He never told anyone about what had been in Hermann's note – not Otto, not Maulwerf, not even Lita – not until he met the Turk again, the man to whom Hermann had entrusted the note in the first place, who gave it to Otto to give to him. Philbert met the Turk many times later, but never asked, not until after many years had passed.

'You were so young, Philbert,' the Turk said then, 'I knew Hermann a long time, and back then Hermann didn't know if you would understand. He wanted me to hold onto it until I deemed the time was right. Not that I had any idea of what he was planning to do, only that I knew things were going wrong again and that you were special to him, and that folk like us would always be a little apart from the crowd, different inside our skins.' He'd raised his eyes then, settling them briefly upon Philbert's taupe as if it represented every kind of otherness. 'But I do know this . . .' the Turk went on, '. . . that there was only one time in Hermann's life when he felt he truly belonged, only one time when he could truly, actually, be close to other human beings, including Hannah, as I'm sure you already know. And he believed you gave him that time and that, once over, he didn't want you taking the blame for it. He didn't know if you were ready, but I did. He left me the choice, and I made it.'

He'd looked at Philbert with his by-then old man's smile hiding behind his by-then old man's beard, and added his last three words.

'Was I wrong?'

We all make choices, the grown-up Philbert thought then. *We all push at the boundaries of other people's lives, sometimes breaking right through the bubble that separates us, without us even knowing it.*

And he knew the Turk had been right, had taken the correct decision. Philbert still had Hermann's ring about his neck. He'd almost lost it once, the story of which far surpassed any of the supposed miracles of Kwert's making, and whose consequences had gone so much farther than any of them at the time would have thought possible.

14

The Outside In, the Inside Out

By God, but it was cold. Philbert huddled by the brazier in Maulwerf's tent. It had a flap in the roof to let out the smoke, but there was still a faint miasma of it hanging in the air. During the weeks following Philbert's bringing of Hermann's note to him, Kwert had stepped up his teaching of how to read for Philbert and Lita. Tomaso had quit the task entirely, his animosity towards Philbert unabated since the invasion of Hermann's tent that he'd taken for his own, spending all his spare time with Madame La Dentellière, the lace-maker, learning other kinds of words, studying bobbins, spools, skanes and chains and all the other intricacies involved in her trade, eager to absorb it quick as he could so he could leave the Fair. This desertion bothered Philbert and Lita not a whit, happy Tomaso was gone from their immediate circle. A bad boy, they both agreed, and a hard one, and one they could well do without.

On reading nights Kwert would take out his book, the *Philocalia*, a book, he explained, whose pages were filled with all that was beautiful in the world, the wise words of the Ancients lathered across its pages like honey. He told his two attentive pupils of Ephrem and Evagrius Ponticus, of Grigory of Palamas, Symeon and Cyrus, all gathered together by Nicodemus of the Holy Mountain, and latterly Macarius Notoras of Corinth who, by so doing, had squeezed out the primal truths from the old patriarchs' texts as a gizzard does with the seeds it swallows, absorbing the good, spitting out the bad.

Philbert and Lita tried to decipher the words that wandered the yellow pages of the *Philocalia* like hair spread out and tangled over an oft-used pillow. Every night before they started, Kwert took out his book and held it up to the light so the letters on its old brown cover stood out like a shower of golden worms. Carefully he turned the first page and read out the warning citation, lifted from the *Cloud of Unknowing*:

'Fleshly janglers, flatterers and blamers, ronkers and ronners,' Kwert would solemnly declare, 'and all manner of pinchers; cared I never . . .' and here he would pause, looking searchingly at the two bright faces before him, assessing but never judging, and then went on, 'cared I never, never, that they saw this book.'

After this ritual warning he would pass the volume over to his chosen pupil of the night who would open it where Kwert had placed a marker, and start to read.

This particular night, this cold, cold night in Finzeln, it was Philbert's turn, the book coming open at one of Symeon the New Theologian's Hymns.

'*The monk has made of his cell a heaven,*' Philbert began slowly. '*His mind is fixed in the Light of God, as an arrow in a wall. The thief cannot steal it, even if he should slit open the monk's belly and rummage about his intestines as in a purse . . .*'

Stirring stuff, and mostly short words, but not so easy to read as Philbert hoped. He went at it as a sandpiper moves towards a favourite stone – backwards and then sideways, jumping this way and that, cocking its head and jerking first upwards and then down again. When Philbert got stuck, Kwert would mime the answer so he had to think the harder of the word he'd stumbled over, make a mental image of it in his mind, fix it like the arrow to the wall, the star in the firmament. Or so went the theory. Philbert juddered along reasonably well until he hit *intestines* – a word as folded and complicated as its meaning. Kwert began to mime its action out, mimicking Maulwerf at a meal, Philbert saved by freckled Hannah popping her head into their tent, telling them it was time to go. Kwert tapped his finger at Philbert's head to remind him this was a word he was going to need to come back to, Philbert smiling, always eager, always keen, Lita nodding at the command to go. They strapped on their rabbit and squirrel skin boots, their cloaks and coats, scarves and gloves, before setting off into the cold, dark night, heading for the synagogue of self-imported Italian Jews and the *Chamishoh Osor bi-Sh'vot* Festival – the New Year Service of the Trees – to which everyone, no matter their creed or beliefs, were welcome, at least in Finzeln. It was a time of thanksgiving for the woods on which the town depended, for the oaks that provided the tannin and timber needed to make the leather-topped furniture for which they were famous.

The synagogue itself was long and thin, the huge oak doors that fronted it now thrown wide, steps already filled with people pushing back hoods, stuffing gloves into pockets, chattering all the while. The place was only as wide as the over-large doors and filled with loose wooden chairs. Chaos seemed to be the prevailing seating arrangement, the only stricture being that anyone who was actually Jewish was allowed to sit at the front, women – if they were veiled – to the left, men to the right, the rest piling in as they came, sitting wherever they could. The Fair's folk often came here in winter, but this year they had an extra member of the congregation to introduce, namely Frau Fettleheim, who would not be denied, cheeks flushed the same colour as the flowers upon her dress so enthusiastic was she to attend, her cart heaved up the steps and into the synagogue, everyone having to wait until the turmoil of her bulk subsided and she and her cart were straddled across the central aisle. By the time Lita and Philbert got in behind her there wasn't much room, so they squeezed in behind her cart, leaning against its strong wheels.

Hush then, as the huge wooden doors were closed, a ragged silence ensuing, broken only by whispers, sneezes and phlegm-bound coughs. Everyone held their breath while the candles of the trendled chandelier – big as a cart wheel – were lit, watching reverently as it was hoisted inch by inch, foot by foot, creaking and smoking, into the vault of the synagogue's ceiling, making the gold stars dotted amongst the blue paint shine and twinkle like the real thing. And then, at the front, the Rabbi appeared like a magician: tall hat, beard spilling from his chin like unruly black wool. He raised his hands high and began to chant, his voice deep and magnificent, bouncing around the walls and ceiling arches, reaching his audience like the echo from an underwater cave.

'Behold and Bless the Lord, all you servants of Jehovah who stand in His house in these night seasons. Lift your hands to the sanctuary and bless the Lord and He will bless you accordingly out of Zion, even as He made the heaven and the earth . . .'

Philbert had never been in such a place before, nor attuned to religion of any kind, his eyes wandering about the cavernous space; but the more the Rabbi spoke the more Philbert saw this tall thin room as its symbolic reality, the candles setting off the stars a treat, the smell of damp soil rising from between the chairs, the tapers on the great round hoop of the trendle flickering and winking in the hidden currents of air that wrapped themselves about the beams, folding and stretching in and out of the shadows: Heaven and Earth, indeed. The praying continued, the Kiddush soon done, the Rabbi beginning a variation on his usual Day of the Trees speech.

'Welcome to you all here in our place of worship. We are happy to have so many join us to partake in the glories of *Chamishoh Osor*, to thank God and the very trees around us for being our salvation . . .'

The Rabbi was emotional, had to wipe the tears from his cheeks as the choir began to sing the *Hashkediyah*. Amidst the sniffles and muffled coughs a few sought out the rhythm and soon everyone was clapping to the words and some were stamping their feet, and by the end of the *Atsey Zeytim Omdim*, the crowd was on the brink of full-blown song and dance. Rabbi Ridente took his chance then to move amongst his congregation, hugging and shaking hands with friends and strangers, winking at Maulwerf as he passed, nodding at Frau Fettleheim and Lita, and then was back at the front, hands held high as he began to hum low and loud, on and on, until all other noises ceased, his head raised, eyes closed, beard quivering, one note reverberating around the hall until it seemed to fill the air entirely. Behind him, way at the back, half-hidden by a long, gold-coloured curtain, a small man could be glimpsed sitting in front of a huge box to which all sorts of bells were attached by a complex cats-cradle of strings and cords. By pressing pedals and pushing large keys with both feet and leather-clad hands, he could ring out a note inside each bell. And as the Rabbi hummed, so the bells rung, just two notes, on and on, the bells not pealing but expanding their single sounds like ripples of soft satin lifting in the wind. Slowly the Rabbi's hum became a chant as he began the words of the psalm, all on a note, an even rhythm, the bells keeping tone all around him:

'*The Lord reigns; He has robed Himself in majesty;*
Yea, He has girded Himself with strength,
And the world is set firm and cannot be moved . . .'

Not so for Philbert, for whom the world had already begun to tilt and shift, an odd sensation growing inside him as if he were ringing with the bells, as if his head was being slowly stuffed with new-spun wool.

'*The streams have lifted up, Oh my Lord,*
The streams have lifted up their voice . . .'

Philbert's knees began to tremble, his head buzzing as if filled with flies in a summer sycamore; his taupe felt filled with thin jelly that was sloshing slowly around and around, as in a whirlpool . . .

'*The streams lift up their roaring;*
More mighty than the voices of many waters, mighty waves,
Breakers of the Sea . . .'

Philbert's legs gave way completely and he sank almost noiselessly to the ground, his eyes fixed on the stars above, the flickering of the candles, the sound of the bells surrounding him as if he was that bell and the rest of the world the clapper with which he was being continuously struck. He didn't know it, but on his downward slide he knocked the brake from Frau Fettleheim's cart and now his weight was against the wheel, pushing it forward, tipping it over a plank-edge, giving it leave to pick up a pace, sending it jerking down the tilted wooden walkway between the flanking rows of spectators and chairs, Frau Fettleheim letting out a short shriek and waving her arms as she gained momentum, her movements causing the cart to tilt and twist the more, sending the seats flanking her skittering out from beneath the knees of their occupants who were by now scrambling to get out of the way, knocking over their neighbours in all directions, the cart crumping off the wooden gangway a few seconds later, tipping Frau Fettleheim unceremoniously into a heaving lap of splintering chairs and cursing congregation. The bells stuttered to a stop as everyone started shouting and standing, pushing and looking, people trying to hoist Frau Fettleheim free from those squashed beneath her. There were gasps and yells, wind-milling arms, running feet, and the candelabra above began to sway dangerously as people tripped over the ropes that held it steady, and in amongst the mayhem could be heard the loud booming laughter of Rabbi Ridente as he stood on the topmost step, seeing all going on before him but completely unable to stop it, quaffing mightily from the large gilt cup of wine whose metal glinted in the swirling light; laughing and laughing, until the ceremonial breastplate split from his chest and clattered to the ground.

~

'Well, Kapellmeister Corti, what do you think?'

'I think, Rabbi, that perhaps the boy needs a sip of your wine.'

'He's a bit young, don't you think?' queried Ridente, keeping a firm hold of the cup, 'and his head looks like a yeast pudding. I'm not sure wine would be good for him in such a state. And where have all those Fair people got to?'

Philbert could hear them talking but they sounded far away, as if he was trapped inside a bottle, unable to move. The man called were looked anxiously around the emptying synagogue for help, but everyone had flooded away to the doors, following Frau Fettleheim and her cart as they were hauled back down the steps, this being apparently far more interesting than the small boy with his weird head who'd been discovered collapsed in amongst a tangled load of chairs.

'He must have got an awful knock for it to come to such a size in so short a time,' said Corti, the bell ringer, with concern.

'Where's that Maulwerf?' Ridente replied, sitting atop the step beside Corti, who was cradling Philbert's head in his lap. 'Can they still be heaving the Human Mountain back onto her plinth?'

'Rabbi, please,' Corti admonished. 'Such cruelty! You should have more care. You know people cannot help their stature, myself included.'

This was certainly true in Corti's case, whose arms were half the length they should have been, stumped off at his elbows

from which his hands exuded without need of lower arm or wrist.

'Kapellmeister Corti,' said the Rabbi, brushing another slurp of wine from his lips. 'I wonder sometimes if you should not be the rabbi instead of me.'

'And leave you to play the bells? Are you mad?' Corti sounded angry, snatching the goblet from Ridente's hands, placing it to Philbert's lips. 'You'd have the roof down in seconds, and half the congregation on their knees praying for mercy.'

Ridente laughed and the Kapellmeister shook his head, started slapping Philbert lightly around the face until, with a crash of the wooden door echoing behind him and a gust of cold air before, Kwert came sweeping down the cluttered walkway towards them, his long grey cloak lifting with every step to reveal the flash of his red habit which, striking as it was, was not so arresting as the intimidating glint in his eye.

'What are you doing to the boy?' he demanded, Corti and Ridente exchanging glances, Corti being the first to answer.

'His eyes are open, but he appears to be unconscious, Signore. I am Corti, the musician here. Do you know the lad? He's taken rather a bump on his head, I'm afraid. You should be prepared for the worst before you come closer.'

'A bump?' Kwert said loudly, and then again a little quieter. 'A bump. . . oh, I see. Oh no. Not at all. That is always there.'

There was a further exchange of glances then, followed by a conversation of shrugs between Corti and the Rabbi, the conclusion being an unspoken, *Well, there you are then. One of Maulwerf's crew. We should have guessed he wasn't going to be quite normal.*

Rabbi Ridente took back the wine and took a long swig just as Kwert drew up beside them, towering above them where the two were sat on the step.

'Signore?' Corti was polite, but carried on holding Philbert's head between solicitous hands.

'Kwert,' said Kwert gazing down on Philbert.

'Signore Kwert,' Corti continued. 'If this is the . . . er . . . usual shape of his head, it is possible my bells have precipitated his little fit. They can set a bowl of water vibrating, and I have seen a melon explode . . . so.'

'Very messy,' Ridente commented, 'and at Sukkah it was too, I believe, took a couple of bottles of peach brandy with it as it went. Very tragic,' he added sadly, shaking his head.

Corti shot the Rabbi a look from beneath pursed eyebrows but continued.

'Even so, Signore Kwert, despite the boy's head being what it is, it might be wise to get a medical opinion on the matter and, as it happens, there's a certain doctor resident here at the moment, a Dottore Ullendorf. He's been here several weeks, taking craniometry readings from each member of our community. I believe he's trying to establish if we differ from the original inhabitants of the area . . . Signore?'

But Kwert was no longer looking at his informant, was gazing off above Corti's head.

'But surely not,' Kwert was murmuring. 'Doctor Ullendorf is here? I can't believe it.'

A small moan from the patient brought his eyes back to the matter in hand and Kwert sat down, gently taking Philbert from Corti, folding him into a sitting position that made Philbert's breathing easier, brought him halfway back to conscious thought. Two strange faces grew from the mist in front of Philbert's eyes: one humorous and darkly hairy, the other fine and round but squashed as if in a vice, hands growing straight from his elbows, and he could make out a third, and with it the familiar yellow grimace of Kwert.

'Philbert,' Kwert's voice was soft and reassuring. 'You were almost trampled in the crush. How glad I am you are still with us.'

With the reassurance of Kwert's voice Philbert relaxed, the

odd faces rolling away, leaving in their place the majestic mound of Frau Fettleheim's behind looming above him, the flowers of her dress billowing over his field of vision like a field of poppies.

'Frau Fett . . . Frau Fett . . .' he couldn't get the words out properly. They stuck to his lips, refusing to unfurl their tails.

'Frau Fettleheim is fine,' Kwert comforted. 'And I'm glad to report that the casualties are few. She's back on her cart and on her way home. And now you, Little Maus, are going to see a doctor. Doctor Ullendorf no less, if these gentlemen will see fit to take us to him?'

'He's staying just across the square,' said the foreshortened Corti.

Another loud crash of the door heralded the reappearance of Maulwerf, rubbing his hands together from the cold as he approached down the splinter-strewn gangway.

'Everything is sorted,' he told them. 'The aggravating Frau Volstrecken and her family, the boy-child of whom appears to have suffered greatly by having his marble-flicking finger crushed in the mêlée, have agreed to be privately entertained in compensation. Several other survivors have seized the opportunity too, so our Little Lita and the Lovelorn Calf will appear at the Volstrecken residence tomorrow afternoon, accompanied by Yours Truly, with his usual impeccable table manners. I assume you will accompany us, Ridente?'

'My dear Maulwerf,' boomed the Rabbi, 'but of course! We have much catching up to do.'

Corti interrupted. 'We really should get this boy to the doctor. He's green as a copper-stain.'

Corti was right, Philbert didn't feel well at all. He was fading in and away as if he were seeing everything through a pool of water. He heard words but couldn't understand them; he saw faces but wasn't rightly sure who they belonged to, his eyes slipping around in their sockets so that only the whites were showing, a sight so alarming that Kwert and Maulwerf wasted no more time. They picked Philbert up, Corti slinging his short-armed coat over him to keep him warm, and together they made their way through the broken-chaired synagogue, the trendle-lights left to self-extinguish in the gloom, going out through the big wooden doors that stretched like trees to the apex of the synagogue, and began to jog across the cold night of the square, a slight mizzle freezing over them as it fell. Corti kept rubbing Philbert's hands as if to coax his own warmth into the child's skin, the Rabbi leading the way to the doctor's house, and soon banging loudly on its door.

After a short silence a light appeared and they could hear a woman's voice.

'*Momento, bitte. Ich komme. Pazienza*!'

The woman carried on grumbling down what must have been a very long passageway, judging by the length of time it took her to reach the door.

'Frau Brenstoffen, it is Ridente!' the Rabbi shouted, still hammering heartily upon the wood, Frau Brenstoffen's reply being not so brief.

'Ach, Rabbi this, Rabbi that, always something; get me this, get me that. It's a wonder my legs aren't worn to stumps . . .'

The door was opened finally by a fractious little woman whose grey hair whispered thinly over her head.

'Frau Brenstoffen,' said Ridente, 'but you're looking as beautiful as ever.'

The little Frau spat, but seemed placated by the compliment.

'Is your good lodger at home?' the Rabbi continued. 'It's urgent we see him.'

'Well, Rabbi, I don't know. He's always locked away in his rooms, so busy. But for you, I will go and see.'

Another long shuffle down the corridor was forestalled by a

door opening and a head emerging from a darkened room.

'Rabbi!' the disembodied head said, alerted by the banging on the door. 'What a pleasant surprise, and I hope you have the Kapellmeister with you. I have the results of our latest experiments. Come in, come on in!'

'Ah *Dottore!*' the Rabbi shouted back at him. 'I'm afraid we're here tonight on business. We've a boy who . . . bring him in, Maulwerf . . . here he is. We had a slight accident during the service.'

Philbert was brought through the door and down the corridor, Kwert and Maulwerf's shoulders banging against the narrowness of its walls, but once they reached the doctor's room they found him already pulling books and papers from a large table at its centre, motioning them to deposit Philbert on its now empty expanse. The moment Kwert released his burden he grabbed the Doctor's hand and began to shake it, bowing deeply.

'So you are Doctor Ullendorf!' Kwert exclaimed with enthusiasm. 'What a pleasure, sir, what a pleasure! I've long admired your work, but never hoped I might actually get to meet you. It is an honour.'

'I am Ullendorf,' said the doctor, his free hand going automatically to brush away the frizz of dark curls that grew like seaweed from his unhatted head, his eyes, nevertheless, fixed upon the boy who'd been dumped upon his table. Kwert was visibly overcome.

'I can't tell you how delighted I am to meet you, sir. My name is Kwert, and the boy here is Philbert. His head has always been like this, a taupe, I understand, and as a craniometrist you must know how unusual that is. In the phrenologist's vocabulary he is quite simply unique, or at least as unique as we're ever likely to see in our lifetimes. What an absolute pleasure!'

Ullendorf freed his hand from Kwert's, surveying Kwert with interest, his hair still bobbing as if in a high wind.

'So you must be the ones travelling with Maulwerf's Fair of Wonders,' Ullendorf replied. 'And a taupe, you say. And born with it? Yes, I've heard of such things, and what an interesting case.'

He took up a magnifying glass then and a single great eye loomed towards Philbert where he'd been deposited on the table like a piece of fish, still vaguely conscious, eyes back to front-ward, seeing all and hearing all but far away, as if he were nothing more than an owl swooping by them, in and out of that stall Hermann had told him was all that made up a man's life. Corti interrupted.

'We think, Dottore, that he may have collapsed due to the carillon. I was holding sustained notes on two bells to give a single assonance which, as you know, during our experiments, can cause deep vibrations in objects of kindred spirit. In this case I suspect the fluids inside the lad's head must have begun to move in resonance with the tone, that his brain is somehow being affected by the internal movement of the cerebral . . .'

'Yes, yes, Corti,' the doctor said. 'You have made a most excellent pupil and learned well, and it is possibly as you say, but I must look closer . . .'

He leaned forward, examining Philbert's taupe with his fingers, pushing at it gently, searching the skin for whatever structures lay beneath.

'Sometimes such things are like a nestful of vipers,' he pontificated as he palped. 'Release the plug and whoosh! They're out quick as a belch and no one can put them back. Other times – just a moment – Corti, hand me my auscultator,' and Corti did, picking out one instrument from the many that lay on a small trolley to the left of the table on which Philbert lay. 'Other times. . .' Ullendorf went on, but did not finish, as he took up the hollow wooden tube Corti had given him, moving it slowly and methodically over the surface of Philbert's taupe, his face creased in concentration.

Everyone else moved away to give the doctor room, Corti to light lamps, Ridente and Maulwerf drawn to the wine-filled pewter jug that was stood on a small ledge beside a book-cluttered desk, Kwert hovering behind the doctor's back, studying his every move.

'Yes . . .' murmured Ullendorf, his ear to his instrument, head cocked to one side in concentration, eyes half-closed as he listened hard. 'Yes, I believe I can hear something, something inside . . .'

Philbert heard the collective cessation of breath at this dramatic statement, although it appeared to him that he wasn't lying on the table at all but was instead tethered to the ceiling looking down, his mind creating the illusion so successfully that he could feel the cobwebs collected in the eaves wafting against his face, saw a couple of discarded fly-wings glinting in the light of the doctor's lamps – as if he were Harlekin watching one of his plays unfold before him on his stage.

'Can you hear me? Philbert, did you say? Are you awake?' Ullendorf went on with his examination. 'It's curious that his eyes are open,' he commented, scribbling a short note in his journal before carrying on with his examination, and indeed Philbert's eyes were now back to normal, responsive to Ullendorf's finger, tracking it as he moved it from side to side.

'Don't be afraid,' he said then to Philbert's prostrate form. 'I am Doctor Ullendorf, and to your left is Corti, and your friends are also here. I'm just taking a look at your most interesting head. You must be rather proud of it. How lucky some people are! Now then,' he handed his auscultator back to Corti, who replaced it on its surgical tray, Ullendorf turning, addressing himself formally first to Kwert and then Maulwerf.

'I believe we need to do a small operation to release the pressure. It's dangerous for the brain to have so much weight pressing upon it. It will be no worse than chiselling a chink into a wall to let in a little light.'

Maulwerf looked dubious.

'I'm not sure, Doctor. I'm certain you're very skilled at what you do, but what if his skull collapses once you stick a needle into it? What if it goes off like a punctured balloon?'

Ullendorf smiled. 'My dear Mr Maulwerf, I assure you that could never happen. The taupe grows directly on top of the skull, and may even be depressing the bone beneath. This is my calling, my area of study. The boy could not be in better hands.'

Maulwerf raised his eyebrows, but Kwert nodded his head gravely. He'd known of this Ullendorf for many years, read every scrap of his work he could lay hands on, and believed in those Ullendorf hands as they examined Philbert's head.

'Below the taupe,' said Ullendorf, reciting from one of his own many texts, 'the bulbiform mass will be normal, I guarantee it. What we need do is burrow through the tumorous protrusion and take a small plug from the skull-bone, thus releasing the pressure that has been building up over the years. It's a good thing this has happened. It has drawn our attention to a need that was already there. If we don't operate, the lad will begin to get headaches and they will get worse; the pressure will build and build, until, crash! Like a dam that cannot hold the force of water it has been trying to contain it will begin to crack, letting the one part flow directly into the other, and then . . .'

He didn't finish his caveat, but smiled down over Philbert, apparently assuming he could see him, which oddly enough Philbert could, having swung down momentarily from the ceiling to the table before going back up again. Corti spoke again.

'Believe me, he's in very good hands, Maulwerf. Dottore Ullendorf is the foremost trepannist in Europe. His skill in diagnosing ailments and the releasing of bad vapours is unexcelled. I have had the esteemed opportunity to be his assistant while he's been here in Finzeln, and no surgeon could have so steady a hand.'

Ullendorf looked over to Kwert and then to Maulwerf.

'Whose charge is the boy actually in?' he asked, Philbert's eyes involuntarily following the man Corti as he crossed and re-crossed the room, watching as he picked up some instrument from the shadows. His attention was momentarily caught by a tray whose surface was covered with tools, shiny silver instruments with ivory handles and toothed cogs, miniature circular saws, a three-legged compass, points sharp and glinting, some part of Philbert realising suddenly what this Doctor, or Dottore, depending on what language you were speaking, was about to do, and that he was about to crack open his head like a duck's egg. At this point he tried his hardest to struggle and protest but his body barely twitched with the effort, and only the strange man Corti seemed to notice this apparent reaction and physically pushed Ullendorf to one side, taking hold once again of Philbert's hand.

'Shame on us all!' Corti proclaimed. 'We are talking about the lad as if he was no more than a frog held down with pins! But it's alright, Philbert. Nothing bad is going to happen to you. The Dottore is just going to perform a simple operation, and it won't hurt. I can promise you that. He's done the same to me, not once, but twice, and afterwards you will feel so much better, like a breeze has blown through your head and swept all the cobwebs away.'

Philbert saw Corti clearly for the first time, that the man's arms truly were clipped off at the elbows, hands growing directly from the joints, and was oddly comforted by it. He saw too the man's face, flat as an iron, though not grotesquely so, and he had such a gentle smile and green eyes that were bright, almost phosphorescent, alive with fire-flies that twinkled in the dim light of the room. A man to be trusted, whoever he was, and Philbert relaxed.

'Well, Kwert,' Maulwerf spoke. 'If you agree, I think we must let the doctor have his way. Not that I hold much with this new-fangled head-holing. I'm not one for peering inside other people's bits and pieces, for Lord knows what you're letting in and letting out. No offence, Doctor,' he bowed his head briefly, but Ullendorf only smiled.

'None taken. And remember, one and all, that curiosity always precedes progress.'

Maulwerf sat back in his seat, taking the goblet offered him by Ridente, the slight sheen of his waistcoat bristling where he'd brushed the nap the wrong way with his hand, Philbert not being immediately at hand to correct it for him.

'And remember too,' Ullendorf added mildly, as he moved away from Philbert and his table and started polishing his instruments on a strop of leather, 'that most of us will tolerate a condition we are suffering until we understand it can be otherwise.'

Maulwerf and Kwert exchanged glances, both thinking of Hermann, as was Philbert, remembering Hermann leaning back from the bridge and letting himself go. And that was what Philbert did too. He let himself go. He didn't feel the leather buckles being strapped about his body and head, nor that Frau Brenstoffen had brought in a pail of boiled water in which the instruments to be used were now soaking. Ullendorf was checking his drill. Kwert was off to one side looking worried. Corti had drawn up a chair and placed himself where Philbert could see him. Rabbi Ridente and Maulwerf already pouring out more wine.

'Of course you'll have read in the Second Book of Maccabees about the brothers who were scalped,' homilised Ridente, as he clinked goblets with Maulwerf, 'and how the skin of their heads was torn off by their hair before they were fried alive in a giant skillet. It used to be commonplace to scalp your enemies, or so I gather. Apparently the natives of the Americas do it all the time.'

Ullendorf was busy retrieving his instruments from the bucket, drying them on a steam-scalded towel.

'Ah yes,' he replied, as if he were in some philosophical salon and not about to perform a delicate surgical procedure. 'Very ingenious. Though in all cultures the process seems very much the same, usually done – in primitive cultures – with sharpened stones, first cutting a line about the cranium, starting in the middle of the forehead and going out on each side above the ears, then down to the back of the neck. One side first and then the other, or – with those very skilled – one complete and uninterrupted circular movement.'

Ridente interrupted, unhappy his tale had been hi-jacked. 'They say it's like skinning a rabbit – a few quick slices with the knife, a few hard tugs, and off the skin comes like orange peel.'

'The Anglo-Saxons did it too,' Ullendorf went on as if no one had spoken. 'And were so skilful that many survived afterwards to tell the tale, at least so we read in the chronicles they've left us.'

'They'd need a good wardrobe of hats and wigs afterwards,' Ridente riposted. 'Though I'm told the English wear such objects for fashion.'

He laughed at what he took to be a good joke, but Ullendorf took him literally and quibbled at the Rabbi's grasp of history and custom as he laid his needed instruments out onto his trolley.

'Oh no sir, far too early for such frivolities, as far as wigs and hats go for the ancients. Though it strikes me often that men today are just as cruel as they were back then. I've read of several jungle tribes who to this day tether monkeys to trees, treating them like pets as they fatten them up, then one day decide this is the time to slice off the tops of their little heads, scoop out their still beating brains, eating them while the monkeys are running around in circles screaming, "Why is my head so cold? Who let in the rain?" And of course there's definite evidence the Polenesiani people eat the brains of their dead relatives and cover themselves in the ground-up ashes of their ancestors' burned bones.'

'Enough!' Corti's voice was not loud, but loud enough to silence both Rabbi and surgeon. He'd found a bottle of brandy and dabbed a little to Philbert's lips as he continued with his admonition. 'Ridente, Dottore, I really don't think you should be speaking of such things, interesting as they might be. The boy's eyes are open, as are probably his ears. What if he can hear you?'

And so he could. Philbert had heard everything and felt the sweat rising upon his skin, trying to wriggle free all this while, to shout and jump from the confines of his infuriatingly unresponsive body.

'Hrrmph,' said Ullendorf, chastened. 'Quite right. My apologies. Philbert, if you can hear me, I apologise. One forgets that the catatonic state induced by pressure on the brain does not preclude conscious sensation.'

Ullendorf loomed above Philbert with his knife and Philbert tried once again to intervene, saw Ullendorf suck in his lips, adjust the lamp, saw him shift his head slightly to one side as he started to wash Philbert's taupe with oil of vitriol. By now Philbert was in absolute panic. He could see, he could hear, and though he could not exactly feel, he knew precisely where he was and what was about to happen.

'Look at me, Philbert.'

It was Corti, gentle and reassuring, and Philbert looked, saw Corti lift a strange contraption onto his knees, what looked like a bunch of dried straw tied together with string.

'This is a reed organ,' Corti spoke directly to Philbert. 'Sometimes called a cheng in China. Each reed has a metal tongue placed inside it and we use this gourd, this calabash, to take the breath, mould the sound, make it bigger.'

Philbert calmed a little, ceased his fight, focussing on Corti and his cheng.

'I'm going to blow into the reeds and I'm going to play them,' Corti said, 'and you are going to listen, and you'll hear a melody of great beauty. Do you understand?'

Philbert did, though couldn't say so, but then Corti began to blow into his instrument and the sound came to Philbert like wind within a cave, like a shell placed against his ear. The knife sliced, and a few drops of blood fell from Philbert's head but he didn't notice, concentrated as he was upon the sounds of the reed organ that was like water tippling over stones, wind through a fallen heap of leaves. Ullendorf took up his knife again and made his T-cut, picked up his pincers, pinched open Philbert's scalp, and Corti's cheng sang like swans going over marshlands as Ullendorf peeled back the skin and placed his miniature tripod, turned the handles, lowered the drill, pushing the central piece down into Philbert's taupe. He retracted it, replaced it with a longer drill shaft and then went on with his operation, drilling down and down through Philbert's taupe until the teeth finally hit bone, a slight smell of burning filling the room. All Philbert heard was the singing of the cheng, the wind and the swans. The drill-handle moved along its oiled coils as Ullendorf went at his task, the grating sound as it went through the bone making Kwert wince. Ullendorf carried on as if he did such a thing every day of every week, a few moments later reversing his drill, brushing his hands briefly on his trousers to wipe away the sweat before steadying the instrument for its final bite. Philbert felt no pain, felt instead as if a hundred thousand butterflies had just been born inside him, taking flight as Ullendorf finally scraped out the circle of his skull with the drill's teeth. Corti played, Kwert paced nervously, Ridente and Maulwerf drank on.

Ullendorf murmured softly to himself, '*Ungewöhnlich* . . . *außerordentlich* . . .' as he retracted the drill bit from his little tripod and then removed from the drill's end the tiny circle of Philbert's skull and, before taking away the retractors that were holding back the skin, Ullendorf took up a thin pen-like instrument and shook it, mixing together a couple of chemicals that released a small light and shone it down the tiny mineshaft into Philbert's head, Philbert sensing the warmth of the little light-pen as it descended, seeing his own taupe like a poke of snail eggs huddling deep inside, thousands of tiny chrysalises row upon row, all pulsating, all ready to hatch, could already feel the millions of memories that were bursting to get out of him like dragonflies crawling up the reeds of Corti's cheng waiting for the sun to warm their blood so they could unfurl their wings and fly. And he knew that when they did they would leave an exact imprint of themselves behind so he would always be able to recall every flutter and scale of every wing as they passed out of him, retain the images of their colours and their grace and the recognition of their changing, and that he was changing, right this minute, just as they would do when their time came. He wasn't sure if anything else could ever feel so real as it did at this very moment. Up until a few seconds ago Corti's music had been his entire world, but that world had changed and could never go back to how it had been before.

Ullendorf released his breath, withdrew his light-pen, removed his tripod and retractors, took the little disc of bone from the end of the drill with tiny pincers, dipping it several times into a solution of salt and iodide before laying it out upon a square of muslin where it lay like an iridescent opal, pale and newborn. He ran his thread through his needle and through the skin of Philbert's taupe and pulled it tight, blinking off the light. A single twist, a tiny knot, and Philbert's visions ceased. He lay like a corpse, unmoving, though could still hear Corti's cheng and Ullendorf's breath like a breeze against his skin, a soft and gentle feeling of twist and fall as if he were an ash key separated from its parent branch, released into the wind. He knew he was falling into sleep but just before he did he saw the bridge at Hochwürden, felt like he was looking up at it from down below, seeing Hermann's body falling down towards him and understood it had not been an ending, but release.

15

The Bowman and Goodbye

Philbert was sitting in the kitchen of Frau Volstrecken alongside her son, Kaspar, the boy who broke his finger during the stramash in the synagogue. The next week the Fair was to perform for this private audience in recompense, with the added coda that Philbert be allowed to consort with Kaspar until then. Philbert would remember that morning, fresh as the bread Frau Volstrecken was removing from her oven, over the years, often visiting the adult Kaspar, their shared bouts of nostalgia having first been preceded by Philbert admiring the astonishing sculpted stonework of which Kaspar became a master. They would sit and drink too much, talk about that small good time they'd had together when they'd first met, and of Philbert's trepanation which had fascinated Kaspar back then. It took Philbert a long while to grasp the full implications of what Ullendorf had done for him, how ever since, every instant, every second of his life, was etched inside his head like an ongoing pageant he could revisit whenever he chose. But always he and Kaspar would talk about that first morning after the operation when Philbert sat with Kaspar in Kaspar's mother's kitchen, Philbert feeling alive in every sinew, every thread of him, everything vivid, kicking with colour and smell, taste and touch.

~

Frau Volstrecken had suborned her two young inmates to test out the cooking she was practising for the opening of the *Buschenschank*, the small restaurant she and her husband were planning to launch the following spring. She would be serving her soon-to-be famous strudels, and her husband his already-famous wines.

'Now then,' she said, placing a steaming golden roll in front of them. 'This is my family's secret recipe for *Krautstrudel*. It's as good as my grandmother's, and no one made it better.'

She cut into the crisp pastry, small shreds of bacon and cabbage glistening amongst the main filling of buttered onions, Philbert and Kaspar eating like men who've been on the march for weeks. They'd already been fed *Nockerls* and noodles, slivers of fried goose liver braised with beef in sour cream and cherries, *Gebachene Mäuse* – sugar, rum, raisins and flour, shaped and fried in butter, little sticks of preserved angelica for their tails – both laughing that one kind of mouse was being eaten by another.

Philbert had never tasted such things before and, though he had them many times down the years, often cooked by Frau Volstrecken herself, they were never so crisp, nor smelt so good, nor held their flavours quite as perfectly as they did that first time, and he would remember those quiet, food-stuffed afternoons with Kaspar with a special passion, as well as the conversation they had later in the Volstrecken's barn.

'So is it true then?' Kaspar asked, twisting a stalk of dried clover through the gap in his front teeth. 'About your head, I mean?'

'Is what true?' Philbert replied, pretending not to know what Kaspar was talking about.

'Is it true that loony doctor actually sawed through your head?'

'Oh yes,' Philbert replied casually, as if such a thing happened every day. 'Right through.'

'Wasn't there loads of blood and stuff?'

'Swept it up in buckets,' Philbert elaborated.

'And what Lita said . . . is that true too? Is your head really filled with marbles?'

His voice trembled with the hope of it and Philbert, who didn't want to lie exactly, nor let his new friend down by telling him the truth, took the central path as provided him by Lita.

'Sort of,' he said, reaching into his pocket. 'Actually, I brought you one.'

Kaspar was up quick as a flea, sick with excitement, his friendship about to reap its reward because he was a boy who loved stones in every form, trawled rivers and streams for them, made of them his life. Carefully, Philbert placed the folded cloth on the flat surface of the bale between them and teased back the corners, just as Ullendorf had folded back the skin of his scalp. And there it was, a small round bead, green as pond-water, just a flick of something red, twisted deep within.

'*Erstaunlich*!' gasped Kaspar, picking the bead up carefully between finger and thumb. 'Is that your actual blood inside there?'

'Blood?' Philbert repeated, a little annoyed he hadn't thought of this particular piece of fabrication himself.

'And this came out of your actual head? *Unglaublich*! Don't they make the most awful noise rattling around inside all the time?'

This level of detail took Philbert by surprise, but Kaspar was too entranced by his little piece of Philbert to notice.

They laughed about this episode down the years, but Kaspar always kept his fascination for Philbert's head and what he kept locked away inside, and also kept that bead with its lick of red; Philbert in return tried to explain what had happened that day, how it seemed ever after as if the whole world was stepping lightly to one side so he could view it from a different angle; how at times he heard a gentle scraping, as if someone was rearranging the furniture inside his head. Philbert had not been alarmed by this, nor had he found it unpleasant, only reinforcing the growing sensation that his taupe was like a deep, deep well, every new experience a stone thrown in, each ripple noted and recorded. It might be mislaid for a while, but as long as Philbert was alive it could never be lost.

~

A couple of winter months in Finzeln always suited the Fair of Wonders well, giving them time to rehearse new acts and plays, polish up their routines, try variations, adapt the old to the new. Whenever they needed money or food and the weather allowed them passage, they would go off in small troupes to the outlying villages, staying a few days here, a few days there, but always returning to Finzeln, like puffins to their burrows. Kwert spent many hours reading from his *Philocalia*, and yet more in meditation. He'd been profoundly affected by Ullendorf's operation on Philbert's taupe and would place the whittling of it – the little circle of Philbert's skull, given to him by Ullendorf – within his palm, staring at it until it became the entire universe, because for Kwert it represented far more than the mere application of modern science. Like every Hesychast, he believed utterly that the human body was a prison cell of skin and bone whose only duty was to keep safe the soul inside, carrying it like a pearl, like a lamp within a vase, and could not help wondering how much of Philbert's soul's light had leaked out that evening Ullendorf had drilled into his head. He'd noted a subtle change in Philbert since, the boy undoubtedly being more thoughtful, more introspective, despite the attentive friendship of Kaspar Volstrecken. Kwert was a seeker of signs and had been expecting something, but not at all what actually came, by which time they'd already left Finzeln a few days behind.

First off, his donkey got sick, hind legs swelling up overnight

139

like mushrooms, great hard cords running their length that budded ulcers at every turn. Kwert, the supposed healer, tended her and stroked her, poulticed and pussed her, but then Kwert got sick too, and every breath he drew was cracked, sounding like leaves being driven up an alley by the wind and, below his jaw, an abscess bled itself black, and he began coughing up phlegm the colour of rotten plums. Philbert and Lita were terrified and tried to help Kwert, preparing and administering the various remedies he dictated through grinding teeth: ointments made from agrimony, chickweed and groundsel, salves of beeswax and softened resin, bitter pills of garlic and ground hemp. But nothing made the slightest bit of difference and Kwert and his donkey lay side-by-side beneath the stretch of canvas pulled from his cart, bundled up with straw to keep them warm, the donkey on her side, legs puffed up like pastry, stinking of pus, burning like a tar barrel. Every boil that died down on the donkey seemed to grow up twice as fierce on Kwert as he moaned and creaked beside her, the boils ballooning and bursting so the air was noxious with their seep and spill. It was the last week of February, and there was no doubt that neither man nor beast were going to make it far into March without intervention. It was Philbert who made the decision, trekking all the way back to Finzeln on his own, bringing back with him the same doctor who had already shed so much light into his own life.

They arrived back on the first day of March, the entire camp anxious and cold beneath the blank blue sky, watching with hands to their brows to shade out the sun as Doctor Ullendorf's carriage grew from a dot in the distance to normal size. Philbert couldn't know that Ullendorf had been tracking the Fair's progress; that he'd been studying all the measurements and notations he'd taken back in Finzeln of Philbert's head and had anyway been about to seek them out. He couldn't have been gladder to see Philbert when he came banging on his door just as Ridente had done a couple of months before, Philbert clinching onto his hand like a crab the moment he appeared, urging him with every breath to get back to the camp and quick.

Ullendorf took one look at Kwert and his donkey and knew immediately what was wrong.

'Get me oak-bark and acorns,' he commanded. 'Get me mistletoe from the apple trees, get me witch-hazel and sorrel and pads of dried moss, cobwebs and honey.'

Lita and Philbert set to, scurrying across the fields like mice, burrowing deep into the woods with their baskets. They returned scratched and torn, Doctor Ullendorf sat by the fire, hands gloved, a long needle held between his fingers, its sharp tip going from red to white in the flames. The astringent was made as he ordered and the honey melted, and then Kwert's arms and legs were held rigid and bare while Ullendorf struck through and through the marauding boils as though bayoneting an enemy.

'Pile on plenty of clean straw,' bellowed Ullendorf, after Kwert's wounds had been washed and dressed. 'I want him hot as a hedgehog in a gypsy's pot. And then,' he said, seeking out Philbert's eye meaningfully, 'I want a platter of dumplings and a casket of Volstrecken's wine. You and I have been travelling more than three hours, young man, and saving lives is hungry work.'

~

All was done as he ordered, Kwert heaped over with straw, blankets and sheepskin rugs, and Ullendorf's food was brought. He sighed as he dipped his dumplings into his cup and swallowed them whole, drank the casket dry, then leant himself against the back of the Kwert Mountain of blankets and went to sleep. Philbert, by contrast, spent a troubled night, for Ullendorf had spoken quite correctly about how long they'd travelled; what Ullendorf hadn't spoken of was what he'd proposed to Philbert during that travelling. His researches in Finzeln were almost done, he told Philbert, all that remained was to draw up his conclusions from the comparisons made between the native German population and the third generation of incoming Italian Jews, who had made their home beside them, integrated but not intermarried, as dictated by their faith. All this he spoke about in great detail to Philbert on that journey, saying it would soon be time for Ullendorf to leave Finzeln and return to his home; and that when he went he wanted Philbert to come with him, an idea too huge for Philbert to think about while Kwert was still at death's door.

The next morning Philbert found Ullendorf at his post, beginning to exhume Kwert from his blankets as Philbert rushed forward to help. Once his body was revealed Philbert was astounded to see that Kwert's boils were dry as bones abandoned on the desert of his yellowing skin. His breathing had broken back to even stride, disturbed only by occasional and incoherent murmurs, snatches of prayers perhaps, foreign words and phrases. His skin was hot to the touch, but no longer clammy, and twenty-four hours later Kwert was sitting up, sucking at pease-soup thickened with curds, the donkey wobbling to its knees, licking at the drips, eager for anything his master could spare. Two days later both were up and about, thin and winter-worn for sure, sag-skinned, slack-jawed, but both alive and both recovering well.

Amongst the Fair's folk Doctor Ullendorf was a hero, more than that, a miracle worker without whose help Kwert would certainly have died. He was a bit of a strange one, that went without saying, for they none of them held much with doctoring, having seen what it could do in the wrong hands. Kwert was a trusted healer, but when the likes of Kwert got sick well, that was that. Or so they'd always thought. Then Philbert had fetched this oafish-looking doctor with his idiot's smile and hair like curly dock, and not only had he dug a hole into the

Maus-Junge's head with the lad living to tell the tale, but now he'd gone on to heal the healer, and the healer's donkey too. Ullendorf explained that the sickness suffered was common enough, called Glanders to those in the know, but the Fair's folk didn't know, and regarded Ullendorf with awe. So when he also told him that the Volstreckens were planning to open the doors of their *Buschenschank* for the first time at the end of the week Maulwerf took the lead and declared they would return to Finzeln with Ullendorf, and there he would be guest-of-honour at the Grand Opening to celebrate Kwert's survival in style. It boded well, Maulwerf told them, that their season had started so auspiciously, so they upped sticks and crowded back along the lanes to Finzeln and to the open arms of the Volstreckens, who were delighted to welcome them in.

It was a night Philbert would long remember, the kind that torqued your heart on a spit just to think on it, and think on it he often did. People always said you can never go back, that what's done is done, and though the latter part of this sentence was as true for Philbert as for everyone else, the first part was not, for Philbert was discovering that he could go back to the past whenever he chose. He couldn't change a thing about it, but he could close his eyes and live it all over again just as he'd lived it then, with every colour, every smell, every touch just as real to him as if it had happened only a few moments before.

~

So back to Finzeln went the Fair, all sat around the tables of the *Buschenschank*, the red and white checkers of the running cloths marching over the boards as Frau Volstrecken lit the lamps. At the end of the long room, lined with barrels all along one side, Kapellmeister Corti waved his orchestra into half-baked order; Herr Volstrecken filled mugs and glasses with wine, delighted to see his friends back again for his opening night; and Frau Fettleheim had a table to herself, piled high with all sorts of dishes and plates, appointed Frau Volstrecken's official taster, Frau Fettleheim having boasted many times of being an assistant cook in her youth at the Imperial Palace. That's what she said, and she was as entitled to her tales as was everyone else. She'd always sworn it was all the tasting for salt and seasonings that had made her the way she was today, and that at one hundred dishes a week to taste it would have done the same to anyone. The rolls of her belly made the table shake as she spoke of far gone days with misty eyes, and no one had the heart to argue.

Rabbi Ridente raised an arm, lifted his glass, calling for hush, nodding to each of the company in turn, and in particular to the large Dr Ullendorf who took place of honour next to Kwert. Ullendorf's curly hair tweaked out from under his hat every time he moved his head or smiled his big open-door smile, and beside him was Kwert, fever-free, the welts on his skin calmed to a sea of pinkish domes like shrinking jellyfish stranded on a beach. The dancing troupe somersaulted a saltambalique across the room, directed by the man they called Harlekin, who always seemed to stand in shadow, keeping his head half-turned so no one could see his eyes. It was all part of his mystique and a part he stuck to rigidly, always standing like the spectre at the wedding feast, reminding everyone that fate is fate and no one can escape whatever theirs might be.

Then Rabbi Ridente was up and speaking and everyone bowed their head, even Harlekin.

'O God, great and mighty, I come before You to render thanks; in our distress we called on You and You did answer; for Your anger is but for a moment and Your favour will last our whole lives through. To Our Lord, our Rock, and our Redeemer, we give thanks. Amen.' It was a short prayer and soon he clapped his hands and broke the bell-jar of silence. 'My friends, let us eat, let us drink, let us thank the Good God that Kwert is among us still, and let us laugh at our misfortunes when they come, in the full knowledge that God will see us right in the end. Corti, let the music begin!'

Corti raised his short arms high as they would go and let crash a cymbal as they fell; his foot started tapping and everyone drew in their breath as the show began. There was an almighty wheeze and creak as a trio of bagpipers began to blow and the Polish Goats – as those strange instruments were called – began to dance, dudelsacks swelling, elbows bellowing, fingers chittering up and down the screeching pipes; a man plucked his zither with a plectrum, making weird high notes screech across the room; the drums were rolled and the paukes were trommelled, and the gongs were rung, and the tambourines sang; the rebeck riribled and danced between its owner's knees, bouncing against the bow as the player leapt now and then from the floor. Corti had attached bells to his hands and feet, and more to his hat and knees, and he clattered around the room like a scarecrow trying to run from his shadow; another man, with a curved board studded with nails and string grabbed a bow and played it like a fiddle, the iron nails vibrating and humming and dashing their strident way amidst the cacophony of sound. The Fair's folk laughed and sang and danced, pulling Kwert up with them even though he didn't look too keen, and Maulwerf flung Frau Volstrecken around the room like a top until she fell, pink-cheeked, hair a-whirl, onto a bowl of *Kalbsvörgel* that her husband had rested on his lap while he clapped and shouted at her progress. The Bowman lay down his fiddle and picked Lita up in his arms and stood her two feet in the crooks of his elbows, launching her around and around as she clung wildly to his ears, laughing and screaming to be put down.

It was a night as stuffed full of good things as Frau Volstrecken's strudels were with apple, and later on Philbert and Lita sat outside in the cool air of midnight looking at the stars, listening to the feast going on inside, and the Bowman sang, and his iron nails rang, and they danced a slow dance outside under the light of the moon. Happiness. No other word for it. Happiness for all there, pure and simple, and especially for Philbert, dancing with Lita, her head on his shoulder, his arms about her waist, Kroonk bumping against his legs as he turned her beneath the turning stars.

Inside, Ullendorf was taking the opportunity to discuss certain matters with Kwert, rather bending the conversation to his advantage, having not long been the saviour – no matter the Rabbi's praising of his God – of Kwert's life.

'Your boy is a most interesting case,' Ullendorf was saying. 'And I must admit I was delighted when he turned back up at my door, and even more so to act upon his summons.'

'I'm very blessed that you did,' Kwert replied, somewhat formally, his neck-bones clicking as he made a short bow of thanks in Ullendorf's direction.

'My pleasure, Mr Kwert,' Ullendorf was hearty, 'my pleasure.'

'And you suspect Kwert's illness was . . . what was it?' Maulwerf broke in. 'I'm not much up on doctoring, but it will be useful to know how to act if we ever come across such a thing again.'

Ullendorf spread his long surgeon's fingers across the red and white cloth as if it were an unopened skull and he was trying to guess what lay beneath.

'Groom's Glanders, without a doubt,' he said. 'The equine disease tears through the lymph system like mucky water through a pipe. It's rarely fatal in horses, or donkeys come to that, but it can be so in the men who catch the disease as they tend them. The contagion is caused, so I've been led to believe, by small animalcules leaping from beast to beast, or beast to man.' He coughed, relit his pipe. 'Once inside the blood the body detects these unknown animalcules and sets out to eject them, hence the eruption of boils: throwing out the rats with the rubbish, as it were.'

'And am I to assume you collect such specimens?' inquired Kwert politely, having already been informed that some of his pus and excretions had ended up in bottles in Ullendorf's capacious pockets.

'Oh yes indeed,' Ullendorf had no compunction about removing parts of other people's illnesses. 'Every living thing is but a myriad of cells, each one capable of reproducing itself, just as you or I can reproduce ourselves in our children.' He hesitated a second before continuing. 'But on the introduction of the foreign animalcule into the body it's my belief that this reproduction goes somewhat awry, and in that belief I fall somewhat between the rival camps of Schwann and Virchow.'

Neither Kwert nor Maulwerf knew who these people were and Ullendorf didn't stop to explain. He was getting to the nub of his thesis, and the reason for his interest in Philbert.

'Diseases are strange creatures, and can move from person to person, from beast to beast. But they can also be engendered by the body itself, not merely from the influence of outside agents. And this is one of my primary fields of study. It is my Collection Principle that the *Knollenförmig*, the tumours, and the *Ungeheuerlich*, those bulbous knobs that can form both within and without a person, are both in and of that individual, and may stand as representatives of the whole. And of course boils and ulcers are not to be sniffed at, for they are all part and parcel of my research, and as such it was a pleasure, as I said before, to become reacquainted with you, Kwert – not that I want in any way to make light of your recent discomfort. But it also brings me back to the boy . . .'

A moment's silence then, as both Kwert and Maulwerf glanced at each other.

'You mean Philbert,' Kwert said, looking a little uncomfortable. 'I am, of course, more grateful than I can say for your intervention in making me well. But can I ask, sir, what more can you possibly want with Philbert?'

Ullendorf rocked back in his chair, the smile on his face so broad it could have swallowed a side of beef.

'I am no sinister butcher, Kwert, no resurrectionist hacking unfortunates to death in back alleys, chopping off a bit here and there in order to further my studies. But you must share my interest, for are you not . . . how shall I say it? A forquidder . . . a Teller of Signs . . . that you read bumps and the like?'

Kwert cleared his throat. He was used to being laughed at, and usually enjoyed it, for it was all part of the show when it came down to it. But this was different. This was a learned man he admired and owed his life to, and he felt the need to hold his own.

'I believe a great many things, Doctor Ullendorf, about the signs the Good Lord gives us. I believe the body is the casement of the soul, and that the soul can express itself through the body. It's like spying out the lie of the land. You look, and you see hills and fields, terraces and forests. And you know that if a man has built his house it is not likely to be built on a marsh. You know that if you see birch and gorse and heather all growing together then the likelihood is that the land beneath them is primarily peat or moorland, whereas if you see beech and ash growing together then the ground will be altogether different, softer, that it will harbour different kinds of plants, different fungi, different flowers. And so it is with a person: the skin can be the outward sign of that which is rooted deep in the substance of the soul within.'

'So what do you think is within the boy, Kwert?' Ullendorf leaned forward, elbows on the table, juggling his empty glass between his fingers. 'Is he a monster or a saint?'

It was Kwert's turn to smile. 'Oh Doctor Ullendorf, it is nowhere near that simple, as I'm sure you must know. There are a great many ways a body can be put together, but the main point is this: the body is but a curtain – a vestment – that conceals the state of the soul beneath. A man's skin hides his

humanity like a nut within its shell. It's a seed that may grow or rot, but has at its outset the potential to do either. And it's that potential I seek to find and interpret.'

Ullendorf moved back against his chair as Kwert raised his eyes to meet his. They stared back and forth for a few moments, two dogs, one bone.

'I don't want to harm him, Kwert,' Ullendorf said. 'All I want is to study him a little, get a living sample if I can. The core I took at the trepanning I took no measures to preserve, and therefore it is dead. But what I want is to look at the living cells of his taupe, observe them at their daily work. It will be like watching ants busy in their formicaries. Like you, Kwert, I have my beliefs, and I believe that every body is composed of millions of cells, but in that head of his I think those cells might be quite different, that they must at the very least work and divide at a greater rate than is the norm. His taupe is like a bulbil, a new bud forming on the side of an old plant, ready to detach itself from the stem and become an independent being entire of itself.' He laughed briefly as Volstrecken reappeared and refilled their glasses, and smiled his wide smile. 'Naturally I'm not suggesting that half Philbert's head is about to jump down and walk off out the door never to be seen again. That would be preposterous! What I am suggesting, however, is that a part of his body is working to a different plan than the rest of ours are . . . has a different time-scale, different aims and different goals, and that perhaps he really is the speciality you so desire, Kwert, after all.'

He pulled a small glass tube from his inside pocket and held it up to the light, shaking it as he did so.

'Is this all that is inside his head, do you think?' Ullendorf said, looking not at the little tube but at Kwert, his body tensed like a string when it is twisted against a hook in the wall. Kwert stared at the tube, at the small cylinder of dark skin held within it, uncomfortably aware that the tiny circle of Philbert's skull

Ullendorf had dug out at the same time was sitting in his pocket, wrapped in silk, and that day after day Kwert had concentrated on it and what it meant, if it meant anything at all.

'Can you really believe,' Ullendorf went on, 'that Philbert's taupe is just an extra handful of earth, serving only to bury his soul a little deeper within him?'

Kwert shook his head. 'What is it you want?' he asked, and Ullendorf smiled again, replacing the tube of Philbert's taupe into his pocket and knew he had won.

'Not much,' he replied. 'I merely want to borrow him for a few weeks, take a closer look at that head of his – maybe see if I can't extract something living from his taupe, see if I can study it properly in the right environs. And you would be very welcome to accompany him, Kwert. The boy need not be alone.'

Kwert looked at Maulwerf, and Maulwerf looked back, inclining his head just a little, for he could see no objection to Ullendorf's plan. Philbert was useful, and had been with the Fair of Wonders long enough to be considered a part of the family Maulwerf created for every waif and stray who happened into it, but he knew too that Kwert had seen something special in the lad and, with Hermann gone, was the closest to a father the boy would ever have.

Kwert closed his eyes. Ullendorf had been right to call him a forquidder, a Teller of Signs, but Kwert was much more than a mere entertainer. He too had long followed the scholastic pursuit of bulbils and bumps, phrenology and craniometry and, as he'd already stated, was a firm admirer of Ullendorf who was foremost in this very field. Even so, Kwert wasn't particularly happy about the plans Ullendorf had for Philbert, but as long as he was willing for Kwert to accompany Philbert every step of the way Kwert couldn't see how he could reasonably object.

'All right then,' Kwert said, opening his eyes again. 'All right. Myself and Philbert will do as you ask, but only on the proviso that we will, at summer's end, be allowed to return to the Fair.'

'My dear Kwert,' Ullendorf laughed. 'You won't be prisoners, but free to leave whenever you choose.' He laughed again, slapping Kwert on the back. 'And so it's agreed.'

And so it was, and had Ullendorf lived long enough he would have bitten those last few words right back into his head.

16

Coming into Anchorage

It was a grey sulk of a morning when Kwert and Philbert left Finzeln and the Fair, all wrapped up in mist, the jolts and pot-holes of the road throwing them into the crushed velvet of Ullendorf's carriage sides. Philbert had never felt so grand nor so sad and excited all at the same time. They left with Doctor Ullendorf to go with him across country back to his home, leaving everything; but for a small time only, Kwert had assured Philbert.

They departed before daybreak having said their goodbyes the night before: Lita still clutching at the Bowman's arm – they were practising a new act together, she announced, him playing his fiddle, she dancing up him like a squirrel up a tree until he threw her wide and somersaulted her back down to her feet. Philbert promised himself that when he returned he would bring a present for her and had already decided what it would be: a pair of shiny little shoes to house those toes that had dangled with him in the water way back in Staßburg. The hardest thing for Philbert was that he'd have to leave Kroonk behind, Ullendorf convincing him that two days travelling confined in a carriage would be tantamount to torture for the poor animal. That he had no place for a pig in his household he didn't mention, nor did he quite appreciate that pig and boy had never spent a day apart in almost five years, which was the most part of both their lives. Philbert hugged her rough red neck and kissed her soft warm snout that smelled, as always, of mud and must. She kroonk-kroonked gently and waggled her tail, putting her head on Philbert's knee, not understanding how long it would be until she saw him again. Unexpectedly it was Lita's Bowman who said he would take especial care of Kroonk in Philbert's absence. His name was Lorenzini Archetto, born in Finzeln, and itching for adventure ever since. He knew all about little *porcellinos*, he said, having been pigman for half the town's population since he'd been knee high to a grasshopper. He knew how to tickle her ears and rub her snout just right. And Philbert could ask for no more.

Dawn found Ullendorf's carriage and its occupants far from Finzeln, rolling through stands of creaking oaks, their old leaves crackling beneath their wheels, new buds barely breaking from their stems. Philbert heard the wind whispering through their branches as they passed, wondering what they said, remembering something the Turk had told him and how his mother's people believed the breeze-blown leaves told tales of things past and things yet to come, if only a person knew how to listen. It was just the sort of nonsense Fair Folk came up with all the time but in this instance, as they passed through that dark corridor of oaks, Philbert craned his neck towards the partly shuttered window and wished it were true.

Opposite him slumped Ullendorf, his hat on the seat beside him, his dark curls leaping up and down with every bump. It wasn't often a child saw the top of an adult's head, especially one as large and tall as Ullendorf, but Philbert could see it now, and realised why Ullendorf was so fond of his blasted hat for there, right on the top of his head, now denuded of bouncing curls, was a large bald patch, round and pink and smooth as the underbelly of the piglet Kroonk had once been. Philbert smiled and turned his attention away, began staring from the window, watching the world slip and change as they moved from dawn into something brighter. They'd reached the end of the vast forests that surrounded Finzeln, the trees having thinned and then shrunk into stubby grey shrubs, listing to orange as the light grew and warmed. Mist rose from the river, drawing fish to the surface to suck at the gnats that clouded the banks, king-fishers flashing streaks of iridescent green and blue right through them like shiny spears, and soon the blackbirds and robins began to sing and the chill fell away from the edge of the day.

Philbert wriggled from his blanket, knocking Kwert from his gentle snores.

'Aaaghlgh!' Kwert yawned above Philbert's head, knees and elbows clicking as he stretched. 'Morning at last,' he murmured, to no one in particular, and leant forward to release the rest of the window blind. It shot up with a crack, the finger-ring tapping at the glass, the quick bright light rousing Ullendorf from his slumbers. Kwert tapped him on the knee with his canteen.

'Something to moisten the morning muggle, Doctor?' Kwert said, handing him a flask of watered wine. 'And for you, Little Maus, how about some reading?'

He was delving into his knapsack for the *Philocalia* but the lifted blind had revealed far too much and already Philbert was pulling at Kwert's sleeve, pointing out of the window, seeing things he'd never seen before, the carriage taking them far from the normal drove-roads and tracks the Fair usually took.

'Look at that tree!' he exclaimed. 'And what kind is that with all those yellow berries on it? And what's that white bird over there? I've never seen one before. And look at that house! Someone has painted it blue! And oh look, look over there! There's a castle up on top of that hill!'

When Philbert had finally prattled himself dry and finished annoying his fellow passengers with his questions and amazements, it was his turn to tumble into sleep. When he woke again an hour or so later he was given black bread and cheese, and was appalled to learn they were less than halfway through that first day's travelling, for the carriage ride that had begun in comfort had lost its glamour, boards become hard as stones, cushioned seats turned into a bed of conkers. Ullendorf began telling his companions about Lengerrborn, where he lived: a small town snuggled between Osnabruck and Bielefeld.

'Only a day's coach-ride from Dortmund and Bremen. Perfect for the chase of *Lusus Naturae*. The Sports of Nature, dear boy,' he elucidated, jamming his not inconsiderable hat onto his head. 'Ullendorf the name, Teratology the game, to use a Kwert-like catch-phrase.'

The more tired Philbert got with the travelling, the more Ullendorf seemed to perk up, telling them in great detail about his home and the laboratory he had built there over the years and how he would have the great privilege of taking another look inside Philbert's head in circumstances far less trying than back at Finzeln. He seemed as excited at this prospect as any Fair-goer paying over his penny to see a new exhibit; he might not know exactly what his penny would enable him to see, but he surely wanted to see it.

Philbert's initial wonderment faded dramatically on the second day of travelling, every bone in his body felt bruised by the bump and jump of the carriage, nothing in the world of interest to him anymore but his own discomfort. It was at least as dark as when they'd left Finzeln when they finally arrived in Lengerrborn and came to a stop. All to be seen outside the carriage were two glimmering torches hoisted high on columns either side of a great wrought iron gate. Ullendorf flung the carriage door open, stuck out his head and breathed in deeply of the fresh night air.

'Welcome to my abode, my friends, to my haven, or my House of Horrors, as it is known hereabouts.'

Ullendorf was jovial in the extreme as he tethered the

carriage's horses to a post just inside the gates, and Philbert was too tired to protest when Ullendorf insisted he and Kwert disembark and take the last few yards up the winding track on foot. They trudged on wearily behind their host, and up a short flight of steps to the wooden door of a house that was hidden in darkness. Ullendorf put out a hand and grabbed at a dangling rope that was weighted with a brass globe the size of man's fist, a mighty jangling ringing out fit to burst lesser heads than Philbert's.

'Like a ship coming into Anchorage, which is the name of my home,' laughed Ullendorf.

Then the door swung open and a huge aproned woman advanced upon her visitors in a floury cloud, the scents of sesame and honey-cake surrounding them as did her fleshy arms, flapping them all in like chicks beneath her wings.

'Brother, brother,' she chided Ullendorf. '*Du knabe unartig*! What on earth are you doing keeping these poor gentlemen sitting on the step while you ring your *schrecklich* bell? Don't you know how cold it is? And who is looking to the horses? And oh my, look at that poor mite.'

The woman ballooned over Philbert. 'You will come down to the kitchen with me immediately and I'll fix you up something grand and hot to eat. Merciful God! That brother of mine is really the end. All manner of strangers and so little warning. But you know men,' the woman chattered on, abandoning Kwert and her brother as she led Philbert away down the lamp-lit hall.

'All alike in my experience,' she continued. 'So long as they've got something they can chew over – talk, talk, talk, their mouths twitching like rabbits at a blade of grass – then they are happy. Those two can sort themselves out with the bottle of port I've left in the sitting room, for no doubt that will entertain those two sots while I see to you. Come along with me, my dear,' and Philbert's hand disappeared into hers, soft and warm as rising dough.

'Oh and Heinrich,' the woman paused briefly at the threshold of the kitchen, turning back as Ullendorf and Kwert began to come in through the open door. 'Welcome home. There's port already out and I'll bring you and your guest something shortly, but first the boy . . .'

Ullendorf laughed, well used to his sister's thwarted leanings towards motherhood and expecting nothing less of her. He shook off his hat, sweeping it in an arc through the air as he bowed deeply to her, his curls unfurling briefly before being pinned back again by the brim of his voluminous hat.

'Always a pleasure to be back, Helge, always a delight. And port you say? Port in the safe haven of home! What could be more apt?'

And with that pronouncement he and Kwert disappeared down the corridor, Ullendorf talking non-stop, his arms gesticulating, Kwert dipping his head as he tried to follow what the man was saying.

~

Once in the kitchen, Helge smiled at Philbert, her face as round as a bun.

'That brother of mine, what can you do with him? Here and there he goes, here and there, and always he comes home without so much as a by your leave. If it hadn't been for Fatzke calling earlier to say he'd seen you on the trail, I shouldn't have known you were coming at all. Anywise, here you are, my duckling. You sit yourself down on that stool by the stove. You must be cold as an icicle, and I'll bet you could use a slice of blueberry pie with a bit of warm custard, so you just wait there while I fetch you a slice from the pantry.'

Philbert sat on the stool and leaned against the edge of the range, glad for the warmth of it seeping into his bones. The kitchen was huge, all painted white, even the flag-stones of the floor, in the middle of which stood an enormous slab of a table. From the ceiling hung racks and pulleys holding washing and hams and bundles of drying herbs, copper basins and black-bottomed pans. Helge returned with a bowl full of pie and poured on some thick, steaming custard from a jug on the range. She gave him a small silver spoon with a figure carved into the handle.

'Lucky for you I've not long taken some to Widow Wilhelm next door and the custard's still hot as a chestnut. You eat as much as you want, my duck, and I'll set a platter for Heinrich and his friend. I think I've still some of that veal and there's plenty of those butter-crumbed eggs . . .'

Helge bustled about her kitchen, bringing out plates of cold meat and potato salads from the pantry, placing them on trays, rattling spoons, arranging dishes, humming all the while. Philbert forgot about being tired and bruised and bad tempered and was soon kneeling on the big chair by the table, watching Helge's hands weave in and out of her dishes, folding slices of meat into slivers of bread.

'Putting the baby to bed, they call this,' she hummed, then began to dip cold dumplings into melted butter before putting them to fry on the stove. She gave Philbert a little taste of every-thing and he sat watching, as warm and welcomed as he'd ever felt in his life.

Helge left briefly to take all her dishes to her brother and Kwert, and when she returned she sang softly as she washed up her pots and pans. When she saw Philbert's eyelids drooping, his head falling down onto his arms, she lifted him up, just as Philbert had many times lifted the piglet Kroonk, and carried him off to bed.

And what a bed! All big and bold with white sheets and pillows, and an eiderdown quilted all over in patchwork flowers. Helge removed the hot bricks she'd earlier placed there from the sheets as Philbert crawled in, and she leant over him for a moment as she tucked the boy in. She put a warm hand on Philbert's cheek, and kissed his forehead and wished him good dreams before leaving. From outside came a caterwauling of tomcats fighting for their territories in the gardens beyond, reminding Philbert of that Bowman sawing at his nail-fiddle, and the tap-tap-tapping of Lita's feet, and hoped to God he was looking after Kroonk as he'd promised; then Philbert slept, and slept deeply. And long, long would Philbert remember the feel of those sheets and those pillows, and every flower of that eiderdown: his very first night in a proper bed.

17

Islands Beneath the Skin

The next morning came crisp and white as the sheets Philbert had slept in, the hoar frost gathered in hard pockets beneath the green bushes of the garden just beginning to melt in the sun. Looking out of the window, Philbert saw a spread of gleaming roofs laid out below him like a dealt deck of cards. Helge burst in just as Philbert was pulling up his trousers.

'Well, my little Philbert,' she said, hands on the hillocks of her hips, 'first thing for you is a change of clothes and then food, after which,' she sighed a little as if the thought pained her, 'my brother wishes to see you.'

Philbert got manhandled into a pair of patched trousers and socks with heels newly darned, a shirt with sleeves so long Helge had to fold them four times at the cuff to make them fit. She puffed and panted, cheeks going red, tendrils of butter-yellow hair escaping her bonnet and sticking damply to her neck, before leading him down to the kitchen where she fed him poached eggs on toast and a cup of hot chocolate.

'There now,' she said proudly, leaning back for a more critical look at her handiwork. 'You look so much better. Are you still hungry?' she asked, parading a plate of toasted and sugared muffins before him as she loaded them onto a tray alongside bread that was dark, dense and hot, jams of wild strawberries and plums spooned in delirium onto a wide pink plate. Helge was humming again.

'The boys,' she commented with disapproval, presumably meaning Kwert and Ullendorf, 'have been in the study for hours. I've already taken them their eggs and coffee, though it's not something I approve of, eating with all those . . . all those . . . specimens . . .' She struggled for adequate words. 'It just isn't nice, not nice at all.'

Helge spat on Philbert's tuft and combed it flat, along with the rest of his hair, and Philbert realised with a jolt she hadn't commented once on his taupe, nor even given it a second look or thought. She picked up her tray of mid-morning snacks and led Philbert down a wide hall that was undoubtedly the grandest place Philbert had ever seen. They passed the staircase that wound up to the floor above, hordes of grim painted men riding on their grim painted horses lining the passageway, enlivened here and there by painted ladies on painted swings and severe looking mountains shading the green and purple landscapes above which they towered so magnificently. At the end of the corridor, Helge knocked on a large oak door, opening it without waiting, plonking down her tray before turning and briskly propelling Philbert in as she left.

'Go on in, my duck,' she whispered, 'and see he doesn't frighten you with all his talk. You come back to Helge if he does.'

The door closed behind Philbert, and he was left twiddling with his buttons, gazing around him. If the kitchen was big, this room was enormous. Cavernous even. From top to bottom the walls were pleated with shelves overflowing with books on one side of the room, bottles and glass jars on the other. A series of tables marched its length, arrayed with tubes and gadgets, pipes and cylinders, springs, microscopes, tanks, vials, ink pots, folders scattered through with pens and pencils and eye glasses of varying shapes and sizes. On the other side of the room, beyond the tables, two vast windows reached down to the floor, showing the same deck of roofs Philbert had seen from upstairs, and down at the base of those windows, thankfully on the other side of the glass, a line of scraggle-backed cats sat looking in, eyes glinting as they turned to watch Philbert wend his way across the floor.

'Ah Philbert, here at last! I see Helge has given you the full benefit of her thwarted motherhood.'

Ullendorf was perched high on a ladder that hung from a rail running the distance of the top shelf. Something red caught Philbert's eye and he located Kwert hunched in a vast armchair, a pile of books tottering at his side, the remains of his breakfast plate on top, a piece of rind draped limply over its edge waiting, just waiting, to fall. Philbert moved towards Kwert, who looked up and smiled, a piece of tomato skin caught between his yellow teeth, a dribble of egg on his stubbled chin. Breakfast, Philbert gathered, had been a hasty affair.

'Welcome to the Wunderkammer!' Ullendorf announced as he extracted himself clumsily from the ladder, both hands clutching a large glass jar inside which something moved. Philbert thought of Kwert's cart and the umbilicus and couldn't help but feel a little sick, especially when Ullendorf brought the jar right up to Philbert's face.

'Want to see?'

Philbert gagged, but kept his breakfast down as Ullendorf strode past him and took his jar to the nearest table.

'As I was just saying to Kwert, Philbert, it was my very good friend Karl Von Basedow who first described the features you can see so clearly in this jar. And only a few years ago, in a quite magnificent paper. He called it Exophthalmic Toxic Goitres. And quite rightly, too. You see here? The gland is swollen somewhat, although a close examination would show the vesicles themselves have reduced in size, the epithelium being long and columnar – obviously caused by the overproduction of thyroxin. But nevertheless a very unusual case. Quite why the eyeballs have begun to protrude is a mystery. One assumes it is something to do with internal fluid pressures.'

Philbert approached the desk. Outside, the cats were still watching, their eyes blinking in the sun. A ginger tom, with only a stub for an ear, viewed the goings on with a look of distaste, then began licking at his paw and cleaning his face, dismissing the world beyond the glass as if it were the tail end of a dissected vole. Philbert gathered his wits, determined not to let himself down in front of this critical audience. No doubt they'd seen it all before, but it was new to him and it wasn't every day somebody waltzes by you carrying the pickled head of a woman, her hair floating loose above her head, eyes sticking out like a snail's, wide open and staring, the whites surrounding the iris like a lily on a pond.

'She was a most unusual case, as I say,' continued Ullendorf, beckoning Philbert closer. 'I had the honour to meet her and give her a good prodding over. The blood supply was so increased there was a positive thrill beneath my fingers when I palpated her neck, and the gland itself pulsated visibly. Her fingers shook, clubbed at the end like spoons and she was forever fiddling, couldn't relax. Picked up everything, twiddled it round and round, put it down, picked it up again. Her husband swore he could feel the blood racing around her body when she was asleep at night, and do you know? You'll never believe this! Come closer, Philbert, take a proper look.'

Philbert edged his way up to the table and gazed at the woman agog in her jar. They stood staring at each other like reflections although Philbert, to be fair, hadn't been severed at the neck and pickled in a jar. At least not all of him.

'And the only reason,' Ullendorf went on, 'that she'd gone to the physician at all and thence was referred to me, was because her husband insisted she was snoring like a troll at night and he couldn't stand the touch of her hands – all hot and sweaty. *More than a loving husband can take*, was what he said. Can you believe it?'

Ullendorf turned and casually patted Philbert's head.

'Prize specimen,' he said, presumably meaning the unfortunate woman. 'Don't worry, Philbert. I didn't chop her into bits with an axe; although come to think of it, I've probably got enough pieces in this room to make a whole body if I could persuade Helge into sewing them into a patchwork. No. The poor woman got knocked down by a carriage just as she was leaving me. An opportunity too good to miss. The husband, distraught as he was, wasn't averse to being paid to let us clean up the mess. I don't believe he ever came back for the rest of her, now that I think of it. You never can tell – there are some strange people in this world.'

Philbert raised his eyebrows. He'd met many strange people at the Fair, but by far the strangest of them all was this man Ullendorf, who had now folded his hands behind his back and was gazing out the window, before turning back abruptly and continuing his lecture.

'Now then, what else was I going to show you? What would you like to see, Philbert? Ah, I know! Come and look at these.'

He took Philbert by the shoulders and propelled him across the room, Philbert glancing back briefly to see the lily-eyes following him with not a blink as the woman bobbed within her glass, her mouth a puckered sigh. Ullendorf took Philbert to his shelves of bottles and lifted him onto a stool. Straightaway Philbert was faced with a line of cats staring at him as they had been at the window, only this time they were like frames of a magic lantern, sliced up and in bits. There were heads and tails, paws, and all sorts of stuff from the inside that he didn't want to think about. Each jar had its label:

Katz: hepatocellular carcinoma with cirrhosis scarring
Katz: intracranial tumour

Katz: cholangiocarcinoma in the biliary tree
Katz: severe ulceration and mange of tail

The labels were appended with dates and various cryptic notations, which Ullendorf happily explained were details of gender, general condition, method of death – if known.

'You see,' he expanded cheerfully, 'Lengerrborn is filled to the bursting brim with cats. We had a brief outbreak of supposed bubonic plague here, oh, it must be twenty years ago now, and some bright spark – whose name is Fatzke – told everyone the plague was caused by rats, and that if only they could kill off the rats the town would be saved. He was not, of course, a doctor, and he chose his moment well, waiting until I was well away on sabbatical. But naturally the man could produce a neverending supply of cats and everybody was soon clamouring to buy them.'

Philbert turned on his stool and looked out of the window. The cats were still there, and Ullendorf was still speaking.

'Believe me, Philbert, there were riots! Every home had to have at least one cat, and the whole town went mad with it. Tallies were erected outside each house with notches to show how many rats their Mauser or Inger or Tiddmuss had caught. Ah,' said Ullendorf, strolling across the room and tapping at the glass of the windows. The cats took no notice and continued their vigil. 'Well, you can guess,' he went on, throwing a hand into the air, 'in no time at all there were no rats to be seen, but pffft! The place was overrun with cats that nobody wanted to feed. Some were dispatched with spades and garden forks but you can never keep a good mouser down, and now they roam the streets in gangs. Gangs I tell you! Frightening, it is,' and so it was, to Philbert at least, turning his gaze from the identity parade of eyes at the window to Ullendorf, who looked anything but frightened as he continued his horrid tale with a dramatic sigh.

'Of course the softer ones among us, mostly women like

Helge, had grown fond of the wretched things, keeping them for company or in case the plague came back. Pah!' Ullendorf swatted at the window, though the cats remained unmoved. 'Little chance of that. I could have told everyone if I was here, for the moment I returned I saw those supposed plague victims, hoping for proper buboes, for what an opportunity that would have been! I've a jarful up here somewhere, but not from anyone in Lengerrborn. Those plague-victims of Fatzke's were nothing more than a few itinerants with a nasty outbreak of boils. He'd gone to the trouble of dying them black and told the fellows to sneeze a lot before going in search of idiots to sell his cats to.' Ullendorf laughed. 'He made a fortune, for it was a jolly good scheme, one way and another. And some people still think him a bit of a hero for taking those old men into his home and nursing them through their final illness, which involved nothing more than a bowl of broth, a couple of coins and a quick ride in the middle of the night to deposit them back from where he'd found 'em.' Another admiring chuckle from Ullendorf. 'Crafty devil. For no sooner had the danger of the supposed plague passed than he set himself up in the cat-killing business, selling poisons and fumigants, catapults and peashooters, or *Katzkriegers* as they call them hereabouts. Very popular still, though I'm not so sure I like that streak in him. Painful deaths, some of those poor cats have suffered.'

The stub-eared tom blinked outside the window, fixing his gaze on Philbert as if he was an over-sized shrew waiting to be caught and devoured. It was unnerving, and Philbert began to move back towards Kwert as Ullendorf wrapped up his story, one that he told almost word for word to any newcomers to his house. Kwert had got the whole of it the night before and paid not the slightest attention.

'As for me, Philbert,' Ullendorf said, tapping at the side of his nose, 'now I use potassium salts; just a little in their food, and poof – dead in a few seconds. Have to net them first sometimes if they're the wild, scratching kind, stick them in a box to breathe in the fumes, which is not so tidy. You get the odd convulsion, which can make dissection harder. Still, once again, as an asphyxiant, you'll get nothing better.'

He started back across the room to the shelves and lifted down a jar or two, showing Philbert more bits of cats and some of dogs, a few rats, several human feet, hands and ears, and a lot of entrails. All had abscesses, ulcers, lumps or bumps of differing kinds. He showed Philbert a hand that could have belonged to Hannah, all sprinkled with freckles and white as Philbert's face now was. And then he brought over his grand finale, this time not in a jar, but a boiled skull with a hole in it the size of a small quince.

'It came from France,' Ullendorf said, 'and is five thousand years old, at an educated guess. Just think, Philbert. What I did to your head someone did to this gentleman all those thousands of years ago.'

Philbert put his hand involuntarily to the spot where Ullendorf's drill had gone through. The skin had sucked over the hole leaving only a small mark like a pinprick, as inconsequential as a bubble in a bog.

'None of your fancy drills and saws then, Philbert,' Ullendorf continued. 'Just a piece of chiselled rock. Obsidian was good, often used in the Americas. Very ancient practice, trepanning; Hippocrates writes about it, and in first century Rome Aulus Cornelius Celsus was a celebrated master of the art. And of course the Islamics knew all about it – the great Abu Quasim being only one of its many practitioners. Now though, come with me Philbert, for I have a bit of a treat for you. Come over here and see the inside of your very own head.'

Philbert went as directed, interest piqued, glad to be diverted from the awful tale of the cats, watching closely as Ullendorf produced a small glass slide, smeared on one side, and slid it into the mounting of a brass microscope. Standing on a stool

Philbert, directed by Ullendorf, looked down the eyepiece, squinting hard, trying to focus, wondering how the insides of him might look. Ullendorf fiddled with the mechanisms of the microscope until all came into view. Philbert was massively disappointed, seeing only a network of squashy squares. Ullendorf for once registered Philbert's reaction and was at pains to explain.

'They may not look very remarkable to you now, Philbert, but when I take another plug from your head, this time I'll be able to keep them alive. And how alive! Imagine those cells you are looking at all moving around, breathing in and out, their little insides wriggling and kicking; imagine them slowly swimming around and around like big soft bellies sliding over one another, growing and expanding before sneezing into two, separating like a pair of half-set jellyfish.'

Philbert tried to imagine such a scenario but could not, but Ullendorf's enthusiasm was infectious, and he listened hard.

'Imagine what we'll find, my dear boy, in that head of yours when we've taken a proper look. There'll be hundreds of thousands of those cells living and moving and growing in their own little word, islands within islands. I'm going to take just a few of them outside of your head and let them grow. And I'm going to introduce you to some of the most famous minds in Europe, and together we will teach them the marvels of taupe teratology . . .'

Ullendorf at last ran out of breath and instead clapped his hands excitedly, and although Philbert wanted to be as enthusiastic as Ullendorf was, wanted to be the prodigy Ullendorf so plainly believed him to be, he didn't really comprehend how that could happen. Ullendorf had already cut a little bit out of his head – for here it was on this microscope slide – looking nothing more than a rather depressing landscape of barren and abandoned fields, with no more life in them than the specimens Ullendorf kept all around this room: that woman with her extruding, lily-pond eyes, those cats in pieces, those human feet and innards, the hand that looked so much like speckled Hannah's. What Ullendorf would have made of Hermann, Philbert shuddered to think. What he would make of Philbert, Philbert was about to find out.

18

Times of Singing and Gypsy Tales

Ullendorf took Philbert's head, clamped him in strong leather bands secured by strong iron buckles; he got out his needle-sharp drills and went once, twice, and many more times deep into Philbert's head, taking cores, as Ullendorf called them – tubules of taupe, each only a sliver in diameter but a good finger's length. He probed his instruments through Philbert's growth right down to the skull, though never back through bone again as he'd done in Finzeln. He went to great lengths to make sure Philbert felt as little of these operations as he could, but Philbert would recall them well, always wondering if those times strapped to Ullendorf's bench in Lengerrborn were the cause of his dark days as well as the ones overwhelmingly filled with light. The dark days were dark indeed, when the older Philbert laid himself out on his bed and drank wine and more wine and saw nothing at all but the dark deeds that had gone before, that he'd precipitated, seeing them, hearing them, witnessing them, over and over again, just as they'd happened then. On the good days he drank less wine, and saw the whole of his life laid out before him like a forest whose every tree was frozen from movement, winding himself through its paths; noting the glory of each memory as if they were bullfinches, robins or golden oriels forever secured upon their branches or suspended in mid-flight as he passed them by, his feet recognising the feel of every stone, every inch of earth preserved on every path he had ever trodden, able – as few were – to access to his past in such detail.

Ullendorf was kind and considerate. He performed only one small procedure every couple of days, stopping the moment his tiny drills hit the bone; and the moment he extracted Philbert's taupe cells and got them growing in the various solutions he'd prepared for them, he ceased his intrusive operations altogether. He continued to take measurements of Philbert's head daily and very precise measurements they were, the conclusion of which, after a month or so, was that the taupe was growing an almost imperceptible amount each day, imperceptible except to Ullendorf's ingenious measuring mechanisms.

Most of the time Philbert was at Lengerrborn he was left entirely to his own devices, Ullendorf and Kwert wrapped up in their studies; he spent much of his time eating Helge's food or prowling amongst the currant bushes in the garden, practising with the *Katzkrieger* peashooter Ullendorf had given him; he never shot at the cats, for Philbert had grown used to them and liked them, oftentimes sat outside while they curled around his feet, loving their purring, and their warmth that so reminded him of Kroonk, whom he sorely missed.

'Terrible, dirty animals,' Helge would say when Philbert brought in one or other of the kittens he found mewling in the bushes in the garden. But even as she said the words she would run her soft hands along the small arches of their backs. 'It really is time someone got rid of them. Always hungry and yowling for more,' she would say, pouring out milk into the bowls she had ready for them, scraping bits of meat from bones to keep them fed. Philbert would come in later to find a spool of little kittens curled up in a basket of old clothes and blankets by her stove.

'Of course it's only sensible to keep a few of them handy,' she would say then, 'just to keep down the mice and the rats.'

'And the plague?' Philbert would ask, and the two of them would start giggling, throwing sidelong glances towards where Ullendorf and his study were, both knowing verse for verse, word for word, the tale of Fatzke and his cats.

Helge taught Philbert the rudiments of cooking and some of the many songs she had known since her youth. They chorused the *Ziguenerlied* together, Helge telling Philbert its origins as a folktale, one that Goethe later retold as his *Gypsy Song*: the story of a boy who lived alone in the deep, wild woods about Lengerrborn and who one day shot dead a cat. But not just any cat, for it was the familiar of a witch named Anna, and she sent her werewolves out by night to catch the boy and tear him to pieces for the awful thing he'd done. It was the first song Philbert had ever learned, and he remembered it for as long as he had a memory, exactly as Helge always sang it, every intonation, every lift of tune, every speeding up and slowing down.

Im Nebelgeriesel, im tiefen Schnee,
Im wilden Wald, in der Winternacht . . .
WILLE WAU WAU WAU!
Wille wo wo wo!
Wito hu!

They sang sometimes like madmen, dancing in circles around the kitchen table, howling like the wolves Anna sent after her foe, drumming on their pans with wooden spoons before collapsing, laughing, into their separate seats, Philbert feeling in those brief moments as if he really had a mother, and Helge feeling in those brief moments as if she really had a son.

~

It all came to an abrupt end when Heinrich Ullendorf got the call from one of his colleagues. By then Philbert and Kwert had been at The Anchorage almost six weeks, Ullendorf bursting into the kitchen one evening as Helge and Philbert were busy *wille-wooing* and pounding out the next morning's bread.

'Philbert, get ready, get ready!' Ullendorf exclaimed. 'My letters have at last been answered, and tonight is the night! You're going to meet the extraordinarily famous Professor Von Ebner of Jena University. He's arrived in Lengerrborn, and just this very minute a message has been brought to me to say he will receive us! We're to meet at the Westphal Club tonight!'

Helge thumped her portion of bread dough on the table and frowned at her brother.

'Oh Heinrich,' she sounded exasperated. 'Why must you continue to go to that awful place? Don't you know how people talk about it? Isn't it enough to get drunk in an ordinary tavern without inviting trouble?'

Ullendorf occupied himself with straightening his hat and propelling a small messenger boy forward to distract his sister's attention.

'Give the lad a crust or two before you dispatch him, Helge,' he said, ignoring her concern. 'And Philbert, you be ready in one hour. One hour, do you hear? This is going to be a most auspicious night!'

Ullendorf departed, leaving a dishevelled lad standing on the flagstones, his cap already doffed, his nose twitching, his stomach beginning to rumble. Helge had no option but to sit him down, begin to sort out the leftovers of the previous night's dinner of venison fillet, warm up some pumpkin sauce with which to serve it and get something ready in the meantime to keep the boy's stomach from growling. Philbert was by now in tune with Helge's need to cook and fuss, and started frying up some cold potato cakes she'd dipped in vinegared plums before handing them to her helper.

'What's the Westphal Club?' Philbert asked, sampling the wares, the warm damson juice dribbling down his chin, making a beeline for what had been a clean shirt. Helge tushed and swept at Philbert roughly with a cloth, her main focus now on the boy her brother had just deposited who was so plainly in need of a good, hot meal.

'It's a very low sort of place indeed,' she answered, 'and yet, according to Heinrich, it's as overrun with clever gents as Lengerrborn is with cats.' Helge smiled indulgently at the small boy who'd brought the message, popping his venison and pumpkin sauce into the oven before grinding poppy seeds and rubbing them with some butter into the dough she and Philbert had been preparing earlier, knocking it hard against the table. 'What he's thinking taking you there is beyond me.'

Again the knock, knock, knocking of the bread, and the small messenger boy kicking his feet against his chair in time, salivating at what he knows will come. She picked up the dough and threw it into a tin, stabbing it harshly with a knife before slapping on some cold milk. 'And who's this Von Ebner he's so excited about anyway?'

'He's a head-doctor, Miss,' piped up the boy. 'Very big in treating hysterics and mad women, so they say.'

'Mad women indeed,' muttered Helge, clattering plates, thrusting the bread into the fiery depths of her oven, checking the meat at the same time before pushing it back inside and clanging the door shut. 'Is it any wonder, I ask you?'

'He's chopped loads of people into pieces,' said the boy, unfazed, hands twitching as Helge searched for spoon and fork with which to serve him his meal. 'He's chopped loads of people into pieces, and says you're only mad on the outside if you're all sort of sick on the in.'

'I'll give you sick, you scamp, if you don't pipe down.' said Helge, flicking the boy with her tea towel. The boy stopped speaking immediately, understanding that Helge could whisk away the marvellous food the smells in this kitchen were promising him. 'And as for you, young man,' Helge said, advancing towards Philbert with menace, tidying his clothes, spitting on his hair and getting it straightened. 'Don't you be taking any strong drink tonight. And tell Heinrich I'll expect you both home by midnight.' Helge rubbed hard at Philbert's face to clean it before running her soft hand over his head as if she might never see him again.

She was more right about her brother's club than even her brother knew, let alone Philbert and Kwert, when they set off from The Anchorage that night, leaving the messenger to his venison and pumpkin sauce and the hot potato cakes Philbert had fried on the skillet.

It's a mistake to believe that the small things surrounding you do not matter a whit, and a bigger mistake to believe that if you withdraw yourself from the world then the world will go on as if you've never been; every action every person takes has meaning, reverberation and consequence, whether or not they understand it at the time those actions are taken.

But there it is all the same: small actions can ripple out and change the world, and this single night in Lengerrborn was no exception.

19

Von Ebner's Nucleus

Kwert and Philbert got into Ullendorf's carriage and went down the long winding road into town, surrounded on both sides by tall dark lines of cypress trees dripping and swaying with the light rain falling on their leaves. They were heading towards the patchwork of roofs Philbert had seen but not experienced, and soon were right amongst them, clopping past white-washed walls, hedged gardens and courtyards. The streets were remarkably busy, this being a warm, soft evening, people able to ignore the sporadic showers by sitting in open-doored porches or beneath awnings pulled out from bars and taverns. Ullendorf's carriage wound through narrow alleys and backways behind the main thoroughfare of the town into the dark, unpopulated streets that made up the less salubrious parts of Lengerrborn, where the houses were shabbier, the cats scrawnier, the gas-lamps dimmer – if they were there at all.

A short while later the carriage drew up, hooves clattering on the cobbles. Ullendorf flung open the door and threw himself out telling his driving-boy not to wait but to come back at midnight, wrapping his cloak tightly about his shoulders, making sure his hat was on fast and sure, beckoning Kwert and Philbert with him up a mean ginnel set between two rows of tall-stacked houses. It was dark, their footsteps echoing dully between the flanking walls, the recently fallen rain splashing against their legs when they stepped into unseen puddles. Ullendorf stopped at a break in the wall, tapping at a small narrow door with his knuckles – rat-a-tat-tat-tat, rat-a-tat-tat-tat. A small window opened in the wood, closed again, then the door opened, Ullendorf and Kwert having to bend in half to get through, Philbert nearly getting stuck trying to step over the high ledge at its base. And then they were in, a mangle of wet capes and hats, the door closed quietly behind them, two large bolts drawn over to keep them in.

Philbert could see very little, but was aware of murmurings and scraping noises and the strong smells of beer and tobacco. Ullendorf handed over his cloak, talking *sotto voce* to the man who'd opened the door to them and who was eying Kwert and Philbert with suspicion, looking them up and down and round and round before eventually nodding. He jangled a large set of keys as he took all three through an arched tunnel, like those found in beer cellars. At the very end of it, he unlocked another door.

The noise was immediate – the place chock-a-block with well-attired men, tankards and cups before them, candles burning at the centre of each table, chair legs catching at the stones set in the earthen floor as they were constantly pulled back and forth as people moved amongst themselves. Ullendorf stood tall, shading his eyes to concentrate his search, but before he found what he was looking for he was addressed by a man clothed entirely in black velvet who grabbed Ullendorf by the arm and pulled him on.

'Doctor Ullendorf!' said the man. 'What a pleasure! Come, sit. Von Ebner's not here yet, but your fellows are.' He barged his way through the small crowd, pushing people aside with ostentatious requests to make way for Von Ebner's special guests and, moments later, they were all three seated, Philbert launched onto a cushioned pew so that he was able reach the table, hands already reaching towards the platter of trotters and potatoes at its centre, which delicacy was soon matched by the arrival of a stack of napkins, two pitchers of ale, a large jug of wine and three men, after which the velvet man slipped away like steam from a kettle, like Harlekin from the stage. Ullendorf took his place and introduced Philbert and Kwert to his newly arrived companions, everyone shaking hands. The first, Herr Federkiel flipped back his coattails and sat next to Philbert, lifting a potato from the central platter to the light of the candle.

'A prime example of a parabolic frustum section, I should say, shouldn't you, Philbert?'

It sounded good, so Philbert nodded, adding that the potato tasted fine. Federkiel laughed and picked up another, which he handed to Philbert with the words 'rhomboidal tetragon', at which Philbert nodded gravely and wished him good health in return. Federkiel smiled and put a hand on the boy's head, informing the company that he'd studied under the great Cuvier in Paris and had a passion for all things geometrical and the names they bore.

'I measure everything I see,' he elucidated. 'I can't help myself – the length of bones, and boiled vegetables, and boys' heads.' He held his hand to one side as if to frame it. 'I've seen the crystal skulls of the Indians of the Andes, and the netsuke skulls of Japan with their ivory frogs for eyes. I've seen the bones of four thousand Capuchin monks resting in the subterranean vaults of Santa Maria in Rome and another, even older, that is purported to be of an ancient Adamic race, but never have I seen a head like the one that sits here before me in the humble confines of a Lengerrborn crypt. I can barely wait to get out my callipers and start sharpening my pencil.'

The second man at the table held back Federkiel's arm, the hand of which was already delving into the bag by his side. 'Let's wait a moment, Federkiel, before you begin your metrological analysis. We have all night, after all, and tomorrow to measure as much as we wish.' The man turned to Philbert and propped a pair of pince-nez on his noise. 'You must forgive us, Philbert. We're all as old and crusty as the hills, only impatient lest we drop dead before we can see all the marvels of this world, of which you are surely one.'

Philbert smiled, wiping trotter grease from his chin, surprised at the interest these friends of Ullendorf were giving him. The man with the pince-nez handed him a napkin, presumably liking his marvels clean, before speaking again.

'I am Professor Schnurrhenker, a physiologist, come all the way from Berlin to see for myself this great head of yours, young Philbert. I gather my colleague Ullendorf has studied you under his microscope – a pleasure I surely hope to replicate, and so I'm delighted to meet you, Philbert,' Schnurrhenker made a small formal bow over the table and grasped Philbert's two hands in his own. 'I'm sure we're going to be the greatest of friends.'

Kwert seemed amused by these proceedings in which he was being so obviously ignored, and Ullendorf was rocking back on his chair, arms lifted behind his head, chest thrust out, a great smile spread over his face like a folded pancake. Abruptly Ullendorf brought his chair back down to the ground and laid his large hands on the table, turning towards the third man.

'And what of you, Zwingerhahn, what's your interest in the boy? For you are no doctor, of that I'm sure.'

Zwingerhahn sipped from his cup and took his time swallowing, licking his thin purple lips in a rather unnerving way.

'You know me, Ullendorf,' he said slowly. 'I like to know who is coming and going, and why they're doing what they're doing. Times are coming when we'll need to get organised, so it's always necessary to know who is who and what is what.'

Schnurrhenker and Federkiel coughed, sipping noisily at their drinks, tensing themselves in their seats for the diatribe they knew would come. Zwingerhahn ignored them and shifted his gaze from Ullendorf to Kwert.

'You're a stranger here and, I gather, a traveller. You must have seen things up and down the country the rest of us have not had the privilege to encounter.'

Kwert nodded uneasily, shooting a quick glance at Philbert who wasn't listening but instead sinking his chops into another pig's trotter. Zwingerhahn went on regardless.

'In Silesia the workers are overthrowing factories and burning down their workshops. The weavers in particular seem ill-used. I personally spoke to several being held on charges of treason and sedition, if you can believe it. And they were honest men,' he growled, 'forced out of their trades, or to work for a pittance and a crust of stale bread. They're craftsmen, men used to supporting their families without breaking either their backs or their spirits. Not that they were against the new machinery, not at all. They keep their harsh words for the princes and over-lords who are tithing them out of their own businesses, shackling them into bonded labour to pay invented debts. It seems to them, as it does to many, that the time has come to throw down the *Landsadel* who presume nobility and possession, not only of the land but of the men who live on it.'

'Property is theft,' quoted Federkiel, before adding, rather sheepishly, as Zwingerhahn swivelled his head and nailed him with a glance, 'so said Proudhon, or so I believe.'

'Ah yes,' Zwingerhahn nodded, maybe with approval, maybe not. 'Proudhon. And Lafayette. Let us not forget Lafayette, yet another great man who cast off the shackles of his birth and proclaimed liberty to be the due of his people. I remember toasting all of them at the Festival of Hambach in '32, when thirty thousand of us stood before the gates of the castle to demand a free and united Germany; the Red, Black and Gold wrapped about us as our standard.' Zwingerhahn took a large swig of wine, keeping his gaze on the table around which the others kept a stiff uncomfortable silence as he went on. 'Proudhon, Lafayette . . . the martyred Marat . . . all heroes of the Revolution. And of course, Saint-Just, whose words no one can ignore: *With whatever illusions monarchy may guise itself, it remains an eternal crime against which every man has the right to rise up* . . . Strong words,' he said, 'strong words and so very true.'

'For a Frenchman, at least,' added Ullendorf lightly, drawing Zwingerhahn's eyes back from their vision of the past.

Zwingerhahn looked curiously back at Ullendorf as if not quite understanding what he'd said and gulped once into the hovering silence.

'Quite right,' he repeated, in a tone that was about as humorous as he ever got, 'for a Frenchman, quite right.'

It was the sign for general conversation to break out, much to the relief of everyone, especially as Zwingerhahn chose that moment to stand up and take his leave, regretted by none.

'Sorry about that, Kwert,' Ullendorf said. 'Old Zwingerhahn does get rather carried away. The right of what he says is not disputed, for maybe it is time for a free and united Germany. All of us think so gathered here. But the likes of Zwingerhahn would pick up arms at any moment and do the dirty princes to death with his bare hands if he could. He still sees the Treaty of Tilsit as the divider of the country, the dissolution of the Empire and all that, but most of us just meet up here to talk out ideas, keep up with what's going on, discuss our business uninterrupted in a congenial atmosphere.'

Ullendorf filled Kwert's glass, and those of his companions. 'And you really do have to go where the great minds gather,' he went on. 'Myself, Federkiel and Schnurrhenker, are only here because Von Ebner is one of the great minds of Europe. We ourselves are hardly activists but Von Ebner is a die-hard – like Zwingerhahn – and this is one of the few places he will agree to meet.'

Ullendorf sighed, Federkiel and Schnurrhenker nodding in agreement, as did Kwert, though he'd not the faintest idea what any of them had been talking about. It was true he tramped the country up and down, as did most of the people who attached themselves to the Fairs, and it was true too that many of the Fairs' people were well up on the politics of the land – Maulwerf's own troupe of actors were proof of that – but in truth, most of them just got their heads down and did what they did, hoping to make a small living out of it. And what Ullendorf said next went right over his head.

'Von Ebner used to know Karl Follen and be in with the Burschenschaften in his youth. Claims he's still dogged by Metternich's spies, though God knows they must be ancient by now if they're still following him around after all these years. But, but,' Ullendorf went on, interrupting himself, trying to get his point across to Kwert, 'his expertise is invaluable. As a physiologist Von Ebner is first rate. He is way ahead of anyone else in terms of brain research and function. One glass of beer with him will give you as much knowledge as a week's worth of lectures by anyone else in the field.'

Nods and more nods from Federkiel and Schnurrhenker, who now took over where Ullendorf had left off.

'He has this theory about the growth of cells in tumours,' Schnurrhenker said excitedly, 'on which all of us have been corresponding.' He produced a letter from his inside pocket and flourished it with pride. 'We've been wondering if such cells might be harnessed to heal other parts of the body otherwise damaged, serve as energetic storehouses for the higher functions of other organs.'

'Hence our interest in Philbert,' Ullendorf took over the gist of the conversation, jiggling ever so slightly in his seat as he took the letter from Schnurrhenker's hand and pushed it towards Kwert. 'And when I told him of Philbert, Von Ebner was most excited, most excited indeed. People with a condition such as

Philbert's are rare indeed – and only ever present to the medical profession as adults, when their teratology has become a burden interfering in their normal lives. But Philbert . . . Philbert is still a child, still growing . . . an opportunity none of us have come across before.'

Kwert frowned, would have spoken, but Federkiel suddenly stood up, waving his arm.

'There he is!' he said. 'By God, Ullendorf, it's really him. It's Von Ebner!'

A flurry at the end of the room confirmed Federkiel's analysis as a tall man – made taller by his stovepipe hat – threaded a graceful way towards their table, the black-velveted Zwingerhahn practically pushing people out of his path. Ullendorf stood up.

'Von Ebner, dear fellow!' he shouted, smiling and waving his hat, Schnurrhenker and Federkiel hastily rearranging chairs so the great man could take the centre place. Kwert didn't stand but leant over the table and bade Philbert drop the trotter, dabbed at him with napkins and straightened his coat and shirt.

'Doesn't hurt to make a good first impression, Little Maus,' Kwert whispered urgently. 'I think we're about to meet someone very important, and the only reason he's here at all is because of your head. So sit sharp, be polite, answer any questions you're asked exactly as you're asked them, and with any luck we'll be able to get back to the Fai –'

There was an eruption of noise and movement like a bottle of Herr Volstrecken's wine blowing its cork in an unguarded cellar, everyone shouting and trying to run, getting in each other's way, tables getting shoved and knocked, candles rolling to the floor, setting fire to spilled spirits and the cloaks and coats slung casually over chair backs. The loud commotion had begun at the Club's outer door but was soon moving towards the inner sanctum with every second, metal clanking as if the ropes of Helge's kitchen racks had been cut and all the copper pans sent crashing to the stone flags below. Philbert saw the newly come Professor Von Ebner rising above the crowd, his hat askew, then heard the sharp sizzle of an explosion, the man and his hat falling sideways to the floor. Ullendorf gasped, cried out in panic and then crouched down quickly as a barrage of soldiers pushed their way in, unmistakeable in their uniforms, barging through the central passageway, flinging men out of their way with wide sweeps of broadswords. Philbert heard pistol shots, smelled the newly discharged gunpowder that was rank in the air, dragged without warning from his seat as Kwert bundled him beneath the table. An awful moment then, when all Philbert heard was yelling and shouting, shots and more shots, horror when Ullendorf's large body fell onto the table above Philbert's head, the wood splintering and giving way, pinning Philbert to the ground. The noise was tremendous and confusing, the air filled with swirling smoke-dust and gloom as the candles were extinguished with the movement of burst tables and men, but Kwert did not lose his head and dragged Philbert out from beneath the broken Ullendorf and his broken table, everything lit now only by the flashes of the marauding soldiers' guns and the trickles of brandy caught to flame by the candles that had been tipped to the floor.

'You've got to get out, Philbert!' Kwert spat into Philbert's ear. 'You've got to get out. Go towards the kitchens just over to the right at the back. Keep yourself down to the floor and don't stop for anyone, don't speak to anyone, no matter what you see. Get yourself to Helge, but go now, Philbert, you have to go right now!'

And Philbert went. He'd been caught by the noose before and needed no persuading. He took time only to grab Kwert's knap-sack from the seat and sling it over his shoulder, glancing back for one millisecond, seeing Kwert rolling Ullendorf out from beneath the broken table: hat gone, dark curls stained darker by his blood, fine coat ripped and torn. Then he was away, scampering down the short passageway as Kwert had directed, blood beating at his bones telling him to be gone. He reached the kitchens, saw the small window in the wall and was up and through it, catapulting himself out into the night where the clear air fell down on him like the breath of God. But even then he didn't stop. He clutched Kwert's bag close to his stomach and ran down the wet streets like a rat, ran until he had no more breath, until his body told his head that enough was enough, no more in him, time to stop.

～

The soldiers stamped their way through the Westphal Club as if they'd nothing left to do, which indeed they did not. Not that any of this was their idea. They'd known about the Westphal Club for years but it had never seemed a threat, just a load of local boffins going to drink in a place they thought was secret, but was about as secret as the fact that the sky is sometimes blue. The Schupo themselves, the men nominally in charge of keeping order in the town, drank in here themselves, finding it convivial, the one place in Lengerrborn where folk didn't stiffen at their arrival, where everyone was taken for what he was, everyone accepted, everyone as keen as they were to keep themselves to themselves. The Schupos therefore knew the place inside out, and were not happy to have been co-opted into the storming of the Westphal Club by outside soldiers despite the order from their direct superiors, and all on the one tip that one man, namely this Von Ebner, deemed an enemy of the state, a revolutionary who needed to be stopped, had arrived in Lengerrborn. The town's Schupos had colluded in this duty only because they were given no choice, the result being this raid, this massacre and mayhem, the apparent cutting down of revolutionary ringleaders from outside. But friends and family were friends and family, and a great many of Lengerrborn's own lost their lives in the tumult, and not many of the local Schupos were happy about that.

~

Philbert stood with his back against a wall. He breathed hard
and was terribly afraid. The rain fell, runnelling off him, and
he'd no idea of which direction to take. This wasn't the first
time he had been alone, set adrift without oar or rudder, nor
was it the first time he'd seen people shot by soldiers, but it was
the first time he'd seen people he knew shot down in such close
proximity and was appalled, having no idea whether Kwert or
Ullendorf – or Ullendorf's friends – were still alive. There was
nothing to do but get as far away as he could, and when he ran
out of steam with blind running he walked, stumbling over wet
and uneven cobbles, tears pricking at the backs of his eyes,
focussing his mind on Helge and her kitchen, that oasis of
warmth waiting for him in this bleakest, darkest of nights. But
he'd no idea how to get there. The hill to The Anchorage was
hidden from him and soon he was too tired to walk, too tired
to think straight, and he slipped from the wall against which
he'd put out his hand to brace himself, huddling into a crouch
on the unknown street, the rain tip-toeing down the shop-
window opposite him as he wished himself safe inside, behind
its glass, cut off from the wet and the horrendous turn the world
had taken against him. He didn't think it possible that he could
have slept but he did, and when he opened his eyes again a
sliver of dawn had begun to climb into the sky, just enough for
the shadows behind the glass of the shop windows opposite to
take form. He saw hams peppered and hanging, sausages black
and curled and speckled with fat, dusted with white mould.
They reminded him of dead things and Philbert retched and
spat before hauling himself to standing, moving off slowly,
following the gutters that ran along the edge of the street,
tangling his feet in its muck. His throat was tight, his face aching
with unspilled tears. All Philbert wanted was to curl up in that
wide, white bed at Helge's, knowing Helge was down in her
kitchen cooking up splendiferous wonders waiting to be piled

onto plates, and that Kwert and Ullendorf were still in Ullendorf's study, watching the cells from Philbert's head growing wildly in their little dishes, wanted the solidity and warmth and companionship of Kroonk at his side, wanted Hermann to be alive again and be there to tell him that everything would all be alright.

The sun rose a fraction in the sky and Philbert's eye caught a patch of gold shivering in the gloom, a shine of brass, an edge of red, and he slowed down, stopped and took a couple of steps back. He held his sleeve against his nose to catch the drips and then slowly crossed the street he'd been walking down and was up against the window, hands a visor across his eyes as he tried to see more clearly what was inside. And what was inside was the Uhrmacher's clock with its six sides of glass, the very same one – or one the twin of it – that he'd seen on the stall of Zacharias Holzhauer at Dortmund, the man who was companion to the Turk. Philbert fingered Hermann's gold ring beneath his shirt that the Turk had delivered to him, and made a decision: no more running not knowing his direction. Against all the odds Philbert had seen something he recognised, and here he would stay, for if one of the Uhrmacher's clocks was really in that shop window then maybe the shop owner knew the Turk and would look kindly on him, tell him the way back to The Anchorage and Helge.

~

Philbert stood his vigil, unaware he'd fallen asleep in the shop's doorway until woken a half hour later by a hard kick, followed by the unpleasant sensation of wet fur rubbing against his face.

'What you do here, boy? You not know it is 'gainst the law to go sleep in people's doors? *Geht*! *Gehen Sie*! Go way!'

Two more kicks had Philbert scrambling to his feet.

'Ayiee! Your head look bad! You have been in fight I think. You find a doctor before it go bang.'

Philbert moved to one side as the girl with the big boots fumbled in her skirts for a key. She was a few years older than Philbert, maybe thirteen or so, wrapped in a cat-hair-covered shawl with a shabby looking tabby on one shoulder and a little ginger wrapped like a tiny stole about the back of her neck. Philbert blinked and took a few moments to gather himself.

'I'm looking for the Clockmaker,' he said, his voice a little indistinct, his mouth desperate for a rinse of water, a rub of mint leaves, but he managed to catch the girl's attention by tapping at the glass behind which the clock sat shiny on its box. 'Der Uhrmacher,' he tried again, 'or the Turk.'

The key the girl was fiddling in the lock stopped, and she turned her dark eyes towards Philbert, taking in his wet and bedraggled appearance and the lump of his taupe.

'The Turk?' Philbert repeated desperately. 'Is he here? Or do you know where I can find him?'

It's an odd truism that coincidence doesn't exist for the young when it seems the natural way of things, the world fitting together like it should, and yet that same coincidence – when you're older and understand the odds against it – sends a shiver down your spine no matter how well explained by one fact or another, that it's no coincidence at all, just a line of logic locking one part of your life to another. Like the fact that the Clockmaker and the Turk had storehouses up and down the Rhein, outposts peopled by subsets of their families from where they could collect or store their goods; like the fact that Ullendorf had heard of Philbert and sought him out and hadn't been in Finzeln by happenchance after all, that in fact he'd learned of Philbert right here in Lengerrborn where the Turk and the Clockmaker had one of their bases, even frequenting the Westphal Club where they'd mentioned Philbert's head.

Neither Philbert nor this girl with her cats knew any of this.

'You know Abdal Bey?' the girl asked of Philbert, looking at him with a curiosity she'd previously lacked, seeing only then a raggedy boy taking a kip from the rain in her shop's doorway.

'Eröglu Erivan Abdal Bey,' Philbert nodded enthusiastically, 'and Zacharias Holzhauer, the clockmaker,' he added for good measure.

The girl looked the boy up and down. She didn't disguise the fact of her looking mostly at his head, for she could guess this was the boy in the tale told her by the Turk earlier that year about the man who'd chosen to take a dive off a bridge. Philbert was about to speak again, try to explain about the Westphal Club and what had happened, but the girl turned away.

'Enough,' she said, swinging the shop door open, jingling the bell as she pushed it far as it could go. 'Poor thing's hungry,' she added, disentangling herself from the tabby. She beckoned Philbert in behind her, making him sit on a stool by the counter before closing the door and put out some food for her kittens before speaking again.

'The Turk,' she said then. 'Very kind to me. My friend's cousin's cousin. Give me job looking after this place. And I think you the boy the Big Doctor has up the hill, but I already been to bakery and hear bad things happen in town. Best you get back to your friends.'

Philbert nodded. He wasn't surprised that everybody already knew about what had happened at the Westphal – Lengerrborn was a small place, and gunshots ringing through the night could not have been ignored – but he was surprised and a little perturbed that everybody, or at least this girl, knew he was biding up at The Anchorage, for never in all the time he'd been there had either he or Kwert strayed away from Ullendorf's home.

'You look for the doctor?' the girl was speaking again, fussing about her kittens, checking till and counter. 'His house up top the hill. Look,' she said, directing Philbert's gaze out of the window, past the small glass clock that sat upon its velvet stand, its little cogs ticking out every second followed by the next, for all to see.

'Up there,' the girl pointed, and as she did so her shawl loosened, tumbling the little ginger kitten to the ground. It made a pitiful squeal as it fell and Philbert scooped it up, the girl taking it from him with a smile that brought her face alive. Philbert looked away and out of the window where she'd pointed and, now that morning was truly established, he could see there indeed was the hill and the little track winding its way up through the cypresses, and Philbert was so relieved he jumped down from his perch, thanking the girl and taking his leave, quitting the shop's door on a run.

The girl dipped her chin and carried on with her morning as if nothing out of the ordinary had happened at all.

20

Loosed from the Pier

Philbert knew something was wrong before he reached The Anchorage. Coming up the last stretch of hill he could see the big iron gates were hanging open, the door at the top of the drive agape. He went on anyway, through the gates, up the driveway and the steps to the door; but there was no Helge standing at the porch to greet him, only a blood-spattered apron huddled on the floor just a couple of yards inside the house. Philbert moved forward, picking it up, hugging it to him, a small puff of flour dusting the air. There was a noise behind him and Philbert turned, saw a small brown woman creaking up the steps behind him, hovering in the doorway, nervously playing with the sleeves of her tatty cardigan.

'You must be Philbert,' the woman said. 'Never mind the head, I'd recognise that jacket anywhere. Used to be my Georg's. Can't tell you how many times I've cleaned and patched it. But you'll find no one here. They took Helge away last night. Went through the entire place. Broke everything up. And then I saw them dragging Helge out.'

The widow from next door wiped her eyes, which nonetheless sparkled with fear and excitement once she took away her arm.

'There was trouble last night in the town,' she went on. 'They say the soldiers caught a traitor – the leader of those Westphal scum. That they killed as many as they could and took the rest to the gaol. But poor Helge! What must those soldiers be doing to her now?'

Her voice rose a pitch, her eyes glowing. 'You know what they do to women who won't talk? Well no, you're too young. But mark my word, it isn't pretty and if you can, then get off and go home. They'll be back for the doctor if they haven't got him already, you see if they don't.'

Widow Wilhelm had said her piece and went away, trotting down the hill into town. The things she had to tell her friends at the bakery! She could hardly contain herself, no thought anymore of Philbert treading gently over the broken glass of the tall barometer that had once hung on the wall.

Philbert moved through the hallway, the pictures there all askew, the big coat-stand felled and broken, trying to comprehend what the woman had been saying. There was mewing coming from the kitchen and Philbert followed it. He held his hand to the stove – still warm – and saw Helge's kittens on the table, their paws dipping into the spilled cream from the jug that had fallen to its side and broken. The remnants of a meal lay broke-boned before him and Philbert threw some of the scraps onto the floor, the kittens jumping easy-pawed from table to chair to follow them. Only then did Philbert see what was all around him: lots of plates on the table, a bowl of sauerkraut, another of coleslaw. The widow woman said the soldiers had been here and he realised Helge would have tried to feed them, as she always tried to feed anyone who made their way through her doors. And no one could possibly do anything bad to Helge, so most probably she'd gone with the soldiers to the gaol to see if her brother was there, Kwert having no doubt helped Heinrich, staunched his wounds, the two of them explaining why they'd been at the Club – all to do with Philbert's

192

head and nothing whatsoever with uprisings or traitors. They were probably right now at the gaol, filling in the forms needed for their release. And gaols were easy to find; they looked the same in every town Philbert had ever been in; the best plan was for Philbert to go and meet them there.

He gathered up some bread and a half-gnawed knuckle of smoked ham, wrapping both in Helge's apron. There was a bit of wine left in a bottle on the table, so Philbert plugged it and stowed it in his knapsack – or rather Kwert's knapsack. He was about to leave when he saw his *Katzkrieger*, his little peashooter, lying on the floor by the hat-stand. He picked it up and, as he did so, noticed the door to the study was open. Thinking that perhaps Ullendorf and Kwert were already back, Philbert ran towards it, swinging himself into the room before coming to a sudden stop, utterly dismayed by what he saw: a massacre of glass and toppled instruments flung in apparent fury to the floor, books lying like battlefield corpses, their spines cracked and broken, pages loose; the pickled woman's jar was still intact, and she looked down from her top shelf onto a deluge of shattered glass and deliquescing body-parts, equivalent to a flood of moon jellies stranded on a shore. The smell was strong and sharp, like over-boiled over-salted spinach, and Philbert stood for a moment in disbelief, then latched his eyes onto an unbroken decanter on one of the desks. Something of use then, and he poured its contents into the bottle of wine he'd taken from the kitchen, filling it right to the brim.

After that he wasted no time. He closed the study door behind him and took up one of Doctor Ullendorf's hats from the broken stand by the door and put it on. On any other boy's head but Philbert's it would have been like shoving a hollowed-out melon over a mouse, so large Lita could almost have used it as a bed, but for Doctor Heinrich Ullendorf with his unruly hair, and for Philbert with his taupe, it was perfect. The hat was of soft green felt, the colour of one of Maulwerf's waistcoats, the brim-feather blue as the spots on Hermann's fish. Another sign, as if he needed one.

~

Once in the town, just as predicted, Philbert had no trouble finding the gaol, for he'd already spotted it coming down the road, its high walls throwing a shadow over the small adjacent square. Once he'd reached the Platz Gefängnis he was in no doubt, detecting a smell the early lime-blossoms couldn't hide, and a kind of graveyard hush all around the walls that made people whisper and cross themselves as they moved quietly by. Not that many were abroad this morning, apart from a single man sitting on the other side of the grimy window of the decrepit *Kaffeehaus* opposite, who showed no interest as Philbert walked slowly down the length of the prison wall until he spied a small crack and could see a shard of light the other side. Using the end of his *Katzkrieger*, Philbert forced a way through the crumbling stone and put his eye to the spy-hole he'd excavated. He saw men sitting listlessly on the few stone benches and against each other, drawing coats tightly around themselves, the cold of the night having seeped into their bones. One of them might have been the man Federkiel from the night before, or maybe Schnurrhenker, but Philbert couldn't be sure, couldn't remember which one was which, if it was either of them at all. Blinking away the stone dust from his miniature excavation, Philbert screwed his body around to get a different angle, digging away more of the small aperture in the rotting mortar before he at last made out the dull bundle of red sat slightly apart from the rest. Kwert. It had to be Kwert, for he was kneeling just as Philbert had seen him down by the river that morning, doing his meditations. Philbert moved along the wall until he guessed he must be almost opposite Kwert and began to poke out another hole. It was harder this time, the only soft bit being barely a foot from the pavement, but he managed it with the help of a sturdy twig. He loaded the *Katzkrieger* with a couple of the small pebbles scattered liberally on both sides of the divide, stuck the stem through and took his aim. He repeated the operation four or five times before Kwert finally noticed the plinking of the stones about his feet, and looked around with bewilderment. Philbert hammered at the hole with his fist and scraped at it with the *Katzkrieger* until it broke in two, but suddenly there was Kwert in front of the hole, ghastly pale where he wasn't bruised, his robe ripped and stained, hair coarse with dried blood.

'Kwert!' Philbert whispered fiercely. 'It's me! It's Philbert!'

'Little Maus?' Kwert's voice was strained and croaky, a shred of its former self.

'I've come to get you out,' Philbert said, a sob choking its way up his throat as Kwert wheezed and cracked in vague intimation of laughter.

'Ah, Little Maus,' Kwert said, leaning himself against the stone so as not to arouse attention. 'I'm not sure anyone, even you, can do that.'

He started to cough and couldn't stop. Philbert heard his ribs creak with every spasm.

'I'm going round to the front,' Philbert said, rubbing his fist against his eyes to stop the tears no longer coming from brick dust alone. 'I've some food and wine for you here that surely they'll let me give you.'

Kwert waved a feeble hand to stop him but Philbert was already on his feet, heart thumping as he rounded the wall of the yard and approached the steps leading to the entrance of the gaol. The door was huge and heavy but was ajar, and Philbert could smell the dank coolness coming from inside and heard voices too. He straightened his knapsack and went in.

There were three men there in the lobby of the prison, chairs pulled out a little from the walls, bottles at their feet, uniforms open at the collar, chins stubbled and unshaven, one small and fat, another small and thin, the last sitting a little straighter in his chair looking to be the one in charge. All three lifted their heads as the door creaked open a couple of feet and Philbert slipped inside.

'Aha!' said the fat one, in a dull, slightly slurred voice. 'Is this another prisoner to add to the fold? Or no! It's a gentleman! Look at that fine hat!'

He spat as his skinny companion laughed. The third man, who had his chair tipped backwards, two legs off the floor, looked towards Philbert curiously, beckoning him in.

'Tell me, Junge,' said Schupo Ackersmann. 'What are you doing here? Don't you know this is the most feared place in all of Lengerrborn? No one will come here this morning. Nobody dares to speak to us – not even my own wife.'

''S not her fault,' slurred the fat man. 'I wouldn't come here myself if I wasn't already here. Those bastard soldiers coming in and leaving us to do their dirty work. 'S not right is what it's not. Bloody bastards.'

He picked up his bottle, swirled the last drops at its base and swigged them down, then fiddled with the pistol tucked into his belt.

'So what do you want, boy?' said Schupo Ackersmann. 'Come here to dance for us?' He clunked his chair legs back to the floor, putting his elbows on his thighs, bending so his eyes were on the same level as Philbert's. 'Come on over here by the table,' he said.

'I've brought some things for Kwert,' Philbert whispered, moving one foot forward cautiously. 'He's out in the yard.'

The fat policeman laughed. 'Out in the yard! Ha ha! That's where he is all right!'

'Shut up, Böllduch,' said Ackersmann, who was indeed in charge. 'Get a hold of yourself.'

Schupo Böllduch winced, uncomfortably aware he might just have crossed a line, and fell silent.

'Come here lad,' said Schupo Ackersmann, 'and let's see what you've brought for your friend.'

Philbert undid the buckles of Kwert's knapsack, taking out the bundle of Helge's apron, placing it on the small table by Ackersmann's side. Ackersmann pulled back the corners of the apron, the smell of bread and smoked ham drifting across the room as Philbert delved once more into his knapsack and brought out the bottle.

'Ah,' breathed Ackersmann softly, shaking his head. 'Bread and wine. If ever there was a symbol then this is it.' He looked at Philbert's small offerings, noting a couple of red splotches on the apron's edges that might well have been blood, and shuddered.

'Right,' he said decisively. 'Your friend's name? Kwert, was it?'

Philbert nodded.

'Up with you, Böllduch, you drunken shit,' said Ackersmann. 'Go and fetch him. The poor sod can have a bite of bread before the rest of the merry-go-round is set in motion.' He turned back to Philbert as Böllduch got grumpily to his feet and headed for the door that led into the prison yard. 'This man a special friend of yours?' Ackersmann asked, and once more Philbert nodded. 'Well then,' he said, unexpectedly taking Philbert's hand in his own and patting it. 'I'm truly sorry for what will come next. But we have our orders, not that I expect you to understand. I have a lad about the same age as you, and Lord knows I don't want him to understand either, but this is just how it goes sometimes. We'll all be pariahs after this gets out. Those soldiers should have finished the job themselves instead of galloping out of here on their fine horses to go and bust up someone else's town.'

'We ain't really going to do it Chief, are we?'

It was the thin man, the quiet man, the man who so far hadn't spoken a word. Now he'd lifted his head Philbert could see his cheeks were streaked with tears, despite his previous strained laughter. Ackersmann gave no answer and instead placed his hands upon Philbert's shoulders, forcing the boy to look upwards, despite the large brim of the overlarge hat.

'I don't know how much you know of what's going on,' he said, as much to the skinny man as to the boy he was addressing. 'But all those men they pulled from the Westphal Club last night? We've got to shoot them, see? Every last one of them they said. They beat all sorts of names and shite out of them last night and then scarpered with the best of them. And now we've got to line the other poor buggers up against the wall and shoot them down like dogs. And I know most of these men, grew up with them.' Ackersmann groaned and shook his head, but did not release Philbert from his grip, holding onto the strange boy with his huge hat as if somehow the lad could save them from what they had to do. Silence fell on them, making the skinny man's snivelling all the more unnerving, and then they heard Böllduch's slurred shouting out in the yard.

'Kwert!' he was yelling. 'The man Kwert! Come 'ere! Yes, you! Get 'ere, and get 'ere right now!'

'Grew up with nearly all of them,' whispered Ackersmann, at last releasing Philbert, one hand lifting his Schupo's cap and brushing at his hair. 'My wife's cousin's out there . . .'

Böllduch came back and with him was Kwert. He was stooped and stained, raising a sad smile as he fixed his eyes on Philbert, revealing gaps where several of his front teeth were missing.

'Little Maus,' Kwert said, before Schupo Ackersmann cut him off.

'Prisoner Kwert,' said Ackersmann, trying to sound stern, though plainly feeling otherwise. 'This child has brought you food and drink. You can take it out to the yard with you, eat it yourself or share it, it's up to you. But you need to say goodbye to the boy now, for you won't see him again.'

Kwert and Ackersmann looked at one another for a few moments, understood, tore away, and then Kwert bent down on one knee and Philbert ran to him, burying his face – as far as his hat would allow – in Kwert's red habit, understanding there would be no form-filling, no swift return to The Anchorage, that this was the end of Kwert and Ullendorf's road.

'If you don't mind, Herr Kwert,' Schupo Ackersmann spoke gently, 'we'll leave you the vittals but we'll take the wine. We're not easy with any of this, I want you to know that. God knows we don't want to do this, but if we don't then someone else will – and we'll try and do it quick.'

Kwert hugged Philbert to him, hugged him hard, hugged him long, cleaving to this last human contact, knocking away Philbert's hat. Kwert understanding: the Westphal Club routed by soldiers of unknown fiefdoms, some of its leaders killed, others taken away. Left behind were all the rest: the locals, the hangers-on, folk in the wrong place at the wrong time, just like Kwert himself. And these poor Schupos given the order to shoot the lot of them dead. Kwert's life of Hesychastic meditation was stripped back to the bone but he would not be found wanting, nor would he be bowed.

'Bless you, Philbert,' Kwert whispered and kissed the boy's head, all the while looking at Ackersmann, hoping he would at the very least let the boy go free. Ackersmann nodded, and closed his eyes, opened them again.

'Right lads,' he said. 'A couple of swallows of the boy's wine and we'll need to get ready.'

Kwert released Philbert and stood back a pace, his hands on Philbert's shoulders.

'Thank you for bringing me the food, Philbert,' he said, putting one palm to Philbert's cheek, trying to avoid the huge hat Philbert was ramming back on his head which, God forgive him, he couldn't help but find comical even in these circum-stances. Ackersmann saw the gesture and took his moment, took up the wine bottle from the table and passed it to Böllduch, his intention being for them each to take a swallow and then pass it round to Kwert for his last hurrah. But Böllduch was greedy, needed steeling for the awful task ahead, his skinny, snivelling companion equally in need of fortification, and when the bottle came to Ackersmann there was not much left, but what there was he drank down to the dregs, desperate to prolong the moment. Kwert, meanwhile, took the bread and ham and was heading back to the prison yard when the entirely unexpected happened. The Schupos' legs began to kick, their throats drew tight, skin beginning to blotch beneath their itchy uniforms; they retched and coughed, salivated and spat like angry cats. Kwert turned back abruptly, staring wildly at the Schupos writhing and squirming on the floor, the skinny one already dead, warm piss seeping through his trousers, hands wet and loose, splayed out beside him.

'My God, my God!' Kwert was aghast, elated, terrified. 'What did you do, Little Maus? What did you do?'

Philbert looked around bewildered, could give no explanation.

'My god, my god!' Kwert whispered again as he picked up the bottle Ackermann had been holding in his hand only moments before. He caught the smell at once, though it was well hidden by the deep, dark wine. 'But it's potassium cyanide! You gave them potassium cyanide!'

Kwert's shock rendered him at once utterly calm on the outside, but writhing inside like a mass of worms. He shook himself once, twice, threw off his stupor, clothed himself in a quick prayer, then dashed quick as he was able to the prison yard door and undid the heavy bolts, turned the key that was still in its lock, yelling and gesturing to the inmates as he flung the door wide. Then he grabbed Philbert by the hand and ran back through the lobby, past the Schupos twitching on the floor, crossing himself briefly as he did so, then it was out the door and down the steps and out across the plaza, running like a hare with a pack of hounds on its tail.

21

The Grey Man and the Seamstress

Kwert found the running hard, every bone cracking and creaking within him, his two broken ribs a torment; and to make it worse he kept tripping on his robe where the blood had dried it stiff. He had to stop. He was panting hard, leaning on the dog-spattered lamp post. Philbert pulled at his sleeve to try to move him on, but Kwert was coughing as if his lungs were filled with tar and shook his head, unable to speak. But luck was on their side as Philbert, looking desperately around him, recognised the corner of a street twenty yards down and tightened his grip on Kwert, pulling him forward.

The shop door opened with a jangle, the small bell vibrating on its spring, the Turkish girl looking up from the pile of sewing on her knee, standing up quickly, letting it all fall to the floor.

'*Allah qorusun*! May God protect us!' she exclaimed, her hand going briefly to her throat as she struggled for the right words. 'What is this? What goes on . . . who are . . . ah, yes, I know you,' she pointed an accusing silver-thimbled finger at Philbert as his hat parted company from his head as they tumbled through the doorway. 'What you do back here again? Not find Doctor?'

Kwert tried to straighten up, to focus, draw in air, but the movement sent him into another spasm of coughing.

'We've nowhere else to go,' Philbert said, more loudly than he'd meant to. 'We have to find the Turk . . .'

The girl was moving forward, pushing Kwert onto a chair, fearing he was about to fall. A few seconds after this kindness he managed to hold onto enough breath to speak: short, broken sentences, spat out like stab wounds in the air.

'Apologies, Fraülein . . . there's trouble . . . problems with . . . soldiers . . . with police. Please. If you know – how do you know? But if you know him . . . we must . . . speak with the Turk . . . we beg you.'

His voice was a rattle, rising weakly between the wheezes so she had to stoop to hear him. She looked from the man to the boy and back again, taking her time, measuring the odds, weighing up the balance. Then she decided.

'I am Kadia Odev. Eröglu Abdal Bey is my friend's cousin's cousin. I will help. What can I do?'

'A thousand thanks, Fraülein Odev,' croaked Kwert. 'A thousand thanks . . . a glass of water . . . please . . .'

Kadia Odev disappeared through a beaded curtain and they could hear liquid glugging into a jug. Behind them the door tinkled again and, as Kadia came back through the curtain, a man appeared through the door. He was small and grey – whiskers, boots, felt hat, jerkin, all were grey, even his skin had the quality of smoke in shadow. They all froze as in a tableau: Kwert with his hand at his throat, Kadia grasping the jug and pewter goblet so tightly her knucklebones were visible through her skin, Philbert clutching his green hat like a grassy hummock to his chest. The newcomer took in the scene at a glance, nodded a brief bow towards Kadia, and broke the silence.

'I am Fatzke,' he said, his voice loud in the confines of the small shop, 'a friend of Ullendorf's.'

Kwert let go his air and whispered, 'Ullendorf is dead.' A small tear wound down the darkening bruises of his face.

Fatzke sighed. 'So it's true then.' He looked hard at his boots.

'It's true,' Kwert said, his head hanging. No one spoke for a moment. Kadia came forward, gave Kwert the goblet of water. He sucked at it slowly, wincing as the cold air hit the empty spaces in his gums, choking as the liquid squeezed its way down his tight throat.

'I don't really understand what happened . . .' Kwert said, looking up at Fatzke, who stood with his head to one side like a chicken in a dirt-yard.

'No,' he said, 'I don't suppose you do. And you're not alone.' He moved his head to the other side. 'It's that club. The Westphal. The soldiers have been keeping an eye on it. Political dissidents, crowd stirrers, traitors, that kind of thing.'

Kwert looked at the floor, his brow a furrowed field, puzzlement lessening.

'Like that Zwinger . . . whoever,' he mumbled, 'like him.'

Fatzke nodded. 'Exactly like him.' Kadia poured more water, Fatzke pushing a cat away from him with the toe of his boot. 'But last night the big fish were there. Von Ebner, to be more specific. Away from his home ground. Away from the support he's grown used to. Perfect time to nab him, I would suppose, if I'd been a soldier and on his trail for months.'

Nobody responded. Fatzke crossed in front of Kwert and leant against the shop counter. Kadia collected up her sewing, having understood very little of the conversation, more interested in saving the pins that had spilled from her little velvet pincushion.

'Shame to get you all mixed up in it,' Fatzke added.

Kwert held out his hand a moment, a hand caked with dried

blood. 'Please sir, if you're a friend of Ullendorf, then help us. We must get out,' he spoke slowly, watery lines waving down his dirty chin, 'especially the boy. They'll think he did it deliberately, with the wine I mean.'

Unexpectedly Fatzke laughed, the short sharp sound of a terrier coming at a rat.

'Aha!' he said, looking delighted. 'Well I can tell you that Schupo Ackersmann was alive a few minutes ago, though not the other two. Dead as last years doings they are, and no doubt about that.'

He looked intently at Kwert then before going on.

'Schupo Ackersmann is a bit hazy on the details, but he remembers you. "The Man in Red" is what he said and I can see what he meant. He's been babbling away like a fountain about the Last Supper, and there was talk of angels. They took him away after that.'

Kwert nodded his head sadly. 'They didn't deserve to die. What he was told to do to us? To the prisoners? He didn't like it. Oh God,' Kwert closed his eyes, shook his head. 'What are they going to do now?'

Fatzke cleared his throat. 'First things first. It won't take them long to trail a man in a red robe wandering through the streets, not once they get their act together. There's talk of calling the soldiers back into the town, and nobody is keen on that, not even Ackersmann, and certainly not me.' Fatzke shook himself and rubbed his hands. 'Time to get you away,' he said. 'Kadia here is a seamstress. She can give you something to cover yourself up or you'll be spotted quicker than a cat can steal your milk.'

'And you?' Kwert's words were muffled as Kadia caught the drift and began to pull his dirty red robe over his head, looking around for something she could use to replace it. 'How did you know we were here?'

'Aha! There you have it!' said the grey man. 'I've a nose for

205

things going on. I've been following the boy since early doors. Heard about the trouble at the Westphal – who hasn't? – and went up to see Heinrich. He's always been good to me, as has Helge. But no one was there, except for that infernal widow from next door snooping around. Can't stand the woman. Always trying to entice me in. Would slap a leg iron on me soon as I'd hung up my hat! She's an evil woman and no mistake. So I slips round the back of the house into the bushes to see what I can see. Thought Heinrich might have got away or Helge might need some help,' he hoisted his thin grey behind onto the counter, ignoring Kadia's tuts as he drummed his little felt heels against the boards. 'That's my stock in trade, see. I help. Help people when they're sick, help 'em if they've got too many rats, or too many cats come to that; help in all sorts of ways, I do. And here I am helping you.' He took off his hat and swung it through the air. 'Saw the boy arrive and recognised him as one of Ullendorf's little . . . subjects. Saw him feed Helge's cats, picking up this and that, followed him down to the gaol. Saw him go in, and what do you know? A short while later I hears noises – people rustling in the yard, talking, jostling – it's unusual, I can tell you. Prisoners are usually such a quiet bunch. And then you all came running out the front. Well! I sees you heading out first and I sees the boy, so here I am.'

He chuckled, the noise of an un-greased treddle, two pink spots appearing on his grey cheeks as he enjoyed the telling of his tale. He spat on his hand and brushed it over his trousers, might've been any man in the morning.

'Anywise, news is spreading slowly, no one wanting out. But when I sees you come here? Well. I knows the Turk and I likes a few drinks with old Zacharias, and Kadia here's an honest girl, despite being unhealthy fond of cats.'

Kadia snapped her cotton briskly, clicking her thimbled fingers. All the while Fatzke had been talking her needle had been shuttling in and out of a length of material, adapting some garment to the needs of Kwert's disguise. Fatzke talked easily, sitting on the counter, winding his grey-felt ankles the one around the other, dottling his pipe but not lighting it.

'And I thinks to meself as I follows you,' he went on, 'now then, a pretty pickle these two are in – a stranger in a red robe and a boy with a head like a boot – no offence, lad, and the hat's a nice touch – but how far are you going to get? The Polizei Reserves have already been sent for, and once they've figured out one end of a musket from the other, they'll be on your heels. You don't exactly blend into the background. Be easy as pulling a thread and unravelling a knitted jerkin. They'll get here and soon, so here's what you've to do.'

Ten minutes later they were creeping out the back of the shop, Kwert with a new habit of muted brown, a cowl about his head to hide the bruises, and a stick to make his walking easier. Philbert was still in Ullendorf's hat, though Kadia had snipped a good length off the brim and blacked it with dye. He'd added to his knapsack the food and canteen Kadia had prepared for them, and in his head was the map of directions from Fatzke.

'When they come here looking for you, which they will,' he said, just before they left, 'they'll find me and Kadia passing the time of day, and we'll both swear you came in on the off chance and we sent you packing off some other way. They'll believe old Fatzke – I've nothing to hide. They all knows me. I've sold them all sorts in the past and they'll need me to sell them all sorts in the future. And Kadia – well, she's just a seamstress and a shop minder, what would she know? She'll be busy sewing me a patch on my jerkin and I'll be advising her on how to poison cats. Ouch!'

Kadia withdrew her needle and waved her visitors goodbye. Philbert looked back and saw them: the small grey man – a revolutionary in his own way – and the girl who had been helped and so helped others when they needed it. A bold philosophy, one Philbert was grateful for and tried to adhere to. Like engenders like: be kind and others will reciprocate. Not infallible, of course, for nothing is. But if you've ever been caught in a trap not of your own making and someone goes out of their way to let you out of it, then the onus is on you to lift the trap from someone else, if and when you're able.

22

The Crypts of Leiberkuhn

The rain came down again, which was good, meaning they could draw their collars tight, hats down, scuttle along like everyone else trying to get where they're going without getting too wet. They threaded their way through the narrow streets of Lengerrborn, Kwert going a little easier since Kadia had strapped his chest with a tight band of cloth to keep his ribs from moving too much. Still, they grated every now and then and they had to stop so that Kwert could catch his breath, overhearing the gossip going the rounds.

'Did you hear about what happened at the gaol? They say a band of men in red came breaking in, slaughtering the Schupos and cutting their throats from ear to ear . . .'

'No! Is that right? I heard there was a magician in with the prisoners and he put the Polizei to sleep with just a few waves of his hand.'

'Don't be silly, woman. Whoever heard of a magician getting arrested? It's nonsense, I tell you. What happened was that the two Sergeants got blind drunk, and Captain Ackersmann tried to shoot all the prisoners by himself like he'd been told, and then shot himself in the foot, and those that were left legged it from the yard.'

'Now then, that's not right. Nobody heard shooting. But didn't you hear about the boy? Had a head like a rotten pumpkin, all swollen and hairy. They say he brought in bread and wine, gifts for the Schupos, and poisoned the lot of them like cats in an alley.'

'Gracious heavens, who'd have thought a boy could be so wicked!'

'Oh dear me yes, boys have always been wicked. I should know. I've five of them at home and all they're good for is stealing food from their mother's mouth and whipping her when they come home drunk. No good lot are boys. Ah, that God had seen fit to give me a girl . . .'

'They'll hang 'em when they find 'em, that's for sure, boys or no boys, throttle 'em till they're black in the face and their legs kick their shoes right off their feet. Saw a man hanged in Hanover once, screamed like a rabbit he did, shouting out for his mama to forgive him. It was a grand spectacle, looking at that man, his legs all thrashing, eyes coming out his head so you thought they'd pop, tongue near pulled from its roots. Aye, that's what they'll do all right when they find 'em. They'll hang 'em. That's what happens when you murder Schupos. Always been so, always will.'

They hurried on as best they could, following Fatzke's complicated directions, Philbert recalling them with ease, like they'd been tattooed inside his skull, and eventually arrived at a crumbling old church, its dedication board half splintered away by brown twines of ancient wisteria, all that was visible being some faded lettering and the outline of a painted shell.

'This is the place,' Philbert said, whispering, as he'd been whispering ever since they left the shop whenever he needed to urge Kwert on or tell him left or right. Kwert's skin was the sickly green of sun-bleached leaves, and it was left to Philbert to push his way through the overgrown plants and lichens that hung in dirty ropes from the arch of the lych-gate. He beat his way past them and up the nettle-grown path to the porch, relieved to find the church door partially cracked open, its topmost hinge hanging loose from the frame. There was enough of a gap for Philbert to push Kwert on before him, straight into a miasma of cobwebs and the retreating tic-tic-tic of tiny feet skittering away beneath floorboards and walls. Kwert was terribly tired, but all the pews had been ripped out leaving only flat, greasy stone and tired earth scabbed over with liverworts and mould onto which Kwert sank in a wheezing heap.

'Stay here,' Philbert said, as if Kwert was going to do anything else. He looked around him at the broken font, the roof domed above him like an inverted bowl, the worm-riddled beams showering them with peels of paint and dust motes, enhanced here and there by minute flickers of gold – all that remained of the Protecting Hand of God, once a magnificent fresco vaulted over the congregation's heads. He saw the stones marching up the nave and aisles all inscribed with illegible names and words, depictions of the tools of various trades, some with skulls and angels. A large wooden altar leant and wobbled on its legs of stone behind a sagging reredos, the baldacchino tattered and torn almost into nonexistence. Philbert saw the little door to the right of the altar leading into the sacristy, just as Fatzke said, so in he went. A small room lay beyond, empty but for a crude straw mattress, a bench, and a woodstove that was giving out a perceptible, if slight, quiver of heat. Philbert retreated hurriedly, helped Kwert in and onto the mattress he kicked a little closer to the fire. He then laid down the satchel, retrieving the package of food Kadia had given them, unwrapping it to find several pastries stuffed with crumbled cheese and olives, a few hard-boiled eggs, some lumps of rosewater jelly, chewy and sweet. Philbert managed to get Kwert to eat a little, worried at how thin and tired he looked, the large bruise stretching over his face like a tent, pinioned by bristles on cheeks and chin.

The effort of eating was too much for Kwert and soon he was asleep, his breathing relaxing, and for a while Philbert sat beside him, glad of the warmth of the wood burner, comforted by the scritch scratching of mice and beetles scurrying through secret chambers, reminding him of nights with Hermann. A few minutes later he caught a faint sound coming from the wall at his back. The noise was curiously familiar to Philbert, and he took off his brim-shorned hat and placed his ear against the stone, and there it was again. He couldn't be certain, but it sounded so like the Wille Woo song Helge had taught him that he took a chance and rapped his knuckles against the stone in the rhythm of the song's chorus, jumping back in fright to hear the rhythm repeated, the echo taking on a life of its own, carrying on the tune. He was so intent on listening that he near leapt from his skin when he heard a voice quietly intoning the first line of Helge's song, feeling its mists and snow clamping itself around him as if he'd been snatched into the world of ghosts.

'*Im Nebelgeriesel, im tiefen Schnee . . .*'

Philbert whirled around, and found a very thin man standing there in a patched and worn cassock, his neck sticking out of his habit like a cabbage stalk in winter, cheeks deep-pocked as if sunk with seeds.

'So what have we here?' the spectre said. 'Someone coming uninvited into my home? Someone who brings supper and then eats it all before his host has time to arrive?'

Philbert got his breath back, realising he was dealing with a man of flesh and blood, a mouth filled with teeth that were blackened to their stumps and breath abominably offensive. Philbert lifted the flask and wordlessly handed it over to the stranger, who might have been as thin as a wraith but had a thirst no ghost ever could, slugging down a good few gulps before delicately wiping the rim, replacing the stopper and handing back the flask.

'Well thank you, my boy. And do you have a name, this person who knows the songs of my childhood? And who is this?' He pointed at Kwert. '*He whose sleep is very sweet and which he has a right to*, as Goethe's Hatem said to the cupbearer.'

The man seemed to have taken no offence that Kwert was on his bed, and sat down cross-legged at its corner, Kwert stirring not an inch, Philbert finding his voice.

'My name is Philbert, and this is Kwert. Fatzke sent us to find you.'

The man inclined his head. 'Fatzke,' he repeated slowly.

Philbert nodded.

'And you're in trouble?'

Philbert nodded again.

'What kind of trouble?'

Philbert saw little need to hold back. Either the man would help them or denounce them, but either way he'd already calculated the man could be knocked over by a swift shove, so slight was his body weight, and Philbert had already marked out a couple of stones fallen from the walls that would help if he needed defence. So Philbert briefly told the tale of how they'd come to Ullendorf from the Fair, how Ullendorf had taken them to the Westphal Club, the soldiers choosing that night to raid the place, that many people were already dead – including Ullendorf, for Kwert had not been able to revive him after all – and that some had been taken away, others, like Helge, disappeared, the rest holed up in the gaol awaiting execution until the moment of dramatic escape.

'Ah,' the man breathed out a long sigh. 'I'm deeply grieved to hear it, and most especially about the Ullendorfs. I taught them both in the village school along with Fatzke. And it's Fatzke wants me to guide you through the crypts?'

'It is,' Philbert nodded.

'And for some reason you've brought me a cat as a gift? In Lengerrborn?'

Philbert frowned, following the man's gaze to his satchel, out of which the scrawny head of a ginger kitten was poking. The man plucked it up by the scruff, stretching its whiskers from its pink gums, Philbert quickly taking the kitten and placing it on his shoulder – just as Kadia had done – where it began a gentle purr, licking at Philbert's hair with its rasp of a tongue.

'I take it you're Pastor Gruftgang?' Philbert asked, relieved the man hadn't snapped the kitten's neck while he'd had the chance.

'Oh my goodness,' said the man, 'but I haven't heard that appellation in a long time. Pastor,' he repeated. 'It sounds good. But call me Amt Gruftgang. That's how I'm known now: defrocked defender of the deconsecrated church of St Lydia-of-the-Dyers. My Lady St Lydia, first Philippi heathen to convert to the teachings of St Paul. The walls here were painted purple for the dye she sold – not that you'd know it now. Her sign is the snail shell into which shape the church was built. Lord! But how many sermons I used to give in my younger days on the value of her blessed signs and symbols,' he went on, getting into the drift of those sermons, Philbert the first congregation he'd had for a long time. 'The purple kingship of Christ, the snail to recall the soul trapped in the body and the sleep of death before resurrection. How proud I was to shout out the words of my blessed Lydia: *if you have judged me to be faithful, come into my house and stay.*' Amt Gruftgang blinked away a tear and shook his head. 'Long gone. Long gone. My sermons too Latin, Lengerrborn too Lutheran. The building too costly to upkeep. A pastor past his best, who talked too often of saints and miracles to people who'd witnessed neither for generations.'

'But you stayed here?' Philbert asked, the old pastor squeezing his throat to stop his tears of anger, frustration and regret after his tirade that had been oft in his head but never spoken out loud, not to another person.

'I stayed,' he said, 'but oh, you should have seen the place back then. You could access the undercrofts from outside, before the wall collapsed. We'd gather on Our Lady's Saint Day, tolled forward by the bell, all carrying our torches, singing out the verses of her Conversion.' He gave Philbert a scratchy versions of these verses:

Et quaedam mulier nomine Lydia,
Purpuraria civitatis,
Thyatirenorum, Colens Deum, audivit.

'Good days, good days,' Amt Gruftgang said. 'I'd lead them through the chambers built beneath the church, right into the middle, me chanting from *The Windings of the Cochlea*, a little book I had the joy to compile, telling how the chambers replicate St Lydia's blessed snail shell, our wanderings through life's spirals . . .'

Philbert twitched with relief when Kwert's groans stopped Gruftgang's lengthy reminiscences, ending by directing one last blessing at Kwert:

'In *Nomine Lydia purpuraria* . . . may you be well again.'

The lamp Gruftgang had brought with him spluttered without warning and went out, leaving only the dim light from the stove for them to see by. The neglected building seemed to sigh of its own accord, jogged briefly into life by the old man's fading memories, finished now, and the only thing left to do being to fold itself back into silence and fall into a dreamless sleep.

23

Through Shroudways and Narrow Tunnels

Kwert was awake. He managed to push himself up on one elbow, looking around him in the dark. He made out Philbert leaning against the wall, eyes closed, and an old man sitting at the bottom of the filthy mattress, his back against the cooling stove. He'd no idea what time it was or how long they'd been here. He could hardly remember getting here at all, only the torture of movement, the fear of being discovered, the vague hope that help was at hand now they'd got to where Fatzke had directed them. He forced himself to sit, grimacing with the pain in his ribs. He knew that if he didn't move soon he would never want to move again. He was thirsty, saw a flask on the floor and lifted it to his lips, but it was empty. He picked up the wineskin that was lying by the old man's feet and took a sip, but Christ how it burned! Like drinking naphtha straight from the ground. His eyes watered, his cheeks puckered, but after a few moments he felt the strength of the spirit in his blood, his heart no longer slack but tight with a fast drumming that made him want to get to his feet and get on their way. He knew it wouldn't last long, this feeling of betterment, and so he shook Philbert awake. Philbert was alert in a second, pleased to answer Kwert's question that yes, he was ready to move, but was Kwert?

Kwert smiled. 'It's that dirty wine of our new friend over there. I don't know what he puts in it but yes, I do feel stronger, though I fear it will only be a brief respite. But if we can get going now I think we should.'

Philbert was pleased Kwert was up and ready for the go, but worried by the colour of him, too vibrant, too red, as if the glanders where running through him all over again. But no time to waste. They took a few minutes to waken Amt Gruftgang, for he'd been drunk on the liquor of his own making, had been drunk almost from the moment he'd been defrocked and the church deconsecrated, two decades since. But once up he found candles that they lit from the woodstove, and soon were heading down the slimy steps leading to the undercrofts and the maze of crypts and corridors dug into the ground beneath the church.

It was dark and dank, room only for single file, Kwert and Philbert following Amt Gruftgang's swaying candle and the tapping of his stick and the hollow sound of his voice as he slipped back into the past again, intoning the prayers of St Lydia as he led his congregation of two through the crypts. The tunnels were low and dark. Philbert held out a hand to the dripping stones, disturbed every now and then when, without warning, the walls would open up into a niche of mouldering bones and black-grown ferns that dripped a liquid too viscid to be plain water. He worried that the old priest was not only drunk but mad to boot, and leading them so deep into this labyrinth they would none of them ever get out again. Kwert was struggling to keep up. Whatever good the pastor's home-brew had done was evidently wearing off. There was one comfort to be found down here in this subterranean meandering, and that was the little kitten that purred away like an engine at the back of Philbert's neck and never seemed to stop.

On they went through the shroudways and narrow tunnels,

the pastor's pace erratic – sometimes fast, sometimes slow – until finally the tunnels became a little wider, the air less foetid, the darkness less profound, small intimations of true light appearing ahead between the lumbering, stumbling form of Gruftgang ahead; the whiskers of Raspel – as Philbert had chosen to call the kitten – began to twitch as the air became fresher. Then suddenly they were out, fighting a last battle with a curtain of spiny brambles, faces pale as limpets, eager for the light.

Never had the evening air been so glorious to Philbert. He might have been reborn. All around a faint rain drip-dripped through the branches of trees, heightening the sharp scents of pine and bay-willow, tinted by the sweetness of early blooming may-blossom and daffodils. Amt Gruftgang had sobered up considerably during the half hour it took to guide his wards through the mile or so of shroudways from the church to here, and pointed to a faint path rippling through the trees and un-flowered bluebells that would take them down to the lake.

'There'll be a boat moored under the large holm oak,' he said. 'Take it over to the island that lies just to the right of you, and there you'll find the Hermit. He'll shelter you for the night until you make your plans.'

Kwert clutched Gruftgang's arm, his back creaking as he bent to kiss the fingers of the man who might just have saved their lives.

'How can we ever repay you, my friend?' Kwert said, swaying with every word, plainly having difficulty staying upright on his feet.

'Pffht! It is nothing!' Gruftgang's halitosis was almost lost in the fresh evening air. He too seemed rejuvenated by the adventure, but what he'd done, Kwert knew, was not nothing by a long chalk. Caught giving fugitive murderers a helping hand would see his cabbage-stalk neck strung up in a rope, and no one to take care of St Lydia's legacy then. But Gruftgang was at heart still a pastor, only wanting a flock to care for, and that was enough for him.

'Perhaps, when you pass again,' was all he said, 'you will call in on old Gruftgang; bring him some decent food and brandy, some slices of venison, a haunch of wild boar, some apple sauce, some truffles . . . those old eggs of the earth.'

Philbert wanted to please this man who'd helped them so much, and the request seemed a small one.

'I ate snails' eggs once,' he volunteered, misunderstanding the reference to earth eggs, 'and will surely bring you some if I can,' and then he took off his hat and swept it low to indicate how much he appreciated Gruftgang's help.

Gruftgang, who had been about to turn back towards the tunnels, mindful of the falling night, looked at the young boy, seeing only now how unusual was the shape of his head.

'You've . . . eaten snails' eggs?' he asked, uncertain he'd heard correctly, looking from the boy to Kwert for confirmation.

Kwert interposed before Philbert could say any more. 'A custom, Amt Gruftgang, nothing more. No disrespect to your church or your saint. They're said to bring wisdom to the foolish and youth to the old.'

Gruftgang's thin face mottled, the pockmarks on his cheeks reddening as if there were raspberry pips just below the surface of his skin. He stood quite still. No movement at all, except for the rain dripping through the branches of the willows, releasing their soft scent of bay. Kwert looked anxiously at the old man, hoping to God Philbert hadn't offended him. Then suddenly Gruftgang laughed and held out his hand, his nails black with the dirt of the winding tunnels through which they'd just passed.

'Blessed Lady Lydia!' he exclaimed. 'But is it any wonder you were sent to me, for the egg is a world within a world as is the snail within its shell, and so it must follow that the egg of a snail is a world within a world within a world. And you, boy! You!'

His finger moved back and forth like an eye that cannot focus. 'You now have all those worlds within your head! It's a sign, the sign I've been waiting for all these years . . .' He did turn then, almost running for the tunnel, laughing like a man possessed. 'I must return at once. I must make my oblations, dedicate myself once more to the Blessed Lady whom I had almost forgotten but who this day has taken the shroud from my eyes!'

Kwert and Philbert watched him go, then mooched on towards the lake, picking their steps through the coolness of evening-closed anemones, a shiver of ghost-moths rising from the damp grass hovering and settling like clouds in a valley.

'Let that be a lesson to you, Little Maus,' Kwert said, 'never to take strong drink. It addles the brain and does a man no good at all.'

Philbert smiled. This was no time to mention the quash Kwert brewed and drank so freely. But he did look back, saw Amt Gruftgang on his knees beside the entrance to the hidden passageway. Perhaps he was praying. Perhaps he'd dropped his candle or was looking for his wineskin. Either way, he raised his head and waved, watched his miracle walking away into the distance, big hat on his big head, ginger kitten on his shoulder, sniffing like a gourmet at the air.

What Amt Gruftgang chose to see in his two fugitives was anyone's guess. Sometimes there just comes a time when believing a sign has come from God is preferable to any other alternative; and it was not an odd delusion, not for Amt Gruftgang given his years of solitude following the desertion of his flock. What was odd was that he was not alone in his delusion, as he would soon find out.

24

The Islet of Langer Hansnarrwurst

It didn't take Kwert or Philbert long to forget about Gruftgang and his exclamations of signs and faith, for the green of the woods soon gave way to the edge of the lake, the wind sporadic but stronger now, wrinkling its dark waters with foam-flecked waves, the small islands dotted on its surface looking grim and far away. Once out of the shelter of the trees, gusty swirls of dust and grit plucked at their clothes, stung their skin and eyes. Raspel retreated back down Philbert's arm and into the satchel, and Philbert pushed his hat down harder on his head. They found the skiff beneath the large holm oak swinging back and forth upon its weed-hugged rope in the recess of a small bay, the oars carelessly hidden in a nearby bush. Dark clouds had begun to race across the sky, dimming the last half hour of sun, and they were acutely aware of how little light they had left to them, how little time they might have to get from water to island. They struggled to thread the oars onto their pins, the skiff spinning in wild circles as Philbert dragged it into deeper water, Kwert's ribs grating as he fought to get aboard without tipping the whole thing over. Philbert got himself onto the narrow, splintered seat while Kwert huddled at one end so that he could give directions. Then Philbert went at the oars with gusto, scooping a spray of water into the boat with one stroke, skimming the lake's surface uselessly with the next. Happily, the wind broadsided them right, Philbert using the oars as rudders before beginning his rowing proper, getting into the rhythm of it, Kwert keeping the island in view, hoping it was the right one, signalling direction with weak waves of his arms.

By the time they scraped into the dark spray of the island's shallows the wind was strong enough to heave Philbert off his feet as he stepped out to drag the skiff in. The slippery boulders shrugged off the noose of rope again and again, and Kwert had to get into the water to help haul the boat up a few yards of sharp shingle so they could get it high enough to loop the rope around a tree bole. The sun had given up completely, hidden behind a dark rolling of clouds and the effort of sliding and slipping in the mud was too much for Kwert. He collapsed on the slime of the strand-line, pulling his shivering body into a knot, his breath fast and thready, unable to speak, let alone move. Philbert tried his best to haul Kwert away from the water, but the muddy shingle sucked at his boots, and the rain was coming down hard on his back.

'Kwert!' Philbert shouted, hating to see the thin white shanks of Kwert's legs as his tunic rode up, hating more the moaning of the branches above them in the rising roar of the wind. Kwert did not respond, and Philbert squinted through the beating rain and swirling leaves and thanked God he could see a faint, far-off glint of light somewhere up beyond the bank. He grabbed his satchel just as Raspel stuck out his rat-thin face and yowled, fur wettened into points, nose cold and clammy against Philbert's hand as he shoved the kitten roughly back beneath the burlap. He started a mad scramble up the muddy path between the boulders heaving away from the bank, and from bank and boulders into the trees beyond. He had a vivid memory of the miserableness of Herr Groben's barn, Huffelump's mother lying in her filth, saw the outline of Kwert abandoned on the beach and hauled himself upwards however he could, grabbing at stumps and roots until he could stand and then run, and then off he hurtled through the growing storm until he could clearly see the outline of a shack and the warm light flickering from its rattling windows. He didn't wait for niceties but hurled himself through the door and fell inside, breathing hard. And who was more startled of the two on this mud-wrung island in the middle of a lake in the middle of a storm was moot – the hermit, on seeing a small boy bowl through his door out of nowhere, hat gushing water, small ginger kitten shooting from his bag like a marble, running in ragged circles as it spat with damp and sneeze; or Philbert, finding a man round as a blown bladder, skirts hitched up about his knees, reed pipe in one hand, drum in the other, a line of tiny puppets wriggling on his bare toes. Either way, the door clattered behind Philbert and the man leapt up, dropping his instruments, startling the kitten which lunged at the little figures dancing at his feet.

'Is it some kind of weasel?' the man blinked, snatching at Raspel, missing, steadying himself against the wall as he surveyed his sudden visitors. 'You seem rather wet,' he began but was interrupted.

'Kwert!' Philbert shouted, as the wind thwacked the shack with such force that all the wall-boards creaked and the balding rug onto which Philbert had initially rolled began to rise as he got to his feet.

'Come on!' Philbert shouted, gesturing with his arm before running back out into the storm. The round man heard the desperation in the boy's voice and followed, scrambling away down the path towards the lakeside, his large bare feet scattering puppets as he went, burying them in the mud. Kwert was lying just as Philbert had left him, though now a thin stream of water was building up about his body, which was acting as a dam for the wind pushing the water on, and it was covering his neck and part of his face.

'Gracious me!' exclaimed the large man as he leapt down the bank, expertly avoiding the boulders, immediately picking Kwert up, slinging him around his shoulders like a goatskin and stamping back up the hill, balancing himself on wide-straddled legs, the dark mud oozing between his naked toes, Philbert shivering and slipping on behind him.

They got back inside, barred the door, and at once the man stripped Kwert of his filthy, sodden clothes and couldn't hide his shock when he saw the welter of bruise and batter on Kwert's yellowing skin. The hermit said nothing. Instead he went to his bedchamber and took up a sheet, ripping it into lengths and dipping them into the cauldron that was hanging over the fire, wringing each one out, using them to gently wash away the worst of scab and grime. When he was done, he lifted Kwert onto his pallet, covered him with eiderdowns and blankets and then whistled. From the gloom at the farther end of the barn came two gleaming white goats who came up and nuzzled his hands like puppies, taking the bits of bread he held out to them before going, on his command, to Kwert and lying down contentedly, one either side of him, and went immediately to sleep.

'Hansel and Gretel,' said the hermit for explanation, looking around him to find the boy leaning against the door. 'Over here, lad,' he commanded. 'Come on over to the fire. Best take your things off too, get them dried. I've more blankets, if not more goats.' Philbert did as he was bid, stripping down to his under-clothes, piling everything in a sodden mess.

'Grandfather here looks very sick,' the hermit went on, 'so I'm going to make him some ginger and horseradish tea. You should have some too, warm you both up a bit.'

Philbert nodded and sat down by the fire, leaning against a sofa built from wooden pallets bolstered by sacks of hay and straw. The hermit set a small pot on the gridiron, stirred it, dropping in bits of this and bits of that, and the next time he looked over he saw the boy had slumped into a sleep so deep he didn't stir a muscle even when the hermit, whose name was Langer Hansnarrwurst, gently took off the rest of his wet clothes and lifted the lad up, placing him on the sofa before covering him up.

~

Philbert woke naked, cosy and hungry, Raspel a warm bundle on his neck, tantalising smells of coffee, bacon and frying pancakes strong in the air. He looked up at the low roof heavy with beams pricked over with hooks, then shrugged off all his covers but the last, knotting the sheet about him and clambered to his feet. The hermit sat on a stool close to the fire, looking as big and round as the night before, but with slippers – instead of puppets – on his feet, that resembled birds' nests: woven plant stems felted with wool. He was ladling out bowls of soup, hunks of rough bread squatting like soldiers on a low, hand-hewn table.

'Well, well,' Brother Langer said brightly, his big belly rolling like an ocean swell beneath his rough-spun habit. 'So you're awake. I'm afraid grandfather over there hasn't come back to us yet.'

He nodded at Kwert, who was lying slack-mouthed and gaunt in his blankets by the fire, Langer having shifted his pallet – Kwert, goats and all – closer to the warmth. He motioned Philbert to sit, and Philbert went down on the floor next to Kwert, appalled at the rotten melon-skin blotchiness of his face. Philbert was uncertain and frightened; the sequence of events of the last thirty-six hours bewildering and confused. Brother Langer Hansnarrwurst was no more certain. He was a self-elected hermit, but denying his curiosity was not a part of his seclusion, and the arrival of these two waifs was tickling him. He had noticed the large growth on the boy's head the second the lad removed his hat, and also the concern with which the boy regarded the old man, wondering how and why they had washed up on his island. But he was a wise man, was Langer Hansnarrwurst, and asked no questions. Instead he handed the lad a bowl of sorrel and fennel soup, big chunks of back-bacon breaking through its surface, a roll of pancake shoved in like a straw, and it intrigued him that the boy didn't immediately dive in and eat, but instead pinched off a few bits of the pancake soaking in the soup, feeding them first to his little ginger kitten before taking any of it for himself.

'Enough?' asked Brother Langer when both kitten and boy had taken their fill.

'Enough,' Philbert repeated. 'Thank you.'

'Do you have names?' Brother Langer asked.

'I'm Philbert,' Philbert whispered, 'and that's Kwert,' unable to stop a couple of tears leaking from his eyes as he saw how pitiful Kwert was, how bereft of command, wanting nothing more than for Kwert to wake up, take charge and tell him what to do.

~

Langer shifted uncomfortably. He wasn't good with emotions or small boys, or people in general come to that, and he was unsure how to proceed.

'Why don't you tell me what happened to you and how you came here,' he said after clearing his throat. 'Here,' he added. 'Your clothes are quite dry now, so maybe you'd like to get dressed first?'

Philbert didn't answer. He couldn't take his eyes off Kwert, whose laboured breathing was as bad as when he'd got the glanders, but no Ullendorf to come to his rescue, for Ullendorf was dead. It felt like his whole life was made up of a series of disasters – small or otherwise – interspersed by short pockets of calm before the next one came along, each time growing in strength. It was only by pure chance or through the kindness of others that he'd got out of them at all. And now it was all happening again.

He blinked, and then spoke, giving Brother Langer an abbreviated version of leaving Staßburg, getting to Lengerrborn, the Westphal Club and the soldiers, the prison and the running; of Fatzke sending them to Amt Gruftgang and Amt Gruftgang taking them through the shroudways that led down to the lake. Considering the extraordinary nature of the tale, Brother Langer took it remarkably well, merely nodding his head here and there as Philbert talked. But when he mentioned St Lydia's Langer frowned, looking closely at the boy brought to him by the storm that had blown out of nowhere and gone the same way back a few hours since.

'It was Amt Gruftgang brought you through the crypts?' he asked, Philbert nodding assent. 'And so your story becomes both clearer and more obscure at the same time.'

Philbert was used to Fair people's patter and absorbed the contradictory response without comment, but he did lift his eyes, looking properly at Brother Langer, noting he didn't look quite right, though couldn't quite put his finger on what was wrong. Brother Langer saw him looking.

'We're not a world away, you and I,' he said. 'You can probably see I'm not like most men, but I'm sure too from what you've said that you've seen many such as I, yourself included.'

Brother Langer brought his face from profile to full moon, and plain as day then, the two sides didn't match, the left side out of sync with the right: one ear too high, one eye too low, one cheekbone far too flat. The recognition of these differences had Philbert feeling at home, as used to oddity as most were not and he smiled, Langer responding in kind.

'You've told me your tale,' Brother Langer said, 'so let me tell you mine.'

Philbert shifted and got comfortable, eager to hear the story, Langer obliging.

'I was always intended for the church,' he said, 'being the youngest son and without prospects, but glory, how I hated all that praying and kneeling, all that kneeling and praying. And being with other people with no privacy really bothered me. I hated it, the never being alone of it all. And so I ran away,' Brother Langer spoke in a low voice, as if fearing he would be overheard. 'Scaled the walls of the enclosure, scrambled down a scraggle of peach tree, legged it to the nearest village, hid out in a cowshed, begging for work on land that was already overrun with vagrants and unemployed labourers far stronger and older than I was.'

He stopped briefly to stir at the horseradish and ginger tea he had on the fire, pouring it out into small wooden cups with large spoonfuls of honey at their bases: one for Langer, one for Philbert, before going on.

'I took to steeple-jacking and tiling,' he said, 'having a head for heights as very few do, training next as a tree-lopper and then a thatcher and then – and this, Philbert, you might find hard to believe – I went on to be a freelance funambulist with a passing fair . . .'

Philbert clapped his hands, couldn't help it, this sudden swerve to the story dovetailing so much with his own.

'Oh but you clap, Philbert,' smiled Brother Langer, ex-steeplejack, ex-thatcher, ex-tree surgeon, ex-funambulist, 'but that was my downfall, quite literally. I took a show where the wires had not been strung as taut as I'd briefed them to be, and I fell. I fell,' he repeated, with a dramatic sweep of his arm, 'broke both my legs and flattened half my skull, hence the way you see me now.'

A sympathetic and gratifying gasp from Philbert, just as Brother Langer would have cued it if he'd been directing the show.

'But,' he went on, lifting an admonishing finger, 'that terrible accident was my salvation, because the fairs' folk I was working with took me to the monks, to the very same Abbey – with the same old scraggly peach tree leaning against its walls – from which I'd escaped a few years previously. And God bless them,' he added, 'for they took me in as if I'd never left. Nursed me and cared for me and looked after me, and within the year they had me back at the praying, though kneeling was out, at least for a while. But the entertainment business is not lost from me, and still I carry on . . .'

Langer laughed softly, taking from his pocket some of the little felt puppets unsubsumed by the mud and storm of the night before, shrugging off one bird's nest slipper and popping them onto his toes, wriggling a brief performance so ridiculous Philbert laughed out loud and long.

~

Brother Langer told Philbert others things that morning about his life, about the island, and the more Philbert listened the more Philbert admired the big lopsided monk, enjoying the asymmetrical crinkle of his mouth when he spoke, the awkward way he moved, as if his skin was struggling to contain a bouncing ball; but more than that, Philbert admired the way Langer tended to Kwert, who two days later had still not woken, not that Langer gave up on him. He spent every spare minute coaxing sustenance and fluid into his patient, placing a small funnel into the side of his mouth and constantly drip, drip, dripping soup and ginger tea down Kwert's gullet so he would not dry out, so that his body had enough fuel to heal, which – thanks to Brother Langer – it finally did.

25

A Great Good Still To Do

Kwert woke, weak as water from his long sleep, hardly able to raise his head above his blankets, Brother Langer seeing to all his bodily needs and waste excreta without comment, judgement or disgust. Never had folk like Philbert and Kwert been stranded upon his beach, but once there they became his primary concern, his only duty being to care for them until they were well enough to leave. The Öde Insel, as his island was called, was in the ownership and bailiwick of Langer's Abbey and therefore as much a sanctuary for anyone pitched up within its gates.

He was an odd combination, Philbert came to understand, hermit on the one side, socialite the other; quiet as a mustard seed one moment, spilling out his life story like grain to a goose the next. All year round he was alone on his island, apart from sporadic visits by Gruftgang and occasionally Fatzke, and even more occasionally by strangers directed from the Abbey to seek his wisdom; until once a year – and once a year only – when he threw himself out into the world with the energy of a coiled snake Then he went down to the Cloth Market at the Abbey, putting puppets onto his toes to make the children laugh, collecting the annual stipend of food-stuffs to last out his solitude for the year that would follow.

And now here were Philbert and Kwert on Langer's Öde Insel, picked and polished like driftwood beneath Langer's juris-diction, biding with him and his goats and the fish that teemed in the lake beyond. These last Langer caught, gutted, salted, smoked and ate, as did Philbert whilst he was with him. They also made bread from sacks of thick, bran-brindled flour rubbed through with butter and water and griddled into scones on the fire, or made into pancakes, or strange-tasting strudels topped with honey and cream. He also had his bees and a small orchard; too early for fruit, but still a few apples stowed for the winter in wooden boxes in the barn, and pickled pears and cherries, sugared apricots, dried plums and peaches, walnuts and almonds, all of which Langer gave freely to his guests.

And because of Langer's largesse and care Kwert awoke on their third morning, and a few days later was able to get up, the purple bruises on his face and body faded into yellow, although it seemed to Philbert that his skin had got thinner, as if wasps were coming in at night and scrape, scrape, scraping little slivers of it away like they did to wood to make their nests. The first thing Kwert did, once conscious, apart from introductions and effusive thanks, was to have Philbert read to him from the *Philocalia*, which Philbert did, Brother Langer being the one this time to help out with words he didn't understand, intrigued by the discovery that Kwert was a Hesychast, admiring the independence of that diasporic order who valued private meditation with their God above all else. A week later, Kwert still couldn't walk without wobbling hopelessly on his crane-fly legs, but Brother Langer's mention of the upcoming Cloth Market spurred him on.

'The perfect time for us to sift into the crowds and disappear,' Kwert proposed, at which point Brother Langer asked Philbert to come and help him in the smokehouse, but stopped before opening the door.

'You should stay,' he said. 'You and Kwert. I know he's intent on taking you off, but he's very frail for such a journey and I can be back in a few days. Fatzke always takes me and brings me back, and we only ever stay a night or two at the Abbey.'

Philbert wore his Ullendorf hat to keep away the gnats that rose like a mist from the damp of the orchards in early evening and rippled across the shallow waters about the island, dancing on the backs of newly emerged dragonflies sleeping on the reeds. He shuffled his feet, not knowing what to say. Brother Langer opened the door of the smoke-house, began to flip the fish on their shelves with wooden spatulas, his shadow large, suddenly engulfing Philbert as he turned.

'You must know,' Langer went on, 'that Kwert will go if he is given the opportunity. He knows how unhappy you are, how much you want to find your Fair.'

Philbert winced. He'd not thought he was so easy to read. Langer sighed, cracking his knees as he suddenly squatted down.

'He wants to protect you, Philbert, but he's not strong. If you go, it is you who will have to take the burden if he gets ill again. And he will get ill again.'

He tilted Philbert's hat back with a fish-wielding spatula so he could look the boy in the eye. From any other head than his the hat would have fallen to the ground, but it was jammed onto Philbert's and did not much waver, no more did Langer's direct gaze.

'We sometimes have to make decisions we don't feel ready for,' Langer said, 'but this decision, Philbert, has to be yours. Not that you need make it right now. But please think about it, take a little more time to plan what you must do and where you must go.' He put a hand to Philbert's cheek for a moment before releasing him. 'Just promise me you'll think about it.'

Philbert did, trying to untangle the jumble of packages that lay unsorted in his head, to untie the strings and scrutinize the contents, get everything in its proper place. Go or stay, his decision. He thought about the little trapdoor removed so skilfully by Ullendorf from his head, the great gift Ullendorf had given him by allowing the rest of the world passage in; how ever since he'd been slowly realising other people did not exist as mere adjuncts to himself, but that he was an adjunct to them; everything he did, every move he made, could have consequences for those around him, and no more so than now. He'd killed people, real people who had names and families and lives beyond his own; and the longer he stayed on this island the more likely it was that someone would eventually come looking for him here. And if that happened, when that happened – for he was suddenly certain that it would – then the consequences for those who'd helped him – for Kadia, Fatzke, Gruftgang and Brother Langer – could be dire. He'd already had more good luck than anyone had a right to. Time then for Philbert to stand up and be strong. Time to take his life in his own hands and not look for others to save him, time instead to put others before himself. Decision made.

~

Their last night on the island, and the fire was burning low, scarlet streaks across the western sky, tree bark glowing orange, grass a deep and vibrant green. They stared into the failing light of the flames as Philbert began to read a passage from the *Philocalia*, one Kwert had helped him choose and rehearse especially for Brother Langer, from the words of John Chrysostom:

> *Would you go into the abode of goodness, and the tents of the blessed?*
> *Then go into the mountains, the forests, and the deserts.*
> *See the birds flying, feel the breeze through the trees and the soft wind blowing;*
> *Bathe in the streams flowing through the ravines.*
> *For here is a man's solitude and his strength;*
> *A time away from the ever rolling waves.*

233

All was quiet as Philbert read those words, Kwert hunched over his makeshift crutches by the campfire Philbert had built and lit, Brother Langer poking at the ash with his bare toes, drawing up his cassock over the round hills of his knees.

'That was beautiful,' Langer said after a few moments silence.

'It's you,' Philbert said simply, and Brother Langer smiled his lopsided smile.

'I wish you wouldn't go,' he said. 'You could stay here and be safe.'

A few more moments of quiet between them all while the embers smouldered and sighed, and the night birds made soft squawks in the reeds around the island's bays.

'You have moles,' said Kwert, changing the subject, pointing at the small brown archipelago on Brother Langer's calf. 'Shall I read them for you?'

Brother Langer laughed. 'Why not, sir? Every man is entitled to his trade.'

Kwert creaked a little closer to his reading, moving his broken-nailed fingers over Brother Langer's isles.

'You are loyal and generous and have travelled far.'

'You astound me, Kwert,' the Brother replied, 'but have I not already told you so much myself? Why not tell me of other things yet to come?'

The tospirologist in Kwert could not help but take up the challenge and he bent to look the better, shifting his head to catch the light of the dying fire.

'You have sought and you have found,' he said, easing himself into the patter. 'And you have two larger moles with four smaller clustered around.'

He paused a moment, looking hard at Brother Langer's leg as the evening dark began to spread its blue across the sky, then made a small noise in his throat, as if having a sudden revelation.

'There's a great good in you still to do,' Kwert said quietly, 'and it will not be long in coming.'

Philbert smiled. It was a common trick Philbert had seen Kwert perform a great many times. In a moment Kwert would turn back and gaze intently at his subject's face and come out with some short and pithy homily about man doing good to man; but not this time. Instead Kwert shifted his gaze across the water, seeking out the shore on which they'd arrived.

'A great good,' he murmured. And that was that. Philbert raised his eyebrows but Kwert would not look at him. Langer laughed obligingly, his belly rolling, and pulled his cassock down to cover his legs and his moles.

'Not me, Kwert, old friend, not me. The only good I do out here is for myself. The moles have got it wrong.'

'The moles are never wrong,' Kwert retorted quickly, his soft smile hidden amongst the fading flush of his bruises. 'Are they, Little Maus?'

'Never!' Philbert replied earnestly, just as he'd been taught. Of course they could be, as could any one of a million predictions given by fortune tellers the world over, but in the case of Brother Langer, Kwert was proved exactly right.

26

Crossing Bridges

They left the island on the day of the May Fair, rowing across the lake at first light, someone waving to them from the opposite bank.

'That'll be Fatzke,' informed Brother Langer. 'He brings his pony cart to ride me into town.'

Also there were old Pastor Gruftgang, an old donkey at his side, and Kadia, in a cornflower blue dress, face smooth as an olive, eyes the gold-flecked brown of tench-backs fresh from the water. Fatzke grabbed at the boat line immediately they threw it ashore, shouting excitedly before they'd even landed.

'Good news, my friends, oh but I have such good news! Schupo Ackersmann is alive and well! He's alive, but has gone quite mad! He's given up the Polizei and cashed in his pension. He keeps babbling about meeting angels, if you can believe it. Says the angel stayed his hand, stopped him from murdering all those prisoners and having their blood on his hands the rest of his life.'

Gruftgang came forward, splashing through the water, dragging at the keel of the boat to get it grounded.

'An angel that looked like a boy,' he panted, looking from

Philbert to Kwert and back again. 'A boy with a head like a conch hidden in a hat of green . . .'

He grabbed Philbert out of the boat and hugged him hard as dodder to a tree. Fatzke started up again, displeased to have his narrative broken.

'The Schupo says the poison was his Cup from Christ, purging him of evil,' he said, tying the boat to the oak tree. 'And I was right there when he said it. *An angel*, says Ackersmann, *stopped my hand and took my evil from me.* Well Schupo Ackersmann, I said, if it was poison you wanted, you should've come to me. I could've given you enough to kill every cat in Christendom.'

Gruftgang clapped heartily at Kwert's shoulders, making him wince with the pain.

'It's a miracle!' Gruftgang added, taking up the tale, Fatzke popping up over his shoulder every now and then to say, 'That's right! I was there! I saw it all!'

'The angel,' Gruftgang went on, boring Philbert through with eyes like beetle larvae going at rotten wood, 'told Schupo Ackersmann to build a shrine, and what a shrine!' His breath caught in his throat before going on with quiet reverence. 'And the shrine is already there. It's St Lydia's. He's going to rebuild St Lydia's. Who could have foreseen such a blessing?' His voice was rising as if he were already standing at his lectern, red-pipped cheeks going in and out like bellows. 'Says he is risen back to life, and called me to him. *Help me Gruftgang*, says he, *help me build up the least of God's churches into glory, and we will carve both our souls into lamps for the light of God.* That's what he says.'

'That's what he said, that's what he said!' piped up Fatzke, 'I heard him myself, I was there, and that's what he said.'

'Priest in my own church again,' whispered Gruftgang. 'Whoever would have thought it? Ah, what a glorious blessing to have seen the Angel of the Lord.'

Kwert was frowning deeply, but Brother Langer clasped Fatzke in one big arm and Gruftgang in the other and led them off.

'Sounds like we need a celebration!' Langer exclaimed. 'Who's got brandy? It's a cold morning, never mind all the rowing. I knew something was up when Philbert told me you'd taken them through the shroudways, Gruftgang. You've not been down there for years.' He winked at Kwert, who followed the little procession shaking his head, glancing at Philbert as he went, not that the boy had taken any heed of this conversation. He was off a few yards up by the trees with Kadia, who was attempting to pin a bunch of bluebells to her shawl. He brought out the little ginger kitten.

'You must have wondered where he went,' Philbert said, Kadia stopping her pinning and looking at him.

'Ah, *hayvancik*, my little one. I think he runs away.' She put out a finger and tickled the kitten beneath his chin, Raspel purring loudly. 'He is fatter, yes? In just these few weeks. I think you keep.'

She moved forward, picked up the kitten, opened the flap of Philbert's bag and pushed Raspel gently inside, a little whirl of ginger hair catching at the buckle. Philbert felt the animal settle, curling up for sleep as if this satchel was his home and Philbert his owner, and Kadia smiled at Philbert and Philbert smiled at Kadia, and they heard absolutely nothing of what the others were talking about until they piled into the cart and began moving off.

'Of course I shall have to get the roof repaired and painted, and the sign. And the garden will have to be seen to. And pews!' Gruftgang was saying. 'That'll be one of the first things needed. We can probably make do with benches at the start. The Schupo's already given orders to the carpenter. And I shall need somewhere for the choir. Ackersmann absolutely insists on a choir . . .'

He murmured on, but soon his eyes closed in reverie and no one liked to disturb him, so they sat there, happy in their seats, listening to the stones knocking together beneath the pony's hooves, Fatzke whistling tunelessly with every breath, Philbert watching the dragonflies shimmer and dart, the slender shadows of fish below the water. Herons lifted lazy wings as they disturbed them with their passing, reminding Philbert of what Kwert had once said, that if birds didn't fly in the sign of the cross they would plummet to the earth and die.

A long while passed as they travelled, broken suddenly by a shout from Brother Langer.

'There it is! The Abbey! I can see the point of its spire! Ah, it still has a homely look about it. Every year, every year.'

The Abbey flitted in and out of sight between the trees until, rounding a bend, the woods all at once gave way to lesser banks of hedge and scrub sprawling an unruly mob down the brae. It took them all by surprise when the Abbey bells rang out a halting arpeggio, the lower notes slow to catch up with the higher, seeming to stay a little longer on the breeze.

'Nine of the morning,' intoned Brother Langer, 'official start of the Cloth Market.'

'Not quite,' said Fatzke, looking at a small contraption he'd fished out of his pocket, 'a little early, I should say. I wonder if your monks would be interested in a batch of these pretty things – ring-dials, they're called. Work just like sun-dials, only you can carry 'em around for your convenience.'

'Not very convenient when it's cloudy,' declaimed Langer, 'nor at night.'

'Hopeless for telling how long your sermon's been going on,' dreamed Gruftgang, his mind still attached to St Lydia, like a ligger pulling at a pike.

'Bah, Philistines the lot of you,' grumbled Fatzke to the Hermit, the Hesychast and the Priest, folding down the gnomon and snapping shut the lid.

The hill fell steeply away within its banks of yellow gorse and soon they reached the corner of the Market that lay just this edge of town. The great grey walls of the Abbey blocked the sun from the streets immediately beside them, a monk stepping out from a gate-turret to collect tolls from everyone passing into town. Sheaves of flyers held down by stones were stacked on his little booth, and he handed them one from each pile. Langer picked up the first and read out loud:

Brought to you by PRUNKVOLL'S CIRCUS OF MARVELS:

We Have The JONGLEUR OF JOUBRILLE who can balance an onion on the end of his nose and a chair upon his chin;

We Have, all the way from YELLOW CHINA, The AMAZING ACROBATS, men so small and smooth they can toss each other through the air like balls;

We Have A TROUPE OF DANCING DOGS who jig upon their hind legs and are dressed in the latest fashions, and bow and curtsey to one another in the politest of ways.

'I wouldn't pay a pea to see a bunch of dogs cavorting around a bone on a stick,' said Fatzke, still disgruntled by the non-impression made by his ring-dials, of which he had a further fifty in his saddle-pack. 'And as for men from China, why I saw them last year – they're nothing but a bunch of boys who've shaved their heads and painted their skins with dyers' broom. Now what I'd like to see is the jongleur balancing a boy on his nose, never mind an onion, that would be something to see alright.'

Brother Langer put that paper to the bottom and uncovered the next, which had a picture of a horse tapping at the ground with its foot, and read on.

ALL THE WAY FROM LONDON, who would have believed it, A HORSE THAT CAN COUNT!

All you have to do is ask him a question and he will tap out the answer with his hoof!

What is the number of days in a week? How many seasons a year?

How many full moons will there be this month? How many quarts of ale before a man falls to the ground?

All these questions answered, and many more!

'Pfff!' snorted Fatzke, the pony turning its head in its trap as if to agree, or maybe to wonder what all the fuss was about – counting was easy: one, two, three, one, two, three. Simple – oats, hay, water; water, hay, oats. What more was there to life than that?

They turned the corner of the Abbey and were immediately confronted by a barrage of stalls and noise. Lined up against the walls were wooden trestles protected by awnings of myriad colours and patterns, and piled high up on the trestles were bolts of cloth. Men stood close by doffing their hats as people passed, deafening them with shouts describing their wares and the remarkable bargains on offer for the first morning of the Cloth Market. Men leaned in, fingering the corners of the cloths, asking about colours and cotton contents; wives bustled, saying 'Not this one, let's try that one; this one has the warp all wrong, and look at that nap! And that colour! What are you thinking! Now that one over there . . .'

Their voices wove themselves together around the travellers, the cacophony rising in pitch as they closed upon a stall, fading again before they reached the next. On the other side of the street food-sellers were getting ready, frying potatoes and cutlets of lamb, setting chickens steaming on spits, strong smells rising from the *rippenspeer* – the smoky pork ribs people ate by the dozen dipped into this sauce or that, or smothered in salt and pepper. Brother Langer leapt down from the trap to take the lead, bringing them through a tall gate into the Abbey's grounds, where immediately the noise dropped in volume as he closed the gate, the walls holding it from them like the arm of a dam. Once inside the Abbey's courtyard they dismounted, the young monk ceasing his languorous pumping at the fountain and walking briskly towards them, smiling broadly.

'Brother Langer! How good to see you!'

'Brother Jaspis,' Langer replied warmly, taking the proffered cannikin from him and handing it to Fatzke. 'Still here then, I see.'

'Still here,' agreed Jaspis, 'thanks be to God, and to you, Brother.'

Langer beamed at him. 'I was helped as I helped you, as you will help another; thus the Light of God finds its way into the world.'

The monk in Brother Langer was re-emerging, and young Jaspis led him and his hangers-on to the guest-houses where they were to stay, apparently unconcerned by having to billet extra bodies besides the ones expected.

The Abbey had a calm about it despite the crowds outside, the stones seeming to sleep in the early morning light, murmuring gently as the bees came and went from between their nooks. Brother Langer departed with Brother Jaspis, and Kwert fell asleep the moment he laid himself out on a bed-roll. Kadia was eager to take a quick look at the cloth stalls and Fatzke took his pony and Gruftgang's donkey to the stables to be fed and watered and allowed to practise their mathematics in peace. Then there was only Philbert and Gruftgang sitting quietly on a bench outside the lean-to building the Abbey had for guests. Spread out before them was the infirmary garden, a purple cloud of fumitory smoking up the shins of its ancient walls, pushing past the leaves of speedwell and herb-robert that grew self-seeded through the paving stones. Gruftgang leant his bone of a back against the warm stone, his pipped cheeks sucking in and out as he breathed deeply, eyes closed. Philbert watched two rove beetles meet between his feet, their long bodies arched into scorpion-shapes, circling each other, waving their tails, then agreeing to pass on.

'The Schupo told me more, you know,' Gruftgang suddenly came to life, though he stayed leaning against the wall, his eyes now open, gazing into the deepening blue of the sky. 'Oh yes, he told me much more, that I haven't repeated to anyone.'

He turned then, and gently lifted the hat from Philbert's head, placing it down on Philbert's knees. 'He saw quite clearly the hand of his deliverer, felt the Flame of God pass through him as he swallowed that wine you gave him.'

Philbert shuddered, looked around him, was stopped from leaping up by Gruftgang's hand steady upon his arm.

'You've nothing to fear from me, lad, nor from him. The doctors say his visions are mere after-effects of the potassium-salts he ingested, but I know what he told me when he called me to him.'

Gruftgang looked at Philbert then, so hard Philbert couldn't look away.

'He told me,' Gruftgang swallowed, had difficulty speaking the words, his gaze so intense it seemed almost to be burning somewhere deep inside Philbert's head.

'Ackersmann told me he had seen the Face of God.'

He leant back against the wall and Philbert took advantage to take hold of his hat, began to lift it, but Gruftgang stopped him, put his face close to Philbert's as he leant down. His breath had not improved despite the renewal of his calling, but for the moment Philbert could not pull himself away.

'It is a wondrous thing, Philbert, when a child spreads his innocence abroad like seed strewn on a field of tares. A wondrous thing indeed, no matter how it came about. The ancients tell us that angels are all around us, and take many forms . . .'

Philbert heard the words but was no happier about them than Kwert would have been. Certainly he was glad that Schupo Ackersmann was alive, but the fact remained that his two companions had not been so lucky, and the authorities were not about to let the whole thing drop just because Ackersmann had found his God, and all this talk of angels was only going to keep the story alive and kicking. Philbert went to stand but Gruftgang moved his hand to the boy's shoulder and forced him down again. Philbert looked around wildly for some mechanism of escape; all he could come up with was a worthless question about what type of flower it was growing in a hummock by their feet, which at least had the effect of pausing Gruftgang in his speech, making him frown, lean forward obligingly. For a few moments he peered hard at the small green and white flowers, then threw back his head, knocking it so hard against the wall it made a thump as it hit, and then there was a sound in his throat like someone trying to pull on a leather boot that has been abandoned for years on a step in the rain.

'Oh Lord!' Gruftgang wheezed, wiping his eyes with his finger-knuckles, Philbert wincing, wondering what he had set in motion.

'Oh my Lord, my precious God!' Gruftgang was gasping for breath, but at last he managed to squeeze out an answer. 'Those, Philbert, are only open when the sun is shining. They call them Stars of Bethlehem, which, just like you, have led us back to God.'

Philbert's turn to frown, frightened by the man's belief; the first time he'd come into contact with so fervent a convert who would assert black was white and white black if he thought he'd received a sign that told him so. Philbert was a murderer, but to this man he was a miracle and there was nothing Philbert could do or say to make him change his mind. The responsibility of this realisation was enormous, and for the rest of the day Philbert stayed within the confines of the Abbey, hoping Kwert would wake up, hoping that he could get him out of here before anything else – miraculous or otherwise – had a chance to take root, take a life all its own; hoping, more than anything, that Amt Gruftgang, when he finally left, would not come back.

27

Into the Shadows

It was evening, and all were sat on logs outside the guest rooms, the fire jumping over lumps of spitted lamb and beef, eaten down to the bone. The smell of charcoaled meat wafted over them as they burned fingers and tongues on blackened chest-nuts just scraped from the glowing ashes. Fatzke had invested in a few pouches of exotic aromatic tobaccos and the plug he was smoking gave a pleasant hint of aniseed to the air. It was still light, but only just, the sounds of the thinning crowds milling about the town rising and falling with the opening and closing of tavern doors. Monks could be heard singing the psalms of compline:

In pace in idipsum dormiam et requiescam . . .

In peace will I sleep and rest, for Thou, O Lord, have established me in hope . . .

They'd stuffed themselves with roasted meats, pickles, turnips and wine. Kadia was leaning against the wheel of Fatzke's cart that had been brought into the yard to pile on the linens, grograms and wools she'd bought for her sewing back in Lengerrborn. In amongst those soft piles were Fatzke's sacks of useful implements – as he called them – acquired in exchange for some of his ring-dials and mouse-traps and whatever else he'd brought along for the purpose. For them another night and day awaited in the Cloth Market, but Philbert was adamant that in the morning he and Kwert would be away.

He'd figured out how to intercept Maulwerf's Fair of Wonders, assuming they followed their usual route. It wouldn't be immediate, but it was possible, and this much he'd told Kwert earlier that afternoon, after which Philbert had taken a brief foray out into the fringes of the Market to pick up any news, avoiding the one or two he thought might recognise him from previous fairs, but eager for news of Maulwerf.

'So what did you enjoy most, Philbert?' asked Brother Langer, his belly wobbling as he practised his dancing puppets on his toes. Philbert considered.

'I saw a man who stuck pins and needles in his body without crying out,' he replied. 'And an enormous brindled cat in a cage who growled and roared when people poked at him with sticks. And there was a black man sticking his hands in molten lead, burning all his skin away before curing himself. I know it's a trick, but I can't figure out how he did it.'

Kwert laughed feebly, his thumb going automatically to the gap in his gums, which still bled a little, and spilled the beans.

'It's all to do with expectation and sales pitch. The basin is painted to look red hot over its fire, but has an insulated base to keep out the heat. And it's not lead inside but quicksilver, and the man has a capsule of vermilion hidden between his fingers. He puts his hands into the bowl, screams, splits the capsule as he lifts his bleeding hands to the crowd. Then out comes the magic potion, which is nothing more than rubbing alcohol to remove the dye, and hey presto he's cured and everyone clamours to buy his secret elixir. Old as the hills,' Kwert finished. 'Old as the hills, and no miracle but by the Grace of God's great world.'

Philbert nodded, filing the information away, pleased to have the mystery solved, interrupted by Fatzke who started prattling about a new kind of jug he'd bought with its spout halfway down the side so it poured the milk before the cream, the gravy before the fat, thinking it was a grand idea until it was pointed out to him that the inventor had got the thing the wrong way round, because everyone knew the best part of the milk was the cream, and the best part of the gravy was the dripping. Fatzke sulked, shoved in another plug of tobacco and set it to light, sending the smell of burning cherries into the oncoming night. Philbert was sorry for Fatzke. He liked the man and owed him a great deal, so decided to distract the little crowd by reading a couple more of the fliers they'd been given when they'd first arrived.

'Let's see what's on tomorrow,' he said, for only he and Kwert knew they'd be leaving at dawn. 'There's the counting horse, the talking dogs, the acrobats and jugglers, the funambulist on his high-wire, four identical girls playing four identical tunes on four identical mandolins . . .' Shuffling through the flyers he came across a couple he'd not seen before. 'There's this cow of the desert that's called a camel,' he began again. 'It's got a hump on its back like an oversized saddle and can apparently go for three months without drinking any water . . .'

Fatzke spat and Brother Langer smiled.

'Go on,' Kwert encouraged. 'Your reading is getting really good, Philbert.'

Philbert beamed, picking up the last sheet, which looked the dullest and the most covered in writing. He cleared his throat in the manner of a town crier, but didn't get too far.

'Decree from the Militia of the Crown Prince of . . .' He stopped, having come across several words he couldn't pronounce, skipped over them and went on, '. . . announcing that in view of . . .' He paused again, more words he didn't recognise, curiosity goaded by the picture below that showed a man in a cage hoisted from a pole sticking out from one side of a building, looking ruefully at Kwert who smiled and took the flier from him.

'I know, I know,' Kwert began, 'I should never have tempted fate by – ' Kwert's eyes scanned the contents of the page. 'But, my God,' he said quietly. 'I can't believe such barbarity in our own country. Why would men do such things?' The others turned as Kwert held out the piece of paper to no one in particular.

'Does anyone know anything about this?' Kwert asked, a hint of his old strength back in his voice. 'Fatzke? You always seem to know what's going on – have you heard about this?'

Fatzke took the paper and looked at it upside down, eyes skittering over it as he shook his head. 'I can't make out the letters,' he blustered, unwilling to admit he couldn't read. 'It's getting dark and the writing's very small . . .' Brother Langer took pity and fetched the paper from him, tilting it to catch the light from the fire.

'Decree from the militia . . . yes, yes, a-hum . . . shall be dangled in the cage for the three days of the Market and then . . . may the Lord have mercy . . .' Langer's voice was very quiet and he crossed himself. 'I do believe they mean to kill the poor man.'

'After they've tortured him,' Kwert said hotly, trying in vain to push himself to his feet, hands flailing for his sticks, 'and no doubt he can tell them nothing. The poor soul probably had nothing to do with the Westphal Club.'

'But Kwert,' Brother Langer nodded his head towards Philbert, who was sitting very still before the fire, Ullendorf hat low on his brow. 'What if he was there? What if he knows? You can't expect him not to say anything. Why, he may have told them everything already.'

Fatzke puffed impatiently at his pipe.

'You may be more educated than I,' he grumbled, 'and the light may be a little dark for my eyes, but there's no need for you to speak in riddles. What does the dratted thing say?'

Brother Langer dropped his arm, his puppets falling over, forgotten in the dust.

'Ah Fatzke, it's yet more of this thing from Lengerrborn.'

Brother Langer glanced at Kwert and Philbert. They'd told him the broad outline of their misfortunes before the island, but none of them comprehended the true consequences of what had happened to Ackersmann and his men. He'd only just learned it himself from Jaspis. He'd meant to broach the subject this evening, but it had all been so peaceful, and Philbert had left the Abbey only for a half hour or so, so where had been the harm? He grimaced, then filled them in.

'Brother Jaspis told me that the soldiers took some of the Westphal prisoners with them for interrogation to the fort over the hill there, most still interred. The monks give them food and water through the bars, but they're badly treated, some chained to the walls upside down. And now, well, I don't disbelieve it after this,' he indicated the piece of paper, sighing deeply before going on. 'This is a decree, stating that one of the prisoners is being kept in a cage in town, strung at just the right height so people can throw stones and spit at him and the like in support of their country. He's to stay there for the Market's duration when – assuming he's not already dead – they'll string him up like a sausage on the last night, for the general entertainment of the crowds.'

Fatzke sucked at his pipe and nodded his head as if it happened every day; Gruftgang tutted loudly and Kadia went white as a newly washed sheet.

'There is a proviso, of course,' Langer went on, 'and that is to compound lies with treachery. They want to know who murdered the policemen in Lengerrborn, and they mean to make this man tell of the conspiracy or hang.'

Kwert hoisted himself up ineffectually on his sticks. 'We cannot let this happen. I must give myself up. Tell them it was my doing. You can get Philbert away . . .'

Brother Langer laid his hand on Kwert's arm and although the pressure of it was light, Kwert collapsed like a pile of kindling.

'That would be madness, Kwert, and you must know it. The man will die one way or another. You cannot believe they'll actually allow him to go free, and giving them another mouse to play with will serve no purpose at all. But there will be quite a few folk here from Lengerrborn and if they know him, well, they may see things differently. Philbert has been out and about,' he held up his hand as Philbert tried to interrupt. 'Oh, only for a short while, I know that, lad, but you don't exactly blend into the crowd, and there are plenty folk for whom swapping the life of a man they know for a stranger's, even if that stranger is only a boy they've glimpsed once, wouldn't seem so bad.'

Philbert sat rigid, as did Kwert.

'Pah!' said Fatzke unexpectedly. 'Nobody except us knows what the Schupo said, apart from a couple of doctor quacks, and they all have their heads up their own arses.'

'But the soldiers,' Gruftgang said slowly, sucking painful gasps of cold air over his diseased gums, 'they'll know. They left a man, remember? After they'd taken the others away?' He sounded defeated, hollow as his crypts.

Brother Langer shuffled his toes in the ash then rubbed his big hands together. 'We'll get you away in the morning, first light,' he said. 'I'll take you over the canal. Jaspis will help.'

'We couldn't possibly. . .' Kwert began, but Philbert interrupted and leant forward to clutch Langer's hand in his own.

'Thank you,' he said. 'We were going to leave then anyway, but we would surely be glad of your help.'

And that was the evening gone, fizzled out with the fire, nothing left to say. Brother Langer helped Kwert back to his bed; Fatzke and Gruftgang went to check they had tied their loads properly to the cart. Kadia sat with Philbert a small moment.

'You,' she said, and put a small hand out to his cheek. 'I think you look after Raspel and Allah will look after you.'

And then she and her faded bluebell posy were gone too.

Only Philbert sitting there by the fire. He picked up the flier and stared at it hard, cursing himself for not having been able to recognise the words, the import, everything they meant. Then he shoved the paper into his pocket, jammed his hat hard down on his head and took off into the shadows, taking the trace of path that headed from the infirmary garden up to the small guard-house by the midden tip.

'Have to get something,' Philbert said, and the sleepy monk nodded, 'back soon,' and he nodded again.

Philbert rounded the Abbey wall heading back towards the centre of the town, the dull glow of cooking fires flickering and smoking in front of the food stalls, the remains of ox-carcasses and sheep dripping into their embers, men and women sitting around them, drinking, talking, leaning against one other, discussing the day, just as Philbert had done half an hour since. He followed the lanes leading to town's square, homing in on the splashing of the large public pump that lay at its centre and found the place awash with noise and young bloods chucking each other into the shallow pool that formed around it, spoiling the drinking water for the next morning. He'd reached his destination, could see what he'd come looking for swinging gently in the breeze, the untidy huddle inside inert and unmoving. The cage was just above a normal man's head-height and it began to move violently from side to side as it was hit by a barrage of objects flung by the youths as they emerged dripping from the pump-pond: bottles and jars, squashed pumpkins and cabbages and whatever else they could lay hands on. Philbert could make out a face hidden amongst dirty rags, bruises and blood, as if he'd fallen into a mill-grist or been pounded by stones, his clothing wet and soiled, ringed with crusts of blood and pus. The bars of the cage were stuck with bits of rotten vegetables and even from where Philbert stood he could smell the filth and urine. The youths at the pump decided they'd had enough of taunting what couldn't hit back – time to head off back to the tavern to warm themselves up. They flung their last missiles as they left, loose stones from the street, old fruit-pits from their pockets. They set the cage and its contents swinging; they swore and spat, threw horse manure from the streets in handfuls. 'Filthy pig . . . Traitor . . . Murdering bastard!' Never mind that they were probably all three themselves, or would be during the coming years of revolution.

Philbert emerged from the shadows once the group had passed on, laughing and shoving one another, boasting about what they'd done. He moved beneath the cage, saw the close-up knot of flesh, skin pummelled, covered over in cuts like a crow run over by a cartwheel and left to die by the side of the road. The man had been woken from unconsciousness by the youths' barrage and he unrolled slightly, clutching at his prison with grimy fingers.

'No more, no more,' he mumbled, his few teeth wobbling visibly in white gums. 'I can tell you nothing. I know nothing.' His words were choked, drowned by a deep up-welling of phlegm.

Philbert stood beneath the cage as if beneath a crucifix, Christ's sad head bleeding onto one shoulder, the rags of his misery clinging to the bones of his broken body. He took off his hat to take a closer look and, as he did so, the hands at the bars began a gentle tremor, the man choking out a cry, poking a finger through the bottom of the cage, stretching down towards the boy below. And Philbert recognised that finger, or the way it pointed, and he cocked his head to see the man's battered face the better, rearranging the pieces here and there until they fit.

'Is it Herr Federkiel?' he whispered, shocked to see this man from the Westphal Club who'd described the shapes of potatoes and had wanted to measure Philbert's head with his callipers.

'Ah ah,' groaned the prisoner, his voice thick with throat-rust, words scratching out as if with broken nails upon a crumbling wall. 'It's that boy,' another awful rasp, 'but how can it be? How can it be?'

'I'm so sorry,' Philbert murmured. 'I'm so sorry . . .'

The cage rattled alarmingly and Philbert moved away instinctively, fearing it would fall.

'No, no, no,' it was the dripping of an old tap as the man tried to speak again. 'A moment, just a moment,' like warped wood, 'don't go, oh please . . .' A long, long sigh, wind down a draughty chimney, as he got himself together. 'It's . . . it's . . .'

'It's Philbert,' said the boy, tears squeezing from his eyes as he looked at the pathetic bundle suspended up above him in the night air.

'Ah,' gasped Federkiel. 'Yes, yes, of course . . . so much I forget; my head is filled with scrambled eggs. All soft and steaming on hot buttered toast, just like Helge used to make.' He stopped, swallowing a sob. He'd been beaten and interrogated, felt urine seeping down his leg, leaked brown liquid into the seat of his pants, made to lick up his own filth when he didn't tell his interrogators what he couldn't tell. His fine clothes had been ruined, his glasses lost, his precious measuring instruments stamped under uncaring feet. He'd seen his friend Schnurrhenker down on his knees, tired and bewildered, tears running silently down his face, holding up his shackled hands as the padlocks were undone and ripped from him so as not to waste them, the guns being raised, the shots in the woods outside Lengerrborn as dawn broke; the soldiers getting bored with kicking their weaker cargo into movement, watching the corpses rolling down the bank towards the river as Federkiel forced himself on, slipping in the splattered excrement of the soldiers' horses, unable to understand how it had all happened; relieved when they finally got to the fort and were thrown into dungeons so at least they could rest. And then had come a second wave of prisoners, apparently escaped from one prison only to run directly towards another, yet another mystery

Federkiel couldn't understand, yet another sounding out of guns in the woods in the middle of the night; and then the dawn, and the calling out of his name – which had been the only piece of information he'd been able to give them throughout his long hours of torture about the Westphal and its apparent web of spies and rebels about which Federkiel knew absolutely nothing. And, for Federkiel, it all stopped here, halfway between heaven and earth, and somehow here was that boy again, the one with the head, a boy who was running across the square to the pump and bringing back a cannikin of water for Federkiel, which seemed the greatest kindness he'd ever known.

'Ah,' he felt a deep happiness as he drank that water down, as if that single draught could wipe away the misery his world had descended into, and he leant down against the bars and put his one good eye to them so that he could see Ullendorf's wunderkind.

'How excited we all were that night,' he whispered, difficulty in every word he spoke, grinding out of him as flour from beneath a heavy quern, 'to meet both you and Von Ebner – such a great man, and we were to meet him at last.' He coughed, and there was blood in that cough and it splattered down in a fine mist upon Philbert's hat as he held it in his arms. 'Such a mind, such great ideas . . . me and Heinrich often talked after we'd been to the club, sitting at Helge's table, eating Helge's fine peach-dumplings, or the schnitzels she had left for us . . .'

He closed his eyes and breathed deeply, wanting to hang on to the memory, keep it close, taste it, smell it. Then he shook himself, poking skinny fingers through the bars.

'Will you do something for me?' he asked, and he could just make out a movement down below him where the boy still stood.

'Of course,' Philbert whispered, unsure whether Federkiel had heard him, he'd gone so quiet, before starting up with what was obviously a great effort.

'Give Helge a message for me. Tell her what I should have told her years ago . . .'

Philbert's throat was so tight he couldn't speak, and anyway could not have brought himself to tell this broken man that Helge was missing, probably dead, just like her brother.

'Tell her,' Federkiel's breath was fast and urgent, as if he'd thought of these words over and over again and now was the only time he was going to get to say them. 'Tell her she is my nest of spheres, my prism of light, the heptagon of my days . . . can you remember that, Philbert?'

'I can,' he said. And he could. The moment the words were spoken he knew every one of them even if he had no idea what they meant. It was like a song that gets stuck in your head after the one and only time you've heard it. And then Federkiel closed his eyes and closed his lips, and Philbert stood there for a few moments in case there was more.

'I'll tell her,' he said, and lifted up his hand towards the cage but couldn't quite reach those fingers clawed around the bars, untroubled that the very last words Federkiel might hear in his life were a lie. Sometimes lies were better than truth, Philbert knew it now if not before, and put his hat back on and returned to the Abbey, no one having realised he'd been gone.

28

A Great Deed Done

Breakfast the following morning was a hurried affair. Brother Langer boiled up salt-fish and pickles, most of which he packed away for later. Kadia looked worn out, skin-thin, her dress tired and crumpled, her bluebell posy gone. She stroked Raspel for the last time and Philbert gave her a bunch of those Stars of Bethlehem, but Gruftgang had been quite right. Without the sun they were closed and tight and the gesture seemed meaningless, but she took them nonetheless. Fatzke gave Philbert a ring-dial and patted his shoulder, and Gruftgang gave him a quick hug before Brother Langer brought the goodbyes to a close by loading Kwert onto a donkey he'd borrowed from the Abbey, and they were off. Nobody mentioned miracles or angels or men in cages that morning, and everything was quiet and hushed, dawn a bare streak in the sky. They left by the midden gate, now abandoned, clopping their way across the poppy fields towards the bridge that marked the edge of the Abbey's lands.

Once a quarter mile from the dark shadow of the Abbey, Brother Langer tried to lift the mood by telling the tale of the bridge and how, before it had been built, the river used to sporadically overrun its banks, stranding fish, drowning crops, dragging fertile topsoil with it as it spooled away back into its banks. The Abbey had employed a French engineer to do the work.

'A Frenchman! Imagine!' Langer smiled, 'everyone knew how much the Abbot hated the French, having fought against them way back when and never forgave them for it. Still, there it was, the man the Bishop sent was French and the Abbot had to swallow his pride and sit down and listen to the little man's plans.' Langer swept his arm across the landscape, the meadows of poppy and clover that seemed to stretch away forever. 'But he knew his business, and look at it now.'

And as they got closer they could see it was indeed unique. Langer was about to tell them more about the squat Frenchman, glasses perched upon his head, hand slapping at his blueprints, bare-backed monks toiling with their hoes and pickaxes, hacking out the artificial canal to act as storm-drain and irrigator but he stopped suddenly, held up a hand and looked behind him to see Brother Jaspis, habit flapping as he ran across the fields to catch them up, having to brace his hands on his knees once he'd got there so he could catch his breath. They were almost on the river by then, the bridge's four arms spidering over it and its companion canal in the shape of an oblate X, two covered walkways converging from each side and meeting in the middle, crack willows leaning their orange branches down over the water, trailing their newborn leaves upon the surface like weed.

'Soldiers!' Jaspis gasped at last, 'just left the Abbey. Coming this way.' He managed to straighten himself, held his two hands to his lungs like armour.

'Quick,' commanded Brother Langer, taking hold of Kwert by the armpits and hauling him down from the donkey's back while Philbert hurriedly unhooked Kwert's walking sticks from the pack, Jaspis propelling them both up the wooden walkway of the nearest arm of the bridge until they reached the covered canopy at its centre. Once there, Jaspis gave the boy a leg-up into the eaves of the little portico where Philbert crouched, reaching out for Kwert as Langer shoved him after, Philbert having to clutch Kwert fast to keep him from falling, the skin sagging from Kwert's face with the pain of cricking up his knees, clinging to the wooden arches, until they were roosted like a couple of badly balanced owls. Philbert looked down, saw small seats nooked into the octagonal chamber below, a tidy trapdoor that could be lifted to allow a rod to sneak down into the water that hurried and gurgled below between the starlings of the bridge. It should have been calm and peace, but Philbert could smell the fear and panic burning like vomit in his throat, saw Kwert's hands shaking as they gripped the beams and put out one of his own and held it over Kwert's. He could smell the dawn-wet dust being driven up by horses' hooves as they ploughed their way across the fields from the Abbey. Only minutes later came the jangle of bridle rings, the snort of hard-run horses, the scuff of boots against short-haired flanks. Philbert squeezed his eye to a small knot-hole and saw the band of black-clad hussars, heavy and menacing as a thundercloud, charging through the poppy fields, red petals flying haphazardly as they came.

'Now then,' said the leading horseman, as he pushed himself up to stand in his stirrups and glower down on Langer and Jaspis, who were standing by the donkey, faces as calm and nonchalant as if they'd just stepped out of prayers. 'What are you folks doing here so early? Looks like a conspiracy of nuns to me.' He laughed at what he thought a great joke, pulling on his reins, forcing his horse to encircle the men and donkey with his stink and sweat. 'We had a report there were a couple of escapees heading this way. Escapees from Lengerrborn no less.' He spat the name Lengerrborn as if it had stung him and puckered his mouth in distaste.

'A bad business,' said Langer, keeping his large head down,

'a bad business indeed.' He committed himself no further, did not specify which bad business in particular he was alluding to.

'They've had confessions from the revolutionaries captured in that Westphal Club,' the soldier continued, pluffing his nose as if he were the horse and not the man, 'that there was a plot to poison the Schupos there. Naturally the ringleaders have been caught and shot, but you know how vermin are. There's always a few rats escape the trap.' He spat again, looked at the two monks: one large, round and ugly, the other young and handsome and freshly tonsured. 'No one passed this way?'

'No one, sir, and we've been here a small time now,' said Langer.

'No one passing to admire your pretty pile of wood?' The soldier nodded at the bridge, saw it fussy and overly ornate, completely unfitted for the passing over of troops. He liked flat wide bridges of buttressed beams that could fit a squadron riding side by side.

'No one has passed here, Hauptmann,' Langer's voice was calm and steady. 'I imagine it was only we two who were seen.'

'Ah yes. Two brothers, out for a morning stroll,' the soldier drawled, amused at his insinuations, 'practising your little songs together, were you?'

Langer coughed politely. 'Fishing, sir. We are fishing. I am the Hermit from Öde Insel, visiting for my annual stipend. I'm returning to my island later this morning, and Brother Jaspis here was kind enough to offer me a little companionship before I left. We are abroad early so as to avoid the Market crowd. I'm sure you understand.'

The soldier gobbed his spittle, seemed pleased at the pattern it made on the ground beside the ugly brother's foot, looked hard at the river, at the bridge, at the track that snaked away from it through the sedge on the other side. He sat a moment, heels pressed into his horse's flanks, then waved his arm at his fellows.

'All right, clear out, lads. Back to the fort and breakfast,' he twisted his reins tight in his hands, tugging the horse's head into a hard fold, before giving them a last warning. 'Keep your eyes skinned, brothers, and tell us who passes, or maybe we'll skin your eyes for you, the better for you to see.'

He scowled at them, liking his own jokes, the cage in the town one of his best; he'd always known himself to be a humorous man.

They didn't waste time and as soon as the soldiers were out of sight, Philbert was jumping down from the rafters, Langer and Jaspis carefully lowering Kwert and carrying him over to the other side of the bridge where they had already led the donkey. They all shook hands, Brother Langer insisting they take the donkey, onto which he gently lifted Kwert, which was as well; for Kwert could no more walk a few steps than a frog could fly.

'Thank you,' Philbert said as he took hold of the donkey's halter and led Kwert away, waving one last time before turning his face towards the north and to Bremen, and the Maulwerf they hoped to find there.

Philbert would have thanked Brother Langer all the more earnestly if he'd known what would happen next, but that little piece of drama he didn't hear about for many, many months; no way of knowing that Brother Langer did not return directly to his island, instead heading from bridge to town, all day busy with his arrangements, going hither and thither, meeting strange people in taverns, talking to odd people on corners. He never saw Langer chatting to the old funambulist whom he'd known when he'd run away from the Abbey, nor heard him persuading the man to set up the rope for old-times' sake. He would never see Brother Langer climbing the steps of the building from which the rope had been strung, nor the ill-fitting purple jerkin he'd borrowed to cover his cassock, make him look more like the showman he was pretending to be; nor did Philbert see Langer tottering out onto the hemp-line, pretending to dance, pretending to wobble in alarm and then falling, cutting the rope with his knife as he went, knocking hard into the cage Philbert had visited the night before, sending it plummeting to the ground. He didn't see the people down below cry out in alarm and crowd around, nor that the cage was being kicked to one side, its door wrenched open by the tools a couple of members of the crowd had brought with them for the purpose; nor the many hands that had been waiting for just this moment to reach inside and grab the prisoner, hustling and hauling him away moments before the roaming soldiers arrived on horseback, clearing the crowds from the cobbles, the cage open and empty, Federkiel transported away, taken back to Brother Langer's Isle by Jaspis; Brother Langer himself spirited away to the Abbey to set his twice-broken bones. They didn't heal so well this time round, and Brother Langer would always feel the grumble of them at every turn. But back to his island he went and Jaspis went with him, for Langer could no longer manage on his own.

Oft times through the following years Langer and Jaspis sat by their fire on the Öde Insel remembering that day when they had ceased to pray and kneel and took action instead for their fellow men, and boys. And they would laugh softly as Langer pointed out the archipelago of moles just below his crooked knee and what Kwert had said. Federkiel too stayed on the island until he was healed, in body at least; his mind took longer, unable to leave his cage, recalling the boy looking up at him, breathing in his proxy words of love. Lost in the nest of his days.

29

Of Pumpernickel and Pumpkin Heads

'Oh . . . oh . . . on the la-a-zy water, with his croo-oo-ked stick . . .'

So sings the reed-cutter as he punts his way through the knee-bones and knuckles of pools and streams that make up his world. He isn't cutting reeds – too far gone in the year for that, scythes all oiled and put away by the end of April, reed-stems dried and sorted, stooked and counted. Instead, he cares for the sharp green blades pushing up through the short-shanks of last year's growth, watches the cotton-grass bob in the breeze, winds his way through the giant tussocks of sedge grass that hold back the encroaching carr of alder and buckthorn, plucking up any young saplings that have found their way into his beds. He whistles and hums, punts and pulls, at peace amidst the rafts of ducks and moorhen paddling serenely by, listens to the buntings and warblers hanging upside down on thick blades of sweet-grass. The only things that disturb him are the sounds of the drovers a mile or so distant, driving their sheep to the big market at Bremen. A few of them are camped up nearby, taking a couple of days rest, fattening their livestock before the last leg, feeding them on the lush grass of the meadows to the east of the river. It amazes him that people bother to take their sheep so far but apparently it's common practice, so he's been told; better prices, better bargains to be struck, better produce to be bought and taken back to their villages. He worries briefly about his wife at home, separated from everywhere by thick fields and meadows, but knows his son can shoot a straight shot, that his wife can snap the neck of a rabbit with two fingers, and that she and her rolling pin could do a heap of damage to the saggy bones of any drunkard who might come hammering at her door.

He knows they are drunk because he can hear their loud voices, the vociferous laughing, the occasional snort of song sung to an out-of-tune accordion or, more likely, an out-of-tune accordionist. He's heading for his little shack built of stout branches and bunches of reeds, always ready to protect his stacks, which would make easy burning for anyone who happened this way. He starts singing again, and then stops, raises his hand to shade his eyes against the setting sun. He sees figures coming toward him – two, maybe three. He pulls himself up in alarm, cocks his head, can still hear the drovers rowdying over the river so knows it can't be them. He sucks in his breath and poles the punt quick across the water, ready to up a pitchfork and defend his ricks with his life. He keeps the new arrivals in his sights as he skims through a maze of streams and half-grown hedges, muscles knotting, face taut; then relaxes slightly, sighing with relief as he sees one of them point. They've spotted the drovers' fires and have changed direction, beginning to cross the river on one of the many clapper-bridges scattered down its length where the water between the constant pools is wide and shallow, littered with stones, easy to cross. He slows the punt to make sure they are really going over, which they are, and then swirls his pole through the darkening afternoon and begins again to sing.

'Oh . . . oh . . . on the la-a-zy wa-ater, with his croo-oo-ked stick . . .'

~

Philbert was tired, Kwert exhausted – propped on the donkey, barely upright, head lolling with every step. They'd made slow progress since leaving the bridge, the plan was to keep company with the river that would eventually join the Weser and on to Bremen. They'd been on the road for days, detouring when the river stepped into a series of weirs and small waterfalls as it tipped through tussocks into a broad plain of marsh. It had been hard going and wet, but soon the scrubland took hold and the trees grew taller, sucking the spare water into their roots and leaves, shading the travellers from the afternoon sun. Now the river was wending through sparse woodland, widening into pools and reed-beds that made it hard to follow, but they had kept true to its course, the sky dulling into a great copper bowl above them, and Philbert knew it was time to stop. He'd seen the silhouette of a man punting his way through a passageway of reeds, and caught the brief strain and snatch of his song before the sun dropped away and took the man into shadow, when Philbert heard different voices, and the very welcome sight of a fire on the opposite bank. Just a little longer over the nearest ford of popplestones, acutely aware of Kwert's laborious breathing, the complaint of his joints at every move, the slight grinding of his teeth as he fought to stay awake, too weary to do anything but follow Philbert.

~

'Here, Fager, where's that good-for-nothing clodhopper gone this time?'

'He's away in the bushes pishing on his boots again, ha ha!'

'Why in God's Good Name doesn't he just piss by the hedge like everyone else?'

'Eh heh,' laughed Fager, 'you know what he's like – can't fill a finger and doesn't want anyone to know it.'

'Pfah,' grumbled Schtultz, 'you're mighty brave of a sudden. You'd be holding it out for him if he told you to. Not me, though. I'll say what I think to his face. He's a lout. And he's as much guts as a cauliflower. Fancy going off so far just to take a leak.'

Fager looked abashed, wondered if he'd spoken too loudly, but Schtultz didn't bother who might hear him and carried on. 'Big man like that! He's a fool. Can't take a drink and can't take a joke, and what's more, can't look after his sheep neither. You must've seen 'em. Bloody lot of 'em's knackered. Covered in ticks and keds, and I can see blow-maggots crawling in the wool even in this light. And what does that fart-head think about? Nothing 'cepting his next drink, that's what. You're a fool to put your sheep in by his. He's a couple of shiverers in there too – tick-sick, no doubt about it. Be dead before he gets 'em anywhere near a marketplace.'

Fager looked nervous, steadied himself with another mouthful of brandy. A stamping of bushes and the crack of twigs could be heard as someone fell through the hedge close by, swearing loudly.

'By God,' muttered Schtultz, 'but he's a clumsy lump of a man, and he's got a mouth like a pus-hole. I'm off to kip up by my sheep. Can't take him any longer. I'll be away first light, by the way, if you're wanting to come.'

The man Schtultz picked up his lamp and marched along the track, speeding his step as he heard the other coming back.

'*Trunkenbold*,' he muttered, 'no more legs than a fly in a flagon.'

Fager watched Schtultz's light bobbing away in the twilight and would have liked to follow, but that would mean leaving the brandy alone with Nicolas. He could have taken it with him – he'd been the one to fork out for it, after all – but old Pumpernickel had Fager where he wanted him and, heavy and stupid as Nicolas was, Fager wouldn't go against him.

'Ah Pumpernic – ' he caught himself just in time. 'Nicolas,' he amended, 'you're back,' Fager shifted slightly to avoid Nicolas's large backside which came crashing down onto the log beside him, his boots steaming, wafts of urine hazing with the heat of the fire.

'What's to do, Fager? Give us that brandy . . . Ah! That's better . . . and where's that pansy-puppy Stultz got too?'

'Schtultz,' corrected Fager, though the other didn't notice.

'Tha's what I said, Stultz. Where'd he go?'

'He's just out with his sheep . . .' Fager paused before going on, 'Says a couple of yours are shiverers . . .' the sentence hung over a cliff.

'Shiverers? Wha's he bloody mean, shiverers! I'll give him shiverers! 'Course they're bleeding shivering! It's cold as a witch's tits out here . . . ponced-up pimple. Who's he think he is?'

'He was just saying . . .' Fager mumbled, his hands playing with his beard.

'Says this, says that! S'all he bloody does is talk. Wossee know 'bout farming anyway? Only been at it a couple of minutes. I been doing it nigh on thirty year! He's nought but a sodding prick, is what he is!'

Fager didn't bother replying, eyed the bottle dolefully, wishing it wasn't swinging so dangerously in his neighbour's big bullying hands.

'I keeps me farm good as anybody, I does. Not that I gets any help from that bitch indoors – spends all her time on heat, she does. Touting herself around the neighbourhood like a common trollop . . .'

Fager nodded dumbly. He knew how well the farm was kept, had seen its broken-down shacks; was forever fixing fences and digging out the drainage ditches that abutted his own land, blocking hedge-holes so Nicolas wouldn't steal his sheep. He'd also seen Margarete, 'the bitch indoors', humping great stacks of wood, milking dirty-skinned goats, wiping back what was left of her hair, getting thinner and thinner as the years went by.

267

The brandy bottle was thrust at him as Nicolas readjusted himself on the log, nearly pushing Fager off, scratching at his balls with one hand, taking a bite out of a cold and greasy faggot with the other.

''Ere, Fager,' bits of pork-lights flew from Nicolas's mouth, 'what d'you reckon to a bit of play in the village? See what new meat we can lay our hands on? Saw a couple of pretty lasses waiting table in the tavern . . . reckon they'd do it on the cheap. Probably haven't seen real men like us for a long while. Strong, bit of a rutting – know what I mean? They likes a bit of rough-and-tumble, types like that.'

Fager closed his eyes in the dark, but was pretty sure Groben could barely stand, let alone walk to the village and abduct some poor child for a squalid job-and-poke behind a house, hand over the girl's mouth, couple of coins in her pocket after they left her crying in a heap on the grass. They'd done it before, though Fager had only sort of participated, just to keep his friend company. Mates was mates, after all, that's what he told himself, though afterwards he always felt sick and couldn't touch his own wife for a week, and could barely rest his eyes for a second upon his daughter.

'Ay well, ne'er mind,' Nicolas slurred and made a grab for the bottle – missed. 'Give us that brandy, Fager, you greedy bastard. Giz it here before you cop for it.'

Fager handed over the bottle, resignedly filling a cup with beer from the near empty keg. The night was hard down now and Fager would gladly have sidled off for a bit of sleep in his makeshift tent but Nicolas's presence held him fast. He listened to his scratching and hoisting, heard him fart wetly, felt the man shift his buttocks on the log to avoid the ensuing trickle in his pants. He felt sick. He frequently felt sick in Nicolas's presence, but as a boy he'd been bullied into submission and as a man he was bullied still, though now it went by the name of friendship. He looked up in the darkness, thought he heard a snatch of singing but saw only a couple of figures stumbling their way towards them along the track. He nudged Nicolas, who nearly went flying.

'What the bloody hell d'you think you're doing, you balls-head! Nearly had me in the fire.'

Fager pointed up the path. 'Someone's coming,' he whispered.

'So what?' said Groben. 'Probably them lasses from the village. What did I tell you? Gagging for it, they are, hey, hey! They're in for a good night of it!'

Groben shrugged in his sweaty shirt and put a finger below his collar, smartening himself up for imagined impending amorous activities. They both watched, Fager blinking in the dark, swallowing hard, Nicolas grunting in anticipation. Out of the blackness they heard the clip-clop of a donkey, saw a man on its back, a boy leading it on, Kwert and Philbert emerging into the circle of light surrounding the fire.

'Shit!' said Nicolas, baring his teeth, slurping from the bottle, uninterested.

Fager let go a small gasp of relief. He hadn't really believed it would be women, but he knew from experience to expect the worst.

'Good evening,' Kwert muttered politely, the wear and tear of illness evident in his voice, looking like he was about to drop. 'And apologies . . . but we . . . wondered if you might share your fire with . . .'

'Bugger off!' Nicolas interrupted Kwert's stuttered speech.

'Perhaps we could . . . just sit . . .'

'You deaf or summat? I told you, bugger off!'

Fager heard the man on the donkey droop and sigh, steeled himself and intervened. 'Let them sit, Nicolas. They'll do us no harm.'

Nicolas scratched and grunted as Fager motioned the strangers to join them.

'We've nothing to give you, you understand, but you're

welcome to sit by the fire. Cold night, eh?'

'Cold indeed,' agreed Kwert as he slid from the donkey, collapsing gratefully by the meagre flames. The boy sat down beside him, his large hat putting his face in shadow.

'You didn't stop in the village, then?' asked Fager.

'No,' Kwert replied, rubbing his hands, revived a tad by the warmth. 'Came from the other side of the river . . .'

'Hmmph,' grumbled Nicolas, 'no bleeding money, I'll be bound.'

The boy in the hat was looking at him curiously.

'And tell your bloody monkey to stop staring at me,' Nicolas added, 'or I'll wring his neck and teach him to dance.'

Kwert cricked himself towards Philbert, who lowered his head.

'No money, sir,' Kwert placated, 'is precisely our position. But we hope to meet up with friends at Bremen.'

'Ah yes. The Bremen Fair,' nodded Fager, 'we're taking our sheep there. Nicolas has a couple of bulches too – bull calves.'

'Shut up you,' Nicolas was angry. 'You've a tongue that blabbers like an old woman. These two could be looking to rob us blind. You never heard of fishing expeditions? Christ, man, 's a good job one of us can take his drink well enough to watch our skins don't get taken while we sleep.'

Kwert waved his hand wearily. 'You've nothing to fear from us, sir. We just want to rest for the night. We'll ask for nothing more.'

'They all say that,' muttered Nicolas, but even he could see the newcomers didn't look like assassins. Groben's eyesight was made weak and blurry at the edges by the brandy, but something was tickling him. He squinted, leaned in for a better look, pork-faggot breath leading the way.

'Don't I know you, pipsqueak? Hey, boy, I'm talking to you! You with the hat.' The boy looked up, dark eyes wide, though he did not remove his god-awful hat. 'Ugly little bugger, ain't he; but then, mind your Maria?' He punched Fager in the side with his fist. 'Right bunch of bones and squawking she was not long back, always running snot from her nose and playing with her hair. Couple years on and she's ready for the bed, and no mistake.'

Fager's pale cheeks reddened, a shiver running through him from head to toe but he said nothing, recognised the signs, Nicolas finishing off the brandy in one long swig and throwing the bottle into the fire, blue flames playing briefly over the shattered glass as the strangers jumped. The time of drinking when Nicolas would want a fight.

'What you got in your bag, boy? Bottle of brandy perhaps? Flagon of wine?'

'Nothing,' mumbled Philbert, twiddling the strap with his fingers.

'Cunning little shite! Don't you answer me back. Gi's it here . . .'

Philbert didn't move. He wished he'd not led them over the river. The moment they'd walked into the circle of light he knew who Nicolas was, the telescope of memory zooming into Groben's barn, Huffelump and his pitiful mother, before slamming shut. Kwert intervened.

'Please sir, we don't want any trouble. We've no drink, believe me. No drink, no food, no money. We'd give it you if we had it. Come on, Philbert, we'll leave these gentlemen to their fire.'

Kwert went to stand, creaking and cracking, Philbert clutching his satchel in one hand, helping Kwert with the other. Only two yards they got towards the donkey they'd tethered by the river so it could eat and drink, when they heard a rumbling behind them and on came the staggering Groben, hoisting at his *Hödensacke* with one hand, opening and closing his fist with the other.

'Nobody walks away from me like that, d'you hear? Nobody!' he shouted, 'and especially not a little shite like you!'

271

Fager scrambled to his feet and hung behind Groben like a spent breath, his heart hammering beneath his ribs like woodpeckers, lips moving without words. Kwert was shocked into immobility, Philbert gripping his bag-strap tighter, determined not to let it go, Raspel beginning to squiggle inside, bumping against the *Philocalia*. Groben was on them in a second, lumbering into Kwert, knocking him to the ground, yanking away Philbert's hat, fat-glistened teeth bared in recognition.

'I knew it,' Groben growled, 'knew I'd seen that ugly little *pickelkopf* before. You stole my prize calf. . . pretending to be fine gents you were, and all along just common swindlers. I seen that midget girl dancing pirouettes and that lump-calf prancing, raking in a fortune. *My* fortune, you thieving little bastard!'

Groben grabbed Philbert and shook him like a bag of dice, Fager dragging ineffectually at Groben's arm, flung off in a moment, bleating as he fell.

'But it's only a boy, it's only a boy!'

Groben ignored him, heaved Philbert up into the air and threw him with all his fighting strength; Philbert somersaulted, landing mercifully not on hard ground but into a deep pool beyond the popplestones, sank and stayed, bobbed and gasped, arms flapping and floundering, body banging against one rock here, another there, head surfacing every now and then to hiccup in a bit of air, drowning like a puppy in a pail. And then he was up, someone yanking hard at his collar, bringing him to land, choking and coughing, sounds around him of a hundred sheep stumbling and complaining, rearranging themselves, shuffling themselves like cards.

'Stay here,' commanded his rescuer, throwing a heavy coat about Philbert's shoulders before marching away down the track, muttering under his fast-drawn breath, stamping his big boots, heading for Groben's fire; Groben loomed beside it like a venomous bat, spitting drunk and spoiling for a fight, lifting his fists as he saw the man's approach.

'Whaddaya want, old Stultzie? Old farty-pants-farmer Stultzie?' Groben swaggered, invigorated by action, certain he'd righted a great wrong by chucking the kid into the river. Schtultz did not reply, marching on with sure and steady stride, removing a leather glove from his back pocket and fitting it on. Straight to Groben he went, and straight into Groben's face went his leather clad fist, Groben far too drunk and slow to respond, falling to his knees with an audible *oomph*. Schtultz gave him no leave, pulled him up again by his collar, punched him three times more, saying vehemently each time he hit:

'That's for the boy; and that one's for knocking down a sick old man; and this last is for me, because I'm sick of the sight of you, and I'm sick of the sight of your maggoty sheep, and I'm sick of what you do to little girls behind hedges. Sick,' he said quietly, delivering a final blow, 'of your waste of a life.'

Schtultz stopped and stood, breathing hard, releasing Groben who slumped to the ground, nose and cheekbones cracked and bruised, bleeding and moaning in the dirt.

And away to the west, the reed-cutter sits in his reed-house, thinks he hears a commotion coming to him on the breeze; he cocks his head and listens: nothing but the sound of the wind and the water. He puffs his pipe and is at peace.

30

Loss and Gain and on to Bremen

Low grey clouds drizzled over Philbert's world. He was down by the river looking at the laundry pool into which he'd ended up the night before, watching the water as it splayed its toes between rocks and the discarded limbs of trees before losing itself in the shallows and beds of reeds. He saw the dippers darting from rock to rock, and a kingfisher cutting from air to water and back again as if there were no difference between the two, listened to the water burbling sleepily beneath its breath of mist. He slipped along the grassy bank, two green snakes following where his feet pushed through the dewy grass. He found his satchel, snagged and sorrowful, caught on the roots of a tree that had out-grown its bank, Raspel hanging out from beneath the flap, pink tongue smooth and sodden, long and limp, blue eyes cloudy and vacant, fur sogged and draggled into dark points, bones sharp beneath his waterlogged skin. Philbert retrieved the satchel, lifted him out gently and laid him on the bank next to the water-steeped *Philocalia*. So different, his little Raspel, so thin and cold, Philbert weeping for the loss of the warm purr, the companionship of Raspel wrapped about his neck or snuggled in his satchel, Kwert staggering up behind the boy and laying down his sticks, putting his arm around Philbert – cold and thin as Raspel – pushing the large familiar head against his chest and the arrhythmic beating of his heart.

~

It was a slow and sad sojourn to Bremen, Kwert on his donkey, Philbert walking in front, Schtultz taking up the rear, going behind his sheep, driving them on with two switches of willow held in outstretched hands. Philbert's role was to keep the sheep from wandering on ahead, but mostly he just dawdled, kicking stones with his feet, eyes red and bleary, knapsack damp, weighing more though it carried less – only the *Philocalia*, with the flyers from the Cloth Market torn up and tucked between its pages to suck out the wet. The sheep, incurious, kept their heads down and soodled steadily along, ignoring the boy and the odd sobs that escaped him occasionally but soon desisted, Philbert's grief twisting into an anger as integral as the pit to the peach, growing with every step he took, its hardness spreading throughout him like a mushroom spreads its roots beneath the soil, unseen. And he was glad for it, giving him to understand how cruel the world could be, how filled with chance, how the next time it showed itself he would pay it back in kind.

~

They reached the outskirts of Bremen two days later, Schtultz not minding the presence of his two companions, pretending they were being a big help with the sheep as he shared out his meagre portions of food each night. They heard the city long before they stumbled through the hinterland of villages that were caught around its edges like goose-grass to a dog: the noise of cattle bellowing, sheep coughing, the grackles of geese, the howling of dogs, clear as a multitude of clarion at battle's start seven miles distant. The closer they got, the more crowded the lanes became, filling up with animal muck, spilling one track into another – some wide as weirs, others bottle-necked over a ford or bridge – and everywhere the dust kicked up by the folk and animals coming into market carked and choked and cloaked the air, the pale blue of the sky disappearing, all to see being the livestock stumbling all around them and the backs of the men tending them, everything, everyone, pushing onwards, all shoving into one other, until it seemed a miracle any one farmer could distinguish his stock from another's.

They stayed their last night a few miles out of the town and took off in the early morning, the drizzle helping for a while to settle the dust to the earth, allowing an hour or so of cool, clean air. But this soon ceased the moment everyone else started their own forward momentum, kicking up the dust again, great clusters of flies rising in the growing morning warmth that swarmed around both animals and men, settling on their backs, in their collars, at the corners of their eyes. The clamouring hurry-burry of noise was incessant, the dung so all-pervasive that it was difficult to make out any other smell excepting by degrees of stink and shit. As soon as they passed the town's boundary markers every square inch seemed covered and close-packed with hurdle-houses, animal pens, cheese and butter makers setting up their stalls, touting for milk and cream, thick-armed women churning and stirring everything they could get their hands on. Boxing booths opened, gaming rinks were cordoned off, the screams of cockfights and the howls of dogs pitched against chained bears ripped through the air, and every step sent up streaks of pinch-backed rats that had woken up in paradise. Every yard of every street was taken up by stalls selling crooks and whips, poultry, jugs of cream, curry-combs, buckets of dip and dye, worm powders, fleece pullers, shearers, hoers, turnip-cutters, saddle-sellers, harness-hammerers, ox-hoof clippers, tail-trimmers. From all sides came the hurdy-gurdy of sheep's bleating, cattle lowing, chickens squawking, donkeys braying. Philbert had never encountered anything like it, eager to run up every ginnel, might have been landed on a different continent, and so much to explore.

They left Schtultz when they reached his allotted patch, nothing to give him but their thanks, taken with equanimity and a brief tip of his head before carrying on shoving his sheep inside his pens. Kwert and Philbert pushed and butted their way through the crowds until they reached the cooler, quieter back streets, clutching the few coins Schtultz had pushed at Kwert as they had left; in payment, he said, for the labour they had but poorly given.

'My God!' Kwert groaned, wiping his forehead with his sleeve. 'If I never see another sheep it will be too soon.'

They stopped by a coffee barrow, sipping the rich liquid, glad to be still and almost alone. The streets were still awash with shouts and smells, but the further they went from the hurdle-houses, the quieter it got. By late afternoon the noise crescendoed again as stockmen began their early celebration of the various sodalities of Horn Suppers, Whip-Words, Cock-Claws, amongst many other initiatory drinking rites. Needing rest and food, Kwert and Philbert tucked themselves away into the back-haunts of the city, eventually landing at an inn renting out its back yard for cheap night lodgings, and settled down to noodles, gristly meatballs, and gravy-dunked slabs of stale bread. It was late, and dark.

'Read to me,' Kwert's voice was soft in Philbert's ear, but before Philbert could take out the *Philocalia* and its water-smudged pages, Kwert was asleep. Silence then, only the sound of a few snores and grunts, everyone rested and content to have found their small square of peace. He placed his head on Kwert's knees, but his eyes were open and years later he could have told anyone who asked how many cobblestones there were in that yard, and how many people sat around its walls or were curled upon its benches. And if Philbert had ever become a man who could paint – which he did not – he could have depicted every stroke of light and dark that fell upon that place, every star as it appeared in the sky, every colour of every coat buttoned tight, every strand of hair, every wisp of straw; all there in his head as it was then, before he closed his eyes and slept.

31

The Bundle of his Life

Morning came, as mornings often do, cold and stiff and grumpy, but not for Philbert, for this was the day he might find news of Maulwerf.

'It's such a huge to-do in Bremen,' Kwert assured him. 'We're certain to find someone we know and who knows where Maulwerf is or where he's heading.'

Philbert slipped on the slops of stale beer on the cobbles without caring, nor that he got bitten on the shoulder by a hungry mule, or had to queue ten minutes for the stinking water-closet. Nothing could damp his enthusiasm.

'How will we ever know where to look?' Philbert asked as they set off, his eyes sweeping from the tip of the cathedral across the river and its bridges to the plazas, shambles and hurdle-houses, the unfathomable maze of streets and tall, point-headed houses.

'Now then, Little Maus, you know very well that at all sheep fairs there are entertainers, and they almost always congregate in one place. All we need do is find it.'

Philbert helped Kwert onto the donkey. He still had difficulty walking, even with his sticks, but this morning he was buoyant, feeling stronger, something of the old Kwert back in his bones.

They were astonished by the sights and scenes of the enormous city, which neither had visited before. The noise and tumble of people so oppressive the night before seemed today vibrant and alive. There were hats far larger than Philbert's, planted with feathers and flowers, and women with hair much broader and taller than the best of those hats. There were coats that flashed with fur and sparkled with buttons and brooches, capes that swirled around corners, appearing before their wearers, proud and stiff in silver trim. The sounds of livestock chorused through the city streets, pungent smells around every corner, the air stirred up by the miles of bunting and flags that fluttered like washing from every building. At the bleating heart of the city were the animal-greens, where grander colours muted into browns; here, mud-speckled cattle lowed open-throated over fences, sheep shoving each other into wooly-backed lagoons inside their hurdles, squinny-eyed goats head-butting their enclosures as dirt-spattered men and dogs fought to keep everything in.

Kwert and Philbert were soon directed to the vast common grazing lands where the Fairs' folk were settling like goldfinch across the fast-filling fields, all gay and gaudy, twittering at each other as they set up booths, tents and stalls, gossiping, catching up, the townspeople hovering at the edges gawping, coins clinking in pocket and purse, eager to fling themselves into the alternative reality of the Fair, away from the humdrum into a paradise calling out to their hearts' desires. Amongst the push and swell Kwert gravitated instinctively towards the Seers' quarter, following the hierarchies and structures embedded into the large gathering despite the overwhelming impression of chaos. And there was Kwert's old pal Zehenspitze, who could map out your past and future by rubbing his fingers over the soles of your feet.

'Come on, come on!' he was shouting to the sightseers already gathering. 'Let me feel the life-force of your feet, where they have been and where they are going. If you heed their wisdom, your path will be sure. Ah yibbelly yes, yibbelly yes.' Zehenspitze nodded his sincerity, then thrust his head into the air, banging a hand against his heart. 'A fanfare for the feet! A paean to the pod! A song for the spirit of the sole! Let the podognomist divine the direction of your life!'

The first punters were dithering on the edge of Zehenspitze's pitch and he was about to reel them in when Kwert on his donkey tottered into view, his affect so greatly changed for the worse that Zehenspitze cut short his advertisements, advancing with arms outstretched.

'Oh my dear old friend,' he murmured, helping Kwert indecorously to the ground, 'whatever has befallen you? Come, come,' he urged, sitting Kwert on the stool normally reserved for paying customers. 'This last year has not treated you well. Let me get you something . . .'

He shook Kwert warmly by the hand, the other placed on Kwert's shoulder, appalled by the thin brittle of bones poking through his friend's thin skin. He wasted no time, fetched the condiments normally lavished on his more affluent clients – a lit pipe, a glassful of watered brandy, some little cakes and *krapferl* biscuits, Kwert accepting them with gratitude, soon enlivened, and before long he and Zehenspitze were talking fondly of old times, old scams and pitches. Kwert trusted Zehenspitze implicitly, telling him the gist of his recent adventures, his finding of Philbert, the descent on him of the glanders, the disastrous visit to Lengerrborn, Zehenspitze reacting to this last with visible shock and excitement.

'The Westphal Affair! My dear Kwert. There's been talk of little else in the taverns! You're practically a hero for just having been there.'

No point in Kwert saying how little of a hero he was. Zehenspitze was, like most of the travelling Fairs' Folk, bang up to date on the politics of the time. Their livelihoods were dependant on knowing which principalities would welcome them and which would not, which were lax on papers and town-passports, which trouble-spots to avoid. And Lengerrborn at the moment was of the last. No one would go within thirty miles of the place, especially considering what had happened at the nearby Abbey's Cloth Market a couple of weeks afterwards. It was the epitome, Zehenspitze told Kwert, of the instability shaking the country up and down, foreign armies battering at its boundaries and – far more dangerously – the inner prickling of its citizens who, deprived of land and livelihood by famine and feudal taxes, threatened daily to rise up and murder their nominal protectors in their beds. He knew of the cholera epidemic in Silesia that had precipitated a short-lived, hard-crushed revolution, and was amongst the few who'd heard of the Kartoffelkrieg in Berlin when protestors had been run down and shot at like rats. The Westphal Affair, by contrast, was lurid and dramatic. Everyone was talking about it, especially travelling folk like Zehenspitze who cared to keep their heads on their shoulders and their bones inside their skins. The murder of the Lengerrborn Schupos and the daring escape of Von Ebner's supporters from the town gaol were pivotal events for would-be revolutionaries across the land; the cruelty meted out to the recaptured prisoners – especially the one in the cage – made of them martyrs all, and nothing like a host of martyrs to spur a movement on.

'You don't know the half of it, Kwert,' Zehenspitze leaned in closer, lowering his voice, for who knew who was listening on the other side of the canvas or the thin boards of a booth. 'When the Handtheyrker guilds were dismantled they responded by dismantling the machinery taking over their jobs. Such a thing could never have happened a few years ago. And then there's the case of the teamsters ripping out the railway lines they only laid last year. The railway was putting them and theirs out of work, you see. Bringing in cheap goods from elsewhere.

And only a couple of weeks ago some redundant sailors attacked the company steamships on which they'd formerly worked. Caused a great deal of damage before they were ejected. It's sporadic, Kwert, but it's happening. The revolution is persistent and gaining momentum, and will not soon be stopped. And they know it, Kwert, they know it! Did you hear that Prince William of Prussia – the King's own brother – has already fled? Gone to England of all places.'

Kwert shook his head in disbelief, Zehenspitze not surprised. Apparently you could take the Hesychast out of gaol into a world groaning with injustice and suffering – his own included – but you could not make that Hesychast rise up to action. Navel gazers all – quite literally. He smiled indulgently. He'd known Kwert since they were new-come to their respective callings – Tospirologist and Podognomist – meeting by chance when they'd pitched their very first booths side by side, travelling then side by side for two decades before going their separate ways, Zehenspitze to his politics, Kwert to his religion, but friends ever since, meeting here and there, always glad to see one another, always jawing and drinking before diverging back on their separate routes. It occurred suddenly to Zehenspitze that Kwert was not wearing his usual red habit, and it jarred.

'You've left something out,' he stated quietly, no brandy-cloud to his eyes, and obvious to Zehenspitze that Kwert was carrying some unspoken burden.

'I have,' Kwert agreed, after a few moments. 'Forgive me, but I've left out quite a lot. You said I didn't know the half of it, but neither do you. That boy I introduced you to earlier?'

'The one with the hat?' Zehenspitze asked, looking about him, but the boy was gone, no doubt dipped off into the fair like a squirrel after nuts.

'Philbert,' Kwert said, drawing Zehenspitze's attention back. 'He was the reason we were in Lengerrborn at all, and why we were at the Westphal Club. It was he Von Ebner and his friends had come to see. And it was he who slew the Schupos and set the prisoners free, myself amongst them . . .'

Zehenspitze gasped, his eyes and cheeks bright with excitement.

'He didn't mean to do it,' Kwert went on quickly. 'He'd no notion of it, but that was the outcome all the same. And then there's the miracle of St Lydia's to come to terms with.'

Zehenspitze let out a breath and rolled his shoulders. He was a Podognomist of the first order and believed in what he did, but he was also an on-the-ground agitator and Kwert was flinging revolutionary gold dust at his feet.

~

Philbert had thoroughly checked every stall and booth for folk he knew and found no one familiar. He was right at the back end of the fair where it abutted onto the killing-grounds, men squatted like knots of toads on the mud-churned field, some holding down animals or winching them up on pulleys so as to slit their throats, funnelling their blood into barrels, slicing the hoisted animals, gutting them with nonchalance, skinning them down, peeling their flesh away from their bones. The smell was stomach-churning, the sight morbidly fascinating, the grass beneath the lamps black with blood, steaming with the heat of disgorged intestines, spilt guts, the stinking slurry of last half-digested suppers, all poured as filth upon the ground. Heaving, Philbert sat down heavily, spittle awash in his mouth. Down below he watched a man stagger and lurch amongst the several small and dirty pigs he'd got in exchange for his smaller and dirtier sheep. Nicolas Groben. Philbert butt-shuffled backwards into the shadows. The last thing he wanted was another encounter with that man. Instead he encountered another.

'Frightened, boy?' asked the person into whom Philbert had inadvertently bumped.

'No,' Philbert answered quickly, jumping to his feet. 'But the smell's not good.'

'Indeed not,' said his new companion, 'nor is it pleasant to witness the life-force drain from a body, even one so unclean as the pig.'

'Nothing wrong with pigs,' Philbert said, hard and sure in his new bravery. 'They're very clean animals, if left to themselves.'

'Of their flesh you shall not eat, and their carcasses you shall not touch,' intoned his interlocutor. 'You wouldn't eat your pig if you had one, would you, boy?'

Philbert shuddered, and agreed he most definitely would not. He could tell from the man's get up that he was a Rabbi, just like Ridente, presumably here to oversee the slaughtering, elect from whom he would advise his congregation to buy their meat in the upcoming days. Not too far away was Groben, pigs unsettled and nervous. He yanked one up from its tether and got it between his legs to steady it, but it was too frightened to obey. It struggled and kicked, squealing horribly as Groben whacked it several times with a stick on the side of its head, panting hard, thick arms bulging, neck pulsing, legs astride the animal as it dropped. He let go the stick, stuck a knife into the creature's throat, the gut-wrenching screams rising up terrible in the night. Enough for Philbert, who moved to intervene no matter the consequences, but down came the Rabbi's hand on his shoulder like a sack of stones, keeping him still as Groben fought to slice his blunt blade through the struggling, squealing skin, the pig pushing and rearing until Groben cursed, grabbed at the tether and wrapped it hard about the animal's neck, pulling it tighter and tighter about its half-sliced throat until it choked, grunted and lay still. Groben breathed hard, stabbing his knife into the ground, taking a rest before he went at the next one, casting his shadow over the last two terrified, stamping, huffing, squealing pigs awaiting their turn. Groben went to stand, then took a single step to the side, a spasm arcing through his body as he dropped his knife, stood still, silhouetted against the light of the many fires and lamps lit on the slaughtering ground, then down he went, slumping into the hurdles, knocking the tethers from the iron spike in the ground, releasing the pigs who went running, running, a small ripple of confusion as they made their way into the night.

'A good escape,' the Rabbi commented as if he'd been expecting it. 'That man was not worthy to remain in the bundle of his life, his heart torn in two within him. He took blood badly, and now the blood has taken him.'

The Rabbi released Philbert but he didn't leave immediately. He was still absorbing the fact that Groben had presumably had a heart attack, wondering vaguely if he should go for help. Not that the Rabbi seemed bothered.

'Death is forever breaking upon the shores of our lives and can never be stopped.'

Philbert thought about that as he saw the small-bearded Fager running up to the prostrate form of Nicolas Groben. He raised one hand as if about to sound the alarm, before lowering it again. He looked around him but no one was paying attention. He cast his eyes once up the bank but couldn't have seen Philbert and the Rabbi in the dark, nor Philbert's smile as Fager gently lifted the small dead pig and carried it away, Nicolas Groben lying dying, blowing weakly through the mud and blood about his mouth and nose, small bubbles pushing once, twice, thrice, then burst and were no more.

32

Give a Man Luck, then Throw him into the Sea

Philbert had nightmares: a multitude of red Kroonks wading in a sea of blood, Groben laughing, hauling them in with a monstrous hook the size of Philbert's crooked arm. He kicked himself awake, throat thick with panic, skin covered in sweat. The draggled curtain was pulled back suddenly from their cobbled-together tent and Kwert appeared, cheerful as the streaming sun.

'Good news!' Kwert was saying merrily. 'Time to rise, Little Maus, I have the most excellent news!' He passed over a bowl of cold water so Philbert could wash his face and hands. 'Eat!' Kwert commanded, pointing to fresh baked rolls, thick yellow butter beginning to melt beside them. 'While you've been snoring your big head off I've been plying my trade, as has Zehenspitze, and between the two of us we've found us a ride to the north!' Kwert creaked on his heels, and Philbert swallowed quickly at the news, choking on the hot bread, Kwert bashing him on the back without sympathy, impatient at the interruption, whilst he continued to speak.

'We'll be riding in style, in a carriage with a certain gentleman who calls himself Il Conte Umberto Petitorri,' Kwert announced.

'Called who?' Philbert answered, tightening his breeks about his waist.

'Umberto Petitorri,' Kwert replied. 'A Cercatore di Meraviglie – a Seeker of Wonders – travelling around the continent gasping at this and that.' There was a slight overtone of disgust to his voice as he spoke these last words, but not the next. 'And just as well for us, I might add, for he's very anxious to meet you, Little Maus. You and your marvellous head. And we don't have much time – we must pack up immediately.'

This last Philbert understood well enough, and was happy for it. During his previous afternoon's wanderings he'd caught sight of several fliers about the *Murderers of Lengerrborn*. The descriptions were vague – red-robed monk, boy with big head and hat – but enough for anyone to work it out if they knew Philbert and Kwert. He was eager to be gone, disgusted with himself for sleeping so long – despite it being his first proper night's sleep in weeks. Kwert and Zehenspitze had been busy and, through their network of contacts, discovered Maulwerf was heading away from his usual patch, going instead up towards the neck of Schleswig-Holstein, where the land was being tugged apart by the Danes from one side and the Prussians from the other, and apparently in sore need of amusement. The turning up of Il Conte and his offer had been the icing on the cake.

Kwert was already starting to roll their blankets and tie them with cord, stow their few possessions into a bag while Philbert dressed.

'I got a good price for the donkey,' Kwert said, thanking heaven for Brother Langer and his generosity.

Philbert poked at a small place on the base of his foot where a thorn had lodged a couple of weeks before and not yet come out.

'And you think we can trust this Godsend?' he asked casually, Kwert looking over in surprise.

'Well he can't know us,' Kwert said. 'We only got here last night, and by pure chance he came upon us this morning.'

'I suppose,' Philbert agreed. 'And it's a way out.'

Zehenspitze bustled up to make his goodbyes, hugging Kwert, gifting him a pair of new crutches.

'He's an odd one, that boy.' Zehenspitze nodded at Philbert as he began shifting their gear up the way, giving the old friends some privacy. 'Fire and ice in him now, after what he's done. And that, Kwert, can go either way. Just keep an eye out, is all I'm saying. Take care, old friend, until we meet again.'

33

Peacocks and Deep Wells

Kwert and Philbert got to the arranged meeting place on the easterly bridge as it passed over the Weser. Petitorri's carriage was luxurious, lined with red and gold brocade, driven up front by a large-boned, morose lad several years Philbert's elder, and it was this servant, Goffaggino, who found his master's new monkeys dawdling nervously by the bridge, looking around them, hoping the midday appointment hadn't been forgotten. He checked that they were the expected passengers, held open the carriage doors and almost pitched them in alongside their baggage before slamming the doors closed again, informing them that Petitorri was already walking on ahead. Kwert and Philbert exchanged glances, but nothing could take the bright edge off their day.

The carriage swayed alarmingly as Goffaggino hauled himself into his seat but a moment later they were trotting over the bridge like gentlemen, gazing out of the open-sided carriage as the river passed below, watching people clear the way deferentially as they went. They clopped their way through the last of Bremen town, saying goodbye to the point-gabled houses, the spires and the sheep. It was a glorious day, so fresh the air nipped their noses, the sky so clear they could see the land for miles and miles beyond the buildings, and the cloud-pale face of the moon as it dipped towards the west.

They were well on their way out of the city when Goffaggino called out to his passengers:

'That's Il Conte up ahead – the one with the blue stockings.'

They heard him chucking the twin-yoked horses on and craned their necks out of their respective windows the better to seek their patron. He wasn't difficult to spot, and Philbert could hear Kwert chuckling even with his neck out on a stalk and his ribs in tatters. To say the man's stockings were blue was an understatement – they howled out their blueness, they were bluer than the blue sky above them, a turquoise so bright they would have made a kingfisher covetous. And, as he walked, the silk of his blue stockings rippled gently, creases catching the sun like mirrors. His jacket was no less remarkable, its velvet being a deep-blushed scarlet, not unlike the colour of Kwert's erstwhile habit, but so plush it could take a man's finger in up to its second joint. He was a gaily coloured boat bobbing down a stream; heads turned, skirts swept out of his way, men gazed after him open-mouthed, small children ran behind him imitating his undeniable waddle of a walk and the way he twisted his cane around and around in his hand as he went. He was short and well-made, shoulders wide, legs slightly bowed beneath his weight.

'Have you ever seen a peacock, Little Maus?' asked Kwert, 'because if you haven't, look on.'

They both withdrew their heads as the carriage came alongside and kept pace with Petitorri, Goffaggino calling out loudly:

'Will it suit you to get in now, Sire?'

Petitorri turned his head, face shining like a pomegranate beneath a lime-green hat that resembled a squashed-up concertina.

'Ah, Goffaggino. What a morning! As my old nurse used to

say: *Il buon di si conosce dal mattino*: well begun is half done, and I do believe I've started my day just right and it can only get better.'

Goffaggino snorted, but Petitorri affected not to notice and carried on with his exceptional good humour. He puffed himself up, preening the white ruff on his breast and waddled alongside the carriage, thrusting his head in through the window as Goffaggino slowed the horses' pace.

'Aha! So we have managed to meet up with our new friends! I had worried the plan was too vague, but you are surely welcome.' His beetle-shiny eyes swivelled towards Philbert. 'Ah, amicóne, what a truly marvellous hat!'

Goffaggino stopped the carriage and jumped down to open the door for his master, who duly got in while Goffaggino rearranged himself back onto his driving seat, setting the carriage rocking dangerously for the few moments the two of them got comfortable, Petitorri mincing his pointed feet around the mound of his guests' baggage, sighing theatrically, a strong waft of scented violets permeating the air.

'Ah!' he patted himself down and set his stick between his legs, leaning on it with both his hands. 'What a morning! What a pleasure! What a delight to sit down in the company of new friends.' He took a small lace handkerchief from his pocket and dabbed at his temples before extending a plump, purple-gloved hand to Kwert. 'Herr Kwert, I'm sorry our talk this morning was so brief, but today we shall make amends, yes?' Kwert nodded graciously, but Petitorri hadn't finished. 'So many sights I've seen,' said the Count. 'So many fairs have I visited, and yet this is the first time I've had real live carnival characters in my carriage.'

Kwert nudged Philbert and Philbert, on cue, removed his hat, feeling like a Lengerrborn cat-slice in a jar.

'Ah, *caro ragazzo*! Can it be true?' the Count leaned forward and poked a bejewelled finger at Philbert's head, squeaking with delight. 'Sweet Mary, Mother of Angels! What a lucky man I am. I go around the world with my Goffaggino, seeking out wonders and miracles. I've seen Napoleon's Arc de Triomphe in Paris, taken the steam railway from Nürnberg to Fürth, visited the Great Mosque at Cordova. And yet here today the marvels have come to me.'

Petitorri smiled, lips drawn back over small white teeth separated top-middle by a tidy gap that might have been made for firing out melon pips. It seemed a propitious moment for Kwert to bring out a bottle of cherry brandy. Petitorri accepted a generous glug in a silver goblet he produced from a box table – not that it stopped him talking, which seemed to come as natural to him as breathing.

'Twice I've toured Europe since leaving Italy with my half-wit servant Goffaggino.' The carriage lurched as he spoke and Petitorri shouted curses in several languages. 'He dropped me down a well once. Near broke my buttock-bone in two, but I've a special interest in the subterranean. Sewerage systems are the only way forward for civilisation. The towns I have been where the filth is piled and poured into the streets! It is enough to make one slice off one's nose.'

This statement brought Hochwürden and Hermann to mind, Philbert switching his gaze from the chattering peacock to the outside world, following the sun as it smoothed its way across the sky, watching the rosebay and meadowsweet sway on their stems in the ditches by the lanes they were travelling, the moon fading to invisibility as they passed the day by. It was evening when they alighted at an inn, and when Petitorri tucked into his veal and mutton pie he stopped talking long enough for Kwert to put in a few words.

'We really are immensely grateful for your help,' he said, Petitorri waving a hand with largesse, his mouth full of pastry crust. 'And I gather from what you said back in Bremen that you once met Doctor Ullendorf?'

293

Petitorri nodded his head, eyes bright as a blackbird's. Philbert stopped eating, unnerved by this new revelation Kwert had omitted to mention. He didn't like this strange magpie of a man who filled his hours with anecdotes, going hither and thither, without reaching any obvious endpoint.

'Ah yes, Doctor Ullendorf,' Petitorri sighed, having cleared his plate before the rest of them were halfway through. 'I'd heard of his unusual anatomical collection and sought him out only last year at his home.' He lowered his voice to a whisper. 'And to think he took me to that Westphal Club,' he shivered theatrically. 'What a disaster! I don't suppose you've heard, you being on your travels and all, but Ullendorf is dead – shot to pieces. The militia raided that Westphal Club in Lengerrborn a month or so back, having tailed one of those anarchist revolutionaries there on the personal orders of Metternich himself. Von Ebner he was called, the place packed wall to wall with his followers and no better time to strike. What a scandal!' He shook his head. 'Such a pity because – despite his politics – Von Ebner was a great scientist, God rest his soul.' Petitorri crossed himself, and bowed his head. 'Had an intellect you are unlikely to meet twice in a lifetime, and a singular cruelty, to my mind, that he was there to meet Ullendorf – two great minds were crushed by the stone intended only for one.'

A large peach cobbler arrived at that moment, slapped onto the table courtesy of Goffaggino, who'd sat apart all this while, followed immediately by a splatter of custard from the accompanying jug. Petitorri frowned, waiting until his manservant had removed himself again to his own table and the jug of beer he poured freely into a tankard, before going on, Kwert and Philbert uncomfortable at the turn of the conversation, hanging on every word as they'd not done before.

'Von Ebner,' Petitorri continued in the same conspiratorial

294

vein, 'was only there because he'd been invited to Lengerrborn to view Ullendorf's latest wunderkind.'

Kwert fumbled his fork around his plate, failing to prevent the escape of several peas, Petitorri observing without interest as said peas rolled from Kwert's plate to the rickety table and then to the floor. He chose that moment to lean back in his chair and look from Kwert to Philbert and then back again. None of the concerned whisper about him now, nothing but the blank-eyed stare of a bull about to gore a man right through his belly, words picked and precise, chilling Kwert and Philbert to the bone.

'Poor Ullendorf,' Petitorri said, 'obsessed by lumps and bumps, always on the lookout for the next exhibit to slice and dice. He would have loved you, my boy,' gimlet eyes on Philbert and his hat. 'Probably would have chopped off your head and had it pickled soon as he could sneeze – if he wasn't so principled. But I, Philbert, can think of many collectors who do not possess such a strong sense of right and wrong as Ullendorf.'

He dolloped peach cobbler onto his plate, liberal with the custard, Kwert abandoning his fork, Philbert sitting still and tight, both realising that God had not been so good to them as they'd previously supposed.

'It was murderous what the militia did that night,' Petitorri went on, as if in casual dinner conversation, 'and what they did afterwards to the prisoners marched off to the fort. But nothing short of what they deserved.'

He raised his goblet in a cheer, not that Philbert or Kwert raised their own in kind.

'Have we not,' Kwert started hesitantly, 'heard enough of death and disaster? Why not let me tell of the sights you'll see once we reach Maulwerf's Fair of Wonders . . .'

Petitorri blinked slowly and yawned.

'Not now, Kwert. I'm tired and I'm bored and I need a nap. Take advantage. Goffaggino will hie us up when he's got the carriage ready for the next leg. It'll be a good half hour yet. Still a couple hours daylight, but got to rest the horses.'

He finished the last of his wine in one, rolled up his cape for a pillow, lay down on the bench and went instantly to sleep. He looked like a cherub, round cheeks spotted with two bright embers of red, the colours of his costume rustling slightly like a wrinkled rainbow, a soft smile on his face, hands tucked beneath his rounded chin. Kwert, on the other side of the table, slumped in his seat, all the health he had recouped seeming faded, skin sagging, heart beating low and slack, on the verge of giving up altogether. Petitorri's words had hit their mark and he was deflated. Not so Philbert. He understood they were a hair's breadth away from being betrayed, that the garrulous peacock knew all about Ullendorf and Lengerrborn and had fitted the pieces together. He didn't know exactly how, though perhaps Petitorri had been one of the gentlemen invited to the Westphal that night and had leaked the information that set the militia on Von Ebner's trail. Whatever the details, it didn't matter now. They just needed to get away.

He slid off his chair, telling Kwert he was going to check on Goffaggino's progress, see if there was something he could do to help. 'Stay here,' Philbert said.

Kwert nodded feebly, not looking up as Philbert stepped through the dirty sawdust and out the back door into the court-yard. He saw Goffaggino leaning over the crude railings separating one man's horses from the next, his heart quickening as an idea began to grow like a mushroom inside his capacious head.

'Goffaggino,' Philbert said, and Goffaggino turned, and now that Philbert was looking him straight up and down he could see he was younger than he'd first appeared, his large frame and stooped shoulders suggesting otherwise.

'The monkey-head,' Goffaggino spat out of the corner of his mouth, the moniker plainly amusing him.

Philbert played along. 'Funny, Goffaggino. But have you ever seen a monkey with gold?'

'Sure I have,' Goffaggino answered after a moment. 'Old money-pants in there has it in spades.'

'But did you ever touch it – as your own?' Philbert persisted, his great idea faltering as Goffaggino carried on looking at the horses and didn't reply. 'You ever want to get away from old money-pants?' Philbert asked, but again Goffaggino said nothing.

'He wants to sell me to a museum,' Philbert went on doggedly. 'Chop off my head and hawk it to the highest bidder. I'm the Anatomist's Dream, did you know? That's what they call me.'

It was a lie, but it did not seem so outrageous, not after his experiences with Ullendorf and Zehenspitze and what Petitorri had implied. Philbert walked slowly across the yard towards Goffaggino, acutely aware he didn't have much time, knowing he must play his hand right and sure.

'See this?' Philbert asked, taking out Hermann's ring that glinted like a new-born moon on its leather thong. 'You want it?' Philbert asked, seeing a sliver of interest in Goffaggino's eyes. 'It's worth a lot of money. Very valuable. Far older than you or me.'

Philbert moved closer. Goffaggino's hand twitched on the horse's bridle and Philbert saw it.

'If you get those horses hitched to the carriage and out the back, me and Kwert could meet you in five minutes. You could take us a couple of miles along the track and then we'll ditch the carriage, take the horses and be gone. In return I'll give you this ring. You can say we held you up, put a knife to your throat.'

His own throat was dry as dust, but he managed to go on. 'We'll tie you up if you like, make it look like we took the horses by force, that you tried to fight us off, safeguarded the greater part of your master's things. You'll be a hero. And you'll have the ring and the pick of whatever Petitorri has in his carriage, for you can always say we took it with us.'

It was a huge chance Philbert was taking, and he'd no notion how it would go if his plan succeeded but he had to do something, and this was all he'd got. Goffaggino licked his lips, and agreed.

'Two minutes,' he said. Philbert turned and ran across the cobbles, back through the door of the inn, surprised to see Kwert already on his feet, moving towards him, heading for the latrine. Philbert crooked his arm and waved Kwert on, holding his finger to his lips, and without a sound Kwert stalked the short way down the tavern bar, pausing only for a moment as he handed a coin to the bar-keep, saying a word or two before coming on.

'No time to talk,' Philbert said, clutching at Kwert's hand the second he came within reach. 'Come on!'

And on they went, moving fast as Kwert was able, past the stinking shack of the latrine and its piss-trough, the hole dug in the ground where men could squat and squeeze. Goffaggino was already a-perch his driver's seat, the horses in their traces, the long tail of Goffaggino's whip whispering above their backs.

'Get in,' Philbert commanded Kwert, and before they'd even settled the carriage was off, clearing the corner of the inn and into the copse beyond, Goffaggino slapping his whip against the horses' sides, urging them on, the switch of tree branches scratching at the carriage's paint as it cut quick and fast between them. Five minutes forward, and then ten, as Philbert garbled his plan to Kwert as they fell from one side of the carriage to the next. He knew that at any minute Goffaggino would stop the horses. They had a slender chance if they could blend their way into the bushes and scrub that lined the meagre track, be gone by the time someone came looking for Goffaggino.

They stopped. And then Goffaggino's face was at the door as he pulled it open roughly and in a flash he had Philbert by his collar and was dragging him out.

'Did you really think I could be bought so easy?' Goffaggino panted, hard-done from the ride, hand so strong about Philbert's collar he was finding it hard to breathe.

'Did you really think we didn't know what you were worth?'

And then Goffaggino had Philbert right out of the carriage and was dragging him on through the mud.

'This was always the plan anyways,' Goffaggino forced the words out between clenched teeth. 'Maestro knew who you were the moment he clapped eyes on you, and stands to make a pretty fortune selling you both on – one to the head-doctors, the other to the soldiers. Big payday for the supplier of the Murderer of Lengerrborn.'

Philbert struggled, squirmed and fought, but Goffaggino's rough hand was twisting his collar tight and all he could hear was the whooshing of his blood and the croak of Goffaggino's voice directly in his ear.

'But you're right about me wanting a little something for myself,' he said, 'so thanks for setting it all up so nice and orderly. I'll take that ring and be more than glad to beat the pulp out of you, be that hero you mentioned. No one will mind you being just this side of dead before delivery.' Goffaggino hit Philbert hard across the face and they both went down. 'Might even prefer it that way,' he grunted, 'save Maestro the trouble of doing you in.' Goffaggino's knee was pressing hard into Philbert's chest, knees astride him, holding him fast. 'Maestro saw this coming,' Goffaggino panted. 'Told me to take the chance when it came, and so I will.'

Goffaggino ripped the thong from Philbert's neck, scooping Hermann's ring into his hand, Otto's nail from the Wagoners slipping from its loose end, Philbert's fingers scrabbling for it as

Goffaggino was momentarily distracted by the ring; he fetched it up, fixed it between forefinger and thumb and plunged the nail with all his strength into Goffaggino's left eye. Goffaggino screamed, rolling off Philbert into the mud and Philbert picked up the nearest hard object to hand – a three sided granite rock – and hammered it at Goffaggino's head as if he was beating a shoe on Otto's anvil, hearing Otto's gruff voice telling him to mind his fingers, mark the sidings, lean his hand into the swing. Again and again that stone came down on Goffaggino's head, Philbert looking right into his eyes – the blooded one and the good – first hit going lucky, second cracking Goffaggino's skull just above the ear, third one sending streams of blood onto his face, and still Philbert went on, each blow coming easier and a little stronger, his body alive with the power that comes from rage and the fight to survive.

It was only when Philbert saw the small flash of gold in the mud beside Goffaggino's fallen hand that he stopped, his heart beginning to subside into normal rhythm, and he heard the late afternoon birds singing on unperturbed in the trees, felt his knee slipping in the mud churned up by their struggle, hand grazed by the stone and slippery with the inside of Goffaggino's head, the red warmth of it creeping up his sleeve almost to his elbow. He dropped the stone and looked up. Kwert was standing a few yards away, yelling as he had been yelling since the ten or so seconds of Philbert's murderous attack.

'Oh my God, Little Maus! What are you doing? Oh stop, you have to stop! Oh my God, what have you done?'

Goffaggino was dead, no doubting it, face no longer distinguishable, a mere mix of gore, cartilage and flesh.

'Don't ever call me that again,' Philbert growled through clenched teeth, face and clothes splattered with Goffaggino's blood, 'the Little Maus is gone and is never coming back.'

The blood drained from Kwert's face. Looking at Philbert he

knew it was true, and wondered just how long ago it had happened, and who or what had risen up to take his place.

34

Strike to the Core

'We have to go,' Philbert said, grabbing the thong from the mud, putting the ring back on and tying it about his neck with an untidy knot. He fetched up a load of old boughs and bramble runners, piling them over Goffaggino's body, kicking on dead leaves to cover the gaps. Next, he went to the coach and undid one of the horses, gave Kwert a leg up onto its broad sweating back before slapping the other hard with Goffaggino's whip so that it began a mad canter further on down the track, dragging the carriage lopsidedly behind it. Philbert jumped up in front of Kwert, still clutching the whip, and forced the horse into the trees, the two of them ducking beneath the low branches of alders and oaks, birch and beech, Kwert shaking with awful apprehension, expecting capture at every turn. But none came, and on they went until it became too dark to see their way, when they slipped from their mount and Philbert lashed its flanks with the whip, sending it careering off blindly into the night.

Not a word had they spoken, and now they leant themselves against the bole of a wide oak, Philbert dragging the leaves all around to give themselves some warmth. There were no stars nor any sight of the moon, only a low swirling sort of mist that covered them completely, damping them to the skin. Goffaggino had done them a favour by riding on much further than Philbert had intended, and there could be no question of a search until morning came, by which time the horse and carriage must have gone a good way distant before eventually grinding to a stop or tipping over into the drainage ditch beside the track. With any luck, some impoverished passer-by would find it and loot its goods and chattels, all Petitorri's baggage already being on board, and if they did that they would no doubt destroy the cart and use it for firewood, sell on the horse or, more probably, butcher it for its meat so no trace of either could be found by anyone who came looking. Goffaggino had further aided their escape by dragging Philbert some yards from the track so that his body could not easily be seen by someone riding by, disguised as it was, even if they were looking for a dead body and not the wreck of Petitorri's stolen carriage.

Neither could sleep, both looking blindly into the darkness, until eventually Kwert spoke.

'What happened, Philbert?'

Only the rustling of leaves answered Kwert as Philbert shifted slightly at his side, a long pause before Philbert replied.

'The world happened,' he said simply, and those three words said it all. He'd been waiting for this moment, this confrontation; had seen the look of accusation and approbation in Kwert's eyes when he stood useless above his Little Maus as he beat another boy to death – never mind that Goffaggino had been planning to do exactly the same to him. He'd been having the anticipated conversation over and over in his head. *What did you expect?* he'd been planning to say. *You're always going on about my destiny, how I'm to do great things, but I wouldn't have been able to do any of them if Petitorri had his way. And you'd have been sold out as the Murderer of Lengerrborn. Ever think on that?* But when the time came the words had lost their meaning, Philbert's anger spent; all that mattered was the simple fact that what was done was done, and there was nothing anyone could do about it.

Kwert knew it too, and in the darkness the tears ran down his cheeks for the man he had become, weak and sick, entirely dependent upon this boy who lay beside him in the leaves; the boy who had killed in order not to be killed himself and who, by doing so, had saved Kwert not once but twice. And he cried because he was a man who truly believed in destiny, and was heartsick at what that destiny had become. The first time he'd seen the boy he'd had such a strong conviction that great things were in store for him that it never crossed his mind great things are not always for the good; cried too because he knew he'd sought the boy out and, had he not, then he'd most probably have carried on being that quiet Little Maus who toured with Maulwerf's Fair of Wonders, no greater burden to bear than his head, however big that head might be. All gone now. They'd been fugitives from the law before tonight, and now were doubly so.

Great things, Kwert thought bitterly. His meditative way of life was all about silent prayer, dedication to the Christ-child who dwells inside the heart of every man if only he can block out the world enough to find him there. But there was nothing great about the way things had gone this last while. Philbert was right. The world had happened to them both in ways entirely unforeseen even to the Kwert, the Great Tospirologist. No more lifting of the veil between past, present and future, not for Kwert. All he could do now was wait for the world to happen to them again and he no longer looked forward to it, felt only the cold chill of it as it crept inexorably on.

~

They spoke little during their next travelling, going as long and far as they could with each day, taking their bearings from the stars at night, pointing them always on towards the north, towards where they hoped they would find Maulwerf and his

Fair. Philbert knew Kwert was finding the going hard and tried not to show the impatience the young and healthy always have for the old and sick. He wasn't troubled by Kwert's withdrawal from him, had no need of talking any more than Kwert had. They'd been cast into an aloneness neither felt able or eager to broach; it diminished Kwert and caused him guilt, but to Philbert it gave strength, the heady realisation he could be instrumental in the way his life might go. He pushed Kwert on through bushes and forests, resting as often as Kwert needed. At night there was no companionable sitting around a fire, for there was no fire at all, both wanting to remain away from the eyes and company of other men. They didn't read from the *Philocalia*, they ate handfuls of the berries, nuts and roots Philbert procured on their way. They became thin or, in Kwert's case, even thinner, his teeth wobbling and loosening in his gums, arms so weak they could hardly support him on his crutches, at which point Philbert called a stop. He took out his tinder and struck it against some bracket mushrooms and made a fire. He also laid some traps, and eventually snared a squirrel and got it skinned and spitted, and the scent of the apple boughs they were burning on the fire was the sweetest thing either had smelled for many weeks.

'There's a village about a half mile up through the trees,' Philbert said, 'I can hear their cattle in their pens. I'm going to leave you a while, see if I can find out exactly where we are.'

'Are you sure it's safe?' Kwert said, before realising how ridiculous those words of caution were. They'd been travelling for a couple of weeks since Goffagino's murder, passing through what had seemed an interminable forest before going over hill and dale and back into forest again, always keeping away from tracks and villages, to which this was the closest they'd been so far, always taking the harder route that slowed them up but kept them hidden.

'I'm not sure it will ever be safe,' Philbert replied, 'not for us. But we can't go on hiding for ever.'

He left then, Kwert shivering despite the small fire, wondering if this was the last time he was ever going to see Philbert, if he'd finally taken the decision to abandon the old man who was the thorn in his side, slowing him up at every turn.

They'd fought silently through their respective days, both knowing someone would eventually find Goffaggino's body, the remains of Petitorri's carriage or the horses they'd sent off through the woods. And both understood Petitorri was a vengeful man. Folk might blame the bandits who supposedly roamed these woods like wolves, but they knew Petitorri would have scotched such theories at the start, shouting out to anyone who would listen that he'd had in his hands the fugitive Schupo murderers, and now they'd murdered again. What worried Philbert more was that Kwert had spoken so freely to Petitorri of their trying to reunite with Maulwerf and his Fair of Wonders. There was money on their heads, and by getting themselves back to Maulwerf they might be bringing trouble with them. He hoped it would not be so, that if they went by a circuitous enough route and hid their tracks it would not happen. He needed an aim, and the only one he had was to get back to the Fair, see Little Lita, Maulwerf and Kroonk, always Kroonk, his childhood companion – the only reminder of his childhood he had left. She was only a pig, but was a pig to him as others had a faithful hunting dog, and he hankered after her unqualified devotion and affection more than he could say. And he needed someone better than himself to take care of Kwert, and because of it would travel and tramp until they found Maulwerf. What would come then would come, which would most probably be nothing. He understood he'd done things Maulwerf and Lita would not understand, but would have no reason to tell them, neither more would Kwert. And he owed Kwert a way home, for Kwert had nurtured and looked after him, taken him out into the world and, no matter what had happened once he'd got there, by God he was glad he had. And for all these reasons he needed to break cover, for Kwert couldn't go on much longer the way they were going. He needed care and comfort; all the fire and vitality Kwert had once displayed had gone and Philbert wanted to see it back, needed to restore him to the fold. Philbert had changed, Philbert had grown, but at his core Little Maus still resided, and he yearned for the familiar as much as Kwert did, and for both that meant returning to Maulwerf's Fair.

35

The Sylvean Aqueduct

Philbert followed the course of a stream running from their camp towards a mill, and from the mill onwards to the village. Once there Philbert lurked and listened, mostly to a group of old men who were sat gossiping on logs of varying sizes carved into chairs, this being the village pub, such as it was. From this he learned several very interesting facts, the first of which was that they were on the right track. Just as they'd hoped, they'd managed to completely circumnavigate Hamburg, and therefore any news of them that might well have reached that city. He also learned that the beck he'd followed was one of the many tributaries feeding into the vast river of the Elbe; also that the prevalent topic of conversation was nothing to do with murders or fugitives but centred on something called Magendie's Aqueduct, the Grand Opening of which was due to take place a few days hence. Philbert absorbed this piece of information with great interest, for it transpired that a large proportion of this village had left earlier that morning in order to get to this Opening that was to be a very great affair, with carnivals and hooplahs by the dozen, and would be the most exciting spectacle any of them would ever see.

Enough information for Philbert, for what better place to

find news of Maulwerf than where fairs' folk of every stripe would be gathering? And it wasn't going to be hard to find. Philbert returned to Kwert, to Kwert's immense relief, and the following morning, as soon as it was light enough to see, they followed the stream down to the ford on the other side of the village. Philbert could see immediately that a great many people had trod the path alongside the stream, and followed it too, right down to the banks of the Elbe where they arrived two days later. Once there, it was no effort to be unobtrusive; crowds of people thronged the Elbe's sides, eager to cross the water and get to the other side in time for the Grand Opening, which seemed to be all that anyone could talk about. Exactly what this Opening was Philbert neither queried nor cared. He shouldered his way with the best of them onto one of the many paddle-steamers, boats and fishing skiffs queuing up to take people to the other side. The one that took them over landed them just to the east of Brunsbüttelkoog and, as the stream of sightseers began to trail off up the track, Philbert and Kwert mingled in with the crowd. According to the chatter of the folk about them they still had a way to go, all heading north, some-what by Rendsburg but before Kropp, not too far from the Sorge River.

Philbert was decidedly curious now about this marvellous aqueduct, apparently built of wood and stone and spanning a fissure through which had once run a torrent of blood. This last detail hardly seemed credible, and the tales being told about the engineer who had built the aqueduct even less likely. He smiled as he listened to the bits and pieces of the story, recognising patter when he heard it, surmising that the fairs' folk had been busy, sending out trackers to drop this anecdote or that here and there to elicit the greatest interest, bring forth the greatest possible number of attending crowds. And the story they'd engineered about the engineer amounted to this: he'd appeared out of nowhere as a migrant charcoaler, set up shop in the forests bounding the River Sorge and, before anyone knew it, discovered some rare metal – possibly gold, possibly tellurium, possibly both – and gone to the nearest town, bought up the mining rights for a song, everyone knowing nothing was to be had around these parts and that the man must be madder than a hen in a thunderstorm to spend good money on mining rights worth less than the paper they were written on. Except that the man struck it rich; still mad, no doubting that, for what he chose to do with the greater part of his new-found wealth was to build an aqueduct right across the valley, linking two lands, two villages, two rivers, and it was to the opening of this great aqueduct that everyone was now hurrying to see.

Philbert didn't know what day it was, but knew the month to be June because the lime blossom was out and abundant, filling the air with its sweet scent; also that it was close to midsummer, the days stretching their necks further into the shortening darkness of every night that passed. Kwert was struggling, his back crooked over his crutches as they travelled the last few miles, breath shallow and erratic as they tailed the crowds up a short rise away from the track. It was late in the evening but the darkness was little more than shadow, people swinging out like hammocks onto the crest of the hill, whispering excitedly, their lamps pock-marking the brief night, for Philbert had been right. Tomorrow was the summer solstice, longest day of the year.

'You're tired,' Philbert said. 'Why not try to rest up and get some sleep?'

Kwert took his advice and lay down on his blanket, Philbert easing his crutches away, taking off his coat to cover him. It was a meagre bed, but Kwert was grateful for it. He was so thin now that it was hard for him to be warm even here on this crowded hillside where people were lighting fires, chattering excitedly, exuding heat with every breath.

'Thank you,' Kwert murmured, placing his hands beneath his head for a pillow, feeling easy for the first time in several months, happy to be surrounded by other people, one amongst the many, a single pip inside a many-seeded pomegranate, thinking that perhaps things might yet work out well, especially when Philbert lay down beside him, donating his warmth. Within moments the two travellers were fast asleep, unhindered by the chatter of unknown men and women all around them, sleeping all the better because of it. Anonymous, unknown and unrecognised.

~

They were woken by the growing rustle of expectation amongst the crowd, opening their eyes just as the sun slipped up sleek and fat from the waters of the distant Baltic Sea. Everyone was surging up and forward to the crest of the hill Kwert and Philbert already inhabited, pushing and jostling, craning necks for their own look towards the valley opposite. There was a sudden, collective intake of breath as all took in what was spread out before them: the great canvas of land unrolling at their feet, its colours deep and yawning in the pink glow of the new born sun; a hard ravine cleft the hillside ahead in two, dark and vast, hidden in shadow, ripples of forest running out around the lip of a perfectly circular reservoir on the higher side of the drop, a great wall protecting it like a hand braced about its chin; the shorter, closer side of the ravine was carved into great steps, each cupping a small lake shining like polished agate, the green of their surrounding woods glimmering in a thin mist, water-falls tipping from one step to the one below in a silver chain. And across the ravine stretched the aqueduct: magnificent, with its red sandstone chinked with gold in the morning light, the legs of its three spans unequal in length – lofty and tall on the far side, diminishing in height as they strode across the gap to reach the other. Each arch was carved as a branch, topped by a straight and even channel, giving the overall appearance of an enormous tree trunk falling by chance across the cleft, the straight conduit it carried leading from the higher reservoir to the lower lakes on the other side.

All shaded their eyes as the sun climbed the sky like a rope being pulled up a mast, spreading a sail of orange cloud across the horizon. There were murmurings behind Philbert, and the folk who were waiting with them, as more people arrived, but no jostling now, no discord, everyone spreading their blankets on the ground, inviting their fellows to sit so they wouldn't be troubled by the morning's dew. A few ale and food sellers began hawking their wares but their transactions were muted; everyone quiet, everyone waiting for the main event. As were Kwert and Philbert, until Philbert's hat was suddenly tweaked from his head by a scrawny hand and Philbert caught his breath, frightened for what would come, but when he turned all he saw was Tangelrichter – or was in Tingelburg? My God, but he didn't care, for marching up the hill behind came speckled Hannah in a fine patchwork dress into which she'd sewn all the many squares cut from Hermann's shirt, and Maulwerf mopping his brow, leaning heavily on his silver-topped cane, and Otto single-handedly hauling Frau Fettleheim on her cart as others pushed it on from behind, and running beside them all came Lita, tripping over a waddle of red pig, and Philbert forgot he'd become another person, that he'd murdered men and almost been murdered himself. He stood up, shouting like the devil.

'Kroonk! My wonderful Kroonk!' and Kroonk raised her startled head as Philbert began to jump up and down, waving his arms high, hat abandoned. And up they all came, Maulwerf pink and pert, jacket and waistcoat immaculately brushed as usual, lace kerchief dabbing daintily at his brow; Lita laughing and putting her small arms around Philbert's neck before moving on to Kwert; Otto standing back, breathing hard, red cheeks puffing, hands on hips, Frau Fettleheim gasping on her cart as if she'd run up the hill on her own two feet, fanning herself with a handful of enormous feathers; and then there was Kroonk, tripping and snorting between them all, bashing into Philbert's legs as if he were a skittle and she the ball, and he hugged her hard and hugged her again, kissed her neck and kissed her snout, and then they all desisted as everyone around them began to ooh and ah, and all looked down below into the valley whence came a roaring from the fissure as of a thundercloud as the sluice-gates were opened, water streaming from the circular silvered reservoir on the higher side of the ravine, a thin white arm of foam reaching out before it as it was funnelled along the aqueduct as if to lead it on, gushing headlong from the aqueduct's end into one pool, one waterfall, then down to the next and the next and the next. As one man they stood and stared, reunions forgotten as they watched in awe the sword-straight arm of water stretching along the length of the aqueduct, joining the disparate hillsides from high to low, from light to shade, in one continuous glide of motion. And then everyone about them was shouting and whooping, shaking hands with strangers, throwing their hats into the air, delighted to have been here, to be able to tell their children – and their children's children – that they'd been amongst the lucky few to see such a sight. They'd travelled many miles and many days to see the Grand Opening of the Great Magendie's Aqueduct and it did not disappoint. The spectacle may have lasted only minutes but for those there to witness it they would count those minutes amongst the greatest of their lives. Philbert was as astonished and delighted as the rest, but he shook no hands, his own clasped tightly about the red neck of Kroonk and not about to let go, not even once the excitement had died down and he heard the words he'd longed to hear falling like petals from Lita's lips: *Welcome home, Little Maus. Welcome home.*

He smiled, leaving the words of reciprocation to Kwert because he knew the greeting no longer applied. Little Maus was gone, and he could no longer call the Fair his home. At best he could stay with them temporarily, a few months maybe, but the reality of it was that Philbert could not stay forever. The ramifications of what he'd done – of what he'd caused to happen – were too great. He was no longer an inhabitant of their world, had gone to a place they could not and should not go. Philbert apart, great destiny or no, maybe always so, and more now than ever.

36

An Unexpected Coming Together

Tingelburg and Tangelrichter are dressed as bride and groom, Harlekin standing behind them, a stained glass window in his fine patchwork suit. He spreads his arms high and speaks to the gathered crowd:

'*Meine verehrten Damen und Herren*! *Hochgeehrte Versammlung*! We are gathered here today to witness the nuptials of Bräutlich and Bräutigan, to bind them hand and foot in lifelong union, for better or for worse. And here are the musicians . . .'

A loud shout of approval going up from the audience –

'. . . playing stampstok, rinkelbom and rummelpot . . .'

A shaking of tambourines and the beating of pig-bladder drums –

'. . . and their pretty dancers!'

Whistles and calls as Hannah and her friends do a quick two-step across the stage, flicking neatly turned petticoats and ankles.

'And of course, the bride and groom! Where would we be without them? Come forward, Bräutlich, come forward Bräutigan! Take my hands!'

Tingelburg and Tangelrichter make their way across the stage but find their chairs already taken, are reduced to grotesque clowns gesticulating rudely above the real couple's head, who are Lita and her Bowman Lorenzini, for this is the day of their wedding. Harlekin hands them the knotted cloth containing three silver coins, the symbol of marriage in these distant parts, and as they each take one side of the *knottedoek* the whole stage explodes with purple smoke and iridescent flares, and the musicians fire up with renewed vigour as Hannah and her dancers come on again, appearing through the fast-fading billows. Behind them all Philbert glimpses Harlekin standing in his cloak like a ribbon-plaited pole, then all is hidden again as the dancers throw out great clouds of rice from their bundled skirts, and sugared nuts rain down upon the crowd below the stage, and soon everyone is joining in the dancing and singing and the raisin brandy is brought out to wet the heads of bride and groom.

~

The marriage meal was enough to make the tables weep through their tight-knotted eyes, so hefty was the burden they had to bear. The Great Magendie was holding his own celebrations following the opening of his aqueduct, and the addition of a wedding banquet was an extra to be welcomed and fêted. Stall-holders and fair-ground shows added their wares to the trestles already set up beneath the orchard trees, legs secured in the cider-soaked grass, every square inch soon covered with pots and cauldrons, kettles and platters, flagons and kegs, everyone bringing their own contributions to the nuptials so that it was impossible to know where to begin. There was hotchpot of rabbit with juniper and jasmine, cow-heel fried and battered, cockscombs cooked with saffron rice and oil-fried rings of aubergine, sandwiches of rose-petals, of watercress and fresh curd cheese laced with lemon juice. There were sweetbreads grilled on skewers, wrapped in sorrel leaves, stuffed with garlic and snails; lambs' pie and ox-tail mould, marrow bone baked with apple. There was cloudberry jam and heather-flower puddings dribbled with blackberry and hippen-haw syrups. There was mustard bread and sesame buns and soft-set curds flavoured with fennel and pepper, hard-rind cheeses with black cherries, sprinkled with herbs, rolled in oats; napkin-butter and mousses of mocha, strawberry and quince.

And there was Philbert. He'd tried to act like a boy again, prowling the tables with Kroonk, taking a little bite of one thing followed by a smidgen of another, staining his shirt as he'd done with Kaspar in Finzeln with gravy medals of every imaginable colour and shade. But for Philbert it wasn't like it had been before at other feasts and celebrations, and the greasy smiles and friendly chatter did nothing but get on his nerves. It wasn't long before he took Kroonk off to lie together apart from the crowds under the shade of an old pear tree, Kroonk the familiar heavy comfort against Philbert's legs, the two of them happy and content to be back together; Philbert happy and content also that Lita had found her Bowman, for he was so obviously a kind man and a good one, always laughing and smiling and helping others, and had taken exceptionally good care of Kroonk while Philbert was away, just as he'd promised. He watched the whole happy tableaux but didn't want to take part in it. So much had happened in the months he'd been apart from Maulwerf's Fair, so much death breaking upon the shores of his life – as the Rabbi at the killing grounds in Bremen would have put it. Philbert felt as if he'd been shaken up and rearranged, and everyone else felt it too and kept their distance. Maulwerf had asked to see him earlier that afternoon and Philbert had dutifully gone, though it had been an awkward encounter.

'How have you been, my boy?' Maulwerf asked, Philbert not answering directly, which in itself surprised Maulwerf who remembered this child as honest and naïve almost to a fault, and certainly not evasive as he was being now.

'How much has Kwert told you?' Philbert replied with a touch of confrontation.

Maulwerf shook his head. 'Very little. But he is ill, as you must know, and isn't speaking much to anyone. It must have been very hard for you to get him this far.'

Maulwerf put his head to one side, the questions he wanted to ask hovering on his lips, like how the devil Kwert had got into the state he was in and what had happened that they neither of them wanted to talk about. And why had neither mentioned Ullendorf? And how had they wound up here at the very neck end of Prussia when it was the first time Maulwerf had brought his Fair here? Philbert volunteered no more than Kwert, saying only that Kwert had been ill for a while, that their stay with Ullendorf had not been a success, and with that Maulwerf had to be content. He looked the boy up and down as he left, trying to figure out what was different about him. Taller certainly, but not so much in height as in the way he carried himself. He had a confidence to his step, an aloofness that kept others at arm's length, including Maulwerf himself. Maulwerf was the Father of the Fair but he'd wondered, watching Philbert walk away, if he was any kind of father at all to this boy who seemed to have outgrown them all. He was worried. Uncertainty was part of the game Maulwerf had been playing for all his fifty years, but this uncertainty, this disparity between the boy who had left and the boy who had come back, and the unwillingness of Kwert to confide in him – in Maulwerf of all people – had him discomforted in the extreme.

～

Philbert sat beneath his pear tree that afternoon, seeing Lita and Lorenzini in the distance sitting on their cart-stoop like birds perched alone in a tree, the strong wing of Lorenzini's arm around Lita's shoulders, protecting her. It was so intimate a scene Philbert felt like he was spying, surprised when he was roused from the snooze he wasn't aware he'd fallen into by

Lorenzini himself. He presented Philbert with a stick he'd carved, with an impressive swirl of a handle, and Lorenzini proceeded to show Philbert all the tricks he'd taught Kroonk over the past few months: pushing balls through a miniature obstacle course with her snout, flipping them over jumps and through twig hoops; going onto her knees on command then lying down completely and rolling over, waggling her trotters in the air. Lorenzini was gratified to see Philbert smile at Kroonk's shenanigans, evidently pleased and proud of what she'd learned as he took the stick graciously from Lorenzini, asking if Lorenzini could spare the time over the next few days to go through all the commands with him until he had them fixed.

'But of course!' Lorenzini said with enthusiasm. 'And we have this too . . .'

He produced a green velvet vest Lita had tailored to size for Kroonk from a couple of Maulwerf's old waistcoats, sewn over with sequins and beads.

'I do love her, you know, Little Lita,' Lorenzini said, as if expecting Philbert to argue against it. 'She's the most perfect thing in all the world, and it's important to us both that we have your blessing.'

Philbert raised his eyebrows in surprise but did not hesitate in giving what was asked. 'I wish you both every blessing and happiness,' he replied with the same formality the request had been put to him.

'I don't think you need her anymore, Philbert. Not like I do. And I don't know what happened on your travels but I know travel changes people, and that it has changed you.' He shook his head, then shook Philbert's hand and bowed, Philbert bowing back. 'I'm not sure you need any of us anymore,' said Lorenzini as he turned to leave. 'But whatever life has in store for you, Philbert, be assured that wherever me and Lita are there is a place for you too, if ever you have need of it.'

～

The Aqueduct – Wedding feast lasted four whole days. People fell asleep mid-sentence, mid-mouthful, mid-dance, lying down where they fell. The nights were warm enough for everyone to sleep on capes and blankets spread out beneath trees and stars, listening to the water sleek-sloping down the aqueduct in its carved wooden channels, slooshing and paddling into its pools, rocking the small rafts folk made out of branches to launch onto the silvery lakes. The Great Magendie was the name on everyone's lips, constantly tattling about his strange history and this extraordinary creation they'd travelled so far to see. Everyone was eager to meet him, shake him by the hand, goggling at his magnificent achievement of civil engineering, but he never ventured from his home in all the time the hordes were there. What he did do though, to amuse himself, was invite into his company a select handful of guests every now and then, an honour folk would have killed for, eager as dammit, for just like the man who lived there his home was nothing of the ordinary.

It went by the name of *Der Spaltrostamm*, and Philbert was amongst the guests invited to attend on the last night of the feast. Whether the Great Magendie had been keeping the best until last was anybody's guess, but the company Philbert was called into was illustrious. Maulwerf was presenting some new additions to the Fair, including a woman whose hair was so long she had to push it in a barrow before her and a man who could speak twenty-six languages and chattered away in all of them, slipping from one to the next without warning; from Peru had come a bearded lady and an albino who made an odd couple indeed, even more so than Lorenzini and Lita who were also part of the crew. Philbert tagged along behind them like an afterthought at Maulwerf's bidding, approaching the house with the rest up a drive that was screened by tall beech hedges on either side whose trunks had been set close together as saplings so they grew into one another to make an impenetrable barrier, branches entwined and twisted as they fought for light and space. And it was no easy task to get to this mysterious house, *Der Spaltrostamm*, for the Great Magendie had built it right on the top of the lower ravine, reachable only by a complicated zigzag of steps up which the lady with her long hair had to haul her barrow, helped on by the others as they had breath, thanking God Frau Fettleheim hadn't been one of the favoured.

'Two hundred and seventy eight,' panted Maulwerf, as the small party gasped their way up the last leg. 'One for each week of the aqueduct's construction, so I've been told by those who have gone before.'

The language man spoke a sentence in a mixture of Dutch, Norwegian, Italian, Welsh and French that none of them understood directly but got the gist of its true interpretation: *The journey always takes longer than you think, but in so doing makes its goal all the more worthwhile.*

Once they'd finally reached their destination the door creaked open without their ringing the ostentatious bell that hung like an overgrown pine-cone from the eaves. They were led in by two moleskin-clad foot-boys, red hats wobbling on their heads, bunches of iridescent feathers strapped to their hatbands by blue ribbons. Petitorri would have loved it, Philbert thought, all that swank and swagger. He wondered briefly where that man was now, what lies or otherwise he was spreading, for men like Petitorri did not lie down and take defeat without at least some spit and stand. But no time to think on the peacock any longer, for the moment they were in the door Philbert realised he was inside one of the most extraordinary places he had ever seen.

The room was huge, undivided and dark, all made of wood, from the panelling on floor and walls to the sparse furniture, the centrepiece being a massive table lined with knot-backed chairs and laid up with food and wine. Two great fireplaces were lit at either end of what could only be described adequately as a hall, each banked and correctly fuelled so the flames were bright and the smoke directed to all the various foodstuffs hanging from hooks inside the five foot width of each ingle-nook: haunches of meat, bunches of herbs, strings of sausages, tack bread, hams, the carcasses of hares, squirrels and rabbits, several necklaces of yellowing mushrooms and peppers, the grey curl of an ox's tongue.

The Great Magendie himself was sat at the left hand side of the room, a vast chair hiding his withered frame like a walnut within its shell, rough-hewn boards heavy and dark, crudely cut with acorns and leaves as if they'd been chiselled by woods-men's children still practising their craft. The footsteps of his latest guests creaked on the floorboards as they crowded for-ward, ushered on by the red-hatted boys who introduced the visitors one by one, listing their various unusual attributes before urging them to sit at table and partake of what was there. And sit they did, and one by one were called forward by the hat-twirling boys to meet the Great Man himself, Maulwerf first, whose role was only to introduce the rest. The greatest surprise for Philbert was the couple from Peru. The so-called bearded lady was strange indeed, her face and arms felted over with long soft hair. The Great Magendie had her come to him, stroked her hair, asked her to show him her mouth, all of which she did, for apparently not only was she hairy all over her body but also had a second set of teeth set behind the first. None of this was so extraordinary to Philbert as when she returned from her examination and began to sing in her own language, the words unknown to any but herself and her husband and the man who understood twenty-six languages. But for Philbert it was utterly compelling, like streams running over moss, and he could have gone on listening to her for hours if her husband hadn't been summoned forward, at which point her singing ceased. He called himself the White Jester, an albino with a stock of jokes and anecdotes that would have made a stevedore blush. He took his place at the Great Magendie's feet, had his own face poked and prodded, his jokes ignored, a candle shone into his pink eyes before being summarily dismissed. In his place came the woman with all the hair pointing out the delicate intricacy of her braids, followed by Lita and Lorenzini doing a quick dance and turn, replaced – after a short silence from their host – by the language man, who didn't get farther than sixty seconds of his excellent routine before being repelled by a bored wave of the Great Magendie's hand. Philbert was the tail end of the exhibits, doomed – he'd already concluded – to be a huge disappointment after all the others had apparently failed to impress, completely aware that his paltry head was nothing in comparison. He came forward grudgingly, Maulwerf's hand at his back pushing him on.

'Does your hat never move, boy?' the Great Magendie's voice splintered through the air, the first words he'd spoken since they'd arrived. Philbert took off his hat and moved closer to the tiny wrinkle of a man in his huge chair so as to be seen properly. A few months earlier he would have been intimidated by the strange room, the unexpected interrogation, the hard blinks of small windows glittering malevolently behind the man holed up in his chair, but not now. Philbert's small body was taut and hard, his head no longer seeming to pull him to one side with its weight but feeling instead as if it was just right, part of the balance between himself and the world in which he lived.

'Well, my,' said the Great Magendie succinctly as he leaned forward to take his look. 'I can see why you wear a hat.'

Philbert didn't blink but stared back at the sunken eyes of his interlocutor, saw the light of the nearby fire reflected in them beneath their hoods like the splash of sunlight on wood-hidden pools.

'And what's your name, boy?' the Great Magendie asked.

'Philbert,' he replied, the man laughing fit to burst.

'Philbert! Oh but that's a good one!' he said once he'd calmed, poking hard at Philbert's taupe with his finger. 'And what do you keep inside your head, nut boy?'

Philbert took a breath. He didn't like the way he was being looked at, and absolutely loathed the way Magendie had treated the rest of the Fair's Folk as if they were dogs begging for scraps at his table. He didn't like the karking timbre of his voice and certainly not the scratch of the man's nail upon his taupe and, before he'd thought the action through, Philbert pushed the man's hand roughly away, replaced his hat firmly back down upon his head and moved his face nose to nose with the vile Magendie.

'You don't want to know,' Philbert said quietly, though not so quietly that everyone in the quiet hall couldn't hear it. 'There are memories in here that span the world far more than your aqueduct will ever do, and violence enough to make your hair curl, if only you had hair enough to make the exercise worthwhile.'

Maulwerf was at his back, snatching at Philbert's arm but Philbert kept his footing, he and the Great Magendie staring hard into each other's eyes. And maybe the Great Magendie saw a shiver of those memories flickering across Philbert's face for it was he who pulled away.

'Quite a boy,' he murmured, though not directly to Philbert. 'I see I was right to save the least until last. If I had my hammer here I would take great pleasure in cracking open that skull of his, scatter his secrets to the wind.' He smiled, but it was not a good smile, then waved his arm, informed the company he was tired and they needed to go away and not come back. It took the bonny-hatted boys only moments to get everyone in order, shovel the long haired woman's hair back into her barrow, shove a few coins in Maulwerf's hand and then they were off and out, the moleskin boys barricading the doors behind them, Maulwerf leading them sternly back down the twisting steps between the impenetrable hedges of beech, his anger harsh within his chest at the way both he and his prize exhibits had been treated. Only Philbert – of all people – had stood up for them, and he silently applauded the boy. Undoubtedly the Great Magendie had achieved great things, but Maulwerf was disgusted by the privilege he obviously believed his status earned him. He was rather pleased therefore to overhear what the White Jester said to Philbert as they went back down the steps, proud of his protégé, despite their recent lack of communication.

'Oh but well done, my fine young friend,' the White Jester exclaimed, slapping Philbert gently on the shoulder, 'for standing up to that old curmudgeon. He's had me and my lady La Lanuga in there three times these last few days, pinching at us both, pulling her hair and teeth, seeing if my eyes will change colour. And never once,' he added, as if this was the worst of the Great Magendie's crimes, 'has he ever laughed at any of my jokes.' He placed his paper-pale face right in front of Philbert's, his bright eyes pink and merry. 'He might have built the greatest aqueduct anyone has ever seen since the Romans, but there's no doubting the man is an arse of the first order and you, my young lad, are the only person who had the courage to point it out. Hair indeed! And quite right!'

Maulwerf quivered in his velvet jacket. He no longer twirled his silver topped cane. It was obvious to him from that little exchange between Magendie and Philbert that Philbert was no longer some ingénue raked up by the travelling of his Fair. Something deep and dark had happened to Kwert and Philbert when they'd been away, and he meant to find out what that was.

37

The Christmas Factor

Winter ground on, a dog within the wheel of the seasons, bearing frost in its fur and a howling snarl of wind, the snow barely having time to settle on the frozen ground before it was snatched up again, a hound that would not loose the broke-backed rabbit – still squirming – from its hold. For several months, following the Great Magendie's Opening, Maulwerf's Fair toured the provinces of Schleswig-Holstein, a land in danger of losing its identity halfway here and halfway there, no one knowing whether they should make alliances with the Swedish or the Prussians or the Danish. They were not alone, uprisings and small revolutions going on all over Europe, but Lengerrborn had not been forgotten and men were on Philbert's tail.

Philbert didn't know what Kwert had told Maulwerf after their visit to Magendie, but he knew he'd said something, maybe everything. Maulwerf was certainly on his guard, but to his credit never mooted the notion that Philbert should leave, instead was of entirely the opposite demeanour, telling Philbert he was glad he was back, a sentiment spoken, but one of which Philbert was never entirely sure. He listened for every creep and crack of rumour that might tell him pursuers were on his tail, either from Lengerrborn or Bremen. But he heard nothing, and slowly came to the assumption that winter and snow had thrown them off his scent.

~

Philbert woke one night in that strange land of Schleswig-Holstein, teeth chattering with the cold, pushing his feet deeper into his squirrel-skin boots, snuggling closer under his covers into Kroonk's warm side. On his other flank lay Jimble and Jamble, surprise additions to the Kroonk family, engendered whilst Philbert had been away on his travels – a slip on Lorenzini's part, but a welcome one – a family of piglets it had never occurred to Philbert might ever have existed. These two, the only ones to survive from a poor litter, were lying snout to tail, a shiver of dream passing through first one and then the other, trotters twitching in harmony. All was quiet, only the snuffled coughs and grunts that he was used to coming from his neighbours' tents as they snored and sneezed the cold night through. Philbert was lying on his stomach, hand lifting the corner of his tent-flap to peer out into the night. Stretched out before him the land ran down to the sea, combed into straight lines by a bleak procession of knick-hedges, its white flatness broken only by the low rolls of distant dunes and the stark outlines of tumbled, dilapidated tombs left by the Angles many hundreds – maybe thousands – of years before. The water of the lake before the castle was frozen solid, covered with a multitude of Fair stalls; also frozen were its many offspring streams and feeders, no splish nor merry splash, only the hard cold crack and arthritic groans of ice to be heard. The moon shone down upon the land, the one a mirror to the other's pale unconcern, both glistening in the icy light as if the ceaseless murmurings of the distant sea had swept sudden and silent over the fields, flattening all below it, leaving a crystal lattice of salt to glitter in its place as it withdrew again, unseen.

Philbert turned his head, heard the pochards whistling on the brack-marsh, saw the outline of a small dark fox slink beside the reeds, scrawny herons hunched low on branches, ducks scrunching harder into their nests as the fox's scent came and went. The moon veiled its face within a cloud of ice then let fall one, two, three flakes of softest snow. Philbert put out his hand and caught a snowflake on his fingertip, put it to his mouth. He held out his hand again but soon withdrew it as the night suddenly filled with flurries and gusts, the wind beginning to swirl its cloaks of ermine between tent and stall. Behind them, Philbert saw the white-bricked walls of the castle standing solid between the shifting screens of snow. He could hear the champ and chafe of horse and cattle shifting lazily within those walls, safe in byre and barn and beside them, in the keepers' cotts, the keepers' kith and kin, goats and sheep, vying and jostling for the warmth of meagre fires that gently expired upon their cooling hearths.

And up there in his castle was the Aethling Rupert, shivering in his massive bed. He was a Glücksburg, distant descendant of the Danish Monarchy, aspirant to the thrones of Sweden, England and Prussia, if only he could prove his ancestral claims. He'd sent out a public proclamation in the preceding months stating what everyone knew already: that these were confusing times, the need greater now than ever to unite the disparate populations who lived within his lands; to cement this union, his proclamation announced, he was hosting the biggest Frost Fair Schleswig-Holstein had ever seen and everyone welcome: Prussians, Swedes, Danes, even the English if any were to hand – all of whom had been fighting and forming allegiances the one with the other and back again for the past thirty years. But Christmas was a time for peace, Rupert stated, and he was the man to provide it, by presenting the largest, most exciting and inclusive spectacle ever witnessed hereabouts. His aims were to increase his personal popularity, create alliances, strengthen the slippery hold he had on his family's lands and obscure titles and claims. In recent years the soil had begun to shift beneath his feet, as for so many in his position, and he needed the support of the good and the great, of powerful men and their merchant guilds. He had to know which way things were going, if the Danes or Prussians were thinking of invasion, the nature of the vacillations of the Swedish and English merchants, about where the loyalties of the people lay – to the north and Scandinavia or the German-speaking south – or if the tide was ripe for independence to win out after all.

For all these reasons Rupert, like Philbert, could not sleep easy that cold night and was standing huddled in an eiderdown by his window high up in the white walls of his castle, looking through the flurries of snow that were veiling land and lake. At the same moment he looked out, Philbert slipped back into his private warmth of pig and tent, leaving Rupert alone at his vigil, wondering what the next day would bring and how his Christmas Gift would play out, certain he'd advantage on his side: he had a castle, he had the brilliance of winter at his beck and call, he had an Ice Fair, for God's sake, with hairy women and dancing dwarfs.

Nothing, thought the Atheling Rupert, *can possibly go wrong, and soon my claims will be heard in the highest courts.* He stood a while longer before withdrawing back to his bed, heart racing with anticipation, but barely had he nodded back into sleep than dawn was scraping the night from the blue bones of the sky and the Fair and its folk began to wake, and a couple of hours later all was in full swing, shouts heard across the frozen lake and the fields that ran down to the sea.

'Roll up! Roll up! *Kommen Sie, Meine Damen und Herren*, my fun-loving friends, my companions in curiosity! Do you seek the Strange and Peculiar? Do you long to be confronted with the most stupendous spectacles nature has to offer? Are you brave enough to enter my World of Wonders, my living Cabinet of Curiosities? Tents filled with Puzzles and Anomalies just waiting to be explored. Roll up! Roll up!'

It was Harlekin, Master of Ceremonies, marching across his makeshift stage, tolling his bell, shouting out his wares:

'Come see the Strongest Boy in all the World, and the Elfin Lady; or how about the Fattest Woman in all the land? We also have the White Jester, an albino from Peru, and his wife the Dog-Faced Lady who sings like the summer we've all just lost. And we have a boy with a head like you've never seen before, who makes his pig dance like a Court of Ladies' maids. We have magicians to bamboozle you and soothsayers who will tell you your future, musicians to entertain your ears, actors to entertain your eyes. And if all that isn't enough, ladies and gentlemen, then come visit the Carneous Mole. Yes, the Carneous Mole! Here, in our very midst! Give him meat crawling with maggots, give him slugs, give him last year's donkey-chops. He will eat all before your very eyes! This Fair is a Box of Delights to be opened at your pleasure. Come and see it all, Ladies and Gentlemen, see it and believe it. For the Frost Fair is open! *Die Winterfreudenfest* is begun!'

Philbert would remember those words for many years to come, every nuance and shade of them, and all the people who were pouring in from every corner of Schleswig-Holstein. It was as if his whole life was a river beside which he walked, a river that kept the reflections of his memories true and clear no matter what disturbed the waters or how far along its banks he went. His head was a treasure trove of other people's stories, a bottle into which the ships of their lives could be folded and stowed, as if he were a whirlpool at the centre of his universe, sucking in everything about him.

~

The day wears on, the Frost Fair going great guns and, as the afternoon draws to a close, Harlekin leaps onto his stage and stands amidst the yellow smoke to reveal his play. The place is here, in Schleswig-Holstein, and the feeling is for rebellion, the people tugged between the Danish crown and the Prussians, not knowing which way to go, though either might end badly. Harlekin holds Hannah on one arm to represent the beauty of Schleswig, and an able lad – alas not Hermann – on the other for the delights of Holstein. He tells them they have Queen Dämpfdorf of Denmark and King Prügelbaaden from Prussia in the wings; these are Tingelburg and Tangelrichter, in disguise as usual: one spike-thin and warty in an aureole orange dress, the other with his boots too big and a helmet of iron pinned precariously upon an enormous wig.

'If only these two young lovelies could be married they would be happy and there would be no tale, but "if only" never gave a story and you would not listen.' Harlekin wears black velvet, reminding Philbert of the Westphal man who ushered him, Kwert and Ullendorf into destruction. Philbert watches up front with Lita, just as they used to do; Oort, the strong-boy who can lift a donkey above his head, has taken a liking to Philbert and his pigs and is with them too. Harlekin stands centre stage with Hannah, her handsome beau at her side, cupping a hand to his ear as the ugly Queen comes in from the left and screams:

'Give them to me, give them to me, I say! Give me, give me, give me!'

Harlekin cups his other hand to his other ear as the King enters stage right, preceded by his enormous wig.

'What is that witch saying now?' he growls. 'I've told you before, they are mine, all mine, and I will have them both!'

Harlekin moves further down the stage and lets out a huge sigh and many of the crowd sigh too, for they understand perfectly the analogy that is playing out upon the stage, and how the whim of politics is destroying people's lives without doing them the courtesy of letting them know why it is happening.

'Always it is like this,' continues Harlekin sadly. 'Those would-be lovers separated by others who want what they cannot have and, seeing harmony in the offing, must rip it apart.'

And so the crowd reacts: as the Queen comes in from one side and the King approaches from the other, they begin to boo and hiss; it doesn't stop the actors, for they've done all this before in other places to other audiences and have their part to play. They hook their fingers into their belts and stamp their boots and Hannah and her young man cower, as they must do in the face of tyranny. Harlekin turns against the audience and accuses them with his finger.

Just like Von Ebner, Philbert thinks, *the spoon that stirs the milk until it curdles.*

'Is all you can do is boo?' Harlekin shouts. 'Will you let this evil take place? Will you allow your daughters to be ravished and your sons humiliated? No? Did I hear you say?'

'No, no, no, NO!' cries the audience. They are angry, their fists are raised.

'Did I hear you?' provokes Harlekin. 'Will you really let this happy union be dissolved before it has properly begun?'

'NO, NO!' The audience have begun to stamp their feet, the men getting so worked up they're almost ready to storm the stage as if this was real, as if this was not a representation of what is happening to their country but taking place now, in front of their very eyes, and then comes a huge explosion that stops them in their tracks, and through the billowing clouds of purple sparks and green smoke Harlekin re-emerges waving a banner of red, white and blue – the self-declared insignia of the independent parliament of Schleswig-Holstein – his troupe of actors suddenly appearing behind him carrying prop-pitchforks and saucepans as they surround Hannah and her prince, grabbing the King and Queen by their arms and clamping them in chains, leading them off stage in abject and angry humiliation. But the audience has already gone wild and Harlekin's voice is barely heard as he finishes off his tale of successful revolt and matrimony and the crowd whoop and stamp and clap their hands, throw their hats in the air, drowning out his shouts with their own songs, swinging their own home-made banners. It is the winter of 1847 going into 1848 and this is happening all over Europe. There are Ruperts everywhere who don't know which flag is safe to fly; but for Harlekin this is the cue to begin his troupe's singing and dancing and he waves Hannah back onto the stage and the music strikes up, dancing girls at the ready.

'Give us our duchies and principalities!' shouts Harlekin, as he marches his players about the stage;

Hoorah! shouts the crowd;

'Let us own our own land!' interposes somebody from the crowd –

Hoorah!

'And our rights!' shouts another –

Hurrah! *Hurrah*!

'Give us our liberty!' yells someone else, all agreeing with the sentiment –

Hurrah, hooray, hurrah, hooplah!

And then it's too late for Tangelrichter, the acting King of Prussia, and he's dragged bodily from the stage and across the ice, kicked and cudgelled for what he represents, for what he tried to show them, saved only by Hannah and her dancing troupe flinging out their frills and *unterblumen* and the musicians laying in with drumsticks and bows in defence of their colleague.

'Play up!' Hannah yells to the members of the orchestra who still have instruments not lost in the scrum. 'Play up quick and lead out!'

The big bass drums boom and the bagpipes drone, and the fiddlers play – those who have broken their bows beating time out on their instruments' bridges – and all across the ice they go, Hannah at the fore, her dancers behind, clutching hands to waist, legs going in and out like metronome rods, encouraging the crowd until at last, like a snake caught by the head, the men and women of Schleswig-Holstein slither and slide themselves into a laughing line across the frozen lake, shouting and singing, slipping and sliding, yelling out drunken songs of patriotism and revenge, all thoughts of Tangelrichter, King of Prussia, forgotten. They don't know what they've done in this petty charade, nor what will be done because of it; they have no awareness of the hard men camped silently amongst the trees not two miles distant, nor that their spies and scouts are dispersed amongst the crowds, heads already filled with what their mouths will say later.

'*Mein Gott!*' groans Tangelrichter, ex-King of Prussia, as his friends prise him and his bruises off the ice and bear him away. 'Are things so bad here that they have to take it out on me? Look at my helmet! And *Mein Gott*, my wig! Someone rescue my wig!'

His cries disappear into the night as his wig is stamped apart without mercy at its carefully crafted seams, never to be mended.

⁓

And so the scene is set: here is the Frost Fair and the castle and the baying crowds and the men lying wait in the trees. And here is Philbert, become his own Harlekin, one of the few people in attendance who will exit stage left and still remember the script as it plays itself out. He will wonder later about all that led him to this time and place, and all the what ifs the real Harlekin previously mentioned; for if Philbert hadn't had a taupe then maybe his mother and father would have stayed long together and he would have remained in Staßburg, working in the salt mines like his father; and if that had been the case he would never have met Lita and never left Staßburg to join the Fair; he would never have met Hermann and Hermann would never have been cured and then uncured, his only way to peace being his jumping off the bridge; and if that hadn't happened the Fair would never have left early for Finzeln, and if they hadn't been at Finzeln when they were then Philbert's head would never have been subjected to Corti's carillon and he would never have met Doctor Ullendorf, and would never have gone to Lengerrborn; and if he hadn't been there when he had then neither more would Von Ebner, Federkiel and Schnurrhenker, and what happened to them – and what happened to the Schupos afterwards – would never have been, and the revolution Philbert had unwittingly unleashed in Lengerrborn would never have rippled out beyond its borders as it had; nor would he have met Petitorri or Goffaggino, and Petitorri would never have had cause to shout out so loud about the boy with the big head who had murdered yet another man in cold blood and for no reason other than escape; and without Petitorri's witness – for he was exactly the vengeful man Philbert had assumed him to be – the soldiers might have turned back at Bremen, flyers and rewards forgotten, trail gone cold.

The puppets of revolution are many and varied but every puppet needs its strings, and Philbert had unknowingly pulled them hard and kept others tugging at them long after he and Kwert had left the scene. Possibly Maulwerf's Fair of Marvels might have wound up at Schleswig-Holstein anyway; possibly Rupert's political ambitions and hard-done-by peasants would have provoked a small uprising here upon the ice without anyone else's help; but without Philbert there would have been no bounty-hunters and mercenaries hunting the length and breadth of Europe for the boy with a monstrous bauble for a head, seeking out both him and his murderous associates, those responsible for the gaol-break at Lengerrborn and the murder of multiples of policemen, not to mention the brutal slaying of a visiting Italian nobleman's trusted groom. Every story travels as it grows and grows as it travels and Philbert's story got to Schleswig-Holstein before he ever did, as did the band of men who were carrying it. They were no revolutionaries, only men thrown away by other wars, men who liked money and having a good time who had no care for Princes who lived in castles any more than was Rupert the kind of man to look around the next corner to see what his actions might precipitate, whose Christmas Gift Box, as he called the Frost Fair, was to be his rallying cry and its own reward, though not as he'd planned. If asked, Philbert could have told Rupert that things were never what you wanted once you found them, but Rupert would never have asked and certainly wouldn't have listened to the answer if he had.

So here it was: Christmas Eve, the year of 1847 spilling into 1848, and now come the puppets, ready to walk upon the stage.

38

The Night of the Wolf

Everyone who was anyone had been invited and all accepted, eager for the spectacle of the Frost Fair, if not the Prince's patronage. It was the Happening of the Year. The local grandees passed over the bridge into the confines of the castle walls for Prince Rupert's *Weihnachtsgeschenk* without qualm. He'd organised a gathering of something similar every year: a ball or feast to inculcate the loyalty of neighbours and peers, and this year was to be the greatest yet. When Rupert heard that Maulwerf and his Fair of Wonders was in the vicinity he knew it was just what he needed to make this year's celebrations stand out from the rest. Schleswig-Holstein was being ripped down the middle and Rupert had one foot either side of the divide. He'd dithered for weeks over which flag to fly: blue for Prussia, red for Denmark, or the red, white and blue of independence. In the end his flagsmen came up with a design all of their own that included everything relevant: lion rampant, white nettle, field one half blue, the other red, Rupert's family motto emblazoned in gold above: *Aut Bibat, Aut Abeat*: *Let Him Drink with Us or Leave*. He approved this new design, felt it served the sentiment of the moment, and it was time to let these people know who they were dealing with. He was a Prince, by

God, and one who was heir apparent to not one, nor two, but three royal thrones.

Rupert stood on his balcony, leaning over the balustrade, watching as his guests arrived throughout the afternoon. He wouldn't greet them yet. He wanted them to settle, ease in, have a few jiggers of rum from the jugs placed in each of their rooms. He knew how impressive the approach to his castle was; how it shone like a sail above the trees as you rode in towards the east; how the frozen lake stretched away from the track and on down to the sea; how his castle stood suddenly revealed as you came out of the forest, shining white as if it had been carved from the moon, great arms of ghost-thistle and teasel-heads standing straight against the stone, thick stalks of fennel, lovage and monkshood sculpted by the ice encasing them, keeping them upright, lacing the edges of the moat pools, reed-blades piercing the mounds of snow at their feet. And now, this early evening, with the Frost Fair camped out upon the ice and the surrounding fields, the place was the tapissery of winter: sparkles of light from torches and bonfires, the outlines of huts and stalls, the braziers with their curls of scented smoke hinting at haunches of beef and mutton being cloved, spitted and dripped over with honeyed bastes.

It couldn't look better, thought Rupert, as he went inside to dress for dinner. This was his night, of that he was absolutely certain. He knew nothing of the other men out there who hadn't been invited, that there are always other men out there some-where, no matter if you're a prince with ambition or a boy with a head that is sucking in the world around him. You never know who's going to come out of the forest and break into your life even when you thought you'd locked all the doors and drawn the bolts and pulled the shutters across the windows; even when you'd sat down to warm by your fire, imagining yourself the centre of the universe, for even then – maybe especially then – the universe is never thinking of you, and doesn't even know you exist.

~

Over the bridge they came, the participants in Prince Rupert's Christmas Gift Box, over the moat whose ice was broken three times daily so the swans could swim and the carp could rise or hide from the carriages as they clattered across the new-tarred, snow-swept planks. The tower rose above them five storeys high, criss-crossed by hidden servant-running corridors and stairways, cold and damp, shafted through by light or shadow from the recessed windows, their sills bevelled by five-hundred-year-old grooves carved out for the buckets of brimstone and burning oil that now held only oats and barley for the horses stabled far below in their byres. The guests alighted from their carriages, straightening complex dresses, unfurling coats, greeted by the prince's men-of-state one by one, name by name, sorted by title, rank and wealth. As darkness fell, and the Great Hall filled, musicians struck up their tunes, yule-logs spitting in their fire-places, the guests beginning to wander the circumference of the enormous table to find their names gilded onto marzipan swans to mark their places, sitting themselves down. In the centre was a sugar-spun castle on a hill of crystallised grapes, and there was Rupert, opulent in a throne-like chair, looking lean in comparison with Frau Fettleheim who sat beside him on a custom-built couch, a visible symbol of the enormity of his gift and the spectacle that his invited guests were about to witness.

It was the finest night of Frau Fettleheim's life, and she was chattering away like a lark to the princes and barons on either side of her, to bishops and merchants and their jewel-bedrenched wives. The rest of the Fair's folk waited in the under-crofts and kitchens, getting ready for their set-pieces, practising lines, checking they looked their best. Outside, across the courtyard, beyond the bridge-straddled moat, out in the deep dark forest the wild boar hid and stamped their feet, polished their swords, primed their muskets, waiting patiently – just like everyone else that night – until their turn was called.

~

Rupert clapped his hands and called a start, making sure everyone's glasses were filled and everyone comfortable, and then in came the jugglers and dancers to enliven the mood as the guests began their five-hour, fifteen-course repast. Next came the man who spoke his twenty-six-or-seven languages, having apparently learned another one on his way here, reciting poems with lines alternately in Danish, Friesian, German, Polish, English, Swedish and – who would know it? – Mandarin. The woman with the long tresses had been separated from her cart and was walked in like a bride, brown hair twined with ribbons carried by twenty servants, ten on each side, everyone stroking and admiring her shining mane. Next came Lita and her Bowman – no Huffelump as she couldn't take the stairs – but Lorenzini played and Lita danced and sang and pirouetted and stood on Lorenzini's shoulders, her tiny arms held high and thin as craneflies. Then came the soothsayer – in normal circumstances this role would have fallen to Kwert, but the trials of prison and escape had worn him badly, and the farther north they'd travelled, and the colder it had become, the more he'd folded into illness like a piece of paper too often used, just as Brother Langer had predicted. Drafted into his place was one Herr Himbeere, to whom Philbert was now assistant. Himbeere's oiled head shone like a buttered apple, its pike-tattoo seeming to move and ripple across his scalp as he turned in the lamplight: flexing its jaws, flicking its long tail. The calculated air of mystery and ancient rite was highlighted by the hall itself: the thick tapestries hanging upon the gently rounded walls living out their own secret stories, the multiple fireplaces banked on every side by stacks of wood, resin popping and oozing from the heat of roaring flames, great garlands of holly and ivy hanging from roof-hooks and, all around, the skirling of the wind as it tore about the tower.

Himbeere's talent lay in reading fortunes from livers, Rupert having previously selected the Christmas Lamb of God – which a few minutes earlier had been slaughtered in the courtyard below. Philbert came in with its still warm liver, gall bladder dangling, both seeming to pulse in the flickering light; he hoved the offering above his enormous head, Himbeere taking it from Philbert on its silver platter, studying it, slicing it and telling its signs, delivering the glorious predictions his famous patron wished to hear – all strength to the Atheling Rupert being the gist – and then their turn was done and down they went through the draught-ridden stairways, passing the next act who were on their way up.

'Make sure you throw that liver away, Philbert,' said Herr Himbeere the moment they got back down to the warmth of the kitchens. 'That gall bladder was twice the size it should've been and the liver's got flukes – not that it would have done to point it out in such illustrious company.'

The kitchen was jumping like a hornet's nest, every maid and cook shouting out to do this or that: grab plates, hoik trays from ovens, de-pot pies, rub mash through sieves, rib meat into slices, hack ice to rime glasses, check the junket, grate the cheese, chop the vegetables. The place was pandemonium and Himbeere only just managed to squeeze himself into a seat by the fire so he could get at one of the kettles to soothe the soreness of his feet.

'What did you really see?' Philbert asked as he tossed the liver down the rubbish chute, where it would land in the midden heap below for pigs to rootle at in the morning if the foxes and wolves left anything behind. He no longer believed anything these soothsayers had to say, especially not a man who contested he could divine the future in the liver of a lamb, but he was curious.

'That really is the question, isn't it?' said Himbeere, the pike-tattoo on his head moving slowly as he scratched the side of his nose. 'In a better man than the weakling Rupert,' he said, using the pejorative that was common in these parts for said Atheling, 'it might have meant the coming of battle. I detected a distinct hiatus in the Palace Gates, which is usually an indicator of courage. But our Rupert has smaller balls than bladderwort drying on a rack, and less spine than a dandelion. In his case I suspect it means a time of testing, and for him that probably means disaster, since it takes very little to bring a weak man to his knees.' Himbeere wriggled his toes in the pail Philbert had filled for him, watching the water slop lazily up the sides and over his bunions and corns. 'But then again,' he added vaguely, 'perhaps it just means a bad case of indigestion. Who knows?'

He was tired out and wanted drink, meat and dreams in that order. He dragged his feet from the pail, dried them on the drugget-rug before Philbert helped him on with his boots. At this point the strong-boy, Oort, burst into the kitchen having just finished lifting barons above his head and juggling ladies and beer-barrels, muscles still gleaming with the minor exertions his act had caused.

'Coming to watch the rest?' he asked Philbert, grabbing several ox-and-oyster pies from a passing tray. A rolling-pin came down towards his hand but he laughed and flicked it away with his fingers, sending it clattering to the floor. He was not called a strong-boy for nothing, and Philbert was eager as he was to escape the din and steamy clamour of the kitchen.

'Let's go,' Philbert said, Oort quickly pulling him through a side-door towards a thin rise of stone steps. They spiralled up their own little tower and levelled out by a half-planked gangway leading onto the old minstrels' gallery that clung like ivy to the walls of the Great Hall. It was a bit rickety, but they got a grand bird's eye view of the proceedings down below where Rupert's Gift Box was busily being unwrapped, each layer outdoing the one that had gone before. The musicians scraped their way through tune after tune as the rest of the turns came on: a man who threaded wires through his skin and hammered nails up his nose, a woman who played the harp with her feet, a set of sex-tuplets dancing a merry dance, a man girt only in a loin cloth whose skin was a kaleidoscope of multi-coloured tattoos, a parade of monkeys who chittered and jangled in their chains but who apparently gave wise witchdoctor-tips to whomsoever asked; and then came Madame La Chucha Lanuga, the bearded lady from Peru, looking magnificent in green silk, her dress dotted with mirrors, just like the hat she had given to Philbert a while before in tribute to his stand against the annoying Magendie. Her beard was combed and plaited with beads, and she swayed voluptuously as she sang and the musicians lulled and the room hushed as she keened of faraway places and the guests eased buckles and belts and wished they hadn't worn their corsets quite so tight. She sat serenely once she finished her song as her husband Alarico, the White Jester, took over, the blackness of his garb making his albino skin seem like candle-wax in the dim light. Philbert and Oort had heard all his humorous tales before, so back they went along the gallery, stepping gingerly across the rotting planks.

'Let's try and get up to the roof,' Philbert suggested and Oort agreed, Philbert being his new best friend, Philbert – a little absently – returning the favour. They pushed aside the heavy mildewed curtain that separated the gallery from the landing and saw the stairwell continuing up, passageways tunnelling off into the gloom hiding doors and rooms and other runways that riddled the tower like maggots running through rotten meat. They nodded their common agreement and up they went, the way at first lit by a few firebrands set into iron bracelets, feeble flames dimming every colour that might have been to mouse-back grey. They shivered as they passed the last lit corner, feet stumbling on the stairs, pushing each other on, laughing, a little scared and then excited, racing like fleas for the top, bursting out through the trapdoor like jack-in-the-boxes into the clean air and wind of the night. Breathing hard they ran along the gangways between the parapets, throwing snowballs out in wide arcs from the castellated walls, watching them disappear into the darkness as they fell.

'Look, there's the camp!' Oort called and pointed, and they could just about make out their tents, could see Oort's donkey loosely tethered, his head in his beet-bag apparently asleep, and Kroonk next door with her offspring snug inside their wattled shed, Lita and Lorenzini's cart nearby, glinting brightly in the gleam of a fire.

'But look at the lake,' Philbert called out to Oort as he moved around the tower, leaning his elbows into the snow for a better view. They gazed down at the scatter of booths that were huddled on the ice beneath the thick horse-hair blankets and moth-eaten tapestries that served for their roofs. They were lit here and there by fires in bowls jammed on poles whose thin wooden legs were lodged into the ice, people wandering from one place to another, taking slow, steady paces as they headed for their beds, knowing that the spectacle at the castle was the last unwrapping of Rupert's Christmas Box, all trading to cease at midnight, and the following morning all to clear the place and be off far and away.

Philbert turned his head towards the clatter of horses' hooves coming down the lane from the tree-line, iced-over puddles cracking and splintering beneath their weight. Together he and Oort ran around the parapet and leaned dangerously over the edge to watch the latecomers arriving from the track and straight into knee-deep snow, the wind having blown it into drifts now the stable-boys had ceased their labours to sweep it away, believing all the guests to be already inside and everyone staying for the entire night of revelry that would last well towards dawn. These latest arrivals had no choice but to dismount, lead their horses back to the trees where they tied them up before making their way with difficulty back along the snow-bound trail, wrapping their cloaks tight against the wind, finally reaching the moat and over the planks into the courtyard.

By now both Philbert and Oort were shivering with the cold so they headed for the little booth they could see stranded on the wide flat field of the roof, startled when the flagsmen popped their heads out like turtles, having been detailed to stay here the whole night through to make sure the flag was still flying good and true come morning, no matter what the weather flung at it.

'What the . . . ? Who the . . . ?' they said at first, but seeing the two laughing boys they ushered them in, not often having company.

'Escapees from the fairground, I'm guessing,' said the skinnier one, introducing himself as Albert and his companion as Artus, his cousin. They poured the two lads some warm beer into pots and forked up hot sausages from the small brazier that stood at the centre of the small room.

'Unusual for us to get visitors,' commented Artus, offering the boys his pipe, Oort accepting politely, his face turning grey as the hot briar-smoke struck his lungs, handing it back quick as he could, the two men laughing at his attempted bravado. But they were kind enough, showed the two boys card tricks and how to make the red lady disappear, how to grease a corner so she would slip through the pack unnoticed until she needed picking out again. They could just about make out the noises that were drifting up from the Great Hall down below and Albert asked the lads how the show was going, and who they had on display.

'I can do *this*!' offered Oort, lifting up the table with one hand, swivelling it on his fingers.

'Aagh!' yelled Artus, 'mind the beer,' just managing to catch the jug before it fell.

'So we're not missing much then,' commented Albert, taking the beer jug from his cousin, refilling all their mugs. Both men looked up as the wind grew suddenly fiercer, forcing the flag into standing and the pole to hum, making the icicles cut and shift from the mast and shimmy to the ground with the sound of a lonely black-backed diver calling from the lake. The noise from down below had crescendoed and all wondered what new gift the Christmas Box had brought, Philbert being the first to figure out that the greatest of the acts had already gone and that something else must be afoot, and that something was very wrong. And then they all heard the steady thumping of heavy boots on the bare stone steps leading up to the roof and Albert looked at Artus, and Artus looked at Albert, and then both looked at their guests.

'Get under the flags, boys,' Albert whispered. 'There's a whole heap of them back there behind the table. Burrow yourselves in and don't come out until we say.'

Philbert was in mind to stay and stand whatever was coming, fists already clenched, but Artus pushed him roughly back and strong-boy Oort grabbed Philbert's arm and held him down, pulling a load of old and rotting flags and banners over their heads. Oort didn't see the trembling of Philbert's hands, which had already beaten another person to death with just a rock, nor his anger, but Oort was the stronger of the two by far and held his friend pinioned beneath his body as if to shield him, holding up one corner of the flagging heap so they could see Artus and Albert carefully pick up caps and capes and tread steadily out of the booth, leaving the door open, trouser-legs held from the snow by bands of string. Philbert and Oort couldn't see much but could hear distinctly the clanking of iron-tipped boots on stone and the trapdoor being lifted, angry shouts as heavy bodies heaved themselves up and out onto the snow-covered roof.

'There it is, lads! Well don't just gaup at it. Get the bloody thing down!'

They next heard Albert and Artus edging their way across the roof, the crunch of their clogs as they hit fresh snow.

'What's this?' said Albert, and then came the soft sound of whip against wet-hide and Albert's startled cry and a man's voice, deep and loud from a rain-barrel chest.

'So here's who put it up. Don't you know that flag's an insult? Get it down! Get it down now!'

The man who'd emerged with the others from the trapdoor pushed Albert forward, making him stumble in the snow, his own men leaving off struggling with the ropes they didn't know how to work. Artus hurried forward between them, pushing at the men messing with his precious flag.

'Don't pull on the guy-leader, you'll just tangle it ... ooomph!'

One of the men hit him square across the face with a leather-gloved fist, a wet crump as Artus's nose-bone broke, his blood spraying in an impressive arc across the snow.

'Let them be,' growled the barrel-chested man, 'but get that bastard flag down, here and now.'

Albert started grappling at the ropes, unwinding the leader from the double-armed hook and Artus, despite his broken nose, getting up from his knees to help, their cold fingers stiff and slipping on Artus's blood which kept pouring from his nose. But it was a task they'd done a thousand times and soon the enormous flag was down, though still the wind tugged at it and tried to wrap it around the pole. Several of the interlopers grabbed at the cloth, held it fast, one of them spitting on the field of Prussian blue. The barrel-man took a tinderbox from beneath his cloak, struck it to the flag, though it was too damp to burn.

'You!' he pushed Albert, 'go and get your lamp and whatever fuel you've got and bring it here.'

Albert didn't need asking twice and went running as best he could through the tracks he and his cousin had already made, back to the booth. Once inside, he spoke quietly to Philbert and Oort, whose heads were poking out of the heap.

'Be quiet, lads. Don't make a sound, you hear me? Not a sound. And don't come out, whatever, you hear me. Don't come out.'

They could see his hands shaking as he lifted the lamp and dragged out a small barrel of oil, started back outside. Philbert moved in defiance but Oort held him fast and Philbert soon subsided, understanding this was a battle they could not win, no matter how strong Oort might be and how many men Philbert had already murdered. As Albert moved to leave the booth one of the interlopers came in to take the barrel of oil from him. His nose twitched, and he looked curiously at the table that had been set a little skew by Oort's strongman show.

'Sausages,' he murmured, 'I smell sausages,' but before he'd a chance to investigate his leader shouted out for him.

'I'll give you devil-damned sausages if you don't get a move on! We've work to do, you slug-head. And no work, no pay!'

Enough for the slug-head and he retreated back out into the snow with the barrel of oil and took off the lid, poured the contents over the flag, soaking its lion and thistles, staining the green and the white, slicking the snow with dark rainbows beneath. His leader took the lamp and smashed the glass, held it directly to the canvas which took with a whoomph and a firm hold of flame.

'You,' Albert was pulled forward, 'get that back up,' and Albert heaved on the painter and hauled the burning flag high into the night sky, Rupert's lion disappearing in a golden mane of flame. The wind carried the embers over the castle walls, pinpricked the sky with light, but the snow had begun to fall again, hiding it from anyone even if they'd been looking, which they were not. Damp black cinders drifted onto the shoulders of the mercenaries who brushed angrily at them, making the marks worse. Their leader looked up once more and grimaced as the burning flag was let go by the wind and collapsed against the mast with a dull flicker.

'Get rid of them,' he said as he trudged back to the trapdoor and let himself down. 'And be quick about it. Time we were gone.'

Artus and Albert stood in the snow, blood beginning to cake on Artus' chin and cheeks.

'Please,' said Albert, his fingers clutching at the bottom hem of his coat.

'Don't,' said Artus, shaking his head, and no one knew whether he was begging for his life or trying to convince his cousin to be brave. It made no difference to the men who marched towards them. It made no difference to Albert and Artus as those men took out their daggers and slit the flags-men's windpipes one by one. It made no difference to the half-arsed burning of the flag above them, or the wind that whipped the last flames briefly into being before smothering them completely between fold and mast. It made no difference to Philbert and Oort, hidden beneath the pile of mouldering flags, who caught the scent of copper and iron that comes when hot fresh blood is leaving heart and home for the last time, spilling out onto the cold indifference of the snow.

~

Oort and Philbert listened as the men left, cursing and wiping their knives upon their trousers before slipping back down through the trapdoor from whence they came. As soon as he felt it safe Philbert sprang out of the booth to find that the last flicker of life had abandoned the flagsmen, who lay like slaughtered pigs. Philbert took it all in in a moment. He knew it would be futile to check for signs of life but was fighting furious, and as much as he was anxious about what he might find down below he swung himself straight down the trapdoor and went as fast as he could at the steps, cold hands reaching out to the dark walls, Oort lumbering on at his back, a soft whining coming from the strong-boy's throat as he tried not to cry. Philbert got down the stone stairs fast as he was able in the darkness and pushed past the mildewed curtain to gain the rickety planks of the minstrel gallery from where he gazed down onto the great hall, utterly unprepared for what was there. His hands went to his mouth in useless supplication, for surely to God this could not be happening.

The Gift Box and its guests were well and truly unwrapped and undone, some skewered to their seats by lances, the shafts still wavering gently like dying pendulums; others had fallen forward into plates of food that still steamed softly, their necks neatly tied with wire garrottes tightened hard into their flesh. Yet more lay with their heads laid back upon the neck-rests of their chairs, sliced open like so many raw and fat-spotted salamis. Worst of all was Frau Fettleheim, whose great gut had been hacked from side to side, intestines sliding away from her open stomach, the grey-green glisten of them coiling and spilling over her outspread knees, blue eyes half-veiled by a final blink. Away to the wall, where the last few acts of the Fair had been taking their ease by the fire, was Alarico, the White Jester, spread-eagled on the ember-singed hearth-rug, arms flung wide, white skin bloomed with pink for the first time in his life as capillaries burst all over his body, his feet faintly moving as he tried to crawl over to La Chucha Lanuga who was sitting a few yards away upon her stool, head bowed low, the jewels in her dark hair winking in the firelight, the beads of her beard catching at the hasp of the knife that was buried deep within her chest. A horrid rasping came from the White Jester's open mouth as he strained for one last sight of his wife, his wonderful Peruvian rose. The only other movement in the room came from the Atheling Rupert who was cradled in his throne, a sword plunged right through his belly into the grain of wood behind, Adam's apple bobbing weakly beneath his pale skin, eyes upturned, gazing at the two white faces that had appeared between the gallery railings and bizarrely Rupert tried to shake his head, thinking *they shouldn't be there, the floor's unsafe. I always meant to get it fixed . . .*

It was the last thought in his head as his heart gave up the fight and ceased its beat, as did Alarico's and, in the few moments it took Philbert and Oort to get from the gallery down the stairs and into the hall, both men, though warm, were gone. The stench of spilled blood and burst guts was so appalling and overpowering it was all Philbert could do not to vomit, and he needed to go. There was nothing he could do for any of these people, that much was plain. He grasped at Oort's sleeve to get him on the move but the lad had stopped like a broken clock, too horror stricken by what he was seeing to turn away, barely taking in what was in front of him: a hall full of slaughtered men and women slumped around an enormous table scattered with the remnants of their half-eaten feast; people who'd been taken so completely by surprise they'd not even had the time to rise from their seats in protest or move their forks from their mouths, let alone fight off the disaster that had overtaken them.

Philbert had bigger worries on his mind as he started to run towards the service stairs that led to the kitchen shouting for Oort to follow, which he eventually did. The kitchen was deserted of people, if not of the food that had been left scattered randomly across every surface, but the moment Philbert flung open the door onto the cobblestones of the courtyard he went straight into another mess of bleeding bodies, though the vast proportion out here seemed at least alive enough to groan and swear, their women rushing around filling buckets from the pumps to wash out their wounds and bandage them up with whatever they could find.

Disaster was everywhere, no one understanding exactly what had happened, and certainly not why. Some things are simply too enormous to think about, and this was one of them. The uninjured concentrated on keeping the injured alive and breathing. They didn't speak. They didn't communicate the one with the other, they just got on with the task at hand. Philbert could hear from distant cries and shouts that the mercenaries had moved on from the castle to the Frost Fair, no one fit to lift a finger to help. This was the night of the wolf and the wolf had moved on, nothing they could do about it.

Not so Philbert, who took in the scene in the courtyard at a glance, and urged the folk there into action.

'Get the drawbridge up!' he shouted, 'and get the portcullis down if you can,' and it was a strange thing in that dark and bloody night, with the snow falling all around them, that the men and women held within the confines of the castle looked at the small boy in his large hat who was shouting out orders and did as they were commanded, indeed wondered why on earth they hadn't thought to do it already themselves. There was a flurry of folk, mostly women, who went at it with gusto, following the boy and his large friend who were running and skidding for the drawbridge and then were over and across its back.

'Get it done now!' the boy shouted once he'd crossed, and the women went at the ropes, uncertain how to operate the pulleys but thanking the Lord that someone had had the sense to think of it, and soon enough up went the drawbridge and down went the portcullis, and away ran that boy from them into the white apparelled night.

39

Unwrapped and Undone

Rupert's Christmas Box of the Frost Fair had been destroyed long before Philbert got to it. While half the men who'd been waiting in the trees went into the castle – their mission to bring down the bourgeoisie, burgers and the pretender to the throne – the other half had orders to surround as much as they could of the Fair strung out across the frozen lake and clustered on its environs, to attack the moment the flag went up in flames. Their remit was simple: destroy the Fair and everyone in it, for somewhere at its heart lay the murderers of Lengerrborn and, as if that wasn't enough, its acting troupe had been promulgating rebellion of the worst kind with their little plays and attitudes, taking their message up and down the land, pitting themselves against the interests of the great and the good and fostering ideas of independence in the minds of every Schleswig-Holsteiner who'd visited their pernicious performances ever since the Fair had crossed the Elbe.

The men whose task it was to destroy the Fair had little political inclination. Certainly they despised the fat inhabitants of the castle their comrades had just stormed under the guise of late-arriving guests, setting to murder with great satisfaction. The Fair's folk held little fascination for these others, all of the ilk of men who got far more pleasure from upturning braziers than sitting happily beside them swapping tales, and within moments of the burning flag being hoisted – seen only because one of them carried a telescope and had been looking out for it – they were charging forward and throwing lighted brands onto makeshift shacks, laughing when the folk inside shrieked and ran, some of them burning far better than that wretched flag had ever done on the roof. They flattened anyone who got in their way, set as much of the camp to fire as would burn, took pot-shots at the people running away towards the dark edges of the forests, soon joined by their comrades from the castle, pumped up by the action, eager for more, made thirsty by murder and fight and all too soon breaking open beer kegs and stills once they were done, drinking until their knees began to give way beneath them, grabbing any women they could find by their hair and hauling them screaming over barrels while they fumbled to undo the buttons of their breeks. They threw small animals onto fires, barely bothering to cut their throats and bleed them dry. They stamped on possessions, denuded tents from their frames to provide a waterproof base for their antics, grabbed up paltry trinkets and stuffed them into pockets, garnered coins scattered in the snow from broken till-boxes, snatched up purses that lay abandoned open-eyed as they fell. All this was part and parcel of their pay.

Behind them the drawbridge had been raised, the wooden portcullis stuck at half-mast, its under-used cogs seizing for lack of oil, winch ropes frayed and tangled, but enough to keep the marauders out for the night, no way back into the castle even if they'd tried, and no more for Philbert and Oort once they'd crossed over. Oort's eyes were wide as moons in the blank set of his face as he crouched beside Philbert on the edge of the lake. It was obvious there could be no approaching, that there was nothing they could do but watch as sheds, shacks and booths went up in flames, listen to the screams and cries and the loud booming of the attackers' guns, see the dark sky lit up by explosions of gunpowder and the scatter of fires on which God knew what was burning.

Philbert closed his eyes, Oort shivering beside him, and there they stayed for an hour or more while the men held the Fair grounds fast and strong, drinking, singing and laughing until the snow began to fall without relent, at which point their leader, the man who'd been on the rooftop, called his men to order and took them away, led them stumbling off to regain their horses, filling their saddlebags with booty, throwing newly replenished wine-skins over their shoulders. By God, but they'd had a night of it, and away they went down the tracks filled to the brim with it, so that it would take some doing for any of them to melt back into the lives from which they'd come, returning a little richer, a lot crueller, more than ready to do it all again, if only someone would pay the price.

The moment they'd passed by the castle and gone off up the trail into the woods Philbert and Oort emerged from their hiding place. The fires the men had set were burning brightly, the greasy light and smoke twisting through the lazy swirl of snowflakes that had precipitated the men's departure and would continue falling until dawn. They moved slowly, throats tight with the awful devastation. One of the first things Philbert saw was Jimble burning on his back in a fire sustained by the leaking fat from his body, skin blackened with soot and charcoal, gouged out in places where the men had dug for food with their knives. A few yards away lay Jamble, his own fire out, but he was rammed belly-through by a stake to hold him to the ground. His body was still twitching and alive and Oort couldn't take it, went down on his knees beside the piglet, ripped out the stake and swiftly, quietly, snapped its neck, Oort keening and crying, unable to move further, anguish flowing through him like a river.

Philbert found Kwert beneath an overturned cart, curled into

355

a ball, half-buried by the snow, skin so pale and cold Philbert assumed he must already be dead until he heard the small crepitation of Kwert's fast-failing lungs.

'Oort!' Philbert shouted. 'Oort! Come here and help!'

Oort didn't move until Philbert shouted out his name three times more but at last he came over. Philbert had disinterred Kwert from his snow-hole and Oort scooped him up, following Philbert's direction to take him inside the nearest tomb where at least they'd be out of the snow. Oort had always feared these dark, long-tunnelled cairns piled in rocky heaps all across this part of Schleswig-Holstein, but he was too distraught to recall it and went down on hands and knees and entered the neck of the tomb pulling Kwert in after him by his heels, Philbert at the other end keeping Kwert's head free of the rocky ground. In this way they stumbled the ten yards to the little cavern at the centre of the mound, a small clearing in which the ancients had left their dead. And, like most tombs, it still had room for one or two more.

Philbert made Kwert as comfortable as he could and then went back outside to bring in wood and hot cinders to hastily make up a fire. It soon warmed the confined space, the stones sucking in the heat, making it the perfect place to wait out the rest of the night, but not before Philbert and Oort made several more forays into the desecrated campground. It was eerie to be the only living things moving around out there, for they found no one else alive, no animals, no people. Plenty of bodies, many of whom they turned over to check for breath, but the night was so cold those who hadn't already bled out had frozen solid to the ice. The only encouraging sign was that there weren't nearly as many dead as there could have been, and it was obvious from the tracks that had not already been covered by the snow that a great many people must have made it into the dense, dark forests that surrounded the landward side of the lake. They dragged in more firewood and a couple of blankets they found in amongst the broken carts and could do no more, retreating to the tomb, the snow falling thick and fast and the wind rising up to whip it with the sand from the dunes into maelstroms and eddies all along the shore.

Once safely inside, they cosied themselves around the fire, Philbert laying Kwert's head on his lap, stroking his sparse hair, the grey stubble on his chin, feeling his pulse a feeble movement beneath his fingers. After almost an hour Kwert's lips began to move, Philbert bending down his head down to hear him.

'The others,' he whispered.

'It's alright, Kwert,' Philbert said, knowing full well that it wasn't, at least not for some. 'They made it to the forest,' he said. 'We'll find them in the morning.'

Kwert made a brief movement of his head. 'Kroonk,' he whispered, and Philbert closed his eyes and breathed deeply. He didn't want to think about what might have happened to her and refused to do so now, forced that part of his mind to close down like a stone rolled over the mouth of a deep, dark hole.

'Shall I read to you?' Philbert asked, and again there was a small nod of Kwert's head, and Philbert fumbled in his satchel for the little book of the *Philocalia* that had remained with him ever since they'd been on the hermit's island, Kwert being unable to carry even that extra little piece of baggage on top of the weight of his own bones. Philbert laid it on the ground beside the fire, flipping through the pages in an effort to find one with print bold enough to read. Some of the flyers from the Cloth Fair were still sandwiched between its pages after its soaking in the river, and Philbert lifted one up, smiling thinly as he recognised the words.

'*Brought to you by Prunkvoll's Circus of Marvels,*' he said out loud. '*All the way from London.* Who would have believed it? A horse that can count . . .'

He turned the paper over and saw his own bad handwriting there, slowly deciphering the scrawls. '*You are my nest of spheres, my prism of light, the heptagon of my days . . .*' Words Philbert was supposed to deliver from a dying man's mouth to a woman who had almost certainly beaten him there. He stopped reading. The tragedy of it all struck him deeply, and not just this cryptic declaration of wasted love but the whole of it: the journey he'd taken from his home to the Fair, from the Fair to Ullendorf, from Ullendorf to the Westphal, from the Westphal to the prison, from the prison right to this tomb buried beneath the snow on the side of a frozen lake. If there'd ever been a point to it he didn't know what it was; nothing but a promise broken, a flag hoisted then brought down again and burned. He couldn't read another word. He closed the *Philocalia*, the three of them sitting in silence by the fire, waiting for the dawn.

40

New Dawn, New Day

Philbert was woken by Oort shaking him awake. He could hardly believe he'd slept at all but the moment he opened his eyes he knew something had changed.

'It's the Fair!' Oort was saying excitedly. 'I've just been out, and there's loads of them coming out of the forest!'

And so they were. Philbert emerged from the eye of the tunnel and stood up, shading his eyes from the glare of the snow and by God he could see them too, and Oort was pushing up beside him, waving his arms wildly about his head and shouting.

'Over here! Over here!'

It seemed a miracle, that new day, that new dawn, that so many folk were emerging from the trees like hop-legged rooks, struggling through the night-fallen snow, tripping over the hummocks of the dead who had not been so lucky. Everywhere was white, from the camp grounds to the castle, from frozen lake to sea, giving them all a bizarre feeling of hope as it hid the worst of what had been done from their eyes, its new perfection marred only by several blackened circles of cinders and ash where the fires had fought on through the night before finally giving up a few hours earlier, when the snowfall had thinned and then desisted altogether.

Philbert ran out into the morning, calling and waving just as Oort was doing, looking desperately amongst the gaunt faces of the survivors until he found two that he knew: Lita and Lorenzini, and how they hugged each other and could hardly stop talking over each other until they'd clarified certain facts.

'We didn't mean to leave Kwert,' Lita was saying.

'We just couldn't find him,' Lorenzini chipped in.

'He's fine, he's fine!' Philbert assured them. 'We found him last night.'

'Thank goodness!' Lita said. 'How did you get out of the castle? What happened up there? We've no idea what's been going on . . .'

'Kroonk?' Philbert asked, and there was that lump in his throat that seemed to stop him up from stem to stern.

'She's fine,' Lorenzini laughed. 'She came away with us! We've her tethered in the forest yonder until we knew what was what.'

'And what is what?' broke in Maulwerf, panting into their circle. 'What on earth has happened? Why hasn't the Prince called out his men?'

'Because he has no men,' said Otto coming up beside them, large and red-faced as always, and looking very grim. 'But I've just heard word from one of the castle farriers that there was a rumour yestermorning of a load of someone else's coming up from the south, all shod and geared, though not a proper soldier among them.'

Maulwerf shook his head. 'I don't understand. Why would they want anything to do with us?'

'Because of your bloody acting troupes, that's what,' said a woman no one recognised who was kicking viciously at the snow with her sodden boots, her eyes darting all about her as if expecting another attack at any moment. 'You lot travel all over the place and come up here with your foreign ideas, and just look at what's gone on because of it. It's always us locals have to pay the price.'

'And your name, Madam?' Maulwerf asked politely.

'My name be bloody damned!' the woman retorted. 'I came here last night with my husband from the steadings down the road just for a bit of fun, and just look what you've brought down on our heads. And my husband is out here somewhere, buried in the snow and now my children are going to starve, all because of you . . .'

The woman began to snivel, hid her head in her scarf and moved away, kicking at the humps in the snow as she went, hoping and fearing, all at the same time, that she was going to find her husband who hadn't made it to the trees the night the wolves had struck.

'Were we really to blame?' asked Little Lita quietly, immediately enfolded by her husband's arms. Maulwerf shook his head but caught Philbert's eye as he did so, and Philbert knew then that Kwert had told him all about Lengerrborn and what had gone on there and afterwards.

'We don't know,' Maulwerf said. 'We just don't know.'

~

The Fair folk had been, for the most part, resurrected from the forest, but the woman who'd confronted them earlier had been right: the people on the ice took the brunt of the attack, the itinerant pedlars and local villagers who'd come out to hawk their wares. Maulwerf's Fair had been camped on the farther side of the lake and of those who hadn't been up at the castle most made it away before the attack reached them. All were sombre, and there was none of the usual chatter about camp-fires, breakfast and coffee; taking their place were the unpleasant smells of damp cinders, spoiled wood and wool, burned leather, burned flesh. People moved around quietly, scraping the snow away from their wretched belongings, righting carts, hammering wheels back into kilter. They discovered a few survivors who'd remained undisturbed, trapped beneath collapsed booths or hiding beneath prickly blankets, too cold to move of their own accord, and all were greeted with surprise and gratitude. Everyone who was able grabbed hammers and tools, whittling pegs and dowels, began the long task of putting back together what they could salvage from what had been almost destroyed. Others went around gathering clothing and covers, distributing them to those who had lost everything but the wet rags upon their backs. Children kicked excitedly through the dirt and dead embers, picking up anything that glinted, or seemed faintly edible. They stopped abruptly when they came across Huffelump half-cooked, spitted on a broken tent-pole, a great pile of guts frozen over and glazed by her side, eyes dull, haunches hacked away, hooves stiff. They said nothing, but as one they turned and walked away and stopped their scavenging, began helping the adults sort through the many heaps of charred canvas, erecting the best bits they could find onto branches Otto had caused to be brought out of the forest to give some shelter from the elements.

The snow had stopped, but the wind in the following days was bitter, coming at them from the east, going right through their clothes and into their bones. They sent messengers off to the castle but got short shrift the first day, the drawbridge remaining resolutely up, the castle keeping within its carapace, holding to itself the living and the dead. All who'd survived were staff members, set upon only because they'd got in the way of the real goal, which was the men and women banqueting in state in the Great Hall. And into that hall they ventured later on the day following the attack, dragging out the carcasses of the slaughtered, the great and the good, including Frau Fettleheim – which took some doing – alongside Alarico and his wife and the Atheling Rupert. They ripped the tapestries from the walls to be used at first as stretchers and later to fuel the burning of the dead whom they heaped up into a great pile in the courtyard on top of everything flammable they could find, setting the lot to flame and burn, an action they almost immediately regretted, for it left every surface of the castle, every piece of cloth in which they'd wrapped themselves, impregnated with the stench, and sent every last one of them into a frenzy of cleaning, trying to scrub away the stink of blood and slaughter and rotting food that seeped from every floorboard and every stone of the walls, until they could bear it no more and down came the drawbridge at dawn on the second morning, and out went the people who had erstwhile chosen to be trapped within. It was a long time before anyone thought to go up to the roof, and only because the boy with the big head turned up again the moment the bridge came down and suggested forcefully that they do so, finding the frozen bodies of the flagsmen, just as the boy had said they would.

It might be thought that once the drawbridge was down all those erstwhile servants and underlings from the castle would desert but they did not – not for loyalty to the dead Prince, rather because they had been born and bred into the castle just as much as Rupert had and it was the only home they knew. That another would come in Rupert's place was a given, though when and how and who they didn't know, only that it would happen, and here they would stay until it did.

∼

That second morning, Philbert was cheered to hear the rhythmic clanging of Otto's hammer upon his anvil echoing through the dismal day. Maulwerf ordered the survivors well; although his velvet jacket was unbrushed and muddy, his little glasses scratched and smudged with ash, he directed people where they were needed most: fixing up the least damaged carts first, leaving the worst to be overhauled as and when or burned for warmth if they could not be mended. They had everything on site needed for such a task – abundant raw materials and fuel from the forest, farriers and blacksmiths, wood turners and carvers, seamstresses, leatherworkers and toolmakers. Many of the trap-pulling animals had broken in panic from their loose tethers at the first sign of attack and were soon gathered in and Maulwerf set his people the goal of being up and gone within the week. The surviving pedlars and itinerants salvaged what they could and left immediately along with the villagers, taking their dead with them. Everything else that could be salvaged from the ice camp was heaped into neat piles: blankets here, possessions there, the bodies taken to the edge of the ice to be burned. That the castle had already done this to the dead inside their walls was apparent from the horrid plume of dark, greasy smoke going up the previous afternoon, Philbert shuddering to see it go, knowing that somewhere amongst that rancid pyre must be Frau Fettleheim, Alarico and La Chucha Lanuga, and all of the Fair's Folk stopped for a few moments respectful silence, knowing it too.

Their own pile of bodies, including those hacked and melted and dragged off the ice, numbered thirty-one in total. Maulwerf ordered them to be divided into six separate heaps and covered over with wood from the forest under the auspices of Otto, who knew about charcoal kilns and how best to make them burn right back into earth and ash. Onto the last of these heaps went Kwert. He'd survived that first night, thanks to Oort and Philbert, and made it through the following day, but nothing could be done to warm him up again, no matter how hard Philbert tried, and Kwert soon slipped into a cold silence from which he would never awake. Philbert was there to oversee his passing, make sure he was dressed as he should have been – a ruddy coloured blanket that was as close as Philbert could find to the red robes he hadn't worn since Lengerrborn. Lita did her best washing him down but hadn't the stomach to shave his cold grey chin, more stubbled and grizzled than ever. She tied his jaw into place, his eyelids kept closed by a couple of coins Lorenzini fished out of the snow, and then Kwert was lifted tenderly and placed on the pyre and buried with his neighbours in the forest wood. Maulwerf asked if Philbert wanted to say a few words, but he could not. Anything he thought of caught like fish-bones in his throat, and instead he took hold of the lighted brand handed to him by Otto and laid it at the pyre's base, just as others were doing to the other pyres, waiting for Maulwerf, the Father of the Fair, to sound out the signal, which came in the form of him ringing a doleful bell over and over as the brands were set and the pyres were lit, and all the dead were burned into sky, snow and ice. Two nights and one day those fires were kept burning, more wood piled on as was needed, and afterwards the ashes and bone fragments were shovelled up and placed into sacks, dropped into holes bored into the ice of the frozen lake. A few people were never accounted for, found neither in camp grounds nor in the castle, nor out on the ice. It was surmised they must have made their way far deeper into the forest than the others had done, become separated, lost their way, never to return. One of these was Hannah, which grieved Philbert greatly, and he spent many hours looking for her in amongst the trees, but there were no traces nor tracks to follow, not after all the snow that had fallen, and it was an impossible task. By night the wolves howled along their hidden tracks, making people wince at the thought of what they were doing out there, and to whom, in the trees.

The only person found was Herr Himbeere. He'd managed to lock himself inside the wood-cellar below the castle kitchens on the night of the attack, discovered four days later, baying like a dog with mange, ranting about how he'd been reduced to chewing bark for sustenance and sucking water from the soil.

'Why do men do such things?' he asked, returned to the world a mere mannequin of what he'd been, all skin and bone, pike tattoo crinkling across the dehydrated skin of his scalp. 'Why do men do such things?' was all he could say, a question to which there was no adequate answer, no matter how many times the survivors thought on it and talked on it in the coming days. The accusation bandied about by that nameless woman – that the Fair itself was to blame – was not a strong argument. The response to Harlekin's little play on the opening day of the Frost Fair proved only that the majority of folk in attendance already believed vehemently that independence for Schleswig-Holstein was the way to go. The slaying of the two flagsmen on the roof of the castle gave no clues, only that someone somewhere disagreed with the Atheling Rupert's boastful claims to various European crowns. Only Maulwerf and Philbert knew about Lengerrborn, but Maulwerf found it difficult to make a direct connection from what had happened there to what had happened here, from that action to this. The death of two Schupos surely couldn't possibly be worth that much to anybody. But neither Maulwerf nor Philbert knew what had happened at the Cloth Fair after Philbert had left. They didn't know about Brother Langer's daring tripwire rescue of Federkiel, nor that this had been tied in with the Lengerrborn escape and that both incidents together gave the powerful of the region the creeping fear that their authority was losing its grip, as it had already done elsewhere, and this was not to be tolerated. Time to stop this revolution dead in its tracks.

41

Realisation

The news of what had happened at the castle and the Frost Fair began to move and grow, like a sheet of ice spreading from a riverbank in winter, until it crossed the entire extent of Schleswig-Holstein from the North Sea to the Baltic. By then Maulwerf and the rags of his Fair of Wonders had departed, heading back to Finzeln to wait the winter out, mend what could be mended, drinking too much wine in Herr Volstrecken's cellar, mourning their dead.

Philbert, though, didn't go with them. He gave Lita a letter for Corti telling him some of what had happened since Ullendorf broke into his head, and how it seemed to him that some of Corti's music had seeped inside him, blowing through him like Corti's breath through his reeds, making the world a little fuller, a little deeper, everything taking on a significance it had previously lacked. He also wrote about how Ullendorf had died, and how sorely he would be missed, ending by telling Corti of a carillon of cats he'd seen at the Cloth Fair and later at Magendie's, that went by the name of a Felisophone – cats in cages, nails on sticks, sticks attached to buttons that the Felisophonist played to produce a weird chorus of wails and shrieks and hisses.

Everyone's head seems to be like that, he wrote, *or mine at least – a cat-filled cage waiting to be prodded and poked into action, a ramshackle orchestra from which I try to extract some kind of order, and maybe even a durable tune or two.*

Philbert brushed Maulwerf's velvet waistcoat for the last time and Maulwerf shook his hand and wished him well.

'It has been a pleasure, sir,' said Maulwerf solemnly, 'and an education. And I know we'll see you again soon. Great things, I was told,' he added, tapping his stick against the wood of his cart as he geared up for leaving. 'Great things, Philbert, and don't you ever forget it.'

That great things, and not necessarily good ones, had already happened to Philbert and the Fair they neither of them mentioned, and if Maulwerf was relieved to see Kwert's protégé leaving he kept it to himself. Lita cried, clutching at Lorenzini's arm which doubled as prop and handkerchief, but did not attempt to dissuade Philbert from his course. They were the last people to whom Philbert said goodbye, handing over his letter for Corti as he did so, bowing low to them both.

'Until May, then,' Philbert said, for he'd promised he would do his utmost to meet up with them at the next Cloth Fair at Brother Langer's Abbey. Philbert had no idea if he would make it there or not, but it didn't seem a bad promise to make. He had Kwert's knapsack slung about his neck, and in it was the *Philocalia* that held his mission like a nut within its shell. He would take those last words of Federkiel's to Lengerrborn and to Helge, if she was still alive. He knew it wasn't the smartest move, that someone might recognise him and turn him in even these many months later. He had the advantage of having Amt Gruftgang and the surviving Schupo, Ackersmann, on his side, for surely they would protect their miracle, if only to keep the church of their Lady St Lydia alive. So perhaps not so absurd a plan as it first appeared, besides which Philbert saw it not so much a plan as a duty, and one he meant to carry out, one way or another. He was no longer the naïve, knuckleheaded yard of skin and bone as when he'd first joined the Fair. The intervening years had been kind as well as cruel; he'd outgrown himself, older on the inside than on the out, a person who knew his own mind and understood both his limitations and capabilities. He had on his large head the hat that La Chucha Lanuga had made for him with its squares of green silk and little mirrors, and had at his side his companion, Kroonk, and that was all Philbert needed.

He set off on foot down one of the snow-strewn paths meandering out from the castle grounds and the frozen river and into the surrounding forests, heading away from winter towards the west. He looked back only once, to see Lita and Lorenzini clasped together like the two halves of a walnut, Oort and Otto holding up their hammers in a farewell salute, Maulwerf sitting on the bridge of his cart with hand held high. Philbert gave a single wave before turning and disappearing into the forest, Kroonk waggling her red behind beside him: a boy with his monstrous head hidden within his monstrous hat, ready for anything the world had yet to throw at him.

For the first time in his life he was treading his path alone and was not afraid, indeed was happy for it. Life was his for the taking, and by God he meant to take as much of it as he could.

42

Would You Go Into the Abode of Goodness?

The narrow lane going up the hill was just as Philbert remembered, every pock and cobble exactly as he had laid out in his head. The great wrought iron gates were still extant, though rusted now to immobility, overgrown with traveller's joy and errant honeysuckle. Philbert walked between them up the winding drive, the currant bushes on either side wild and leggy. Despite this general overview of decay he could see a dim light in one of the downstairs windows, and the wooden door was stout and strong, though no longer looked so huge as it had once done. The brass globe still hung from its dangling rope and he grasped it without hesitation and swung, the bell ringing deep inside the house. His mouth went dry when he heard a few steps in the hallway that lay beyond the door, his palms prickling, the hairs on the nape of his neck standing erect. The door opened and a girl stood before him, and Philbert blinked, saw the colour of her dress like cornflowers in bloom.

'Kadia?' he asked, uncomfortably aware of how hot his face had suddenly become.

'Oh my!' she said. 'Oh my, oh my, oh but you must come in!'

And in he went, right into Ullendorf's old home in Lengerrborn, and out from the familiar kitchen came a familiar figure and Philbert's throat went tight to see her and he took off his hat and smiled, for there was Helge, statuesque and floury as was only right, smelling of everything that was good. She gasped and put a hand across her mouth, and then rushed forward and grasped Philbert by the shoulders and drew him to her.

'Oh, my little Philbert,' she said softly, hugging him close and tight for a few moments before releasing him. 'Oh my dear child,' she said, and then began to laugh as Kroonk kroonk kroonked about their legs as she waddled in, heading straight for the kitchen as if it was the one place in the world she had always been meant to be.

~

'They took me away that night they raided the Westphal Club,' Helge was saying, now all were seated comfortably around the kitchen table and Helge had retrieved several strudels and other delicacies from her pantry. There was much to explain on both sides, but it was Helge's turn to go first.

'It was a hellish night,' she went on, 'an awful night, Philbert, and I'm not even going to try to describe it.' She shook her head, knowing that bad as it had been it would've been a whole lot worse if she'd not been protected by the soldiers who'd initially come to the house to arrest her, her tarrying and delaying them by feeding them up with as much food and wine as she could find. 'I honestly thought I was going to hang,' she continued, wiping a few tears from her cheeks as the memories came flooding back of the rancid stink and dankness of the cell into which she'd been thrown, and of the terrible man who had interrogated her, a man who took more pleasure in inflicting cruelty than many of his underlings had stomach for, who believed himself a humourist when he made jokes about the same. 'And I'm sure I would have been hanged,' Helge continued, 'except that a couple of days later Schupo Ackersman had me released into his care, just as a group of soldiers arrived from the fort to take me away. And he said the strangest thing to me, Philbert, when we were back in Lengerrborn. He asked me to pray for him – can you believe it? He told me he'd seen an angel and because of it had been delivered and was going to use the rest of his life putting things right.'

Philbert said nothing. He'd closed his eyes as Helge told her short tale, but now he opened them again, and opened them fully. He could have told her he was that angel and thereby, by proxy, both Schupo Ackersmann's and Helge's deliverer, but he did not, because he also knew he was the indirect cause of all that had happened at the Westphal Club and the reason her brother, amongst others, had died. Here it was, stark and plain: the two sides of his so-called destiny laid out like thrown dice – death and destruction on the one hand, deliverance on the other. Nothing great in any of it, all come about by chance, dependent on time and space and being in one place at one moment and not another. Just like everyone and anything else. He'd been singled out by Kwert because he'd been born with a head that grew differently from others and held its own secrets, his taupe a cave in the country of his body into which memories seeped, a cavern run through with tunnels and walkways he could wander at will; hidden pools leading the one into the other, just like the Great Magendie's reservoirs; spirals of a neverending snail that twisted and turned within its ever-growing shell. And if anything was great about him then it was this: his ability to soak up other people's stories, all hemmed into the fabric of the walls within his head, his only job to keep them safe and pass them on so they were not lost. He smiled, and took Helge's hand within his own, and asked only one question.

'And how did Kadia come to be with you?'

Helge and Kadia exchanged a look, but it was Kadia who answered.

'I think a lot about you when I am in the Cloth Fair,' she said, in her imperfect German, 'and about the man in the cage.'

Philbert drew in a sharp breath. He'd been so astonished and elated to find Helge alive, and Kadia with her, that he'd completely forgotten about Federkiel for the moment.

'*You are my nest of spheres, my prism of light, the heptagon of my days,*' he recited slowly, at which Helge nodded, a smile tugging the corners of her mouth.

'Quite,' she said shortly, 'but let's get back on track. Kadia came to me because of you, Philbert, and everything that happened at the Westphal Club – God curse the place. It was she who went to the prison and to Ackersmann afterwards to ask after me.'

Kadia looked down at her cornflower blue dress and glanced shyly at Philbert. 'You give me flowers,' she said. 'No one ever give me flowers before.'

Philbert blushed, remembering the poor posy of closed-up Stars of Bethlehem he'd given the girl before he and Kwert left the Cloth Fair almost exactly one year before. He looked at Kadia, and Kadia looked at Philbert. They were both young then, their combined ages barely adding up to the mid-twenties, but they were not so young they didn't recognise this might be the start of something.

'I'm glad,' said Philbert after a few moments.

'Not half as glad as I,' Helge was smiling broadly, the look that had passed between this boy and this girl not having escaped her notice. 'Better a housemaid than a seamstress,' she added, 'and better a boy with a big head than a boy who has no head at all.'

They were interrupted at that moment by someone opening the front door and hallooing himself in. Philbert jumped up in alarm but Helge placed her hand on his arm.

'We've not told you all,' she said, standing as the kitchen door opened. 'Let me introduce you to my husband, Philbert. I believe you've already met.'

If Philbert thought he could be no more surprised by the turn of events than he had already was then he was much mistaken, for in came a man he certainly had met before, though he was greatly changed. He was spruce, plump and tidy and obviously alive. It was Federkiel, having survived the cage and the island and returned to earth with his mind relatively intact. His reappearance was one of many discoveries Philbert made while in Lengerrborn, not the least of which was that his bid to bring Federkiel's dying declaration of love to Helge had already been delivered by Federkiel himself.

There were many embraces that night at Ullendorf's Anchorage, many glasses of wine poured and drunk, many tales told that took up their new abode in Philbert's head. The story of Brother Langer's rescue of Federkiel was for Philbert the most astonishing. How the man had managed it was beyond his ken, but if ever sainthood was deserved by anyone then Brother Langer had to be head of the queue; and not far behind him would be Schupo Ackersmann, still the Chief Schupo of Lengerrborn, but every last penny of his pay and pension he could spare went into the restoration of Our Lady St Lydia – his route to salvation – Amt Gruftgang spearheading the cause.

The following day Helge took Philbert to witness it himself. He was greeted with amazement and enthusiasm that bordered on adulation, and no matter how many times he tried to explain, both Ackersmann and Gruftgang saw and heard nothing but that Philbert was a Child of God and the instrument of His work, Lengerrborn resurrected and cleansed because of his stepping on its streets.

'You saved me,' Ackersmann insisted, 'and all those people in the prison. You freed them and you freed me, and Amt Gruftgang too.'

Philbert shook his head at these words but there was no changing them, nor the fact that the folk from Lengerrborn were now pouring into the church of Our Lady St Lydia like ants on sugar. Carpenters had volunteered to provide new pews; silversmiths had donated new candlesticks and the vessels needed for mass; seamstresses, Kadia amongst them, had sewn new vestments for the new choirboys who were volunteering by the dozen. The churchyard had been cleared of weeds, the lych-gate now a tidy vista of roses, the board repainted with its shell and dedication, the undercrofts stripped of liverwort and moss, replastered and repainted. Later on in the year, on Lydia's feast day, Gruftgang would once again lead his congregation into the spiral maze below the church itself, right to its heart.

'And it was in Our Lady St Lydia that Helge Ullendorf married her Professor Federkiel,' said Fatzke, appearing on the scene, 'with Kadia as Maid of Honour and me as best man, and fittingly they held their reception in the newly decked out Westphal Club, a snub to every solider and every authoritarian who has tried to keep us down.'

Lengerrborn was a different town from when Philbert had first been there; it was as if the entire place had taken a deep breath and revitalised itself. Philbert supposed that having almost half of your eminent citizens shot for no good reason might do that to a place. God knew, he'd had the same reaction, the breaking of death on his shores and all that. He knew more, and that the most of it was the privilege of still being alive and that no soothsayer in the world could give you a reliable indicator of how long you would remain so. Life was life. You could be here one second and gone the next, no way to predict which way the dice would fall.

~

The day before Philbert left Lengerrborn he went through the shroudways and out onto the shore of the lake and rowed himself over to the Öde Insel. Brother Langer Hansnarrwurst was there, still recuperating from his twice-broken legs, reduced from his former bulk to a thin reed who needed to be rolled out

375

in a chair by Brother Jaspis, Langer's keeper and carer ever since the rescue of Federkiel.

'At least I can still witness the glory of the day,' Langer said, as Jaspis wheeled him around the island, Philbert following. 'And I have the satisfaction of knowing that whatever I've done in this world I've done the best of it.'

Philbert smiled. A saint in the making, just as he'd supposed, spewing more wise words than a frog does spawn. Later, they built a fire and cooked the fish they'd caught in Langer's nets.

'You read to me once from Kwert's book,' Brother Langer said, as the night was drawing in and the fire growing dim.

'I still have it,' Philbert said, bringing the *Philocalia* from his knapsack. 'Would you like me to read from it again?'

'I would,' said Brother Langer, 'that same passage, if you can find it.'

Philbert didn't even need to look, for he remembered the words Kwert had found for Brother Langer as if Kwert was still at his shoulder, prompting him on.

Would you go into the abode of goodness, and the tents of the blessed?

Then go into the mountains, the forests, and the deserts.

See the birds flying, feel the breeze through the trees and the soft wind blowing;

Bathe in the streams flowing through the ravines.

For here is a man's solitude and his strength,

A time away from the ever rolling waves.

'It's always been so,' said Brother Langer, 'always so. And that is why I will never leave my island. For this is my time away from those waves.'

'And what about you, Philbert?' Jaspis asked. 'What are your plans?'

Philbert smiled and shook his head. 'I honestly don't know. Maulwerf told me once to look around, to look ahead, but never, ever, to look back. But I don't seem able to let the past go

– not completely. It all remains within me, within my head, and so I suppose I'll just travel onwards, gathering more.'

'Well, if anyone has the head for it then it's you, my boy,' Langer laughed.

'Agreed,' Philbert nodded. 'And I wouldn't be without it, even if I had the chance.'

~

And that was precisely what Philbert did. He went back to The Anchorage and bade his goodbyes, first standing a while by the big glass window of Ullendorf's study, gazing out over the streets of Lengerrborn down below, at the roofs he'd once thought looked like a deck of thrown-down cards, and still did. The cats still gathered on the other side of the glass, including that same rat-chewed, stub-eared ginger tom flexing his claws, but his look no longer seemed malevolent to Philbert, rather that this cat was a mirror of himself – both were survivors, both ready for what the world was getting ready to throw at them next.

He was Philbert, the boy with the monstrous head, for whom great things had been foretold. Time to throw himself into the ever-rolling waves, take that foretelling with him and shake it by the throat until it screamed.

Acknowledgements

I'd like to thank my family and the RLF for their support when times were at their hardest; Tony Sumner and Michael Fraser for their valuable input, and Laura Longrigg – my agent at MBA. Most of all, my thanks are due to Ed Handyside at Myrmidon for taking a punt on this book. Or perhaps I should say coble – he'll know what I mean.